Smudges on
page edges.
10, Sept, 2015

INTO THE
MAELSTROM

INTO THE MAELSTROM

DAVID DRAKE
JOHN LAMBSHEAD

INTO THE MAELSTROM

Copyright © 2015 by David Drake and John Lambshead

A Baen Book

Baen Publishing Enterprises
P.O. Box 1403
Riverdale, NY 10471
www.baen.com

ISBN: 978-1-4767-8028-3

Cover art by David Seeley

First Baen printing, March 2015

Distributed by Simon & Schuster
1230 Avenue of the Americas
New York, NY 10020

Library of Congress Cataloging-in-Publication Data

Drake, David, 1945-
Into the maelstrom / David Drake & John Lambshead.
    pages cm. -- (Citizen ; 2)
Summary: "The Cutter Stream colonies were at peace. If everyone behaved
reasonably, that peace could last a thousand years. Allen Allenson had
known war; it had made him peaceful and reasonable. He was far too
experienced to believe the same of all his fellow colonists, let alone
the government of the distant homeworld. War was coming, a war the
colonies had to win if they were ever to be more than prison camps and a
dumping ground for incompetent noblemen. Allenson knew that he wasn't
really a general, but he understood his fellow colonists better than any
homeworld general could. He would free the Cutter Stream or die trying"--
Provided by publisher.
ISBN 978-1-4767-8028-3 (hardback)
1. Science fiction. I. Lambshead, John. II. Title.
PS3554.R196I74 2015
813'.54--dc23
                              2014043651

Printed in the United States of America

10 9 8 7 6 5 4 3 2 1

"To the legion of the lost ones, to the cohort of the damned,"
"Gentlemen-Rankers," *Barrack Room Ballads*
by Rudyard Kipling

★ ★ ★

This book is dedicated to all the soldiers
throughout history who fought and died in unremembered wars
for causes long abandoned.

★ ★ ★

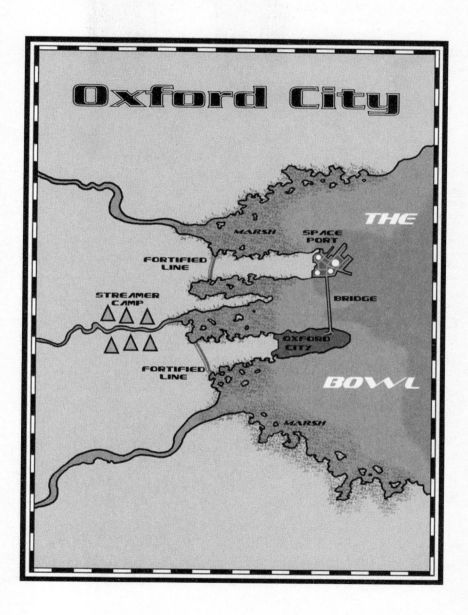

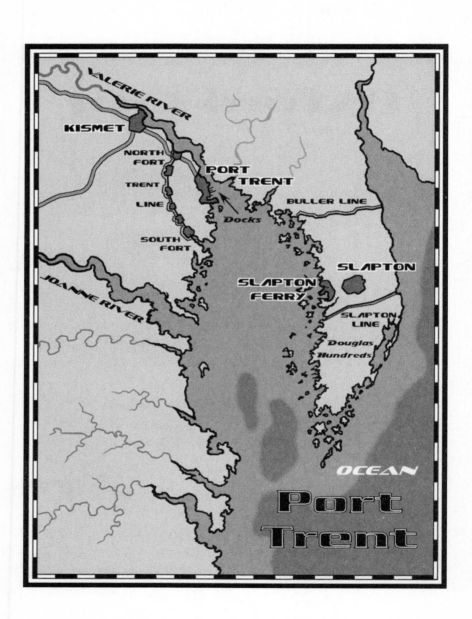

★ CONTENTS ★

INTO THE
MAELSTROM

Magnetar

Tap—Tap—Tap went the claw on the window.

Commander Frisco pressed her eyelids together tighter than a virgin's knees in the hope that the damn thing would go away.

Tap—Tap—Tap.

It didn't—go away that is.

She opened her eyes slowly and very reluctantly. The goblin leered at her from the other side of the airtight screen from where it perched on the blunt shovel-nose of her ship. Triangular was a word that summed it up, triangular and blue. Its head was a downwards pointing triangle ending in a long pointed chin. Its mouth V-shaped with triangular teeth, its chest V-shaped, even its bloody ears were triangular.

Stroppy was another good descriptive word. The creature thrust vigorously upwards with two fingers topped with triangular claws. It made the time-honored Brasilian gesture indicating that she should indulge in sex and travel. She tried not to notice what it was doing with its other hand.

Most of the time the Continuum looked like a seething mass of multicolored energy but every so often ship crews saw and heard illusions. The philosophical postulated that such phantasms were the product of some sort of arcane interaction between the human mind and energy leakage through the ship's field. In truth, no one had a clue why the phenomenon occurred but the illusions were usually specific to each individual.

Such ghosts materialized when one was under stress, causing fears to be dredged from deep within the mind. Helena Frisco was hard pressed to explain why her subconscious might harbor blue goblins with triangular body parts and obscene habits. It was probably Finkletop's fault; most current problems in Helena's universe originated with feckin' Finkletop.

Satisfaction with her promotion to commander and the captaincy of the Brasilian Research and Exploration Ship *Reggie Kray,* nicknamed the Twin-Arsed Bastard by the other ranks, rapidly eroded when she shared her first cruise with Professor Obadiah Finkletop. The good professor held a Personal Chair in Cosmic Evolution at Blue Horizon College. No doubt his peers considered him a learned savant. Helena considered him a pain in the arse.

Finkletop alone she might have coped with but the old fool was completely under the spell of his research student, a curvaceous young lady who went by the name of "Flipper" Wallace. What Flipper wanted, Flipper got and her desires were entirely capricious when looked at from a naval perspective.

The catamaran hulled *Reggie Kray,* hence its nickname, had all the naval equipment including the engines and field generators in the "A" hull so that various "B" hulls stuffed with different scientific equipment could be added or detached as required by the current mission objective. The mission in this case was to convey Finkletop's research group to a neutron star deep in the Hinterlands. The exercise involved gathering "stuff" to test some scientific hypothesis or other concerning nova chains. Finkletop failed to volunteer details and Helena felt no desire to inquire.

The *Reggie Kray* was about as large a ship as could usefully be navigated within the Hinterlands where the gravity shadows of star systems were tightly packed in the Continuum. This stellar proximity channeled chasms, or streams, of boiling energy that made the passage of larger ships too slow and laborious to be viable. Speed equaled range in the Continuum because passage time was capped.

The *Reggie Kray* handled like a pig because of the asymmetric design. On the plus side Helena did not have so socialize too much with the bloody academics. They tended to keep to their own territory in the "B" hull.

A symbol flashed in the area by her command chair reserved for holographic controls. Finkletop desired communication. She sighed and keyed the comm symbol, ignoring a mischievous impulse to activate the B hull emergency detachment bolts instead. The goblin gave a final leer and disappeared. Helena did not recall that the detachment icon was a blue triangle. No doubt that was just as well.

"Ah, Frisco?" said Finkletop's voice by her chair. She had switched out the video. It was bad enough having to listen to the man without looking at a caricature of personal grooming that would cause a Naval Academy drill instructor to self-immolate. She rearranged her features into a neutral expression because he could no doubt see her.

"Professor, what a pleasant surprise to talk to you again and so soon after our last conversation."

"Flipper, Ms. Wallace, needs to be closer to the neutron star. You will move to point gamma-3-alpha-99."

The two ratings on the bridge with Helena froze. They developed a deep fascination with their consoles. It was not normally considered good naval practice to give orders to a ship's captain on her own bridge. Not unless you were an admiral at any rate. Even then an order was usually couched as a suggestion. As research team leader Finkletop had the authority to choose the survey sites but the bloody man could show some deference to her rank.

Helena gritted her teeth and keyed in the necessary course as she couldn't think of a good reason to refuse. She automatically checked storage heat levels as she did so. Ships' fusion engines supplied effectively unlimited fuel but electromagnetic radiation could not pass out through the Continuum field reality bubble to any extent. Waste heat had to be "stored" in heat sinks made of frozen iron cores. Captains worried constantly about heat build-up. When levels got too high there was nothing for it but to find a suitable world with available water to dump heat and refreeze the cores.

Unfortunately the *Reggie Kray* still had an adequate reserve in the sinks. She hit the command key. Her staff would attend to the details of the course change.

"And could you part phase so we can observe the system."

"Why not?" Helena asked, waving a hand to the appropriate minion to indicate that he should comply. "Anything else we can do for you? Brew up some tea and send it 'round to your hull, perhaps?"

"We are too busy for a tea break. Some of us have work to do," Finkletop replied, killing the link.

The bloody man was impervious to sarcasm.

The pilot slowly part-dephased the ship on approaching the neutron star. With its fields at low power the reality bubble enclosing the *Reggie Kray* was subject to a degree of interaction with electromagnetic energy from realspace. That meant that the crew saw into the real universe, albeit in monochrome. In return, light-speed limitations slowed the ship to a crawl. Not an issue in this case as they had only a short distance to travel.

The neutron star was tiny despite its huge mass. It gave off only a dull glow in the visible spectrum. Helena had to look hard to find it against the background star-field but the body's effects were out of all proportion to its size. It probably weighed about 1,000,000,000,000 kilograms per milliliter. That gave it a gravitational field so strong that escape velocity would be measured in significant fractions of light speed.

A large chaotic debris field rotated at high speed around the star. Helena found it unnerving to watch the lumps of ice, metal and rock tracked on the navigational hologram. No doubt similar junk hurtled through the ship's realspace location at speeds too high to be visible to the naked eye. She could create a holographic representation of the bombardment for the crew's edification but doubted they would enjoy the experience.

Deep space made sailors uneasy. Most voyages started and ended on the surface of habitable worlds, the ships phasing within the world's air envelope. Fields enclosed air within the reality bubble so most commercial vessels and small frames omitted an air-tight hull as an unnecessary expense. The naval architects designed the *Reggie Kray* to sustain human life even with the fields off because of its unusual research function.

Massive tidal effects commonly produced swirling fields of junk around a neutron star but this one was positively frenzied. Helena ran an analysis using the limited electromagnetic radiation that penetrated the ship's field.

The comm link lit up. Helena sighed and keyed it.

"We may've found it," Finkletop's voice shook slightly with excitement.

"Oh good," Helena said, wondering what "it" was.

"You must dephase completely and turn off the shields so we can obtain samples."

"Must I?"

"Yes, it's possible the frame field might interfere with the specimens."

Helena touched the "hold" icon while she recovered her calm.

"Have you looked outside at all, Professor?" Helena eventually asked. "You may have noticed something of a debris storm."

"Never mind the paintwork on your ship. This research is too important to be held up by petty military regulations. I'd explain but you wouldn't understand."

"It may have escaped your notice, Professor, but I captain this vessel. As such I am responsible for it and the crew. *If* I decide your request," Helena emphasized the word if, "is too dangerous then it won't happen."

"I shall complain to the Grant Committee!"

"Indeed."

The opinion of an academic grant committee carried about as much weight with Helena as a petition from a delegation of rock apes. She answered to the Navy Board and she doubted they cared a fig what a bunch of academics thought either. On the other hand the Board could be downright unreasonable to captains who smashed up their ships.

"It may also have escaped your notice, Professor, but that is not just a neutron star out there but a magnetar, a star with a massive magnetic field—"

"I know what a magnetar is."

Helena continued remorselessly as if he hadn't spoken.

"—which is why the debris field is so energetic and chaotic. Iron debris is subject to different forces from nonmagnetic rocks and hence has different trajectories. The resulting collisions cause endless fragmentation. It would be like dephasing into a shotgun blast of hypersonic pellets."

Finkletop said. "Well, if you're frightened—"

"Be careful, Professor," Helena's knuckles clenched until they were white.

An officer of the Brasilian Navy could display many faults from drunkenness to licentiousness and still prosper. Cowardice was the one intolerable weakness.

"We'd also have a major problem with magnetic forces such as diamagnetism which is the—"

Finkletop attempted to interrupt. "I know what diamagnetism is but I don't see—"

"—temporary opposing magnetic force induced in materials by an ultra-magnetic field. Our ceramic hull is a good example as it is repelled by the star. Other materials are paramagnetic and will be dragged towards it. Furthermore, while naval architects use nonmetallic materials as far as possible in a ship's construction to limit drag and hence heat build-up while moving through the Continuum sometimes there are no acceptable nonmetallic substitutes. Our large iron heat sinks are a good example."

Finkletop tried again. "Well—"

"So if I dephase at our current location the ship's hull and heat sinks will push in opposite directions while I try to dodge high velocity debris on chaotic trajectories."

Dead silence.

There was a compromise option. She told herself she was all kinds of a fool for even considering it. Unfortunately, Finkletop was stupid enough to insult her honor without seeing that she would have to call him out. That could wreck her career. No one would openly blame her for protecting her reputation. Nonetheless, she would always be remembered as the captain who killed her charge. Actually, she reflected, Finkletop wasn't stupid. A Blue Horizon professor just couldn't be stupid. He was simply incredibly focused and limited in his world view.

"How big a specimen do you need?" Helena asked.

"What? Just a few micrograms would do."

"Very well, I'll harmonize the field of a small jolly boat to pass through the ship's fields. The boat can phase out for the few seconds necessary to recover your sample without endangering the whole ship. Magnetic tidal effects are limited on such a low mass object. It will also present a smaller target to incoming rocks. I won't risk trying to bring the jolly back in through the ship's field as the harmonization will drift out of phase within minutes. We will rendezvous and recover the boat from a quiet area beyond the debris field. Is that satisfactory?"

"I suppose so, seems a lot of stuff and nonsense to me, usual bureaucratic ineptitude, typical of the military—"

She cut the link while Finkletop was still blathering and gave the necessary orders.

The *Reggie Kray*'s field shimmered metallic green when the jolly boat passed through. The phase harmonization with the boat's field was less than perfect. That observation caused Helena little surprise. No human procedure in the history of the universe had ever achieved perfection. She saw no reason to assume that this was about to change any time soon for her benefit.

Finkletop insisted on supervising the sampling personally. Helena had been equally insistent that a naval rating coxswain the small craft, not one of the academics. She watched the boat's progress on a holographic screen. Once clear, the boat adjusted its heading and moved to match speeds with a debris pile. It stopped while the coxswain waited for a signal from the ship indicating he could dephase safely. Well, not safely perhaps but at least without facing instant destruction. Safety is one of those irregular nouns.

Communication was impossible over any distance through the Continuum. Anything not protected by a field rapidly decayed or was ejected into realspace. At short range lasers could exchange narrow bandwidth data. Small open frame crews often resorted to hand gestures and flashing lights.

The ship's information analyzers tracked and predicted the immediate debris field. An icon indicated a break in the debris bombardment. It was now or never. She sent confirmation to the jolly boat.

The boat's field flicked off and it drifted towards the debris. Steering thrusters fired to brake the craft alongside a stream of gravel and match velocities. A mechanical arm extended and took a sample. Sparkles ran along the arm where microscopic dust moving at a high relative speed struck the ceramic surface.

The arm had almost withdrawn when the jolly boat shuddered. Its hull flexed under the impact of particles larger than microscopic dust. A ceramic plate peeled off and spun away. Jets of escaping air distilled into arches of silver crystals that fanned out in the magnetar's strong tidal gravitational and magnetic fields like a celestial peacock's tail.

Helena swore.

The jolly boat should have been safe enough in realspace for that short period of time. The ship's autos predicted a ninety-five per cent chance of success. She should have anticipated that the unlikeliest disaster would happen at the first opportunity. The gods of probability delighted in shitting on mankind's collective head from a great height.

She crossed metaphorical fingers and waited for the jolly boat's field to reform. Survival suits would protect the crew for a while. She counted slowly to three but it never happened. The boat's field generator must be knocked out. The gods were piling improbability upon improbability today. They probably didn't like Finkletop any more than she did but why stick the boot in on her watch?

The boat's crew were in the deepest possible fertilizer. It was only a matter of time before a bigger impact smeared them like raspberry jam across a slice of toast.

"Close and try to enclose the jolly boat in our Continuum field," Helena ordered. "Finkletop you feckin' lunatic," she added under her breath.

The *Reggie Kray*'s pilot swung the ship around as if it was a one-man frame and accelerated smoothly. They reached the boat just as its field unexpectedly flicked back on. The two energy bubbles interacted dynamically in a sharp release of violet lightning. The boat couldn't penetrate the ship's field because its field had drifted out of phase during the off-on transition. The debris strike probably hadn't helped either.

The ship pushed the smaller vessel with its field like a ball on the edge of an avalanche.

"All halt," Helena said, trying to keep her voice calm.

Then something happened, something unfathomable, something she had never witnessed before in all her years in the navy.

The boat imploded soundlessly leaving nothing but a black stain. Helena had the impression of spreading darkness. A dark spear thrust into the *Reggie Kray,* collapsing its field like a pin going into a balloon. The ship rang like a bell struck by a hammer. That's not possible, Helena thought, we're only semi-phased. Nothing that powerful can penetrate our field. A deep chill froze her bones and the lights went out.

Helena felt cold. Her throat hurt like hell. Water vapor condensed from her breath. It hung in the air like a superior's admonishment. Only the glow from instruments leaking across the cabin broke the darkness. To top it all she had one hell of a headache.

"Status?" she asked.

Well, she tried to ask but what came out was a croak.

"Fusion motors decoupled. Trying to get them back on line before our batteries fail," said a voice.

Helena located the source of said voice. Seckon, the engineering officer, stood against a console stabbing down at a screen with both forefingers. The rating who should have operated it was on the floor. Blood matted his hair. He stared at Helena with open sightless eyes. An icicle of frozen saliva hung from his lips. The poor bastard had frozen to death, making her wonder how long she'd been out.

What was the engineering officer doing on her bridge? What was she doing on the deck? Unanswered questions orbited around her mind. Nothing made any sense.

She pulled herself upright using her chair as a crutch. She realized she had missed some important piece of information. What had Seckon said? The motors were out, that was it. The emergency power must be on or she would be floating under zero gravity.

A loud crack sounded and the deck twanged like the skin on a kettle drum. Helena gripped her command chair tightly. Oh God the motors were out. That meant the field was down and they were still in the debris stream.

The lights snapped on. The ship suddenly hummed with that faint background vibration that was so normal a part of her life that she never usually noticed it at all.

"Getting there, ma'am, field on," Seckon said triumphantly.

"Good man."

Helena sat down and activated her chair. The navigation hologram sprang to life. She switched to damage status, causing it to light up with red and orange icons like New Year decorations in a shopping arcade. Her ship was a bloody mess but what struck her as odd was the temperature. Parts of the ship were well below freezing. She boosted power to environmental control to start hot air circulating.

"That's not right," said Seckon, frowning.

"Which of our many failed systems do you mean?" Helena asked.

"The heat sinks, ma'am. They're . . . well, have a look yourself."

Helena triggered the necessary controls and did a double take.

"My screen says they're empty, stone cold empty," she said.

"Mine too," replied the engineering officer. "But they can't be. The monitoring system must be faulty."

"Great. Any sign of the jolly boat?"

"Haven't looked, I was too busy starting the motors."

Helena activated a scan. Scanning while semi-phased was inefficient but the boat should be close enough to detect. There was no sign of it at all, not even wreckage from the hull registering. She couldn't tarry as for all she knew the heat sinks could fail at any moment. She consulted her navigation charts then pressed the icon for wideband communication.

"All crew, this is the captain. We have sustained considerable damage but essential systems are functioning."

Helena crossed her fingers at that point, for real not metaphorically. She had no idea what state the ship was really in or how long anything would function. She couldn't trust her instruments so she was blind, but it didn't hurt to boost the crew's morale. If something vital failed then they were all dead anyway and her people's morale would cease to be a concern.

"We passed a habitable world some two hours normal sailing time away and I propose to head for it. We'll be traveling slowly so as not to test anything to destruction but we should make landfall in just over three hours. Captain out."

She looked around the bridge for the pilot. He sat up and was noisily sick on the deck. Helena sighed.

"Please stay on the bridge, Mr. Seckon," she said to the engineering officer. "It looks as if I will be conning the ship personally and I would like you to nurse the motors for me."

"Aye, aye, ma'am."

Helena found a small river on her landing approach. It was bordered by trees restricted to within a few meters of the water so she set the ship down on nearby scrubland nearby, not wishing to push her luck with the strained hull by trying for the tree-lined bank. That meant extra work for the crew in rigging a hose to the river but she was in no great hurry. She wanted every system thoroughly tested before they began the long voyage home.

The *Reggie Kray* supported its bulk on proactive self-levelling landing struts that balanced the stresses affecting the hull. Most ships dispensed with such expensive technology but most ships landed only on perfectly flat reinforced starport pads or on the water. A research ship needed to be able to land on any vaguely flat surface so it devoted valuable carrying capacity to rough terrain landing gear.

Helena observed the semi-desert terrain with a disinterested eye despite its forlorn beauty. She had stood on so many alien worlds that the novelty had long passed off—seen one wilderness, seen them all. She barely even noticed the change in smell from the tang of the sterile filtered ship's air to the mix of organic aromas associated with a living ecosystem. She disregarded the subtly different spectrum of the sun overhead from the Brasilian standard light used on the ship.

She walked around the vessel to check the hull. It was extremely unlikely that she would spot anything not already revealed by whatever instruments were functioning. Nevertheless, a flight check was traditional and would reassure the crew.

What was left of the crew, she corrected herself bitterly. Out of fourteen naval personal she had lost two in the jolly boat and had four more casualties on the ship. Three of those lay in induced comas in sick bay until they reached civilization or what passed for it this side of the Bight. She doubted if more than two would ever be revived even with proper hospitalization. Not even modern medicine could do much with the burst cells of a frozen brain. The fourth was already dead.

The research team was harder hit as the B Hull had been closer to the jolly boat. Only Flipper Wallace and a young male technician survived. Flipper wisely kept out of Helena's path but the technician was a practical sort who made himself useful to the shorthanded crew.

Her datapad chimed where it was hung off her belt.

"Yes," she said.

"We've rigged hoses into the river and are ready to start pumping, Captain," said the mate.

"Very good, carry on."

"Aye, aye, ma'am."

Helena backed up so she had a better view of her ship's dorsal vents. The blue-white sun shone brightly, causing her to shade her eyes when she looked up. She should have brought a sun shield. She should have done many things including not letting Finkletop goad her into crazy plans.

The heat vents opened. She waited for the white rush of condensing steam from the water flushing out the heat sinks. She waited but nothing happened.

After a few seconds she touched her datapad.

"What the hell's going on, Seckon? Why aren't the pumps working?"

Seckon was at his station in Engineering.

"They're working fine. The water's running straight through."

"Hold on."

Helena ran back to the ship and peered underneath. River water gushed from vents under the A hull and trickled across the dry yellow soil.

"It seems the instruments were quite accurate when they indicated that the heat sinks are cool. We can leave any time you order," Seckon said.

"But that's not possible," Helena replied. "Heat doesn't just disappear."

"Nevertheless."

Helena could almost hear the shrug from her engineering officer.

"Find that bloody girl and send her to me—now."

"Aye, aye, Captain."

Seckon did not need to ask which girl. Whatever he did to insert a squib up Flipper's arse clearly worked. She shot out of the ship and scuttled over to Helena, moving at a faster speed than she had hitherto employed since she came aboard.

"You asked to see me, Ms. Frisco?" asked Flipper

"No, I didn't ask to see you. I summoned you," Helena snarled in reply. "What the hell has Finkletop done to my ship?"

"The professor doesn't like me talking about our work," she said evasively. "He has enemies and rivals."

"Finkletop is dead so all his problems are over. Yours are just beginning if I don't get some answers. You address me as Captain or ma'am. As I have co-opted you into my crew you are subject to naval discipline up to and including summary execution for mutiny. Am I making myself clear?"

Helena glared at the girl so hard that she backed up a step. Actually, Helena was not up enough on military law to know if that interpretation was correct but she rightly assumed that Flipper knew even less about military law than did she.

"Um, yes," Flipper said, flashing frightened eyes.

"Aye, aye, Captain," Helena said, remorselessly rubbing the girl's nose in her new pecking order.

"Aye, aye, Captain."

"So explain that explosion to me."

"I'm not entirely sure."

"Indulge me, speculate wildly."

"Do you know anything about the professor's work?"

"No, carry on."

"Well he was working on subatomic physics."

"What?" Helena was astonished. "I don't claim to be up on the latest thinking but that surely went out with bows and arrows. The ancients explored that cul-de-sac pretty thoroughly and a fat lot of good it did them. They ended up with more fairy stories than a children's nursery book. I mean, we're talking bloody quantum bloody mechanicals or some such."

"Quantum mechanics," Flipper said didactically.

Helena raised an eyebrow, which was all it took for Flipper to take the hint and hurriedly proceed with her explanation.

"It's true that the ancients had the weirdest superstitions about the natural world but they also carried out a number of empirical experiments with interesting results. They had these high speed accelerators that they used to smash atoms apart."

"Is this going somewhere?"

"Well, you know that the heavier an element is the more likely it is to decay?"

"Yes, so what? The heavier elements are radioactive so completely useless and bloody dangerous."

Flipper became more animated and confident now she was on home territory. She waved her hands to illustrate her description.

"The ancients found they could make small quantities of artificial heavy elements by smashing lighter ones together. The products were ridiculously unstable, decaying in microseconds. However, the ancients' mathematics predicted an island of stability where stable ultraheavy elements could exist around element 126, unbihexium. They never had the technology, though, to reach this island."

"Go on," Helena said, becoming intrigued despite herself.

"Their theoretical understanding of what was going on involved superstition about magic subatomic particles called neutrons and protons that behaved as waves. In their system unbihexium was the 126th element because it had one hundred and twenty-six protons arranged in what they called a closed proton shell and around one hundred and ninety neutrons in a closed neutron shell. Nonsense of course."

Flipper paused and gazed unseeing at the ground, no doubt pondering how stupid were ancient people or indeed was anyone over the age of twenty-five. Helena tapped her foot. The action startled the student back into the real world.

"But their mathematics was sound if used simply as a descriptive empirical construct. The professor tried to interest academia in building a modern more powerful version of the ancients' accelerators to see if we could manufacture these stable heavy elements. The grant committees balked at the cost."

Flipper's expression of contempt no doubt reflected her late professor's opinion of nitpicking milksops who whined about money when knowledge was at stake. Actually, Helena sympathized with that view to some degree. The naval budget was always being squeezed to the detriment of The Service.

"How much would it have cost?" Helena asked.

"About half a million crowns not counting the cost of hollowing out a mountain."

Helena's sympathy evaporated.

"I can see why the proposal generated resistance," she said dryly. "This is all very interesting but get to the point."

"Neutron stars," Flipper said, as if that was supposed to explain something.

"What?"

"It's all about neutron stars. You know they're formed by exploding white dwarfs or collapsing massive stars?"

Helena nodded.

"The professor predicted that if a binary supernova—"

"A death star like the one that caused the Ordovician extinction on Old Earth?"

"Yes, if a death star's gamma beam struck a collapsing massive star—something normally big enough to form a black hole—then the massive energies involved would create a powerful magnetar combining lighter elements into the super-heavies. Most would decay almost immediately except for those in the island of stability."

"So you were looking for Element 126?"

"Yes, a stable superactinide with unusual properties."

"Properties like what?"

"Well for one thing Continuum fields would cause it to become unstable and decay. That was why samples could only be collected in realspace. No frame fields until we got it in a magnetic bottle."

Helena wondered if she or just the rest of the world was mad.

"You had us out in a frame ship hunting for nuclear bomb fuel triggered to explode by a frame field? Was Finkletop rug-munching crazy?"

"No, no," Flipper shook her head emphatically. "My calculations showed no release of energy. It was simply that the field would catalyze the breakdown of unbihexium into lighter elements."

"So what happened?" Helena snapped, becoming thoroughly fed up with going around the academic houses. "What went wrong?"

"I have been going over the maths again and again."

So that was what she had been doing, Helena thought.

"I think I got the calculations wrong," Flipper whispered. "Unbihexium is weirder than I anticipated. Its decay isn't energy neutral but it doesn't lose mass and release energy like every other radioactive material. When unbihexium decays, the products weigh more than the starting material."

Helena looked blank.

"Don't you see? It gains mass. That's why it's normally stable. It can't access the necessary energy input."

Helena still must have looked as baffled as she felt. Flipper spelled it out, step by step.

"The coxswain must have switched the boat's field back on before the professor finished sealing the sample into the magnetic bottle."

Helena interrupted.

"Wait a minute. I agreed that the frame field would be switched off just for the time necessary to get samples, not to leave it off while Finkletop buggered about with his equipment. He lied to me?"

Flipper looked evasive.

"Not lied exactly, he was just economical with the truth."

Helena snarled wordlessly.

Flipper rushed out more words. "He thought you wouldn't agree. The field had to stay off until the unbihexium sample was completely isolated."

Helena took a deep calming breath before speaking.

"No doubt the coxswain would be more concerned with being splattered by a meteorite than by the professor's activities."

"Yes, the coxswain must have disobeyed the professor and turned on the field prematurely," Flipper said, repeating herself.

"Damn right!" Helena said. "He did the right thing."

"No doubt he thought so but the boat's field initiated unbihexium breakdown when it activated. Radioactive decay got the initial energy input from the frame field. I suspect the reaction ran wild after it started. It sucked in the necessary power from the surroundings, causing the implosion."

"Impossible, something can't suck in heat," Helena said.

"That's not entirely true. If you blow bubbles into a highly volatile liquid through a straw—"

Helena wondered where fizzy drinks came into it. "What?"

"—you freeze the surroundings. That's how a 'fridge works. Energy absorption is the only explanation I can come up with. The ship's field was interacting with the jolly boat's so—"

"So this negative energy wave," Helena said, for want of a better description, "went through the jolly boat's field into the ship's field where it froze the ship, stalled the motors and drained the heat sinks?"

"It's not really negative energy . . ." Flipper stopped upon seeing the look on Helena's face and merely bit her lip and nodded.

The girl's face brightened.

"It takes a lot of energy to make a little bit of mass. The reaction must have been short lived or we would have been taken down to absolute zero. This is going to make quite an impressive publication," Flipper said, eyes shining with academic fervor. "I might get it in Brasilian Science or even the Terran Universe Journal. I think Tee Yu would be best as it has a higher impact rating."

"Publication, in a Terran journal, are you mad? You aren't going to publish this anywhere," Helena said, looking at the girl in astonishment.

Helena touched her datapad.

"Mr. Grieg?"

"Captain?" replied the mate.

"Ms. Wallace is to be placed under immediate close solitary arrest. She is not to be harmed in any way. I make you personally responsible for her welfare but she is not to talk to anybody or have any access to communication devices until we hand her over to the NID."

Grieg responded as if the order was standard routine. "The Naval Intelligence Department, ma'am?"

"Correct, give her a fatigue suit and place all her possessions in a case locked with my authorization code."

Helena turned her datapad off but flicked it on again when a thought struck her.

"And all of Finkletop's stuff, as well."

"Aye, aye, Captain," said the mate, unperturbed by orders from officers no matter how peculiar.

Flipper gazed at Helena blankly as if she couldn't understand what was happening. The girl really didn't have a clue.

★ CHAPTER 2 ★

Rumors of War

"All rather different from when we were young men," Destry observed, glancing around the dock.

Port Newquay's syncrete aprons glittered white in the bright Manzanita sunshine. The amber field in front of Rayman Destry's eyes lightened and darkened as he turned his head. It responded to the changing strength of the polarized waves of light and ultraviolet bouncing into his face from the perfectly flat surface.

This year the fashion among the upper classes was a field shaped like a great curved visor hanging in the air ten centimeters from the face. Hints of smoky fractal patterns in darker brown formed and disintegrated seemingly at random.

"Yes, there was just Port Clearwater then. It impressed me when I first saw it fifteen years ago," Allen Allenson replied.

Port Clearwater was still there, a kilometer or so along the shore of Lake Clearwater. Wealthy tourists and business men alighting at the trans-Bight terminal would not have their vision polluted by its appearance but it was close enough to move goods to and from. Port Clearwater catered for the tramp ships and barges short-hauling freight around the Cutter Stream worlds along the edge of the Bight.

The conversation between the two old friends was surreal, not least because it was likely to be the last. There were many things Allenson could have said, even should have said, but the words wouldn't come. There was a pause in the conversation while both men studied the massive rectangular gray box of the Interworld liner. It floated, moored to a long solid quay projecting into the lake.

It was difficult to grasp the ship's true size, as the entry ports were mostly closed so the vehicle was featureless. Even the field support rods projecting from every surface gave little clue to scale.

"I envy you, Brother-in-Law," Destry said quietly.

"What?" Allenson asked, startled. "Why?"

"You started with every disadvantage . . ."

"Hardly," Allenson interrupted. "You make it sound like I was born in a stable."

"Of course not," Destry waved a hand in denial. "I didn't mean to suggest that you were one of the great unwashed but you didn't have my advantages."

"Very few people did have your advantages," Allenson replied, with a smile to show he meant no offense. "Mind you we Allensons did enjoy a link to Gens Destry when my brother Todd married Linsye."

"Alliance with the Allensons was definitely one of our better decisions. It was down to my sister you know," he said, turning to face Allenson. "Father was initially reluctant to sanction the match as he had plans for her to marry on Brasilia. Linsye can be most forceful when she chooses."

"I know," Allenson said, making a rueful face. "She gave me one hell of a wigging when Todd died on Paragon. I wallowed in self-pity but she knocked me out of it."

"I watched the conversation from a window," Destry said.

"You never said."

"No, well, I've been on the end of Linsye's tongue far too often myself to bait a fellow sufferer. I never wanted to discuss her advice to me with a third party so I saw no reason why you would."

He gave Allenson a sly grin, which he switched off after a tenth of a second.

"I envy you because you have achieved so much while I have stood still my whole life."

"That's nonsense," Allenson said forcefully. "You played a critical role in the Rider and Terran Wars and have well-deserved combat and campaign medals to prove it."

"We did do rather well, didn't we?" Destry asked.

"Indeed, we did!"

"But you know what I take most satisfaction from?" Destry asked.
"No?"

"That first trip into the Hinterlands with you and Jem Hawthorn. The Harbinger Project set up the exploitation of the new worlds and *we* achieved that—just the three of us. And dammit, Allenson, we were young and everything was new and such fun."

For a moment they were both lost in the past.

"What I most remember about that expedition is fear," Allenson finally said, as much to break the silence as anything.

"You, afraid?" Destry snorted derisively. "I recall you charging a pack of renegades single-handed. You remember. Your gun crashed so you whirled it 'round your head like a club."

"You mistake stupidity for bravery," Allenson said dryly. "But it wasn't death I was afraid of."

Being afraid of death always seemed pointless to Allenson. After all, it was the one inevitable in life and at least then all your problems were over.

"I was afraid of failure, of disgracing myself in the eyes of my peers since I had no idea what was going on half the time let alone what I should do about it."

"You always know what to do," Destry said simply. "That is why you are so successful."

"Rubbish, I'm just a gentleman-farmer who got lucky and inherited my brother's estate."

"A shrewd businessman who is now one of the largest landowners in the Cutter Stream," Destry corrected sharply.

Destry's eyes focused on infinity and he cocked his head, listening to a private holographic message that only he could see or hear.

"Sarai is going aboard," Destry said.

The Interworld liner was fueled, loaded and ready to sail. Destry and his wife would join at the last moment. Even in first class, room on an Interworld ship capable of crossing the Bight was extremely limited, with much space given over to fusion motors and iron heat sinks. Metallic elements like iron created enormous drag in the Continuum. Drag must be overcome by power, power that created heat, heat that needed heat sinks to dispose of, and so on and so on. When it came to ship design, everything was a compromise.

The trans-Bight colonies only existed because of a major chasm, the Cutter Stream. Chasms were permanent rivers of energy flowing through the Continuum. This one linked the Home Worlds to the colonies. Without that free push across the Bight, colonization of the Cutter Stream Worlds would have been uneconomic as there were no intermediate inhabitable worlds to use as stopovers.

The liner was scheduled to sail down the edge of the Bight to the Brasilian colony of Trent. There it would shed heat before joining another chasm that would boost it back across the Bight to the Home Worlds. Its first class staterooms looked luxurious enough. Clever camera angles appeared to show spacious lounges and restaurants but that was all an illusion. By the end of the journey Destry and his sensual wife would barely be on speaking terms. So passengers boarded in reverse order of rank, stateroom guests last.

"I fear Sarai is disappointed in her marriage," Destry said. "Disappointed in me."

"That's nonsense," Allenson said, somewhat curter then he had intended. "Sarai lucked out when your families agreed to the marriage contract. As Lady Destry she has enjoyed far more status and luster than she could ever have hoped to attain as the daughter of a Manzanita merchant. If she is disappointed in that then the fault is with her not you."

Destry shrugged. "Her family had money but little status. Mine, as you know, lacked the financial wherewithal commensurate with membership of one of the ruling gens of Brasilia. That was why my great-grandfather came out to the colonies in the first place—to make his fortune. My marriage alliance with Sarai was a good match for both families. We have both fulfilled our contractual commitments but sometimes I wish she could show me the affection she has found for others."

Allenson struggled for an answer. He had grown acquiescent if not entirely comfortable in Sarai's presence but it hadn't always been like that. Old memories, old feelings long suppressed rose unbidden from the swampy depths of his memory—feelings of guilt and shame but most of all passion—terrible all-encompassing passion.

"Cocktease am I?" she had asked throatly. "What makes you think I am teasing?"

Her thin orange gown tore easily under his hand and she had opened her legs in blatant invitation.

"You and Trina enjoy a good marriage," Destry said.

"That is true," Allenson agreed, mentally shoving the past back in its box.

"She clearly adores you."

Allenson stared at his friend. Trina was a loyal, attentive and affectionate wife, he supposed, but that was not what he meant by a good marriage. She brought money and useful connections to the contract. Over the years he learned to rely on her good sense and political instincts but he had never hungered after Trina as he had after Sarai. Perhaps that was one reason it was a good marriage.

"I hope you will speak out for the Stream back in Brasilia," Allenson said, changing the subject.

"Of course but I doubt anyone will take any notice of my opinion," Destry said. "Trance is convinced there will be war. That is why he has put up the money for Sarai and me to go home."

Trance was the Paterfamilias of Gens Destry which made him one of the hundred or so most influential people on Brasilia. When Destry spoke of "putting up the money," he was not just referring to the cost of the liner tickets, expensive though they were, but of the purchase of an estate on Brasilia suitable for the dignity of Destrys, albeit minor colonial offshoots of the gens like Royman and Sarai.

"No one who has experienced war wants to go through it a second time," Allenson said. "Let's hope Trance is mistaken."

"Yes, but he rarely is," Destry said. "Probably because he is one of the people whose decisions mold the course of events so his opinions tend to be self-fulfilling."

"Is that why you have decided to go home?" Allenson asked. "Because of the rumors of war?"

"Partly," Destry replied. "And partly because I think Sarai and I need a new start. Maybe she will agree to children if it goes well."

A low wheeled car slid out of the terminal and drove towards them.

"That's my transport," Destry said. "Goodbye, Allenson."

They solemnly shook hands.

"Sod it," Destry said giving Allenson a hug, to his astonishment and no little embarrassment.

The chauffeur opened the door of the car for Destry to climb in. He held up his hand, preventing the door closing.

"Promise you will look me up, Allenson, when you visit Brasilia."

"Of course," Allenson replied.

Destry removed his hand, letting the door shut. The car pulled smoothly away and Allenson watched it drive out onto the quay. In his heart he knew he would never see Royman Destry again.

He was going to miss him.

Allenson's chauffeur attempted to open the door of the carriage but Allenson waved him back to his post at the front of the vehicle. The carriage looked a bit like an open sleigh, roofless and resting on two skids. The chauffeur sat in a small open cockpit with a control screen by his left elbow and a small stick on the right. Black rods projected out at forty-five degrees at the sides of the coachwork.

Trina already sat on the leather-upholstered bench seat at the rear. His wife was petite, a little plumper than current fashion dictated but attractive in a motherly sort of way. She watched him climb in beside her but she said nothing. She correctly gauged his mood as not conducive to chitchat. She was good at that, judging his mood. She knew when he wanted to talk and when it was best to leave him be.

"Home, sar?" asked the chauffeur, turning around.

"Yes, Pentire," Allenson replied brusquely.

The chauffeur said nothing but turned back and busied himself turning on the power and keying the carriage's automatics to Port Newquay Control. Even the damn chauffeur knew when Allenson was out of sorts. The fact that everyone could anticipate his humor so easily did nothing to improve Allenson's mood. Neither did the fact that they sat stationary for second after second.

"If we don't get clear soon we will be trapped for hours by the liner's lift sequence," Allenson said irritably. "The new Control's automatics were supposed to stop these pointless bloody traffic jams. Heaven knows Brasilia charged us enough to install them. I suppose we've been ripped off again."

Trina unfurled a bright yellow parasol and adjusted the angle so she disappeared under it. The chauffeur switched on an eye shade colored a hideous bilious green through which swam the dark orange silhouettes of naked girls.

"Ping control, Farant, and tell them that Delegate Allenson demands priority."

"I've just done that, sar."

"Then bloody do it again."

"Yes, sar."

The chauffeur touched the control screen and leaned forward to mutter something into a microphone. There was no point, Allenson reflected, in having authority if you didn't abuse it occasionally.

A hum from the centrally-located motor was the first sign that Control had acquiesced to Allenson's queue jumping. Balls of green and blue light rolled down the rods and out onto carbon filaments that extended from the rods like spreading ice crystals. A faint shimmer in the air like a heat haze was just detectable around the carriage. Frame fields were theoretically invisible if exactly adjusted but when was any machine perfectly tuned? Not in the Cutter Stream, that was for sure.

The carriage lifted from the ground and turned away from Port Newquay, climbing slowly until it levelled out at a thousand feet. Trina fastened her lap belt and gazed at Allenson stonily until he did the same. Allenson was pleased to see that Farant kept his right hand on the control stick and his left on the screen even though they were on full automatic.

Farant was a competent and careful man. That was why Allenson bought his contract when he decided Trina needed a new chauffeur. That, and because the man was a proficient shot with an ion pistol. Allenson paid the indentured servant a generous salary that gave him every expectation of buying out his contract in a few years. Farant had every reason to be solicitous of Lady Allenson's future good health.

Control routed them around the edge of Lake Clearwater to avoid flying over Manzanita City. That flight path was forbidden ever since an overloaded lighter frame with burned out batteries came down onto the island despite the one sober crew member pedaling like mad to generate power. It hit one of the villas along the shore, killing the young mistress of a Member of the Upper House.

The surviving crew member, the sober one, was carefully questioned before being exiled to one of the more unpleasant Hinterland colonies. The interrogation revealed nothing that was not already known. The local frame technology was unreliable and half the stuff imported from Brasilia was crap. Brasilia did not permit its colonies across the Bight to trade freely with other Home Worlds.

Streamers had to put up with whatever Brasilia's merchants chose to dump on them. Reflecting on this didn't calm Allenson so he concentrated on watching the world go past.

New settlements were springing up all around the shores of the lake. Land on the original island shot up in value as Manzanita City grew in prosperity and population. Middle-class citizens decamped out to the new suburbs on the mainland. With no Rider attacks on Manzanita in living memory, the need for a defensible island site became irrelevant. The island was now home just to the Cutter Stream local government, the wealthy owners of the villas on the shore and barracklike buildings for the poor who provided the necessary cheap labor.

They passed over the site of a new settlement still under construction. Allenson was intrigued to see that it was not just utilitarian blocks of cheap flats but also more upmarket houses in terraces with individual gardens. The jetty was already up and being used to bring in materials and labor by boat.

There was still only one causeway running from the island to the mainland where it ended in Port Clearwater. Unused by anyone, that is, anyone who mattered, it slowly fell into disrepair. Nothing ever came of the talk of putting in a new causeway to Port Newquay. Myriads of small private boats, ferries and lighters weaved backward and forward across the lake linking Manzanita City to its suburbs. Far too much money and hence political influence was tied up in waterway transport for a new causeway to get backing in either the Upper or Lower House.

The power supply in Trina's carriage had been retrofitted from a Brasilian military lighter that Allenson had used his influence as Colonel of Militia to acquire. Terran Home World technology was state of the art so Allenson had every confidence in its reliability. Nevertheless, he was pleased to see from the movement of Farent's shoulders that he was pedaling every so often to keep the batteries charged. The chauffeur was indeed a careful man.

Allenson checked Farent's background carefully before employing him. The driver wound up in the Cutter Stream after having been caught defrauding his employer to pay off gambling debts. He was addicted to betting on which dog could run the fastest. He became an indentured servant when his labor was sold to provide compensation for the theft. Farent was spared temptation in his new home as the Stream colonies had never felt the need to import racing dogs across the Bight.

Competent people in the colonies were always in short supply, especially if they had saleable skills. You either paid ridiculous sums of money to persuade a qualified young employee from the Home Worlds to work on a short-term contract so he could build up a nest egg before going home or you took what you could get. And what you got could be pretty undesirable. Better an indentured servant exiled from the Home World with a known vice you could live with than an unskilled local or worse, an incompetent immigrant.

This terrible social system hobbled colonial society. It might have been designed for maximum inefficiency, but you worked within the system you had. Most people in the colonies never gave it much thought. After all, they knew nothing else. The wealthy, of course, had no incentive for change because they were already at the top of the tree. Sometimes in an idle moment Allenson dreamed up better ways for mankind to spread across the Bight but he was a pragmatic soul and recognized the pointlessness of fantasizing.

Brasilia's main Home World rival colonizing across the Bight was Terra, still licking its wounds from losing the last colonial war. They used convicts as forced labor in their colonies rather than indentured servants. It was a distinction without much difference and just as inefficient.

The carriage rose and fell, overtaking slower-moving traffic. Trina keyed the screen beside her elbow. Background noises cut out and they could converse without the driver overhearing.

"I shall miss the Destrys, too," she said, squeezing his arm.

Allenson managed to smile at her.

"Yes, it was nice to have one friend who wasn't after anything. Someone could be relied upon to tell me exactly what he thought even if I didn't want to hear it."

"Sarai was extraordinarily kind to me when I was sick," Trina said.

Somehow it always came back to Sarai. Allenson could not decide whether he was sorry or relieved that Sarai was out of his life forever. Perhaps he was both. The Destrys were regular guests at Pentire when they had business in Manzanita or Sarai wished to visit her family. In return, the Allensons occasionally stayed with the Destrys on Wagener when Allenson was required to sort out whatever mess his stepmother was currently making of his late father's demesne.

He and Sarai behaved as would properly be expected between in-laws with no overt impropriety. But there was always the glance, the touch on his arm, the flash of her eyes: things that Trina and Royman Destry carefully failed to notice.

"She was good at that, caring I mean," Allenson said. "She nursed me once."

"I know. She told me," Trina said, squeezing his arm again to show it was all right.

"Maybe Destry is better out of it the way things are going," Allenson said absentmindedly, still remembering Sarai's tears when he married Trina.

Sarai never could see that a liaison was impossible. She married Royman Destry, his friend, and that was the end of it. A properly discreet fling would have been socially acceptable. It did not matter even if everyone knew provided no one acknowledged that they knew. But it would never be just a fling between Sarai and him. It would never be just another meaningless adventure. The passion ran too deep, burned too fiercely, and Sarai was incapable of discreetness.

Sooner or later she would have precipitated a crisis. Destry would have been publically cuckolded. He would have had to call Allenson out or be humiliated and dishonored. Whatever happened then would ruin four lives. He had been right to end it almost as soon as it began. But sometimes, just sometimes, in the dark of the night he remembered her legs opening beneath him like the petals of an exotic flower.

"Why do you say that?" Trina asked.

Allenson dragged his thoughts back to reality.

"What?"

"That maybe the Destrys are better off leaving."

"Because of the political crisis," Allenson replied.

"Oh that! Isn't there always a political crisis? I mean, crisis seems to be the normal state for our political system. What makes this one any different from all the others?" Trina asked.

A soft beep sounded and an amber triangle came up on Trina's screen. She turned away from him to touch it with a finger.

"Pardon the interruption, ma'am, but we have permission from

Control for free flight. I propose to phase out," said Farent's voice over the intercom.

"By all means, carry on," Trina replied, removing her finger from the screen to break contact.

"It's the new taxation proposals," Allenson said.

Trina shrugged.

"No one likes paying taxes. It's not unreasonable that the colonies make some contribution for their defense. We couldn't expect the Brasilian taxpayer to shoulder the burden alone indefinitely. Why should this tax be so more unpopular than any other?"

Allenson almost snapped at Trina for asking such a damn fool question but bit back the jibe. Increasingly over the years, Trina looked inward to her family. Her role as matriarch of a great estate meant she took little interest in politics and events of state, content to leave such matters to her partner. For that she should not be blamed. She had much to occupy her attention.

Her son, Reggie, took after his biological parents. He combined his mother's charm with the cheerful irresponsibility that marked his father's life. Money slipped through his fingers and any sum "lent" to Reggie must be marked as permanently lost. He occasionally "borrowed" sums from his stepfather's study without troubling Allenson by asking first.

The list of schools from which Reggie had been expelled read like a guide to the finest education establishments this side of the Bight. Trina had tried enrolling him in everything from a military academy—Reggie had taken out one of the dormitories with a homemade fifty centimeter mortar constructed to celebrate his birthday—to a liberal arts academy—where he had been caught running a protection racket among the younger boys.

Trina's son was always contrite, always apologetic when rebuked for his misdeeds. He faithfully promised never to repeat them. To be fair he rarely did. The next catastrophe would be something novel. Trina doted on the boy and could rarely be cross with him for long. Allenson gave up trying to apply discipline early on since Trina robustly defended her son against such interference, even scolding Allenson in the boy's presence.

Allenson quickly realized that further efforts on his part to constrain Reggie would merely further undermine any authority he had left with the boy and drive a wedge between him and his wife. He contented himself with a stepfather's duty of good stewardship of the lad's inheritance until he came of age. He had no expectation of a good result long term but that would be neither his fault nor his responsibility.

And then there was Trina's daughter, Minta. Poor beautiful sweet Minta, another victim of the genetic damage from the biowars that preceded the collapse of the Third Civilization. The terrible legacy of bioweapons struck too close to home. He suppressed the thought, packing it neatly in a mental box marked "do not open here be daemons."

"You are very preoccupied, husband," Trina said.

"What? Oh, sorry, my dear. I was just ordering my thoughts to answer your question. It's not the tax as such. As you say, the colonies would eventually have to take over the cost of their own infrastructure spending. It's the way the tax is being applied."

"Indeed?"

"Look, if you'd asked me twenty years ago, ten even, how we'd govern the Brasilian Trans-Bight colonies like the Stream, I'd have confidently assumed that Brasilia would be withdrawing its governors and officials. I envisaged the Home World gradually replacing them with diplomats and technocratic advisors. Instead they are moving in the opposite direction and curtailing the powers of the Manzanita Houses. Local government's become little more than City Councils arguing about how often the ferry boats run and how many life belts they should carry."

"Taxation without representation." Trina said, looking at him.

Allenson got out his datapad.

"That's a rather pithy phrase, my dear. I must make a note of that."

★ CHAPTER 3 ★

Pentire

Farant smoothly phased Allenson's carriage into the Continuum. Manzanita monochromed and faded away to be replaced by a sea of colored streamers. The predominant background tint was deep indigo. The calm Continuum conditions provided Allenson with at least a quantum of consolation.

He hated traveling by carriage. He would much rather have used a one-man frame but social position restricted his choices. Carriages rocked and corkscrewed cyclically in any sort of Continuum energy disturbance. Too small to crash through the waves and too big to ride over them, carriage travel caused Allenson dreadful motion sickness. One of the most irritating truisms about the things was that the driver at the front got the best ride. The pampered owners at the back suffered an exaggerated pendulum effect.

Carriage design was just another of life's inefficiencies that a gentleman was obliged to endure. Allenson toyed with having a novel design of carriage constructed that reversed the positions of passenger and driver but shrank from the amusement it would cause. He already had an unwelcome reputation for eccentricity over such matters as the absurdly high living standards he supplied to his indentured servants. He actually paid them reasonable wages. As it would be intolerable to his conscience to adopt the norm in matters involving his personal honor, he felt obliged to be conventional on less important issues of mere personal comfort. It was, he thought gloomily, just another example of his moral cowardice.

Trina broke the silence.

"Do you wish that we were going home?" she asked.

"We are going home, aren't we?" Allenson asked, puzzled.

"You know what I mean," Trina said, allowing a measure of exasperation to enter her voice. "Going with the Destrys to the Home World across the Bight—going home to Brasilia. You recall where that is?"

"Yes, sorry, the question took me by surprise." He considered. "I suppose Brasilia's truly home for the Destrys but it wouldn't be for us. You have never been there and neither have I. We don't know anybody in Brasilia. What would we do there? How would we live?"

"I just wondered," Trina said.

"We'd be mad to leave Manzanita. Everything we've built and worked for is here. I don't want any other home."

"I'm glad, neither do I."

Trina slid across and squeezed his hand. He was forgiven for his poor mood.

Allenson managed a smile for her.

"But it'd be nice if Brasilians treated Streamer gentlemen as equals. I'd like us to receive the respect due to our social rank and achievements and not be regarded as colonial flunkies fit only to carry bags."

"You're thinking of Destry's Brasilian nephew?" Trina asked, with a grin.

"Yes, among others," Destry replied.

The eighteen-year-old nephew in question had made free with his opinions about colonials on a visit to Pentire. Allenson put up with sneers and condescension from this sprig of Brasilian nobility for Royman's sake. Matters came to a head when he caught the chinless twit attempting to cane a serving girl for rudeness.

The nephew wasn't having it all his own way as the girl was putting up a spirited defense. She had already bloodied his nose. Allenson was a large fit man whose notoriously short temper had been pushed as far as it would go. He seized both cane and nephew. Holding him face down over a table with one hand, he vigorously applied corporal punishment with the other.

The boy's humiliation was complete when Royman Destry flatly refused to call the Proctors to arrest Allenson. Instead Destry offered the opinion that the boy was lucky Allenson abhorred dueling. Royman apologized profusely for the lout's behavior and promised to write to his father. But then, Allenson reflected, Destry had always been first and foremost a gentleman in his dealings with others.

"Of course, there's always an upside to every bad decision," Allenson said. "If Brasilia weren't so short-sighted, the colonies would probably be preparing to fight one another over conflicting claims in the Hinterlands. Instead we're gathering in Paxton to discuss a common response to Brasilian demands. There's nothing like having a common enemy to inspire political unity."

"Enemy is surely an unnecessarily emotive word," Trina said. "Brasilia is our Home World so how could it be an enemy?"

"Of course you're right, my dear," Allenson replied in a conciliatory tone. "There's no point in inflaming the situation. I should have used a more measured term."

A scintilla of doubt wriggled in his mind like a worm in an apple. Trina was absolutely right. "Enemy" was a word better suited to a demagogue than a gentleman so why had he used it?

"The Destrys will be all right on Brasilia," Trina said doubtfully, breaking his train of thought.

"Of course. As I said it's their home and they've family there."

Privately Allenson had his doubts. Royman Destry represented a very big fish in the little pond of Manzanita society. Few equaled him in rank and he had no superiors this side of the Bight. All that would change when they went home. In Brasilia he would just be an impoverished cousin from the back of beyond. Sarai would not react well to being patronized as the daughter of a colonial who was "in trade."

A chime indicated that the driver wanted to communicate.

"Connect," Trina said without turning around to the screen.

"I've a lock with your private beacon ma'am. We'll be phasing over Pentire shortly."

"Thank you, Farent, carry on," Trina said. "Cut link."

The carriage locked onto an auto that would land it next to Trina's private entrance to their complex. The villa autos would guide all other demesne traffic out of the way to ensure a speedy arrival.

The Continuum decolorized as the carriage phased into reality. Allenson leaned out to observe Pentire. From the sky he obtained a panoramic view that displayed the estate to a single sweep of the eye, allowing him to properly appreciate its balanced proportions. The carriage phased in slowly. Phasing could be near instantaneous but the sharper the change the more disconcerting it could be to human physiology. Farent prided himself that his passengers got as smooth a ride as technology could provide.

Pentire appeared like a monochrome blur from an old memory. The image hardened, sharpened and saturated with primary color before decohering into the subtle shades of nature. Allenson stiffened. For a moment he thought he could see an unnatural line running through the red-lime bushes planted on the reverse slope of a hill. He quickly waved his datapad over the edge of the carriage. The line disappeared when the full complexity of the real world was revealed.

He considered ordering Farent to phase in and out again so that he could check the observation. A glance at Trina dissuaded him. She was tired and deserved to get home without him mucking about. She wouldn't protest or complain at any delay. That only made it more necessary that he anticipate her needs to give them proper priority. Nevertheless the memory of that line irritated like an attention-seeking child plucking at its mother's skirts. The thought of the line spoiled the enjoyment he normally found in his demesne.

A rectangular three story house formed the heart of Pentire Villa. Communication equipment and three point-defense lasers filled the flat roof. He chose to have three lasers because one was sometimes hors de combat while they waited for spares to be shipped in from Brasilia. All too often a tube failed after a short burst. Of course each laser had three independent tubes firing in sequence but . . .

The potent defense system was generally considered to be another example of his eccentricity. Manzanita hadn't seen an enemy in living memory. Allenson was inclined to agree that the lasers would probably never be fired in anger but he had seen war. He had inhaled the choking smoke, heard the screams and smelled the burning flesh. The merest, slightest whiff of an outside chance that this might happen to his household was all the incentive he needed to dig deep into his pockets.

Allenson had added two-story wings at right angles to the house. A high back wall enclosed a wilderness garden in the center. The children he planned to have with Trina could have safely played and explored there. Another thought best tucked away and forgotten.

Traditional red brick hid the villa's syncrete walls. Similarly, a veneer of natural wood covered the exterior surfaces of the window frames and doors. Allenson reproduced the texture exactly when he expanded the structure, including artificial weathering. The villa sat at one end of a small village of cottages where the estate servants and employees lived. He provided a club, school, health clinic and meeting hall for their social and other needs.

His neighbors shook their heads at such wasteful extravagance. Indeed, some took the view that Allenson risked undermining society and the natural order by indulging the lower orders so generously. He tried explaining how a content workforce was a productive workforce. Monies invested in a comfortable life for the demesne staff repaid themselves many times over.

Mere facts were as raindrops against the armor of fixed opinion. Why this should be so was a mystery to Allenson. He tended to change his mind if new data suggested he was wrong. Apparently, this was another mark of his eccentricity.

The protective hedges around the Pentire living quarters kept unwanted visitors out, not the servants in. An indentured servant had not run from the complex for many years. The last case had a love affair at root. Allenson solved the problem by buying the contract of the other party in the affair, finding them both a position on the estate. It was not unusual for servants to request to stay on at Pentire as employees when they had worked off or bought out their contracts.

Beyond stood the utilitarian warehouses and barns required by a working agricultural demesne. The Fleek paddocks occupied an isolated position, located suitably upwind to the prevailing weather.

Only one entrance pierced the gunja plants forming the hedge around the buildings. An angled and narrow approach restricted and slowed access. The reinforced gate stood open to allow estate vehicles in and out. It could quickly be shut, sealing off the compound. Two men in the green and white livery of Pentire Demesne stood each side of the gate, lasercarbines slung on straps from one shoulder. Allenson was pleased to see them upright and hence reasonably alert.

Two similar armed guards stood by the low wall running around the roof of the main house. All four watched the carriage descend into the formal garden. Farent hopped out and opened a carriage door so Trina could alight. Trina's maid hovered at the entrance to the east wing where his wife had her apartment, alerted to her arrival by the automatics. The new wings were more comfortable than the old building and the rooms cozier if less impressive.

"If you'll excuse me, my dear, I need to pop up to my office to check something."

"You go ahead," Trina said. "Eight convenient for dinner?"

"Eight, right," Allenson replied. That didn't give him long as it was already late afternoon, Pentire local time. He went into the old building and ran up the back stairs two at a time to the first floor where he had an office. Shrugging off the uncomfortable formal jacket and loosening his necktie, he tossed the datapad onto his desk and turned it on.

In the room the pad could draw on the greater analytical capability of his desk. He put up a solid hologram that showed the view of the estate from the air as the carriage phased in. He ran the video backwards and forwards, changing the mix of frequencies from ultraviolet to microwave until a linear shadow across the red-lime bushes clearly showed up.

One had to be a little careful of overanalyzing pictures. One could easily create artifacts but unfortunately he had no doubt this was real. He overlaid a schematic of the new drainage system fitted last year to this part of the estate. One of the pipes ran directly under the shadow.

Allenson swore softly under his breath. The damn pipe was leaking something that affected the plants. It might not be particularly toxic to red-lime but that wasn't the point. He had paid premium price for inert long-life ceramic pipes imported from Brasilia. The blasted things were breaking down in the Manzanita soil after only a year: so much for the manufacturer's guarantees.

It might just be an unfortunate and unforeseeable chemical interaction but it was more likely that his Brasilian supplier had dumped second-grade stock on him at first-grade prices. In theory, he could sue but—all the way across the Bight—in a Brasilian commercial court?

Fat chance!

He thought he might as well check through his letters and skim through the various reports accumulating in his in-tray. As usual, there was more than he had anticipated. Well not anticipated, make that more than he hoped for.

Time passed.

A cough from the doorway caught his attention. Allenson groaned inwardly at the sight of Bentley, Trina's *majordomo*. Bentley was bald and middle aged. He had probably been born middle aged but that was no excuse for being bald. Appropriate genosurgery was hardly expensive and, God knows, Trina paid the man enough.

"The mistress asked me to remind sar that dinner is at eight," Bentley said.

"What time is it now?" Allenson asked.

"Seven, sar."

"Then I've plenty of time so go away."

Bentley failed to disappear.

"Was there something else?" Allenson asked.

Bentley coughed again.

"I've run sar's bath and laid out suitable evening clothes," Bentley said. "The mistress was most insistent that I should remind sar of dinner in good time so sar did not have to rush sar's toilette."

"Tell me Bentley, do I smell?"

"No, sar."

"Then I do not need a bath, rushed or otherwise."

"If you say so, sar," Bentley said with a carefully blank expression.

The *majordomo* left, shutting the door behind him.

The blank expression worried Allenson. He could live with Bentley's disapproval but a blank expression raised alarm signals.

"Bentley!"

Allenson crossed the room in two strides. He flung open the door, to find himself nose to nose with the servant. Clearly Bentley expected him to have second thoughts.

"What is it you know that I don't?" Allenson asked.

"I really couldn't say, sar, since I don't know what sar doesn't know," Bentley replied.

"Bentley, stop pissing me around. You only put on that blank expression when you think I'm about to make some dreadful social cock up. So what don't I know?"

Allenson spelled out each word of the last sentence slowly.

Bentley unbent.

"Possibly sar has forgotten that sar's sister-in-law is dining here tonight."

"What, Linsye?"

"Lady Destry, yes sar."

"Dining with us?"

"Yes, sar."

"She's here?"

"Obviously, sar, or she could not dine with sar," Bentley said patiently, as if explaining teetotalism to a drunk.

"Why did no one tell me?" Allenson asked.

"I put it in sar's social diary some two weeks ago myself," Bentley replied.

"Ah," Allenson said.

He had erased the social diary from his desk after it had interrupted his work with a reminder about something of such monumental unimportance that he just could not recall what it had been about. It was not impossible that it had been about Linsye's visit.

"Possibly I should dress for dinner," Allenson said.

"Yes, sar," Bentley replied.

"And you've put something out?" Allenson asked.

Bentley's eyes gleamed.

"On the mistress's instructions, sar, your blue dinner suit with lilac ribbons and accessories including your lemon ruffed shirt and stack-heeled two-toned boots."

"Oh dear God!"

"I look like the doorman of a second rate brothel with upmarket pretensions," Allenson muttered.

He examined himself in the mirror with something akin to horror. This year's fashionable colors in Manzanita society were, if anything, even more garish than usual. The suit tied across the top with a complicated white silk loop. Allenson experimented in fixing it in various ways, settling eventually for a granny knot at the base of his throat. At least he would be fashionably clothed for his funeral if he choked on the damn thing.

A discreet cough sounded at his elbow.

"Did you cough, Bentley?"

"Yes, sar, if I may assist."

Without waiting for a reply, the *majordomo* retied the ribbon in a complex flat bow and positioned it over Allenson's right breast. Actually it did look better. Now he could pass as the doorman to a first rate brothel.

"And your campaign medals, sar?"

"I think not."

Allenson shuddered. Medals reminded him of war and of people more heroic than him who had failed to return to wear any. Bentley looked crestfallen.

"I suppose you spent half the afternoon polishing them?" Allenson asked.

"Not quite half the afternoon," Bentley replied carefully.

"Very well, just this once," Allenson said.

Bentley brightened up immediately and carefully arranged the medals to hang over Allenson's left breast. They were such innocuous looking little ceramic and crystal rods in the Manzanita colors of purple and gray shot with gold threads, recreating symbols of Old Earth. Each one represented blood, pain and sacrifice. The medals held no more glory than the battles they represented.

He made his way along the corridor to Trina's dressing room. She stared thoughtfully at herself in a full-length mirror, turning to left and right to check the folds in her rose-colored dress. A necklace of polished chromite and serpentine crystals from one of the Hinterland worlds set it off. Her maid fussed with her hair but she already looked wonderful. Trina had taste. She knew what to wear and how to wear it. She knew how to blend colors for best effect. By the standards of Streamer gentility, she dressed with understated elegance.

"How do I look?" she asked.

"Perfect, as always," he replied truthfully.

"You look very distinguished as well," she said, lying politely. Or perhaps love really was blind.

He held out his hand and escorted her out of her apartment and into the formal dining room main building. They stopped in the atrium to wait for their guest. Bentley served wine fortified by plum brandy in small crystal glasses.

Linsye arrived in the atrium at exactly the prescribed four minutes after her hosts. A tall, rather gaunt woman, she was striking rather than beautiful. Her clothes were expensively tailored, probably Brasilian imports, but chosen for convenience rather than fashion. People like Linsye set the fashion rather than follow it. When she could be bothered, that is.

Bentley bowed deeply as he held the door for her, far deeper than he would for Allenson, who only paid his wages. The *majordomo* raised snobbery to a fine art and Linsye was a full Destry-by-blood. Allenson and Trina represented mere colonial gentry only related by marriage to true Brasilian nobility. Hence Bentley's determination that Allenson should be at his best. It came to something, Allenson reflected, when your clothes were chosen to please a servant's sense of propriety.

Linsye kissed Allenson lightly on the mouth, the appropriate greeting for an in-law of the opposite sex.

"How are you Allen? My you look dashing tonight."

Allenson replied appropriately

Linsye continued. "May I introduce my son, Todd? He arrived home in the same ship that Royman and Sarai left on."

Todd stood to one side, arm outstretched. Allenson hadn't seen his nephew since he had been sent away to be educated in Brasilia at his Uncle Royman's old prep school and college. He would have been what, twelve?

Allenson looked at Todd in shock. The boy was named after his father, Allenson's older brother. Subconsciously Allenson expected a younger version of Todd senior or at least an Allenson. But Todd junior was a Destry. No. More than that; he was the spitting image of the young Royman Destry when Allenson first met him on his arrival at Port Clearwater. History seemed to be repeating itself.

Todd bowed deeply and looked at Allenson, waiting for his host to say something. Allenson gaped like a rube at the country fair.

He pulled himself together. "Welcome indeed, Nephew. You are quite the young man now."

Todd replied with a smile. "Age tends to do that to one, Uncle Allen."

"Ah, yes, I suppose it does," Allenson said. "Shall we go in?"

The dinner ritual normally demanded fifteen minutes of drinks and small talk in the atrium. However, Allenson needed a moment to order his thoughts and the walk into the dining room would allow that. He indicated to Bentley that they would go straight in. Protocol demanded he escort Linsye while Todd offered his arm to Trina.

Left to Bentley the four would dine on a full table so far apart that they would have to converse by datapad. Allenson laid it clearly on the line how far he was prepared to go even when dining with his aristocratic in-laws. He demanded that most of the grand dining room be shut off by a folding wooden screen. The demesne carpenter had crafted it from highly polished alternating strips of amber and vermilion-colored wood logged from a forest on a Hinterland world that had not yet been named.

The material imparted warmth, reinforcing the mellow atmosphere that Allenson preferred. Many of his guests commented favorably on the effect. Allenson considered experimenting with a crop of the trees on the estate.

He sat Linsye on his right in the lady of honor's place. Todd looked after Trina. Bentley positioned himself behind Todd's chair where Allenson could catch his eye. The man was in his element. He devoted his life to perfecting a series of complicated rituals that Allenson thought as tedious as they were pointless

To be fair, Bentley was invaluable when Allenson hosted political dinners. The skills of a *majordomo* went unnoticed by the more sophisticated guests from the Manzanita Upper House. They would nonetheless have noticed their absence fast enough. Bentley's talents usefully impressed members of the Lower House. In Allenson's experience, the more a politician claimed to be a "man of the people" the less they wanted to be treated as one. One of life's depressing little truisms.

Allenson nodded and Bentley touched his thumb and forefinger together, triggering a communication switch concealed in his white gloves. A new maid with an apprehensive expression entered via the kitchen door with a tray of appetizer. She glanced in Bentley's direction before presenting the tray to Linsye, who selected a couple of items without looking at her.

Social convention insisted that Trina and Todd were served next with Allenson last. Trina murmured a polite thank you and Todd gave the maid a wink that elicited a pretty blush. He had Royman's easy manner, so different from the Allenson dourness.

When the maid left Bentley went round the table with a bottle of a light blue alcoholic liquid. He started with Allenson who duly tasted it although he never quite knew what he was supposed to be checking for. Allenson nodded approval and Bentley proceeded anticlockwise.

Linsye held her glass up to the central light over the table, swirling it to examine the contents before carefully inhaling the vapor.

"I suppose this is one of your experiments," she finally said.

Allenson smiled. "In a way. We grow the juniper fruit here on the estate and I have an industrial chemist in Port Clearwater interested in the fermentation process."

"I see," Linsye said.

Allenson had a policy of serving Streamer produce at his dinners, preferably from his own estate. His neighbors considered this one of his more harmless eccentricities. Brasilian grape strains could not be successfully cultivated on any of the Stream worlds. At least not well enough to produce anything drinkable.

Allenson prompted Linsye.

"Why don't you try it and give me your opinion."

His sister-in-law displayed the expression of a woman going to the stake. Nevertheless, she tasted the contents as was proper for a guest enjoying hospitality. She rolled it around her mouth and then drank deeply.

Allenson awaited her verdict. His sister-in-law was familiar with the very best vintages from the Home Worlds. She often expressed herself robustly on the subject.

Linsye gave her judgment.

"At least it's not a concoction of fruit juice, alcohol and sugar. I taste a light crisp flavor reminiscent of an acceptable white table wine, albeit a young vintage. It's not going to win any awards, of course, but it is palatable. I believe I will have another glass."

Praise indeed. Allenson started to signal Bentley but the *majordomo* was already off the starting blocks, bottle at the ready.

Todd downed his glass in three drafts.

"Mother's a little harsh. This's actually very refreshing."

Bentley shot around the table to refill his glass as well.

"I'm glad you like it." Allenson said. "I will have a case loaded on your carriage when you depart."

"Thank you, Uncle." Todd inclined his head politely. "I've brought a small gift for you back from Brasilia. This seems an appropriate moment to present it."

He handed Allenson a small wooden box that lay lightly on the hand. Inside were three slides, carefully stowed in slits in the velvet lined interior, and a modern black plastic cube. Allenson gently pulled out one. It was archaic, mineral stained by its time underground, and chipped on one corner.

"Are these originals?" Allenson asked in wonder.

"Absolutely," Todd replied. "They turn up every so often. A friend of mine was looking through an unsorted collection for his thesis and found these. I knew of your interest in the Third Civilization and thought you would like them."

Allenson held the slide up to the light.

"Very much, I like them very much indeed. Thank you, Nephew, can they be read?"

Todd pointed to the black cube.

"I included a decoder in the box as I wasn't sure you would have the right tool to hand."

Allenson replaced the slide and examined the black cube.

"Thank you, Third Civilization records are stored in such a strange way. All dots and dashes don't you know."

"Indeed," Todd said. "The slide you looked at is particularly interesting, a collection of fine resolution video stills of ordinary Third Civilization life by some ancient called Paul Weimer. Some are only document records."

"A delightful gift," Allenson said, wondering what he had done to earn it.

Todd waved a hand languidly, brushing aside the praise as if it were cobwebs.

"I would have thought that someone would have produced suitable vine strains to grow wine grapes in the Stream by now," Todd said, changing the subject.

"It wouldn't be impossible," Linsye agreed, "but the genosurgery is apparently tricky. We don't have sufficient technical infrastructure to spare so the work would have to be done in Brasilia."

Allenson grimaced. "Where's the incentive? Why should a Brasilian wine merchant set up competition? Much more profitable to flog us the finished product at a hefty mark up."

The appetizer plate vanished under Allenson's left arm to be replaced by a dish containing soup. Left to his own devices Bentley would have paraded around the table with a bowl ladling out soup to each guest individually. Allenson killed that notion. He wasn't all that bothered what was in his soup but he did like it hot and the host got served last.

Linsye dipped her spoon, holding it just clear of the plate to cool.

"I could tolerate the mark up if one was sure of getting what was on the label."

Trina stirred her soup.

"Surely wine labelling is tightly controlled?"

Linsye sighed.

"In theory, but half the time the vintage is substituted for something cheaper."

She waved her spoon for emphasis.

"The Carinas served Pinot Chaasuar last time I dined at their demesne. It may have been a Pinot but it had never been closer to the Chaasuar than the nearest chemical laboratory."

Todd winced.

"Did you feel the need to point that out to them?"

"Well, obviously," Linsye replied, clearly wondering why he asked such a stupid question. "They needed to know that they had been cheated."

Todd looked sorrowfully at Allenson.

"Generally, I only escort Mother somewhere twice—the second time to apologize."

Even Linsye laughed.

The dinner progressed with the usual small talk. When Allenson was young he had considered such conversation to be a waste of time. Experience and Trina taught him how useful gossip could be. People revealed details in dinner conversations. Details that when put together provided invaluable information about the shifting political and commercial alliances within the Stream—insofar as the two could be separated.

Bentley presented the platter of the main dish to Trina for her approval, which was duly given. Allenson forced down the urge to scream. Wine to him, meat to Trina, what an utter waste of time? His life used to be so much simpler when he was young.

"Wildfowel in jaffa sauce," Linsye exclaimed in delight. "One of my favorite dishes."

Trina smiled: the choice of menu was always tailored to the tastes of the honored guest. One had to be careful praising a dish too highly in company or you could find yourself served it at every dinner party for the next year or so.

"The jaffa fruit is from your own demesne," Trina said. "Your estate manager flew a crate over last harvest."

Jaffa was a Streamer crop in demand in Brasilia where it fetched ridiculous prices. Home World farms grew the crop but wealthy aficionados declared the taste inferior to imports from the Cutter Stream.

"I hope the wine is real?" Allenson asked. "It cost me enough."

Trina frowned at him. Bentley's expression went professionally blank. It was not done to discuss the cost of such things over dinner.

Linsye rolled it around her glass and inhaled the bouquet before tasting.

"Quite genuine," she pronounced. "Perhaps a little past its best but we can forgive that as the bottle has traveled far to grace our table."

"Oh good," Allenson said. "I won't have to shoot my supplier."

Todd looked at his uncle quizzically as if trying to work out whether he was joking or not.

"Ignore him, Nephew," said Trina, shooting Allenson an exasperated look. "My husband has a peculiar sense of humor. He wouldn't really shoot his wine merchant."

Linsye said, "Quite right, sister-in-law."

She tapped her finger on the table for emphasis.

"Shooting is too good for a wine fraudster."

She definitely wasn't joking.

They applied themselves to the meal.

"Tell me, Linsye?" asked Allenson between courses. "Were you not tempted to join your brother and go back to Brasilia?"

Linsye cocked her head to look at him.

"I thought we covered this a long time ago on Paragon. In my opinion there is no future for my children and grandchildren back in Brasilia. That is why I chose a marriage alliance with a promising local family even if they were social inferiors."

Todd coughed into his hand at this point. Linsye ignored him.

"My children do not carry the Destry name. Even if they did, there is nothing more pathetic than impoverished relatives living off the charity of other members of a Great House. Their gens association would be a curse, not a benefit."

Trina asked, "You think Royman has made the wrong decision?"

Linsye hesitated.

"My brother must do what he feels is best for his situation," she replied delicately.

"You refer to Sarai?" Trina asked, pushing the conversation to the edge of what was acceptable.

Linsye half nodded before canceling the gesture.

"Not entirely, Royman does not, I think, possess the appropriate skills and interests for life across the Bight but as this is a private family gathering then, yes, I refer to his marriage."

Of course, there were servants present as well. Linsye like most Manzanitans of "the better sort" tended to regard them as part of the house fittings, forgetting that they were furniture with tongues.

Allenson tried to remember where he had heard that expression. It may have come from the slave economies of Old Earth. The destroyed bureaucratic Third Civilization had left such copious records in so many different formats that vast amounts of data about their doomed world was extant. Much of it had never been properly collated and put into context even to this day. However, enough was known to outline their history and culture. Such a bold and self-confident society—and so blind.

His train of thought drew an uneasy comparison between the indentured servants of Brasilia and the slave economies. The comparison, he assured himself, was not apt. Indentured servants were not slaves. They were people with legal rights albeit restricted ones. Their contracts could be bought and sold but the people were not property. They could hope to buy out or work off their debt. An irritatingly rebellious component of his mind reminded him that even the old slave economies had the concept of Freedmen.

There was no doubt though that the indentured servant system used by Brasilia to dump its unwanted population on the colonies displayed all the wastefulness and inefficiency of a slave society. Not that Brasilia's colonial problems were unique. The harsh realities of

Terran society ensured an excess of convict labor making their colonies just as shambolic.

Trina deftly changed the subject. She engaged Linsye on the subject of a play she had seen in Manzanita City by a promising new *avant-garde* playwright.

Linsye asked, "How did you find the work, Allen?"

Trina had insisted on her husband escorting her to the theatre.

"Most, ah, stimulating," Allenson replied.

Trina cut in. "Really, I thought you dozed off."

"Just resting my eyes to concentrate on the dialogue," Allenson replied.

"I see," Trina raised an eyebrow. "Are you aware that you have developed the habit of snoring when resting your eyes to concentrate?"

"I sympathize, my dear," Linsye said. "His brother was just the same. Todd declared that the word culture always made him want to reach for a laserrifle."

Wasn't that another quote from some ancient philosopher, Allenson wondered? No, it couldn't have been. Their strange superstitions about the physical nature of the universe precluded them developing the technology for laserrifles.

Allenson turned to Todd to include him in the conversation. "How did you find school and college on Brasilia?"

"Oh it had its ups and downs but I fitted in tolerably well," Todd replied.

"You weren't bullied at all because of your colonial background?"

"There's always a degree of good natured banter, Uncle," Todd said without further elaboration.

Allenson struggled on.

"How did your studies go? Let me see, you read . . ."

Allenson's memory balked at divulging the necessary information.

"Politics, history and anthropology."

Todd deftly lifted Allenson out of the hole he'd dug for himself.

"I took a degree but barely scraped a third. I regret that I'm not academic material unlike Uncle Royman."

"Much good it did him," Linsye remarked somewhat sourly.

"It did all of us a great deal of good against Terra," Allenson said, perhaps rather more tartly than he had intended, but Royman had stood his ground with his comrades. "Indeed, Royman's contribution as intelligence officer made him possibly the one indispensable man in our army."

Todd said, "Praise indeed especially coming from you, Uncle. Most people have suggested to me that you were the indispensable man."

"Most people are ignorant," Allenson replied, without heat.

Todd raised his glass.

"Well then let's drink to Uncle Royman's new life in Brasilia."

So they did, which neatly changed the mood at the table. Trina conferred a smile of approval on her nephew's tact.

Allenson put down his glass and examined him.

"You look rather well on university life."

And he did. Todd was not particularly tall but wiry without a gram of excess fat on his body.

"I won a racing dark blue," Todd said.

Blue Horizon athletic teams wore dark blue uniforms.

Allenson was impressed.

"Indeed?"

Todd added diffidently, "I rowed power wheel on the University Eight against the light blues."

Blue Horizon's main rival were the light blues. These, the two oldest and most prestigious colleges of Freelanding University on Brasilia, held an annual frame race. As most of the ruling families were educated at one or other of these institutions the race received media attention more suited to a major sports event. The whole world watched. A great deal of money and prestige depended on the result. Competition for a seat on one of the two frames was accordingly intense. You either had to be well connected or very, very athletic—preferably both.

Allenson asked, "How did your team do?"

"Not too badly, uncle," Todd replied.

Linsye said with a mother's pride, "They beat the light blues by five lengths."

"I see, congratulations," Allenson said, raising his glass once more but in Todd's direction. "What do you intend to do now?"

Todd opened his mouth but Linsye cut into the conversation before he could speak.

"I thought he could be your aide."

★ CHAPTER 4 ★

Pounce Predators

Allenson sat in his office and pondered. So now he had an aide. Well what could he do? Linsye had ambushed him well and truly and the lad was family. Allenson, as paterfamilias of the Allenson gens such as it was, was expected, indeed obliged, to further the career of his relatives, but he had not intended to appoint an aide, let alone one from Brasilia.

He had severe doubts about Todd's suitability. The lad seemed bright enough, well educated and with the necessary coating of sophistication. Blue Horizon College had seen to that. He was physically fit, but did he have the right attitude? Todd looked so much like Royman. Superficially at least, he behaved just like him at that age—like a young Brasilian gentleman. Royman was a decent chap but his temperament hardly made him aide material. Ah well, time would tell; it usually did.

Thoughts of Todd made him try out the slide reader and the slide Todd recommended. He juggled the interface between the decoder and his desk a little until they had contact. He couldn't locate an index so he picked a still at random and projected it up as a sold hologram.

The result was a mess. He wondered whether the slide was too badly degraded to read. These objects normally had a near infinite life span. Resistant to chemical weathering, even cracking didn't necessarily destroy their records beyond retrieval.

Inspiration dawned. He was looking at a two-dimensional image in three dimensions. He flattened the hologram and Weimar's picture snapped into focus.

It showed a night scene, or at least a twilight scene. The sky was still pale blue. A faint orange glow backlit towers clustered together in a concrete coppice. Rows of lighted dots of windows gave the huge and brutalistic towers scale. In contrast, artificial light bathed the tops in gold and amber as if rejecting the darkening sky. In its way the artwork was a metaphor for the doomed civilization.

Weimar's picture summed up the power, the confidence and the sheer naked aggression of the Third Civilization at its height. Here we stand and here we stay the towers proclaimed; nothing can touch us. It didn't last of course. Entropy always has the last word.

The Third Civilization followed the First—The Monument Builders, and the Second—The Priest Kings of the Bronze Palaces, down into oblivion. At each stage human society climbed higher, becoming more complex, with greater technology and an exponentially larger population. Each time the resulting crash plunged deeper, the death toll worse, the destruction more complete and the recovery slower.

"Look on my works, ye Mighty, and despair," Allenson said softly.

The biowars marked the last spasm of the Third Civilization like the final ejaculation of a dying man. That particular folly nearly erased humanity. The human genome still carried the scars. That was something Allenson didn't want to think about. It was too close to home. His brother, Todd, wasted away from a genetic problem beyond the ability of Brasilia's best genosurgeons to cure.

The high technology of the Home Worlds of the Fourth Civilization did not trump that of the Third in every regard. The modern age ruthlessly suppressed research into bioweapons for good reason.

The logistics of Continuum travel made it impossible for one Home World to conquer another. An invasion fleet arriving unpredictably as a dribble of frames could never hope to defeat a Home World's defenses. Interior lines made it so easy to concentrate overwhelming defensive force at any point on the planet.

Invasion was out, but destroying a Home World's population was easy. Just one invader with a bioweapon in a flask could decimate a continent. A lone saboteur riding a single-man frame onto a world or hitching a lift in a ship was unstoppable.

Mass destruction is a useless strategic weapon, of course. Retaliation is so easy that everyone loses. A technological civilization with competing powers in possession of such weapons has but two options. The first is for everybody to be similarly armed and rely on MAD, mutually assured destruction. The logic is that no one starts a war they can't win.

The problem is that MAD is a well-named strategy. All it takes is for one madman on a mission to get control of a weapon just once. That or normal human incompetence. No weapon once developed had ever remained unused in the history of mankind.

So the ruling families of the Home Worlds showed a rare and touching human universal brotherhood. They banned not only bioweapons but also any genetic research that might lead to a sniff of a bioweapon. When a colony of Terra forgot the lesson it was Terran forces that liquidated its population as a reminder that the Home Worlds really, really meant what they said.

Unfortunately that research embargo also meant that people were still suffering incurable effects from the bioweapon legacy, but that was considered to be a price worth paying.

Allenson's train of thought reminded him of his last conversation with Todd. His brother had scared him to the core by showing that their Fourth Civilization was just as vulnerable as all the others. They thought they could beat the odds and reject the night but then, so had their predecessors.

The Fourth wasn't stuck on a single world like the Third. However, the Home Worlds occupied such a tiny region of realspace when judged by astronomical distances. Just one supernova in the wrong place or some other hitherto unknown disaster and it would be back to banging the rocks together. Assuming there was anyone left to care.

Civilization must expand or die and the only realistic road for the Fourth Civilization was across the worldless Bight and into the Hinterlands. The Hinterland colonies had to grow and become self-sufficient for mankind's sake in case something happened to their parent worlds. That was why he had to go to Paxton and listen to boring speeches from self-important people even though the thought made him want to throw up.

Allenson looked at the hologram again. The artist had made the picture from the vantage of a bridge over a wide waterway. Figures rendered indistinct by the gloom walked away from the artist towards the distant lights of the city. They strode purposefully along a laser-straight stabilized road surface. Why were they all walking in the same direction?

These shadow-people had been real flesh and blood. They lived and dreamed, bred children, buried loved ones, wept and laughed. They hoped and planned but all that they built was dust.

He clenched his fist. It was not going to happen to his world or to his people. He wouldn't let it.

Allenson knelt at the base of one of the large fleshy-lobed yellow-ochre plants that served Pentire demesne in lieu of a compound fence. He got as close as he could without risk of contact. He could just see fine hairs sticking out of the brown nodules spotted across the plant. The hairs caused stings as painful as they were bloody dangerous. They injected a complex toxic biochemical mix containing lysosomic enzymes. These rapidly broke down the polymeric macromolecules that made up animal tissue.

Gunja plants were native to Rafe, one of the recent Hinterland colonies. Allenson had initially imported them with some success until an outbreak of spotfly caterpillars devastated the crop. A specimen crawled up the stem of the plant as he watched. It humped its purple and orange striped body as it climbed.

Spotflys were herbivores native to Manzanita. They laid their eggs in the mouths of carnivorous plants where they were protected against predators. Gunja plant venom and the hydrolases in Manzanita carnivorous plants were apparently close enough in chemical composition to confer immunity on the caterpillars. To spotflies, a gunja plant fence was a well-stocked larder.

A peeling section of bark on the plant stem waved gently in the breeze near the caterpillar. An oddity, as the air was as still as a cat watching a mouse hole. Not that the caterpillar cared, being incapable of noting anomalies in cause and effect. The caterpillar had the excuse of a tiny brain consisting of a sliver of nervous tissue. Human beings could claim no such excuse but many still shared the caterpillar's issues with cause and effect.

A pincer on an extending arm like an angle-poise lamp shot out from under the bark peel. The sharp tip impaled the caterpillar. The insect wriggled and twisted in a fruitless attempt to escape but was lifted off the stem. The bark peel raised itself on four stubby legs. It retreated backwards deeper into the vegetation, dragging its lunch after it.

Allenson's estate manager clapped his hands together excitedly.

"See, I told you it was working."

"It seems you were right, Frederick," Allenson said.

"I thought the heavy armor on mealy bugs gave them an even chance of surviving even gunja plant stings."

"Yes, my only concern now is that we have imported an exotic species. We need to keep a close eye on developments in case something unexpected unravels."

"Like at Frempton?" the manager asked.

"Exactly like at Frempton," Allenson replied.

"The Frempton disaster was something of a one off," the manager said, frowning. "But I take the point."

Frempton was a colony farther up the Stream. Its economy had depended heavily on a cash crop of a popular recreational narcotic exported back to Brasilia. Some local entrepreneur imported a goat strain and released it into the wild to provide sport as Frempton lacked anything worth hunting. Unfortunately the goats ignored the bushes provided for their sustenance and took a liking to the cash crop instead. The goats weren't even good sport for hunters as they tended to lie around stoned most of the time after feeding.

By the time Fremptoners grasped the scale of the problem the goats were past culling. The genius involved then imported an exotic predator to control the goats. The predator was so-so about dining on stoned goats but developed a voracious appetite for a native predator that fed on the rat infestations. Wherever humans colonize you sooner or later get rats.

The resulting overpopulation of starving rats broke into the fleek enclosures to steal their eggs, spreading a variety of diseases. The bird populations, ever susceptible to disease, were decimated. The narcotic crop duly rotted in the fields because there were no fleeks for the harvest.

Biological control might be elegant in theory but had a propensity to spin out of control in practice.

Frederick Elberg, the Pentire estate manager, was one of Trina's second cousins who had fallen on hard times. When the bank foreclosed on his plantation, Trina put his name forward to Allenson.

Allenson had not considered employing an estate manager. When he did consider it he found the idea distinctly unwelcome. But although Pentire was a legacy from his brother, Allenson had inherited little in the way of capital. His development and expansion of the estate was funded by Trina's family money so he felt obligated to fall in with her wishes. He rather hoped that her cousin would stay out of his way and drink himself quietly to death somewhere. Incompetence coupled with indolence was generally harmless compared to energetic bungling.

Elberg tuned out to be both energetic and competent, which was something of a shock. In Allenson's experience such paragons were rare as fleek's teeth. Dynamic proficiency took some getting used to. He had come to increasingly rely on Elberg to oversee his ideas for improving the estate. Indeed, he would be a lot less happy about traveling to Nortania without knowing Elberg would be here to watch over the demesne.

Nevertheless, he needed to reassure himself with one last tour of his small empire in the estate manager's company just to make sure that Elberg was on top of matters. They rode on a four-wheel-drive electric scooter. Currently the transmission powered only three wheels which made steering challenging, especially on slopes.

Allenson stopped outside the fleek enclosures to examine the beasts through the windows. Fleeks were birdlike organisms about the size and bulk of an ape. They came from a world that had never evolved mammals so birds filled all the mammalian ecological niches. Colored feathers covered their bodies, forming patterns of metallic blue and green. Non-flyers, they possessed only vestigial wings and ran on long sturdy legs with a backward-facing knee joint.

A heavy beak mounted on a flexible muscular neck had evolved to probe the ground. Buried eggs made up their natural diet in the wild. This life style required good forward vision and a high degree of dexterity so the beaks made excellent manipulatory appendages. Fleeks were not sentient. Their mental development more or less equaled that of a chimp but their bird-type brains memorized and repeated complex behavioral patterns much more proficiently than any mammal of similar intellect.

In short they made acceptable agricultural workers for routine repetitive tasks like weeding or harvesting. Specialized agricultural automatons were more efficient. However, they were expensive and in short supply in the colonies. The ones that washed up on the far shores of the Bight tended to be reconditioned models with appalling breakdown rates. Royman Destry had experimented with importing equipment to assemble robots on his demesne. It had not been a success. The reliability rate of the manufacturing system proved as bad as the imported automatons.

Human labor for such tasks was wasteful. The sort of indentured servants that ended up as agricultural workers had to be constantly supervised to get any work out of them at all. Fleeks filled the gap. Their one big advantage over automatons was that they could be bred to make more fleeks.

But what blessings the good fairy gave with one hand the bad fairy buggered up with the other. Fleeks were inbred to the point of dangerous biological fragility so highly infectious and lethal diseases raged through their flocks. Death rates of ninety per cent plus were not uncommon.

"You have the fleeks silod behind tight firewalls?" Allenson asked.

"Each flock is kept within an air-filtered enclosure. No two flocks are ever used on the same land. Each flock has its own gangmaster and feeders who do not share equipment. No one gets in or out without going through the antibiotic sprays."

Elberg listed the points on the fingers of his hand as he reassured Allenson.

"I can't guarantee an infectious agent won't be windblown from another demesne onto a flock working in the fields, you understand, Allenson, but everything possible is in place to limit an outbreak to a single flock."

"I know it is, Elberg." Allenson patted the man's shoulder. "But fleek plague gives me nightmares. I have seen crops rotting in the fields because of it."

The tour ended at a small field where Allenson was trying a new cultivar of rosehip berries grafted onto the roots of a wild bramblelike plant from the Hinterlands. He cupped a small cluster of flowers gently in one hand and noted that berries were already forming.

"These will be ripe for harvesting in a week or two," Allenson said wistfully. "I shall probably still be on Nortania listening to endless prevarication."

"Not to worry, I shall keep an eye on them for you," Elberg said reassuringly.

Allenson nodded assent.

"Of course, it's just that I would have liked to observe the process."

Allenson glanced surreptitiously at the power gauge on his datapad. They were moving against an unexpected Continuum current. That shouldn't have been a problem. His carriage had been fully charged before leaving Manzanita. It theoretically had power to spare to reach their first port of call, Syma. Now he was beginning to become concerned.

His personal carriage was entirely self-powered and designed for longer hops through the Continuum than Trina's conveyance. It did away with the need for a chauffeur and was navigated entirely by automatics controlled from the passenger compartment. He bought the machine from Synclare of Brasilia. Its specs were impressive but the workmanship was shoddy and it never seemed to hold a charge properly. Perhaps the energy converters were malfunctioning. Whatever the reason, it never achieved the advertised speed or range.

He checked their route in case he had to displace to another closer colony. There were one or two possibilities but they were all backwaters. It was doubtful that they would have the technology to refuel the batteries. He would have been content to dump the carriage and continue on by one-man frame but he was carrying passengers. There was also the matter of his gravitas. Important delegates arrived by carriage. They did not pedal in on a frame.

To his way of thinking, the method of arrival shouldn't matter but he accepted that he was out of step with his contemporaries on this. It was one of those inexplicable facts of life—like why the man had to apologize after a row with his wife irrespective of fault or the relative merits of their arguments.

Todd noticed his concern and turned to engage the other passenger in conversation to distract him from what Allenson was doing. Such matters were an important part of an aide's duties. In this case Allenson thought Todd's intervention superfluous. Renald Buller was not the sort of man who noticed anything except that which was immediately important to Renald Buller.

"I understand you have had a fair amount of military experience, Colonel Buller?" Todd asked encouragingly.

Buller puffed up like an amphibious tetrapod trying to attract a mate.

"Not a fair amount, young man—considerable, considerable military experience."

Buller jabbed a finger aggressively in Todd's direction to punctuate his word, looking like a child poking holes in a pudding.

"And not marching around in pretty uniforms either like you young fops from the so-called better families. I mean real combat experience—up at the sharp end."

Todd smiled. "I heard you were attached to the 12th, sir, but were fortunate to miss the Chernokovsky disaster in the Hinterland."

Brigadier Chernokovsky had led two battalions of light infantry, the 12th and the 51st, on an expedition to eject the Terrans from Larissa. The expedition was ambushed and cut to pieces with all the senior officers killed. Allenson had managed to extract the survivors of the 51st and get them home but the 12th were wiped out to a man.

Allenson glared at Todd. It was not politic to raise the Larissa debacle with members of the Brasilian military, not even ex-members like Buller. Fortunately, the man was too thick skinned to notice the implied slight.

"Had I been there we would have seen a very different outcome young man, I can tell you. A professional soldier to provide leadership instead of a ragbag of chinless wonders and colonial amateurs makes all the difference," Buller said complacently.

He then seemed to recollect Allenson's involvement and held a hand palm up.

"No insult to you, Allenson. Sure you did your best. Not your fault you were out of your depth."

"One tried," Allenson replied dryly.

"What engagements have you seen, Colonel," Todd asked quickly, changing the subject.

"Stormed the Terran colony at Genran with the 103rd. Lost a leg and was out of it for the remainder of the Colonial Wars while it regrew. Then fought with the 103rd when we put some backbone into the Piwis in their revolt against Frankistan. Got a field promotion to lieutenant colonel."

The state of Frankistan occupied the primary continent of Hiwa, one of the less important Home Worlds, which had always enjoyed a close relationship with Terra. Piwi was a collection of islands in the Hiwa world ocean that at various times was part of Frankistan or independent. Mostly it occupied some confused political status of semi-dependence. Brasilia found it useful to aid the Piwi's revolt as a tangential way of eroding Terra's authority in the Home Worlds without actually declaring war. It was a kind of colonial war at home.

Terra responded by sending aid to Frankistan. The war devastated both Frankistan and Piwi before the business wound down to the point where a politically face-saving compromise was possible. It was not clear who had won. Probably, nobody—nobody often did.

"You know what reward they gave me when the 103rd returned home?" Buller asked, rhetorically.

Todd opened his mouth but never got the chance to speak.

"Nothing, that's what," Buller said. "They disbanded the regiment to save money and put me on the beach. They kept Guard popinjays who'd never fired a shot in anger and who'd probably shit themselves in fear if they ever saw a body but the Fighting 103rd was disbanded to save money. We weren't fashionable, you see."

Buller made the word fashionable sound like it described a particularly virulent strain of antisocial disease.

"So I went east as a soldier of fortune and became general and aide to the king-emperor of Quorn in his war against the Syracusan Confederacy. Gave up on Brasilia and emigrated out here when the king-emperor was poisoned by his wife."

Buller appeared to think that the king-emperor had deliberately died to spite him.

"Bought a plantation on Prato Rio. I'm damned if I'll pay taxes to support an army led by popinjays who couldn't protect the Stream from a bunch of society ladies armed with cream puffs."

"Quite," Todd said, faintly, when Buller finally wound down.

Allenson convinced himself that he had enough power to reach Syma but took the precaution of running a continuous analysis of fuel with a warning set if the situation deteriorated.

"That's why you emigrated," Allenson said, joining the

conversation to Todd's palpable relief. "Because you felt your abilities were being unfairly overlooked in Brasilia."

Buller snorted, "Too right, Allenson. Brasilia's run as an old boy network for the dim-witted sons of the well connected. There's a complete block on real talent to cut out the competition."

Allenson found himself sucked into the conversation.

"But is it better here? Brasilian trans-Bight colonies reflect the Home World's social structure, do they not?"

Buller nodded.

"Damn right, which is why we have to cut ourselves off from Brasilia and get full independence."

"I am not sure we could sell that to the Brasilian establishment," Allenson said.

"Hardly," Buller said. "We'll have to fight for independence."

"You mean war," Allenson said.

Buller thrust his chin forward.

"Of course I mean war. You think the ruling families will just sign away their privileges?"

It had always been Allenson's contention that those who had actually seen combat would be less keen on repeating the experience. He began to wonder whether that opinion was optimistic. The smell of war wafted around the Stream like an odor from something that had recently died under the floorboards. Not yet a stench, but unchecked it soon would be.

"And we'll need an army. Need men who'll stand their ground against Brasilian regulars. A disciplined force commanded by a professional," Buller said, striking a fist into the palm of his other hand for emphasis.

"Such as yourself?" Allenson asked, already knowing the answer.

★ CHAPTER 5 ★

Gathering Clouds

Syma shone. No, that didn't do it justice. Syma glowed with a thousand hues and colors. Once it must have been a desert, a wilderness covered in wind-blown dunes. Then a serendipitous catastrophe intervened. A vast flare of energy that fused the sands into a crystalline sheet exploded in the sky.

The learned savants from the Home Worlds still squabbled over the exact sequence, timing or even structure of events. Every few years a new expedition ventured forth to put a new hypothesis to the test. Perhaps a comet exploded in the upper atmosphere. If so, it must have been one of almost unique composition to release such a burst of heat with so little blast. The strangely focused solar flare hypothesis also had adherents, although they failed to agree on the cause of such a phenomenon.

And then came the crackpots, the conspiracy theorists and the plain madmen. Syma allegedly marked the site where, to take the suggestions in no particular order of unlikeliness, an alien faster-than-light starship had crashed, aliens had tested a giant energy weapon, a Home World had tested a giant energy weapon, a secret society . . . well, fill in with your own bogie men of choice.

The catastrophe, whatever it was, changed the regional climate, bringing water to the desert. It seeped into the glass, cutting riverlets, caves and canyons. It washed in colored minerals and pigments. Researchers loved expeditions to Syma not just because it was unique but because it was so hauntingly beautiful. Academia constructed a port on the edge of the glass sheet to the delight of wealthy tourists.

An autobeacon landed Allenson's carriage on the reinforced pad. The sun was high in the reddish sky and it was hot. He adjusted the coverage of his eye shade to keep the worst of the rays off his head and neck. Syma's air smelled dryer than the dust on a corpse.

The pad was completely bare of buildings or fences. The carriage rested by a low rectangular box about a meter long and half a meter high. It was made of some sophisticated reflective white ceramic, featureless except for a chip slot. Allenson noted similar structures dotted around the pad.

Nothing lived on the surface in Syma, human or otherwise. No one met them: no customs officials, no hawkers, no beggars. Allenson's datapad chimed. A holographic arrow appeared, directing him around the back of the box where a hatch opened. A ramp spiraled down into the syncrete surface. The travelers descended and the hatch slid noiselessly closed behind them.

The air in the tunnel was noticeably cooler. Only dim illumination seeped around the spiral, so Allenson turned off his eye shade. He rounded a bend in the corridor to enter a wonderland of glass and light. His body cast many soft shadows tinted in a kaleidoscope of colors. Multiple images of the sun shone through the glass ceiling, each a different color of the rainbow as every frequency of light found its own unique path through the layers of glass.

Vitrified glass lined the walls in frozen raindrops and rivulets. In some places he could see deep into the layers, but elsewhere the glass was near opaque, stained with mineral streamers. Allenson found himself rubber necking like a country bumpkin on his first visit to town.

Buller pushed past him.

"Are you going to serve us or what?" Buller asked an elderly white-haired man sitting unobtrusively on a stool in the corner.

"Your pardon, sar, but I have found that most of our guests prefer to be given a period of reflection to enjoy the ambiance when they first enter Syma," the lackey replied, quite uncrushed. "My name is—"

"I don't give a tinker's fart what your name is," Buller interrupted. "I want to know where I can get a room and a decent meal."

The receptionist waved a hand.

"If you would care to register."

Buller looked on uncomprehendingly.

"Your datapad," Allenson said softly.

Buller pulled out his pad and stabbed at it viciously.

"Hmmph! You have to do everything yourself in this one-frame dump."

Allenson used his own pad to check in. He winced at the prices. He wished to conserve the Brasilian Crowns he carried in case of unexpected demands on his purse. One of the handicaps to interworld commerce was that information could only be carried through the Continuum inside a frame field. Places more than a few days light speed apart relied on packet ships to exchange funds and other information.

"I have an arrangement with the PanStream Bank, Master . . . ?"

"Sederer, sar," said the receptionist.

Allenson didn't catch what the receptionist did but he opened a holographic screen. The man touched a series of icons and Allenson's datapad chimed to remind him that it was downloading information.

"The local branch of PanStream confirms your membership, Sar Allenson. A map to your room is on your pad."

"And an adjacent room for my aide charged on my account," Allenson said, gesturing to Todd.

The receptionist made the necessary arrangements.

"I'm with Colico," Buller said.

The receptionist looked at him without moving.

"I regret that Colico have no branch on Syma, Sar."

"Then I'll have to send you a tab to cover the bill when I get home," Buller said.

The receptionist made no move to accept Buller's booking.

"We accept Brasilian or Terran coin, sar, if that is convenient."

Buller thrust his chin forward. He looked for all the world like a guard dog straining at a chain.

"See here my man, are you questioning my honor."

Allenson moved to defuse the confrontation.

"Charge Sar Buller's room to my account."

The receptionist made the necessary connections.

"Certainly, sar."

Buller nodded complacently.

"Good man, Allenson, we'll settle up back on Manzanita."

Allenson mentally wrote off the money.

"As you find convenient."

"And you need to improve your attitude when dealing with your betters," Buller said, wagging his finger at the receptionist. "Think yourself damn lucky Sar Allenson chose to get you off the hook."

"Oh I do, sar," said the receptionist.

Buller looked at the man suspiciously but the receptionist stared back with a bland countenance as devoid of any hint of sarcasm as it was of concern.

"My carriage needs recharging," Allenson said.

"Yes, sar," The receptionist fluttered his fingertips over the display. "It will be fully charged in two hours."

He stared closely at the screen and sighed.

"As fully charged as the system in your carriage can take at any rate."

"I didn't see any mechanics on the surface?" Allenson asked.

The receptionist replied without looking up, still busy with his display.

"No, sar, the surface is hardly the sort of work-environment to attract skilled employees except at exorbitant rates of pay. We find it cheaper to use automatons. You may have noticed the storage unit by your carriage."

"I see," Allenson replied.

Syma used astonishingly high technology. Perhaps he should have anticipated that at a Home World university research station. He glanced at his datapad and winced anew at the cost of the recharge. Sophistication had its downside.

Allenson's room was splendid but tiny—not something that bothered him unduly as he usually traveled light. One-man frames lacked generous luggage facilities. The glass walls and floor opaqued for privacy but the ceiling let in glass-filtered sunlight. He discovered a control that polarized the glass. After darkening the room he managed a short nap. Something he had learned in the army was to sleep whenever you could for you never knew when the chance might come again.

When he woke up he splashed some water on his face. Then he

buzzed Todd through his datapad to invite him to dine in the restaurant. Todd was only next door but Allenson did not want to wake him if he was still asleep. The receptionist had placed Buller way down in the complex below the sunlit level. Politeness may or may not be its own reward but it cost nothing and did no harm in dealing with people who could exact petty revenge. Never be rude to waiters unless one likes spit in one's food.

Todd replied immediately with enthusiasm. After a moment's refection Allenson also sent a note to Buller although he extended the invitation without enthusiasm. Fortunately he did not get a reply. Todd found the restaurant using his datapad, which projected a holographic arrow to show the route down through a maze of corridors.

The restaurant itself was a circular bowl with terraced seating under a ruby-red ceiling fluorescing from spotlights projecting up into the glass. Streams flowed down from the edges of the bowl. The water meandered around the tables to drain under the kitchen hub in the center. Few staff assisted the diners. One found a table, ordered via datapad from the menu and collected the food in person from automaton dispensers in the hub. It was all rather egalitarian in a high tech sort of way.

Allenson chose a seat up on the bowl where each table was made from a different colored mineral marbled with various contra-colors. The seats were likewise constructed. Allenson scored them ten for fashion but minus several hundred for comfort.

The restaurant was almost empty. Allenson checked his pad and found it was an odd time for dinner on local time. That was the problem with frame travel. The local time zone was usually never convenient but here it had worked in their favor.

Allenson ordered a stew more or less at random from the hologram over the table while Todd chose something complicated from the Terran section. Todd trotted off to get them a couple of beers while their meals were prepared. Allenson was pleased to see that the boy returned with simple lagers only mildly flavored with elderberry.

"I don't understand how Colonel Buller can hope to be put in command of the colonial militia regiments," Todd said, when they had slaked their thirst. "Surely you already hold that position?"

"Indeed, no," Allenson replied. "True I was the last inspector general of Colonial Militia until my retirement but that position was never refilled."

"Why not?" Todd asked.

"Well, as it's a gift within the control of the Brasilian Colonial Office, you would have to ask them. I'd imagine that they saw no useful purpose in a unified military command this side of the Bight once the Terran colonies were defeated."

"But Mother said you were elected colonel in chief of the Colonial Militia Regiments."

"Not exactly, I was elected colonel in chief by each regiment, which is not the same thing at all."

Todd looked at him blankly, clearly not understanding.

"It's not a unified command."

"Sorry, Uncle Allen, you've lost me."

"Maybe an example would help," Allenson said. "Suppose I wanted the Wagener, Manzanita and Prato Rio Regiments to go to, say, Leyland. I would have to give the commanding officer of each regiment a personal order as his superior. Now further suppose I want to conduct a military operation on Leyland in brigade strength. How would I do that?"

"You would have to be present at Leyland to order each regimental CO personally unless the operation was so simple that you could send them out with fixed orders," Todd replied slowly.

Allenson was pleased to see that Todd grasped the problem immediately, not that he expected his brother and Linsye's child to be slow.

Allenson continued.

"In my experience everything is simple in warfare but to do the simple is extraordinarily difficult. In my experience if the enemy has only three different choices of reaction to your plans you may expect it to take the fourth, the one not foreseen in the original orders. Now assume I also want other militia regiments to conduct a simultaneous brigade operation deep into the Hinterland."

"You would need to learn to pedal really fast," Todd said with a grin.

Allenson laughed. "And then some. Sure each regiment will take orders from me personally but only a proper military organization can conduct a prolonged campaign, let alone a war."

"One might almost think that Brasilia planned it that way," Todd said.

"Never assume the enemy, I mean the opposition, is stupid," Allenson replied, remembering his conversation with Trina.

The table hologram flickered and chimed.

"Ah, I think our meal is ready and here comes Buller."

"Oh joy," Todd replied.

The first bite of winter lay on the steppe and a thin smear of frost on the thick grass hinted at the cold to come. The coating was a prelude to the main symphony of thick snow and iron-hard ground. Hawthorn pulled back the heavy wooden door. The chill steppe wind swept gleefully into his workshop. It pried playfully into the nooks and crannies including some rather personal to the owner. He shivered and made a mental note to search out his furs. When he walked back to the counter he limped slightly on his left leg.

Hardwood was at a premium on the steppe so it was only used for the skeletal frame of the building and the doors and window shutters. The walls were made of a lattice of interweaved stems generously coated in a sticky mix of mud, dried leaves and animal dung. The smell wasn't too bad once it had dried. In winter, anyway, things got a bit whiffy in high summer.

A small collection of Riders waited stoically outside, their skin turning blue with cold under their furs and trade-cloth blankets. The first in line was a Rider woman, looking about eighty but probably nearer thirty. Riders aged quickly because life in the wilderness was brutal and short. Those who praised the noble ways of the simple savage from the depths of a comfy armchair would be shocked by the reality.

The woman produced a small statuette, a crude representation of a Rider on a Rider beast. Hawthorn examined it, turning it over in his hands. It had probably been hand-carved by a blunt trade knife wielded by a Rider male too old to hunt. Ivory from the tusk of some animal provided the raw material. In short it was just the sort of one-off unique item that would appeal to a collector in the Home Worlds, where rarity was at a premium. Home Worlders prized imperfect uniqueness, conditioned as they were by the cheap availability of automaton mass-produced perfection.

He offered the woman ten trade tokens using Kant, the lingua franca Riders used for inter-clan communication. The fact that "foreigner" and "enemy" were the same word in Kant spoke volumes about the nature of most interclan communication.

Her eyes widened. Ten was a good price, worth twenty in goods from his own store. Each token was valued at an exchange rate of a few Brasilian pennies. The work would sell for several crowns in a Brasilian art shop specializing in the primitive provided it was accompanied by a certificate of provenance signed by every dealer along the trade route, but that was there. Here, at a trading post deep in the Hinterlands, ten tokens was a good price.

The "box-people" astonished Riders. Why would anyone so imaginably rich in possessions want to exchange valuable items like knives and blankets for a piece of old tat that anyone with two thumbs could knock out in an hour?

The woman elected to take half the payment in a bottle of tonk and some cloth. Hawthorn carefully measured out the length from the roll chosen by the woman. The material was bright red with black zig-zag patterns. Riders liked loud colors, but who was he to criticize their taste? After all, his people paid ridiculous prices for "primitive art."

"Tonk" was the universal word for rotgut gin. Riders had no access to alcohol before humanity crossed the Bight so the human word had found its way into Kant. A little went a long way with a Rider but, in its way, tonk was as useful for keeping out the cold as furs or trade-cloth.

The word originally came from a shortening of Tollins Superior Berry Distillation. Tollins was still a popular brand in the Stream for those with shallow pockets but deep thirsts. Hawthorn drank it himself when he was out of plum brandy. The only thing superior about Tollins product was that it was guaranteed not to actually blind its customers provided they didn't drink too much or they didn't get a dodgy batch rushed through on a Friday afternoon.

Hawthorn served his little band of customers. He traded cloth, tonk and ceramic tools for furs, gem minerals and curios. Eventually he worked through the queue of Riders and was left alone with his thoughts. That was nowhere he wanted to be so he used a trick he had perfected of clearing his mind and just being.

A soft chime switched his intellect back on. He retrieved his datapad from a shelf under the counter. An icon flashed red, activated by a solar powered instrument package on the roof that monitored ripples in the Continuum.

Hawthorn picked up the heavy laserrifle that he kept by the pad. He opened the flap on the counter and made for the door, automatically checking that the weapon was powered up before sloping it across his right shoulder. He held it by the pistol grip, forefinger alongside the trigger. These were habits that had kept him alive but then, life itself was just a habit these days. He had as little to die for as to live for. He just went on, clicking through the subroutines of his existence like an automaton.

His trading post attracted a small shanty town of Riders as trading posts always did. He ignored the Riders' hovels to search the skies. A low, gray cloud base made the sledge phasing in easy to spot. It maneuvered slowly, giving him a good view of the occupants. The driver was a midget of a man but the spare passenger space in the front was more than taken up by the girth of his companion. He was large in every sense of the word. The lemon-yellow padded shell suit covering his ample figure multiplied the visual impact.

He looked like a barrage balloon advertising custard tarts.

"You're early, Shrankin," Hawthorn said to the trader when the sledge had landed.

"Yeah, well, you may have noticed that the weather is closing in early so I made Jem's Shop the first on my circuit this year. Don't wannabe hauling goods through snow."

"Jem's shop?"

"That's what they call this world nowadays."

"I'm flattered," Hawthorn said.

Shrankin, the name of the man worn by the shell suit, jumped out of the vehicle.

"Buggers, get the stuff off the wagon and take it inside," he said to the driver, who climbed into the back without a word.

"Is he really called Buggers?" Hawthorn asked, mildly curious.

"No idea," Shrankin replied. "It's what I've always called him. I've never asked to see his birth certificate 'cause he probably ain't got one. Does his name matter?"

"Suppose not," Hawthorn replied, losing interest.

He took the trader into the back room where he kept his purchases.

They dickered over a price to be paid partly in trade goods and partly in Brasilian crowns. The negotiations were desultory as both men knew what price they would finally agree upon. It was simply a matter of honor to put up some show of bargaining even if they were both just going through the motions.

A loud bang of wood on wood sounded from the shop, followed by a yell and another slam. Hawthorn flew through the door, lips pressed close together. A young male Rider glared at him from the other side of the counter. The Rider insolently lifted the counter hatch and slammed it again so hard that it tore off its hinges. Two of his friends standing in the entrance laughed and said something in their secret clan language.

"Quiet beastspawn or I'll gut you," Hawthorn said in Kant, angling his laserrifle and caressing the trigger so that an orange sighting dot glowed on the Rider's chest.

"Want tonk," the Rider said. *"Got tokens."*

The rider swayed slightly as he fumbled in a cloth bag tied to a greasy loin cloth. Hawthorn was amazed he could stand given the stench of stale tonk on his breath. The Rider extracted rectangular purple and gray trade tokens and tossed them on the counter.

Purple and gray were the Mark of the Stream Administration. Hawthorn picked up one of the tokens and ran a thumb along the edge. A pattern code identified which trading post issued the token. It was not one of Hawthorn's but that didn't matter. Hinterland traders had an agreement to honor each other's credit.

"Shrankin, know anything about O'Zhang's post?" Hawthorn asked, without taking his eyes off the Rider.

"Got burnt out, three, four months ago," Shrankin said from behind him. "O'Zhang lost his hands."

Riders collected hands from their victims as religious trophies. The term was used by people in the Hinterland as a euphemism for dying but in this case Hawthorn suspected that Shrankin meant it quite literally.

"Yeah, that's what I heard," Hawthorn replied, putting his laserrifle carefully under the counter.

He tossed the token back at the Rider. The man fumbled the catch and the plastic rattled on the stabilized earth floor. The Rider attempted the catch with his right hand, which was odd as Riders were invariably left handed. This Rider held his left hand behind his back.

"*Token no good, maker dead so power gone. No tonk, feck off,*" Hawthorn said.

There was a dead silence. The Rider stared at him slackly as if his booze-sodden brain had trouble understanding that he had just been dismissed.

"*Women's piss,*" the Rider screamed and launched his body through the gap in the counter. He thrust upwards at Hawthorn's lower torso with the flint knife that he had concealed behind his back.

It was a beautifully timed strike despite the Rider's apparent intoxication. If Hawthorn had recoiled the blade would have eviscerated him all the way to the rib cage, possibly nicking his heart or aorta before stopping.

Hawthorn anticipated the attack and stepped forward.

He deflected the knife strike with his right arm and pivoted, rabbit punching the warrior in the back of the neck as the man flew past. The Rider smashed head first into a cupboard and went down. Hawthorn put the boot in before he could get up. He kicked the rider in the side of the head and twice in the ribs. Something broke with a sharp crack after the last blow.

Grabbing the Rider's ankles, Hawthorn dragged the unconscious warrior back across the shop. His head left a trail of blood on the floor. Barging past the warriors at the entrance he dropped the wounded man in the dirt outside.

The warrior's two friends looked uncertain. One fingered a hatchet looped to a belt around his waist.

Shrankin loomed like a bright yellow mountain behind them, waggling the discharge end of an ion pistol for emphasis.

"I don't think so, boys."

Hawthorn ignored them. He stomped back into his shop followed by the trader. The Riders disappeared carrying their out-of-it mate.

"You took one hell of a chance," Shrankin said, holding out a flask of plum brandy. "Why didn't you just shoot him?"

"And start a Blood Feud?" Hawkins replied before taking a pull of the liquor.

It stung his tongue and burned all the way down his throat, reminding him that he was still alive. He took a slower slip, savoring the tangy fruit aftertaste.

Hawthorn grinned and handed back the flask.

"Besides, where would be the fun in shooting the bastard."

Shrankin joined him by sinking a generous measure. Hawthorn found a couple of glasses and the trader filled them.

"There may be plenty of shooting soon enough," Shrankin said.

"Really, why?" Hawthorn asked.

"The nobs are meeting at Paxton—"

"On Nortania?"

"You know of another one?"

"No, just surprised at the choice of location. Why not meet at Manzanita or Trinity?" Hawthorn asked.

"How the hell do I know? Do you want to hear about this meeting or not?"

"Sorry, okay, continue."

Shrankin looked mollified.

"As I said, the nobs are meeting at Paxton to organize a joint response and give Brasilia an ultimatum over taxation."

"Why, most of us don't pay taxes?"

"The nobs do," Shrankin replied, refilling the glasses. "I've a mate who knows some guys in the militia. They reckon there's going to be a war."

"I see," Hawthorn said.

"The Colonel of Militia is going to Paxton," Shrankin said, tapping his nose to convey his subtle grasp of colonial realpolitik.

Hawthorn started and put his glass down.

"This colonel, your mate didn't mention his name?"

Shrankin shook his head.

"Didn't have to. Same colonel we've always had. The one who was a hero in the Terran War, Ballysin or something."

"Allenson?"

"That's the bastard."

Hawthorn put his laserrifle over his shoulder and headed for the door.

"Oy, where you going?" Shrankin asked.

Hawthorn turned.

"Have you ever heard of amalgamated vertical business administration?"

"No," Shrankin replied, clearly confused.

"Well, you have now. The trading post is all yours, an outlet for your distribution business. Just think, in a few years they could be calling this place Shrankin's Shop or lemon-yellow land."

"But what are you going to do?"

"I have," Hawthorn said, "to see a man about a war."

★ CHAPTER 6 ★

Paxton

Allenson's carriage phased in over Paxton and began a slow circular descent through a sky crowded with frames. He had read about Paxton and seen video clips but the reality was still astonishing. The population must be four or five times that of Manzanita.

Buller and Todd ignored the view. They concentrated on a heated discussion of the merits of various Brasilian football teams, particularly their chances in upcoming league matches. Both Brasilians were familiar with cities that made Paxton look like a village. Allenson wasn't so he welcomed the chance to play tourist.

Paxton had been founded as a commercial venture by Exoticana Services, a consortium owned by three powerful Brasilian gens. It was really a series of towns strong along the edges of a ria, a drowned river valley complex. At some point the world of Nortania must have been in the grip of a snowball climate. When it warmed, water from the melting ice sheets had carved out steep-sided valleys which subsequently flooded as sea levels rose.

The hinterland behind the city must once been a mountain range but glaciers ground it down, flattening the peaks into a plateau. Rising sea levels then turned the terrain into a flat coastal strip partitioned by deep saltwater channels that acted to mediate weather already temperate.

An astonishingly rich and agriculturally productive land resulted. Soils formed from glacial loess added to the fertility—something to do with varied mineral content, porosity and cation exchange capacity according to the farming manuals.

The saltwater channels served as ready-made canals to move agricultural produce down-estuary to Paxton. Interworld ships could land directly there on the deep-water ria close in to the shore. Waterborne traffic was slow but extremely cost effective. The plants were in no hurry so the canals were still in use despite Paxton's modern prosperity.

A cross-Bight transporter and yacht lay floating at anchor. The cargo ship was docked at an industrial terminal, the yacht next to a bank dominated by the stepped up villas of the local gentry. Lighters shuffled between a dockside warehouse and the transporter, moving bales of plant material.

Paxton was perfect for the growth and distribution of the genosurgeoned crops. That made it ideal for the mass production of high value exotic products such as narcotics, drugs, and perfumes. The low organic content of the soil was convenient as it facilitated the spraying of chemical precursors to fine tune the molecular constituents in the crops. Paxton Freeport prospered until it was one the most important commercial centers this side of the Bight.

The extraction and blending of the target organics in the genosurgeoned crops was done on Brasilia under the direct control of Exoticana. The three families that owned the company shares had little interest in Nortania as such provided Paxton continued to supply a steady output of raw material.

Neither Paxton nor Nortania as a whole had a Brasilian governor because the powerful gens involved hadn't been keen on officialdom poking its nose into their business activities. The company maintained an office and small administration to oversee plant exports. Otherwise the commercial consortium was disinterested in government except in so far as it affected their business so the colonists on Paxton largely governed themselves. The locals had no interest in interrupting the trade on which their prosperity was based so everyone was happy; everyone except for a few political radicals and hotheads who were easily weeded out at intervals and exiled.

Being centrally placed, neither of the Lower nor Upper Cutter Stream colonies, made Paxton an ideal neutral meeting place for the Assembly. The world had a suitably developed infrastructure capable of handling an influx of the great and the good. Such people could hardly be expected to live in tents and dig their own latrines while they discussed weighty matters of state.

Allenson's carriage descended to a commercial area behind the coastal villas. The region overflowed with shops, restaurants and inns. They parked beside Verdant House, a two-story public house built from dark varnished hardwood logged from forests deep in the lands beyond the Paxton agricultural zone.

Buller booked into a different inn, much to Allenson's relief. A little of Colonel Buller went a long way. The man alerted his hotel of his imminent arrival before landing so a complimentary ground carriage awaited him at Verdant House.

Two large animals pulled it. They looked like descendants of an Old Earth tetrapod species although Allenson was unfamiliar with the strain. The beasts stood about shoulder high on the long thin legs of running animals. Muscle was concentrated at the top to lighten the limb itself so it could be swung backwards and forwards with minimal expenditure of energy in reversing momentum. The animals possessed a covering of wiry fur that flowed into long-haired tails and manes.

Animal transport was rare in the Stream as the cost of keeping the animals usually outweighed any advantages conferred by a motor that reproduced itself. Of course, Paxton enjoyed a surplus of animal feed from the unwanted parts of the cash crops—provided the animals in question were plant eaters. This weighted the cost effectiveness of living compared to powered vehicles in the animal's favor.

One of the beasts looked at Allenson reflectively before issuing a tremendous methanic fart as a prelude to depositing a large pile of steaming waste. The composition dispelled any doubt as to the creature's herbivorous habits. Allenson could see similar deposits around the frame park and resolved to watch his step.

"Is that thing likely to do that often?" Buller asked the driver who was busy loading his bags into the carriage boot.

"Old Buttercup does blow off a bit now and then, but don't pay no mind," said the man cheerfully. "Boys come round later and shovel it up to sell as fertilizer."

Allenson and Todd heard Buller complaining loudly over his datapad to his hotel about their complimentary transport as his carriage pulled away. Buttercup, whose ruminations had no doubt been excited by exercise, celebrated their departure with another sonic contribution.

"... where's the proper cars you keep for important guests ..." Even Buller's booming voice eventually faded with distance.

Allenson thought Buller the sort of fellow forever doomed be disappointed by other people's behavior. The universe would always fail to live up to his expectations.

Allenson discovered he was hungry so he went in search of food right after unpacking. He couldn't be bothered to chase around to find a restaurant so he elected to eat at the inn.

"Is it possible to get a table for dinner, mistress?" Allenson asked the Verdant Green's receptionist.

"Of course, sar," the receptionist replied.

The young woman wore a tightly cut employee's uniform that emphasized her slim figure. Her hair was tinted green with orange highlights in shades that complimented her yellow dress. She sat perched on a stool with a holographic screen open beside her. The receptionist peered at it, suggesting her eyesight was less than perfect at close-in focusing. Presumably glasses were beneath her dignity and genosurgery beyond her means.

"In fact we provisionally reserved a table for you—just in case. Will your aide be joining you?"

The girl smiled for the first time. He reflected that he always seemed doomed to travel with men who elicited smiles from pretty girls.

"Ah, no, I believe he has friends in town that he intends to look up," Allenson said, wondering why he was explaining himself when no would have sufficed. Pretty girls tended to have that effect on him. The girl switched off the smile as if a switch had been thrown.

"I trust your room is satisfactory?" she asked.

"What? Oh yes," Allenson replied. "I will need to hire a servant for the duration of my stay. Can you suggest an agency?"

"Of course, sar, I will arrange it."

Allenson pointed to a double door made of the same dark wood that formed the structure of the inn.

"Through there?"

The receptionist nodded and he entered to be seated by a

floorwalker who was another employee. Everyone he met in the public areas of the inn would be employees, which was why the tariff was high. Indentured servants would work out of sight behind the scenes.

The menu sported a variety of Brasilian dishes. He selected one more or less at random that involved fowl covered in fruit preserve. He chose a light fizzy spiced beer to drink while he was waiting. It was so pleasant that he ordered another. The dish when it arrived was a pretty good facsimile of the original. A local white meat substituted for the native Brasilian original but the fruit sauce was perfect, which rather surprised him. Streamer restaurants with pretensions to gourmet standards tended to boast Brasilian cuisine on the menu but the reality was often rather hit and miss.

Not that Allenson cared overmuch about food as long as it was hot and wasn't going to poison him. However, he had attended enough formal dinners to tell a *patina de pisciculis* from an *aliter baedinam sive agninam excaldatam,* a thought that made him wonder not for the first time why it was necessary to write menus in archaic languages. Admittedly *aliter baedinam sive agninam excaldatam* sounded better than "steamed meat."

The empty restaurant slowly filled. A young man brought in an even younger girlfriend who stared adoringly at him as he talked. Allenson sighed. Youth was so wasted on the young, an unoriginal thought but true nonetheless. The waiter and floorwalker pushed two tables together to seat a group of older men and women dressed in conservative business suits. In Paxton, conservative equaled dark green with pink linings.

The party conversed loudly, each trying to outdo the other. The bottles of brandy served to their table were clearly not their first attempt this evening to quench a raging thirst.

Allenson finished his main course and the floorwalker brought him the sweet menu to peruse. He was slightly put off by one of the women in the party flashing covert glances in his direction. He had few illusions about his power of sexual magnetism. The attention was disconcerting so he wondered what she was up to. He glanced casually across to find her in a huddle with her fellow diners. They all turned to look at him.

He felt his face burn and had to resist checking that his clothes were properly fastened.

"Well, I'll do it," a florid-faced man said.

He climbed laboriously to his feet and made his way unsteadily to Allenson's table.

"General Allenson? It is General Allenson, the victor of the Terran Wars?"

Allenson gave a small nod of assent, resisting an urge to deny everything.

"Rosy thought so," the man said, slapping Allenson on the shoulder in a friendly manner. "She saw you at the victory parade on Manzanita."

He whipped out a datapad that he had been holding behind his back.

"Could I have a selfie? It's for my wife, not me."

He turned around without waiting for an answer and held his datapad at arm's length, leaning in close to Allenson to record his meeting with the great man.

The man checked the picture.

"Would you autograph it?"

"What's your wife's name?" Allenson asked.

"Alfred," the man replied.

Allenson scrawled a greeting to Alfred with his forefinger and scribbled an approximation of his name.

"Hey Alf, ask him over?"

"Would you care to join us?"

Allenson saw to his horror that they were pulling up another chair at the double table and signaling the waiter to lay an additional place.

"Thank you but no, I've only just got on-world."

He rose so fast that he knocked the remains of his spiced beer across the table. A rivulet waterfalled off the surface to splash his admirer's shoes. Fortunately the man didn't seem to notice or perhaps he just didn't care.

"A pleasure to meet you," Allenson said, disengaging the man's arm.

He remembered why he had firmly turned down a political career. Glad-handing was not one of his skills. He made a rapid retreat, pressing a coin firmly into the floorwalker's hand as he passed the podium. A flash of purple light as the money changed hands authenticated the coin as a genuine Brasilian crown piece. That was an overtip but the large rectangular plastic tab was the first coin he pulled from his pocket in his haste. Allenson would gladly have paid ten times as much to escape a round of gut-wrenching embarrassment from people queuing to have their picture taken with the conquering hero.

Allenson slept surprisingly soundly. He breakfasted from the preserved food in his room's dispenser, reluctant to brave the private dining room again. He just finished his morning cafay and was dropping the cup in the bin when his datapad chimed.

"You requested a servant, sar," said the receptionist, the same girl as last night going by her voice. She must work long hours.

"Yes."

"I have one in reception for you to interview. I can personally recommend him as he has worked for our guests on other occasions to their satisfaction. Shall I send him up?"

"No, I'll come down."

A short, sturdy man in clean, pressed blue overalls waited for him in the lobby. He was balding but covered his head with a lemon yellow cap that had a bright blue badge advertising an agricultural product new to Allenson.

"You must be Colonel Allenson? I'm Boswell. My card."

The man stepped forward and handed Allenson a small piece of stiff paper. He had forgotten the Paxton habit of exchanging business cards. On reflection, he remembered seeing a similar box of cards with the inn's picture on the front in his room. On one side, the man's card read Boswell's Personal Services and on the other listed a scale of charges. He glanced down to find the costs expensive by Manzanita standards but reasonable for a more developed world like Nortania.

There was a pause while Allenson considered what to ask. He didn't hire the servants at home. Trina handled all the domestic business. He had expected to be dealing with an agency hiring out indentured servants, not an independent contractor. Allenson always found them a difficult economic group to deal with. They were neither fish nor fowl in the Lower Stream's social pecking order.

Boswell had an upturned nose that conferred him with a somewhat irreverent appearance, as if a grin was always near the surface of his features. The man looked him in the eyes obviously expecting Allenson to say something.

"The receptionist speaks most highly of you," he eventually got out, waving his hand vaguely in the direction of her podium.

"I should hope so, guv," Boswell said indignantly. "She's my niece."

There was that half grin again. Allenson laughed. Dammit he liked the chap's style.

"You're hired. Let's start with a week's service and see how we get on."

"Money in advance?" Boswell asked, hopefully, inclining his head and adopting an innocent expression.

"Half now, half on satisfactory completion of service," Allenson said firmly, not wanting to give the impression that he was an easy mark.

Boswell agreed with alacrity that suggested that he expected Allenson to have driven a harder bargain.

"What's first, guvnor?"

"I'm going to take a short walk to clear my head. I want you to unpack my military dress uniform and press out any creases. No doubt your niece can give you a key to my room."

"Right you are, squire."

Boswell touched his cap brim with his forefinger.

Allenson sat quietly in the convention hall, checking through the agenda of the meeting. He was early so delegates still filtered in. Most of them looked at him with curiosity. Boswell had done a fine job with the Honorary Colonel of Militia dress uniform. He managed to get Allenson into it without overly disturbing the knife edged creases. Gold braid around the neck and on both sleeves shone brightly against the purple and gray of Manzanita. Parades of flashes in various colors down his arms denoted the militia regiments of which he had been voted honorary colonel.

Buller was the only other person in a military uniform but he wore a crumpled field combat dress. Perhaps the Brasilian thought the uniform would emphasize his credentials as a regular soldier or possibly he didn't care what image he presented. Either way his demonstration was not likely to impress. The other delegates wore business or colonial official clothes. Some sported brighter garments than Allenson but none were more splendid.

One group stood out in a display of Spartanism and simplicity by wearing one-piece garments of unrelieved charcoal gray. No lapels or cuffs, let alone jewelry or marks of allegiance, disturbed the effect, underscoring the severe style by unadornment. The Ascetics of the Heilbron colonies came from some of the wealthiest and most developed settlements this side of the Bight. Not every Heilbron delegate was an Ascetic but even the independents wore clothes that were somber by Lower Stream standards.

The Heilbron colonies attracted voluntary immigrants in greater numbers than the other Cutter Stream worlds. They tended to be a special sort of colonist, the disgruntled dissatisfied with Home World society or their place within it. These discontents created a social and economic class quite distinct from the impoverished gentry and exiled criminals who had provided the bulk of the lower Stream populations. Ascetics were simply the most powerful group of these radicals.

Allenson had little direct experience of them but from what he read they opposed the activities that ordinary people thought made life worth living. A dour lot, they were sure of their righteousness with an unfortunate tendency to preach. Their social values were of little import to Allenson; of more significance was that they had a strong political ideology favoring independence. They intended to build a new society without social class distinctions and the ostentation that went with an aristocracy.

Personally Allenson thought they deluded themselves that any human society could be classless. The best you could hope for was a relatively flexible class system that allowed reasonable social mobility. Something that avoided ossifying into a caste structure. Any society that left no legitimate path to advancement for talented, aggressive, ambitious young men was doomed to violent revolution. Whereas a society where gentlemen invited potential revolutionaries into their clubs and upper class ladies invited them into their beds was likely to be as stable as anything built by human beings even if it was no utopia.

The Ascetics' desire for independence made them potential allies for Allenson's political goals, provided their radicalism could be kept in check. The Lower Stream gentry were unlikely to take kindly to revolutionary social policies.

The delegate chairs in the Assembly Hall were arranged in a horseshoe with the chairman's podium between the open wings. An outer ring of seats for observers and officials perched on a raised balcony around the edge of the hall. The circular walls were windowless and painted with fantastic agricultural scenes of verdant greenery. The Paxton Ruling Council met here and the artwork presumably reminded everyone where the money came from. Natural light filtered through the semi-transparent crystalline dome of the roof. Strip lighting around the base of the dome reinforced the illumination, eliminating possible shadows.

Allenson surreptitiously checked his datapad for security. Recording and signal nullifiers blanked the hall. Anything said in the Assembly would be confidential.

The chairman of the Assembly, a Nortanian called Evansence, called the meeting to order. His duties included an introductory address welcoming the delegates. He managed to talk for twenty minutes without actually committing himself to anything or even expressing a view. The Nortanian establishment appeared fairly happy with the status quo and just wanted to be left alone. There was a subtext of fear in Evansence's evasions that rippled through the room like a fast flowing ebb tide. Another word for failed rebel was traitor and all-right thinking people agreed that traitors must be punished to the limit of the law.

Allenson understood the delegates' apprehensions and to some degree shared them. He was not afraid of being executed, after the Terran War death held little fear. Once you reached the mind-set of expecting sudden random termination at any moment you either accepted the inevitable or went mad. What did concern Allenson was the shame and ignominy that execution as a traitor would bring to him and by extension to his family. That was not to be tolerated.

A number of "hear, hears" sounded from delegates from the smaller colonies. The Heilbron delegates frowned. One with a face like thunder slammed his hand down and opened his mouth.

Allenson cut in quickly to stop the meeting from falling apart before it had properly commenced.

"If I may make a point."

Evansence looked grateful at the interruption.

"The chair recognizes Colonel Allenson," he said quickly.

Allenson looked at each delegate as he spoke.

"Nortania has a reliable business supplying genosurgeoned crop extracts to Brasilia and it is understandable that Nortanians are alarmed at any threat to this trade."

"Quite," Evansence said.

"The products sell for a considerable markup in Brasilia but how much of that value added accrues to Nortania?"

Falco, one of the Nortanian delegates, jumped in before the chairman could reply.

"Off the top of my head less than five per cent," he said.

"But we just supply the raw material," Evansence protested. "The complex chemistry is carried out in Brasilian factories. That's where the market is."

Allenson tilted his head.

"But suppose you manufactured the finished products here?" Allenson asked. "After all, they're low volume, high value, cheaply transportable organics."

Falco looked thoughtful.

"Then we would get nearer forty or fifty per cent of the markup," he said. "More if we controlled the transport and wholesale distribution to the Home Worlds."

Evansence shook his head.

"But what if Brasilia simply refused to purchase the finished products?"

Allenson replied. "Then you sell to any Home World with the money to buy, but I doubt that Brasilian business would cut off its nose to spite its face by prolonging an embargo."

"But that would take capital that we don't have," Evansence said. "Lots of it."

Allenson laughed

"You don't think that financial institutions all over the different Home Worlds wouldn't rush to invest in such a lucrative business and break the Brasilian cartel's monopoly?"

He sat back and let the delegates argue, confident that he had scored a point. Self-interest and avarice focused minds wonderfully. It was also understood that vested interests in Brasilia would hardly welcome the breaking of their cozy trade cartels so some degree of political rupture with the Home World was inevitable.

Buller ranted for some time on his favorite subject, the injustice caused by preferment of inbred Brasilian aristocratic half-wits blocking the rightful rise of those who deserved advancement due to superior ability. Many of the delegates nodded and muttered "hear, hear" at Buller's eloquence, clearly identifying themselves with the group demonstrating superior ability. Allenson wondered how they would react when their own social inferiors demanded similar opportunities.

A great deal of hot air got expended over what form the governance of the independent state might take. The lower colonies' gentry wished to preserve the status quo while the Heilbronites pushed for social revolution. For Allenson this was like debating the flavor of the icing before you decide how to bake the cake. He let his mind drift with just one small subroutine of consciousness monitoring the exchange.

Allenson came to with a start when he realized that the meeting had gone quiet. Everyone looked expectantly in his direction. He ran the recorder of his memory to extract the discussion. The delegates had been agonizing about war and whether they could ever beat Brasilia. A Heilbron Ascetic with no experience of warfare had announced that one free man could beat a hundred professional soldiers because his heart was pure and his cause just.

A cynical delegate from a Lower Stream world replied that the hypothetical pure at heart colonial would indeed have to be superhuman as there were more than a hundred Brasilians for every Streamer. Buller chipped in that a professional army could only be fought by a professional army with a unified chain of command, a blatant job application.

The reputation Allenson earned in the Terran War, undeservedly in his opinion but there it was, made him the local authority on colonial warfare, to Buller's obvious annoyance. That was why all the delegates waited upon his opinion. Fortunately the prolonged pause before replying made him look statesmanlike and thoughtful rather than slow-witted.

"It depends what you mean by victory," he finally replied. "I take it no one has delusions of crossing the Bight and conquering a Home World?"

This provoked the expected laughter.

"To win we do not have to beat Brasilia. We merely have to survive and make a Brasilian victory too costly to be worth the effort. Military power is eroded by distance and the Bight is a sizable obstacle. Brasilia would have considerable logistical difficulties supplying large conventional forces here given the low industrialization in the colonies. I saw that for myself in the Terran War."

Buller nodded in support, albeit somewhat reluctantly.

"There is also the fact that Brasilia has far more powerful rivals than us to contend with who are much closer to home—Terra for one. For all these reasons then, yes, I believe we could beat Brasilia provided we define victory carefully. I would also add that in my opinion Colonel Buller has a point. Revolutionary fervor is fine but is no substitute for discipline, training and professionalism."

Here he paused and looked around the chamber at each delegate in turn.

"However, no one who has seen the brutality and wastefulness of war would ever want to provoke another one. Provided we are reasonable in our demands and don't push Brasilia too far I believe we can achieve effective political and economic independence while leaving Brasilia a face-saving formula recognizing its nominal sovereignty. Frankly, we are not important enough for Brasilia to go to the wall over. I would add that political negotiation is recognized as completely different from armed rebellion in one important sense. They don't hang you for it or confiscate your property if you lose."

The meeting ground on but eventually broke up for lunch. Allenson noted a messenger hurrying to the Heilbron delegates once the hall doors were unlocked. He idly wondered what could be so urgent. However Todd intercepted him by the door so he put the matter out of his mind.

"No doubt you recall that you have a luncheon meeting with two Paxton bankers," Todd broke off to check his datapad.

Allenson inwardly groaned. The things he did for his country. A networking lunch with a couple of merchant bankers was about as attractive as catching his privates in a rock grinder. Todd flicked his finger over the pad, sifting through pages.

"They are Sar Josson of Bank Agricole and Sar Huang of Emerald Office."

"Fine, lead me to them," Allenson said, practicing planting a phony smile on his face. He would have to master this skill in the next few days.

Todd guided him to where the two men sat in the anteroom. They rose and extended their hands as Allenson approached. Josson was tall and lean, almost cadaverous with sunken cheeks and a concave chest. Huang was physically his opposite, a short tubby roly-poly sort of man who looked as if he would bounce upright if pushed over. In his head Allenson christened them Little and Large as a mnemonic aid. He couldn't help thinking that they would cut an impressive figure if fused into a single body.

The men presented their cards. Allenson patted his pocket prior to explaining that he had omitted to bring his own when he discovered a pack in his pocket. Boswell must have printed some on his own initiative. He sneaked a glance as he handed a card to each man. The style was more florid than Allenson would have chosen but who was to say that Boswell was wrong. The man was on home ground after all.

Allenson glanced over Huang's head, not a difficult task. A tall man with blond hair and pale blue eyes leaned patiently against the door frame. He stood out not just because of his appearance, which was far from the human norm of brown eyes and hair, but also by his casual wear. A line of white hair from an old wound ran across his scalp, almost hidden by his blonde coloring. Allenson blinked, half expecting the figure to disappear, to be a phantasm from his memory. It was still there after the blink, grinning at him. The man raised a hand to his brow in an ironic salute.

"Sar Josson, Sar Huang, I must convey my abject apologies but I regret that something urgent has come up at the last moment. I have to cancel our meeting. I deeply regret the inconvenience to yourselves and assure you no slight is intended."

He turned to Todd.

"Lieutenant, please take these gentleman to the best restaurant in town at my expense and make a careful note of the issues they wish to raise. Then reschedule our meeting at a time convenient to them. They are to have absolute priority."

The last comment was a polite fiction. He was either free or he wasn't but it was politic to smooth ruffled feathers and he did dislike rudeness. He waited until Todd took the bankers from the building and then walked over to the door.

"Hello, Allenson," the blond man said.

"You bastard, Hawthorn," Allenson replied. "Where the hell have you been? I thought you were dead."

★ CHAPTER 7 ★

Old Times and New Beginnings

Allenson toyed with his lunch. He regretted choosing a dish that turned out to be bacon wrapped around some sort of spiced herbal stuffing. Hawthorn eagerly cut his double-sized steak into large chunks. He pushed them greedily into his mouth, swallowing each morsel before it was properly chewed.

They chose to patronize a modest chophouse some way from the Assembly Hall and the prying eyes of other delegates. Allenson studied his friend. Hawthorn had filled out but looked solid rather than fat.

He waited until the man satisfied his immediate hunger before starting a conversation. He wasn't sure what to say. He and Hawthorn had once been as close as brothers having grown up together and fighting side by side in the Terran War. But the man had disappeared decades ago after becoming more and more withdrawn. Hawthorn had always been something of a loner who needed time on his own but he never vanished for more than a few weeks.

"You were ravenous," Allenson said, embarrassed at the banality of the comment but unable to do better.

Hawthorn grinned and paused, waving a chunk of meat on his fork for emphasis.

"If you'd nothing between your teeth for two days but a tart's tongue then you'd be pretty hungry as well."

Allenson couldn't help but smile back despite his disapproval. He knew other gentlemen would consider him a prude because of his opinion on the use of prostitutes. And what consenting adults chose to do in their private life was hardly his business. Hawthorn had the gift of drawing Allenson out of his shell. He had missed that intimacy. He realized for the first time in a sudden burst of self-awareness how much Destry's emigration had affected him. Allenson was a man with many acquaintances but few friends.

"You never answered my question back at the Assembly Hall. Where the hell have you been?"

Hawthorn chewed and swallowed before replying.

"Oh, on some mud ball way out in the Hinterland running a one-man trading station. You won't have heard of it. There was no way of sending a message home and I guess I had nothing to say. I tried to contact you when I got in this morning but the Nortanians had you all incommunicado in your meeting."

"They are understandably worried about security. No doubt they half expect or maybe hope that the meeting will come to nothing. In that case they don't want to be left holding the political baby if Brasilia finds out and demands explanations."

Hawthorn laughed and shook his head before cutting off another generous piece of steak and consuming it.

"What's so funny?" Allenson asked, slightly nettled.

Hawthorn wiped his lips on his napkin.

"It's the naivety of you gentlemen that always astonishes me. You are like children compared to the political *nous* of the average parlor maid."

"And you aren't a gentleman?" Allenson asked rhetorically.

"I suppose so," Hawthorn conceded, "by birth at least but I consort with low folk and it must have rubbed off or perhaps I just have a nasty mind."

He laid down his utensils.

"I would bet you any odds that the head of Brasilian intelligence will have half a dozen independent transcripts of what was discussed this morning before the Paxton clerks have finished drafting the minutes. Terran Security will have copies a month later. At least three of your delegates will be Brasilian double agents. Another three will sell you out simply as insurance in case your plot fails."

"That could help our case," Allenson said. "Once Brasilia sees that we are serious it may bring them to serious negotiations. War's to no one's benefit so, logically, compromise is in all our interests."

"There's going to be a war," Hawthorn said with the air of a man stating the sheer bleeding obvious.

Allenson attempted to protest but Hawthorn held up a hand to check him.

"When have human beings ever chosen the sensible and logical course simply because it is in their interests? Something will go wrong or some hotheaded fool will start shooting on some imagined point of principle—"

Here Hawthorn's lips curled displaying what he felt about those who stood on points of principle.

"—and the fight will be on. When war starts it takes on a life all of its own. Who precisely did Old Earth's Biowars benefit, pray tell? They destroyed civilization and damn near caused human extinction but did that stop the ancients fighting them? Did it hell!"

There was a break in the conversation while Hawthorn polished off his meal. Allenson pushed his food around the plate some more. Hawthorn was always unsettlingly frank with his friends. He had a habit of telling truths people did not always want to hear.

"Why did you leave the Stream?" Allenson asked, carefully keeping his tone flat and unemotional to disguise the hurt. "You took off without so much as a goodbye and I thought we were close friends. I thought you could confide in me."

"We were—are—close friends, you, me and Destry," Hawthorn replied. "That's why I had to leave."

"I don't understand."

"Destry had his societal commitments and you were building the estate and a career but after the end of the Terran Wars I had no purpose. My drinking got worse and the scrapes I got into became more embarrassing."

He shrugged.

"It wouldn't have ended well."

"If you think I or Destry would abandon a friend simply because he caused us embarrassment then you didn't know us at all," Allenson said hotly.

"Of course you wouldn't abandon me. That's the point," Hawthorn replied. "Don't you see? That's why I had to leave before I did your reputations real harm by association. I had to go somewhere far away where you couldn't find me and talk me into coming back."

There was another pause while Allenson digested that information. Actually looked at in a certain way it made a sort of sense.

Hawthorn turned the conversation away from himself.

"So tell me about your life while I've been gone. I guess you and Trina are still married?"

Allenson smiled.

"One of my more successful decisions."

"Then I suppose you have raised a brood of young Allensons. I know you always wanted children."

Allenson lowered his head but there was no avoiding the issue.

"No, we haven't children."

"But Trina is fertile. As I recall she already has—"

Hawthorn firmly shut his mouth before continuing.

"Sorry, living in the back of beyond has eroded my manners."

Allenson lifted his head and looked his friend in the eye.

"You recall there was always a puzzle about where my brother Todd had come into contact with the bioweapon residues that eventually killed him."

"Yes," Hawthorn said sharply.

"I believe the mystery is solved. It wasn't Todd who was exposed to molecular damage but our father or even someone farther back in our shared heritage."

There was a deadly silence. Allenson forced himself to smile.

"Don't look so concerned. There's no evidence that the problem will manifest itself in me as a wasting disease like in Todd. In my case the effect is more subtle."

"I'm sorry," Hawthorn said.

"No matter, what can't be cured and all that, so tell me why've you returned now?"

Hawthorn seized gratefully on the change of subject.

"Because there's going to be another war and you being a damned fool man of principle will be in it up to your neck. Someone has to protect your back while you strike noble poses."

"Indeed." Allenson laughed.

Now it was Hawthorn's turn to reveal private matters.

"Actually I'm still drinking heavily but not so much that a course of genosurgery can't fix any issues. And I reckon that the drinking will take care of itself with some activity to occupy my time more meaningful than measuring out cloth for clan chief's wives."

"You are still a major in the Manzanita militia reserves," Allenson said.

"Am I?" asked Hawthorn, surprised.

"Yes, it's an unpaid commission. However, there will undoubtedly be a rapid expansion of the military. We'd better put you back on the active list and bump you up to colonel so you have some clout over the new boys."

Allenson took out his datapad and made a note. He had taken to making "to do" lists as he got older and his responsibilities multiplied like cockroaches in a bakery. Life was so much simpler when he and Hawthorn were young.

A waitress came and took their order for plum brandy and cafay. Both eschewed pudding. Allenson generally found them too rich and sleep-inducing at luncheon. Hawthorn had already eaten enough for two.

"There was talk of setting up an elite regiment of Hinterland men on one-man frames to act as an independent fire brigade," Allenson said, when the waitress served the drinks and left them alone. "The commander's commission would be at colonel rank. I could swing it for you if you like?"

Hawthorn poured some brandy into his cafay and stirred the mixture while he thought about it.

"You know, I think I might pass on that offer. Colonel isn't really a combat role, is it? From what I remember it's nine tenths office work and one tenth detailing other people to go off and do the difficult stuff and get killed."

"True."

"Which isn't really me, is it?"

"I guess not," Allenson replied. "But I already have an aide, young Todd."

Hawthorn held his hand out palm down three feet above the ground to indicate a child.

"What, Todd Allenson, your nephew but he's just—"

"You've been away a long time," Allenson said gently.

"Todd Junior, well, well, who'd have thought it," Hawthorn said.

"I've another role in mind. You'll no doubt be commissioned as captain general of the colonial army—"

"Probably not," Allenson interrupted. "Colonel Buller sees himself in that position."

"Who the hell's Buller?" Hawthorn asked.

"Regular professional Brasilian soldier with some experience of senior command. He emigrated from the Home Worlds to the Stream after you left."

Hawthorn snorted. "Never heard of him. As I said, you'll undoubtedly be appointed captain general and you're going to need a security service."

"A security service?" Allenson asked, astonished. "Whatever for?"

"To run a bodyguard unit. How long do you think before it occurs to your enemies that it'd be to their advantage if you had an unfortunate but very terminal accident?"

"Oh come on, no individual is that important."

Hawthorn ignored him.

"You'll also need a special unit to plug leaks of sensitive information and to run an intelligence network to find out what your opponents are up to. When I speak of opponents I don't just mean the enemy. You know where you are with the enemy. They're just trying to kill you. It's the smiling bastards standing behind you that present an unknown threat. "

"I suppose so," Allenson replied, a little stunned. He hadn't given such affairs any consideration, but it was clear that Hawthorn had devoted considerable thought to the matter.

"The head of your security force needs to possess certain key abilities."

Hawthorn counted them off on his fingers.

"Firstly total loyalty to you personally without independent political ambitions, secondly the balls to tell you what you don't want to hear and not tell you what you don't need to know, and thirdly and most importantly, enough common sense to distinguish between the two. A cynical nasty mind that sees the worst in everyone coupled with the personality of a ruthless bastard who'll do what needs to be done wouldn't hurt either."

Allenson opened and closed his mouth like a pet fish waiting to be fed while Hawthorn continued remorselessly.

"If you know of anyone else who possesses these qualities to a greater degree than myself then I'll gladly step aside. Otherwise I shall consider myself appointed."

And that was that.

The afternoon session in the Assembly Hall was if anything even more balls-achingly tedious than the morning's. Much time was given to pointless discussions about what form a Streamer army might take.

"I see no need to repeat the mistakes of the past," asserted Horntide, a sallow-faced Ascetic with an irritatingly pedantic manner. "The army should be an expression of the people and as such must conform to the sacred principles of the people. Accordingly it must consist of volunteers who choose where and for how long they wish to serve and under which officers they are willing to serve."

"Quite so and all soldiers should've an equal say about how campaigns are conducted, possibly through a system of referenda," said another Ascetic whose name Allenson hadn't caught.

A murmur of disquiet went around the Hall.

"Are you people bloody mad!" Buller exclaimed. "You propose to take on Brasilian regulars with a poxy debating society? Grow up, you idiots. An army fights because its troops are more scared of their officers and NCOs than they are of the enemy. Soldiers have to obey without question, go where they're sent, do what their told, and kill whomsoever they're told."

Buller jabbed a finger at Horntide, who shifted uneasily in his seat.

"All else is bollocks and if you think I'm going to be humiliated by taking command of a load of bolshy barrack room lawyers who run at the first bit of bloodletting then you can think again. Give me a professional army that can win or get used to forelock touching every time some minor Brasilian popinjay wafts past. You may want to die at the end of a Brasilian rope but I don't."

At that Buller stormed to the door. A commissioner tried to explain that the Hall was in lockdown. Buller pushed the flunky roughly aside with a decidedly unnecessary comment about his mother's sexual habits. He unlocked the door himself and stormed out without bothering to shut it behind him.

Obviously there were limits to Buller's support for egalitarianism.

There was a stunned silence in the hall as the more politically radical delegates digested an unwelcome force feed of reality.

"I thought the point of the exercise was to free ourselves from Brasilian control," said a gentleman from the Lower Stream. "Not to try to create some sort of utopia for the proles. I don't know much about running an army but I do know how to run a plantation and it ain't done by letting the staff vote on whether they wish to work or not."

Allenson could feel the unity of purpose of the meeting slipping way as reality punctured various cherished illusions.

"If I may make a comment," he said, carrying on without waiting for permission. "Colonel Buller is essentially right that an army must be a trained and disciplined organization or it risks falling into armed anarchy. Enthusiasm is no substitute for professionalism."

Allenson paused to let that fact seep in before continuing in a more conciliatory vein.

"However, I sympathize with Delegate Horntide in that a professional army must be under political control. A Streamer army must serve the people of the colonies and reflect their aspirations. I see no advantage in replacing our masters in Brasilia with a local military dictatorship. Accordingly the army commanders, especially the captain general, should be carefully selected."

No one had anything more useful to add, which didn't stop them adding it. Discussion diverted into uniform design and who would get the lucrative contract to supply said garments.

Allenson took the opportunity to tune out and consider his lunch meeting. Hawthorn wasn't the hard young man he had tramped the Hinterland with but then, neither was Allenson—and neither would be much use to the Cutter Stream now if they were.

Hawthorn was undoubtedly right, though. Allenson would likely be appointed to some sort of senior commission in the new army. Not the captain general of course, that was just Hawthorn's loyalty to a friend talking, but some position of responsibility nonetheless. He would need intelligence and that would involve civilian spies as well as military scouts. Dealing with spies was always a tricky proposition. His spymaster would have to be completely discreet and financially trustworthy. He would control sizable unattributable funds needed for bribery and the like.

Hawthorn had spent the last decade keeping his own council in the back of beyond so was unlikely to become indiscreet now. He had never cared enough for money to bother stealing any. Indeed, he rarely got around to spending the modest investment income he had inherited.

Allenson made some notes on his datapad. Hawthorn would need a security pass to attend the rest of the meeting as an observer so he could get a feel for the main players. Allenson thought long and hard about what else Colonel Hawthorn would need to perform his duties as Head of Security.

The meeting dragged out to a desultory close without coming to a decision. Buller had rattled many of the political radicals and they in turn unnerved the plantation owners. The scale of the undertaking and the risks involved percolated into all concerned. The delegates were inevitably a hotbed of cold feet. Allenson wasn't entirely unhappy at the turn of events as such matters had to be faced. It might as well be sooner rather than later.

Todd met him by the door and held out a sealed envelope.

"From Sar Stainman, leader of the Heilbron delegation," Todd said.

Allenson was intrigued. Sealed envelopes were the stuff of romance novels. He slit it open with his thumb nail and read the enclosed single sheet. Then he folded it and placed it carefully in a jacket pocket.

"Convey my compliments to Sar Stainman and tell him that I accept," Allenson said.

Todd looked desperate to ask what was in the message but contained himself.

"Very well, Uncle."

Allenson smiled at Todd's back as he dodged back through the exiting delegates. The lad was learning. An aide was his principal's assistant, not necessarily his confidant.

Later that evening, Allenson idly flicked through the information channels on his pad while he waited in the reception area of the Inn. Nortanian news was parochial even by colonial standards, mostly limited to weather predictions and the fluctuating price of agricultural commodities. The providers seasoned factual matters with discussions about the comings and goings of various local celebrities of whom Allenson knew little and cared even less.

Boswell sat patiently opposite watching some sort of drama on his datapad. Allenson couldn't see the screen but the sound channel conveyed explosions and heavy breathing.

A large carriage towed by four Nortanian quadrupeds pulled up outside the Inn. A brightly striped canvas weather roof supported by four wooden poles protected the Heilbronites who sat within but otherwise it was of open design. Allenson stood up.

"If you please, sar, I believe I should establish your visitors' credentials," Boswell said.

Allenson sighed but acquiesced, as matters had to be done properly. Boswell went outside to confer with the coachman before coming back and bowing to Allenson, winking as he straightened. Once the societal rigmarole was finished, Allenson took a seat in the carriage. He took the precaution of choosing one well to the back as far away as possible from the quadrupeds' rear.

Stainman introduced the other Heilbron representatives. Allenson noticed that Horntide was not amongst them. Strange, the man had been prominent and outspoken in the Hall. They made small talk all the way to the restaurant. A *maître d'hôtel* met them at the door with much bowing and hand rubbing. He had slicked back his hair with perfumed vegetable oil much to the Heilbronites' obvious discomfort. The oil failed to prevent a small snowstorm of dandruff falling onto the wide collar of his dark green suit.

The *maître d'hôtel* intrigued Allenson by conveying the party to a private room that must have been booked in advance. He anticipated merely social networking when he accepted the invitation to dine but it appeared that the Heilbron delegates had more meaty discussions in mind. When they sat down, Allenson noticed that there was one place too many set at the oval table.

Waitresses brought in self-heating tureens filled with various pungent stews. They arranged them in the center of the table alongside bottles of water, imported wine and plum brandy. The *maître d'hôtel* swept the waitresses out with both arms like a man herding sheep. Then he backed out, closing the double doors with a flourish and a final *"bon appétit!"*

Allenson helped himself to portions from two of the nearest dishes without taking much notice of the contents. He poured a small measure of plum brandy into a wine glass, taking the precaution of diluting it with a much larger volume of mineral water. He had the feeling he was going to need a clear head tonight.

The Heilbronites poked around in the dishes in an effort to ascertain the contents before serving themselves. Allenson thought they were wasting their time because in his limited experience Nortanian cuisine favored highly seasoned and spiced dishes whose flavor depended little on the identifiable components. The art of Nortanian cuisine seemed to involve making everything taste like something else.

Conversation was desultory while everyone satisfied their initial hunger.

"Ascetic Horntide not joining us tonight?" Allenson asked innocently.

"He's indisposed," Stainman replied briefly in a tone that discouraged further inquiry.

Indisposed could mean anything from a hot date to an encounter with a dodgy oyster restricting one to close proximity with a water closet. It could also mean being locked in a room with two heavies guarding the door so one couldn't disrupt a serious pragmatic negotiation with unwelcome fanaticism.

"You expressed the opinion that war might be averted," Stainman said.

"Indeed," Allenson replied.

"Unfortunately, you're mistaken."

Allenson paused, spoon halfway to his mouth.

"What do you mean?" he asked sharply.

Stainman looked glum.

"The fighting's already started. I received word today."

"Go on," said Allenson, heart sinking.

"A group of radicals on Trinity staged a protest outside a warehouse at the increase in import taxes on luxuries like tea."

Trinity was the most developed of the Heilbron Worlds so was arguably the wealthiest trans-Bight colony and well able to support a luxury import trade.

"I thought the price had dropped sufficiently that tea was still cheaper than last year despite the tax rise," Allenson said.

"Well, yes, Brasilia allowed us to import straight from the producers, cutting out the middle men. That greatly reduced the price but it was the principle, you see."

"The principle, right," Allenson said, thinking of Hawthorn.

"Things got a little out of hand and the warehouse, ah, burned down."

"Awkward."

"The owners thought so and protested to the Brasilian authorities, who landed a sizable force of regulars to protect private property."

Allenson winced. The next step was as predictable as two schoolboys squaring up to each other in the playground.

"No doubt some of the radicals launched direct attacks on the soldiers."

"Only some minor stone-throwing, although the loss of life when a vehicle went off the road was regrettable."

"And the soldiers retaliated, yes?"

"They shot unarmed civilians," a Heilbronite whose name Allenson had forgotten said hotly.

"Unarmed except for stones," Allenson replied neutrally.

"And hunting rifles," Stainman said, conceding the point.

"That is the current situation?" Allenson asked.

Stainman looked even more uncomfortable.

"Well no, I received another letter by fast cutter. Peytr Masters, who is the senior colonel of militia on Trinity, has called in militia regiments from all over the Heilbron Worlds to besiege the Brasilian regulars in the city of Oxford."

"He's not thinking of storming the city?" Allenson asked, alarmed.

"No. At least I don't think so," Stainman replied, somewhat defensively.

"What military experience does Masters have?" Allenson asked.

"He's very highly thought of," replied the delegate who had already spoken. Allenson now recalled that Tobold was his name. "He was a ship's captain and has a successful import-export business. He's most eloquent in debate."

"No doubt," Allenson replied. "But that does not answer my question."

"Masters was commander of the Trinity Militia Regiment of Oxford when it was part of Levit's column during the Terran War," said Stainman.

"That's odd. I don't remember him," Allenson said.

"Well you wouldn't. Unfortunately he was taken ill when the regiment mustered and had to delegate command to his deputy."

Allenson merely raised an eyebrow and Stainman's face reddened. He would not be in charge of the Trinity delegation if he was an unsophisticated man so he took the unspoken point. The Heilbron colonies had been pitched into outright combat with professional forces from the Home World by a military commander with zero combat experience.

"So the Heilbron Worlds are already at war with Brasilia. You must be concerned that the other colonies will let you swing in the wind through inaction?"

From the look on the faces of the Heilbronite delegates they were not so much concerned as bloody terrified. They looked like small boys who have suddenly discovered that manly actions like plotting insurrection against the headmaster can have awful bloody consequences.

"What do you think of Colonel Buller?" Stainman asked, abruptly switching subjects.

The Heilbronites looked at Allenson sharply. It appeared that much depended on his answer. Allenson broke a piece of bread, wiped spices from his plate, and chewed slowly to give him time to consider his answer.

"Colonel Buller's an intelligent student of war and has considerable practical experience of command."

The Heilbronites appeared to be expecting more but Allenson kept his council until he understood the context more fully.

"But what of his political opinions?" Tobold eventually blurted out, unable to contain himself.

Allenson kept his attention on Stainman.

"In what sense do you ask the question?"

"He's a Brasilian senior military officer, a class that doesn't notably hold egalitarian views. Do you think he's genuine?" Stainman asked, motioning for Tobold to be quiet.

"I have no reason to doubt Colonel Buller's sincerity or to think that he's merely reacting to the failure of his own hopes of preferment through what he considers to be political interest," Allenson said carefully.

"It appears that his love of democracy doesn't extend to the military," Tobold remarked sourly.

Allenson recharged his glass, mostly with water.

"You know my opinion on the matter, gentlemen. Colonel Buller's essentially right even if he's perhaps a little harsh in his tone. Everyone in an army down to the lowliest soldier is deserving of fair and just treatment but I'm not going to pretend to believe that everyone is equally talented simply for political reasons."

A sudden clatter from the kitchen made the Heilbronites jump. They really were keyed up.

"Just a cook dropping a pan," Allenson said gently.

He gave them a moment before he continued.

"An army must obey the legitimate orders of the command structure. Otherwise it descends into an armed mob more dangerous to the community than the enemy. It can't be a debating society, not and win wars anyway."

"So if you were captain general would you demand obedience from all?" asked Tobold.

"If I were in such a position—which I have not sought."

Allenson tapped the table for emphasis.

"I'd be the servant of every citizen of the Cutter Stream. I'd serve my masters to the best of my ability as I have always tried to do and I'd expect the same from those who served under me."

He poured himself another cafay.

"Why're we here, gentlemen? What is it you want from me?"

"You're quite right, Colonel Allenson," Stainman said. "Events've overtaken us in the Heilbron Worlds. The precipitous action of a handful of fools has landed us in a shooting war that we can't win alone."

He rubbed his face with both hands, suddenly looking very old and stretched.

"We need the support of the rest of the colonies. We need a commander who not only has experience of leading armies *but* who will unify the colonies. That means a captain general from the Lower Stream, someone reputable from their own class to reassure their delegates concerned about radical political views."

"Which in practice means a captain general from Manzanita as it is the only Lower Stream colony with the necessary sophistication," said Allenson.

"Yes, Colonel Buller seemed like the ideal choice . . ." Stainman's voice faded out.

"But?" Allenson asked.

"The problem is that he's a braggart and a slovenly oaf," said an elderly Ascetic who had not yet spoken. "Oh, his radical politics could play well in the Heilbron Worlds but their opinions no longer matter as they're committed by events whether they like it or not. It's the lower Stream's opinion we have to court."

"The colony worlds may want independence, but I doubt many of the Lower Stream demesne owners or Nortanian businessmen want to see their wealth divided up amongst their servants," Allenson said, drily.

He stood up and gave a small bow.

"Gentlemen, it's getting late and we have a full day tomorrow. I thank you for a most excellent meal and such a useful exchange of views."

Allenson fished out his wallet.

"In return you must allow me to pick up the tab. No, I insist," he said, holding up a hand, although none of the Heilbronites had made any but a token protest.

Buller hijacked the morning meeting of the assembly. He turned up in the same shirt that he wore the day before, judging by the dinner stains on the collar. He demanded that the Assembly declare independence and appoint a captain general immediately. He also wanted to talk about the remuneration that would be required to attract those with the right military skills. This latter point clearly came as something of a shock to delegates. They were used to thinking in terms of militia who were at best semi-professional and whose officers had other sources of income.

A Trent delegate derailed the vote for independence by proposing a counter motion calling for Brasilia to accept subsidiarity in its relations with the colonies, especially in the economic sphere. Trent was the primary jumping off point for ships returning along the trans-Bight chasm to the Home Worlds. The delegate pointed out that Trent enjoyed a thriving import-export business. He expressed doubts about the impact of full independence upon same. It became clear he also worried about the social and economic revolution that might accompany radical political change.

Allenson surreptitiously checked the dictionary on his datapad for the exact meaning of the word subsidiarity. He noted with relief that many other delegates did likewise. It transpired that subsidiarity meant pushing decision making down to the lowest relevant level of administration to avoid unnecessary centralization. This seemed an eminently sensible strategy but no doubt it generated considerable hostility from all right-thinking bureaucrats on religious grounds.

The chairman called for a vote on which motion to adopt. Unsurprisingly the delegates opted by a sizable margin for compromise. At this stage it was probably the best that could be achieved.

Buller then resubmitted his motion to appoint a captain general of all the colonial militias. Before a vote could be taken, Stainman added a codicil making Allenson the favored candidate. A Wagener delegate seconded the motion so promptly that Allenson suspected collusion. The Lower Stream and Heilbron colonies, who made half the delegation, expressed their support in turn, confirming Allenson's suspicion.

Evansence said, "As Colonel Buller rightly suggested we need to discuss financial terms before the appointment."

Stainman turned to Allenson.

"What remuneration would *you* require as captain general, Colonel?"

"I don't need paying to serve my countrymen," Allenson replied, "although I would be grateful to have my expenses defrayed."

At that the Trent, Nortanian and other nonaligned colonies fell into line so in the end the Chairman declared a formal vote unnecessary. Allenson was appointed unopposed.

He glanced over at Buller. The man glared at him with something close to hatred.

★ CHAPTER 8 ★

The Great North Road

The next morning Allenson held a private meeting with Todd and Hawthorn in his hotel room. First, he checked the suppressor on his datapad was on to guarantee the exclusion of eavesdroppers.

"I need to get to Trinity before the situation blows up in our faces," Allenson said.

"This Masters chappy," Hawthorn asked. "Keen, I take it?"

"Apparently so," Allenson replied, "and very, very inexperienced."

"What do you intend to do about Buller?" Hawthorn asked.

"I ought to give him a senior commission. His military skills are too valuable to waste."

Hawthorn grunted in agreement.

"And it would be better to have him pissing out of the tent instead of in. I suggest you bring him with us as your advisor. He could be useful."

Hawthorn turned to Todd.

"Take note, kid. Keep your friends close but your enemies closer."

Poor Todd looked rather shocked. Hawthorn had that effect on people when they were dealing with him for the first time.

"I can't imagine Buller riding a frame. We'll have to use a carriage and that means taking the Great North Road to Port Trent before turning off for Trinity," Allenson said. "We will have to stop three or four times to recharge the batteries, all of which will take time."

"That might be no bad thing," Todd said, speaking for the first time. "It will give a chance for people on the intervening worlds to see you. That could be very politically advantageous."

Allenson regarded Todd with suspicion.

"You want me to parade through the countryside like a barbarian king conducting a laying on of hands for the peasantry?"

"The kid's right," Hawthorn said, ignoring Todd's flush of anger at his use of the term. "Right now the only pan-Bight institution is the army and the army in practice is you. You have to be visible. I hate to say it but you do look rather impressive in full uniform, quite the military aristocrat. Of course the people glimpsing the splendor won't know the real you as we do."

He winked at Todd, who didn't know how to respond so ran through a few facial permutations before settling eventually on a neutral half smile.

There was a hesitant knock at the door. Allenson nodded and Todd opened it. Boswell stood in the doorway twisting his yellow cap in both hands. Today he wore orange loose fitting pantaloons and a blue and pink striped shirt.

"The replacement carriage you asked me to buy, your honor. I have it outside," Boswell said.

"Replacement carriage?" Hawthorn raided both hands palm outwards in exaggerated inquiry.

"The power storage on mine is stuffed, something wrong with the charging system," Allenson replied. "It would never make it up the Great North Road. We could end up marooned on some backwater mudball with no charging facilities. At best it would be a slow trip."

"So you always intended making a procession through the countryside," Hawthorn said sarcastically, throwing Allenson's words back at him.

Allenson smiled.

"I anticipated it might be necessary."

He turned to Boswell.

"Let's go and inspect the vehicle."

"Yes, sar."

They went behind to where Boswell had parked a large flat rectangular box about ten meters long and colored olive green. Scrapes on the hull revealed the livery of many owners during its no doubt long and eventful life.

"Don't tell me that's it?" Hawthorn asked.

"Ah, yes sar," Boswell replied nervously.

Steps with a single handrail were mounted on the front. Allenson pulled himself up.

A well contained a cycling position on each side and a raised pulpit in the center for the driver. He or she navigated the barge from a standing position; so had an excellent view out to all sides. The middle section was filled in, but most of the hull was given over to a cargo bay at the rear. Walkways and handrails ran down the sides.

Boswell used one of the handrails to swing up besides Allenson.

"The tail gate comes down for easy loading, sar. But the real reason I chose her was this."

He shuffled over to the center section and unclipped a concertina-hinged inspection panel. A series of wired-up control modules and three large cells filled the compartment. The registration plate had a series of letters indicating a Terran military source.

"The previous owner wanted something reliable for trading out to the Hinterland colonies so he acquired this power pack from a sort of friend of a friend who was also a cousin of mine."

Boswell dropped the inspection panel, which slammed shut with a sharp click.

"It's yours if you want it. I know she ain't pretty but she'll do the job."

"That she will. This will do nicely, Boswell, very nicely indeed," Allenson said. "Add ten per cent for yourself as a finder's fee and charge the Assembly."

He turned to look down at Hawthorn.

"Might as well start as I mean to go on."

Boswell jumped down. "I can get seats put in the back and even a food dispenser. It wouldn't take much to rig up a canvas cover and foldaway beds in case you need to camp out."

"Good idea, can you find someone to undertake the task within twenty-four hours?"

"Of course I can, General. I know just the man."

"A cousin?" Allenson asked.

Boswell grinned.

"Nephew, sar, the brother of the hotel receptionist. I find it pays to keep business in the family. That way I can keep an eye on things. Make sure they're done right, if you follow."

"I do indeed, Boswell."

"Captain general?" asked a voice behind Allenson.

He half turned to find a slim man of indeterminate age and swept back oiled hair. The man tilted his head to one side and studied Allenson forensically.

"Carry on Boswell," Allenson said, turning to face the newcomer squarely. "And you are, sar?"

"Timmons Redley, at your service, sar. I practice at the Nortanian Bar."

Which in plain language meant he was a local lawyer.

"The Nortanian delegation at the Assembly believed I might be of some use to you as a special political advisor as I have some little experience of the legal and social customs of the Upper Bight colonies."

Redley wore a sober gray suit of modest cut quite unlike the normal flamboyant Nortanian dress.

"You are not Nortanian born then?" Allenson asked.

"Indeed, no. I went to college in Port Trent. I obtained a masters in law on Brasilia although I spent much of my early life on Trinity."

Port Trent Law School had only been open for a few decades so Redley must be in his early thirties. Theoretically it conferred degrees recognized by Brasilia but in practice no Brasilian academic institution would accept a colonial certification on terms of equality. There were Brasilian colleges that specialized in "quicky" masters for colonials as a way of sanitizing their qualifications.

Allenson shook Redley's hand.

"Well, I confess that, now I consider the matter, an advisor with local knowledge would be helpful, but we will be leaving almost immediately for Trent."

"Yes, General, I know. With your permission I shall come with you."

"So be it. You will need a military rank to be taken seriously, say, colonel. I have the authority to appoint you but not, I regret, to pay you a salary."

"I have no need of one, sar."

"In that case, welcome aboard Colonel Redley. May I introduce you to my aide, Lieutenant Todd Allenson, and Colonel Hawthorn who is my head of SP."

"I see," Redley said, looking up at the massive figure of Hawthorn standing hands on hip on the barge. "SP?"

"Special Projects," Hawthorn replied.

"Special Projects," Redley repeated, pursing his lips.

Allenson noted that he ignored Todd's outstretched hand. Clearly mere lieutenants flew below Redley's radar horizon even when they shared the same surname as a general.

"I heard about that cock-up you made of siting a base at Nengue," Buller said. "Really Allenson, on a flood plain in the rainy season and overlooked by hills as well."

Buller chuckled and shook his head.

"Have I ever told you how I took Castle Aikan by storm?"

"No, I never heard that," Redley said, gazing at Buller in admiration.

"Quite a pretty problem it was. Aikan is sited on two hills with fortified walkways linking half-buried bunkers. A river looped around three sides leaving only one possible line of attack. Of course they had that covered by all their heavy weapons."

Buller arranged bits of the meal he was eating to represent the layout of the battlefield.

"I think I need to check how Boswell is getting on," Allenson said.

He climbed over the engine compartment of the barge using the handrail to steady himself and looked around.

The Brasilian Military constructed The Great North Road at the end of the Terran wars to link the First Tier colony worlds and provide a jump off into Terran controlled worlds. It pacified the Continuum so the ride was reasonably smooth even for such a wallowing transport.

Allenson helped build a road into the Hinterland as part of Chernokovsky's ill-fated expedition. A chain of solar powered satellites in real space created the calmed path through the Continuum. This eased travel, extending the speed and range of frames. More roads like this could open up the Hinterlands to colonization and industrialization. Unfortunately, Brasilia had lost interest once Terra had been driven back across the Bight. Indeed, they weren't even maintaining this route properly. The barge had already crossed a bumpy section probably caused by a malfunctioning satellite drifting out of phase. Another couple of decades and the road would fall into disrepair, triggering something of a recession in the colonies.

The large trans-Bight ships were too big to use roads so there was no particular pressure from the large Brasilian merchant gens to expend taxes on its upkeep. It was only the local Stream traffic that would suffer.

Boswell stood in the driver's pulpit, steering the barge into energy eddies along the road that ran in the direction they were traveling. Dull work but a human pilot could drive the barge so much more efficiently than automatics could. They passed a container truck steered by an automatic pilot that smacked the bow into every stray wave of turbulence. Allenson was so glad that he had hired Boswell for the trip. Smooth sailing was less wearing on the barge's mechanics. More importantly it stopped Allenson from having to swallow motion sickness suppressants or throw up every hour or so.

"Everything okay, Boswell?" he asked, moving to stand beside him.

"She's a real honey, General," Boswell said, waving his left hand to encompass their vehicle.

"Good, good, how long to Samson's World?"

Samson's World had a market town serving the local community; so possessed facilities to recharge the barge.

Boswell ran a finger across the control panel, flicking through pages of data.

"Not more'n two hours, sar. But we have plenty of power remaining. We could press on to Forty-Three. There's a station there where we could stop."

"Forty-Three?"

"The world's navigation almanac number."

"What's it called?"

"Don't rightly think it's got an official name, General. On Nortania it's just called Icecube. Never been there so I don't know why."

Allenson considered. It would be useful to press on while they could but Samson's World was a known quantity. He checked the navigation almanac on his datapad. Forty-Three was listed as a way station not a town or farming community. Oddly enough it was the latter that tipped the balance in his mind. They had already made one stop at a farming community of small villages on a world called Arcadia.

Word of his arrival had spread like wildfire and by evening local time throngs of villagers in dance clothes arrived to throw flowers. They insisted on escorting him to the best, indeed the only restaurant, in the village. He was not sure whether the good people of Arcadia were ardent separatists or simply desperate for any excuse for a party.

Whatever, it was possibly the most excruciatingly embarrassing moment of his life. Certainly up there with the time a girl with whom he was currently besotted persuaded him to sing and play the ukulele in an amateur dramatic performance. Todd, his brother not his nephew, had declared his performance the funniest thing he had seen since someone tried to teach a fleek to ride a bicycle. If Icecube was simply an industrial center, he doubted anyone would have the time or inclination to acknowledge his presence let alone throw flowers.

"I thought I might get some exercise," Todd said, edging past Allenson on his way to a pedaling bay.

"There's really no need, sar," Boswell said. "We have more than enough power in the cells."

"Nonetheless, that's my intention," Todd said, in a tone that brooked no opposition.

"That bad," Allenson said, sympathetically, to Todd.

"Buller's now explaining how he brilliantly ambushed the Syracusan armor at Kesserine Pass using prunes to represent tanks. I don't think I can take any more."

"He's certainly talented as a commander," Allenson said.

"And doesn't he know it?" Todd replied. "Do you intend to go back and avail yourself of more of his wisdom?"

Allenson looked over his shoulder. Buller was on his feet waving both arms and gesturing.

"You know, I believe I could also do with some exercise."

Wherever there is civilization there is a bar like The Leaping Frog. It may be in an inn, a public house, a hotel or even a temple but behind the façade it is always the same: the same barman, large, taciturn, seeing and hearing nothing, the same smell of stale booze and staler breath. The original had probably been located in a stone-age cave with bad drainage. Hawthorn possessed a talent for sniffing out such places. Why he went to them and what he did there was not something he felt moved to share with his friends.

The Leaping Frog squatted in a narrow alley between two warehouses. A dirty flickering neon sign in the form of a two-legged lizard advertised its location. Steel shutters perched on pegs above grimy windows that permitted little inspection of the interior. No doubt the pegs could be withdrawn from the inside, dropping the shutters to seal off the building. The closed door was surfaced with peeling layers of plywood painted blotchy green. Hawthorn suspected it was far more substantial than it looked, probably incorporating mechanisms that could bar it against anything short of a battering ram. The Leaping Frog was not an inviting hostelry but then it probably neither wanted nor expected passing trade.

Hawthorn unceremoniously kicked the door with a toecap reinforced with crystallized silicon carbide. When nothing happened he kicked a bit harder. A hatch at head height opened and a face peered out. It was not the sort of face that would give comfort to small children or swooning maidens—too many scars and contusions for that—but the Frog was not a nursery and any maiden who swooned within its interior was unlikely to retain her maidenhood for long.

"Whaddaya want," Pug-Ugly asked.

Hawthorn gave a name that was not his own to gain entry. The door opened. He walked into the dimly lit interior, ignoring the doorkeeper's hopefully outstretched hand. The bubble of sound in the bar died away.

He stopped in the entranceway and removed a cigarette case from an inside pocket. Selecting one of the contents, he placed it in his mouth, swapping the case for a small disposable lighter with which he ignited the fag. The pause gave him time to take in the bar's clientele although he did not seem to take an interest. They also studied him with equal phony nonchalance.

What would they have seen? A stranger, a tall man, heavily built without much sign of fat, dressed in casual, functional but expensive well-tailored clothes that failed to tally with the scar on his head. They would have noticed that the battered cigarette case was made of a ceramic inlaid with precious minerals. Some might have wondered how such a desirable item might be transferred into their own possession.

A glance at his eyes would dissuade such ruminations. Piercing blue and as cold as church charity, they lacked any trace of gullibility or fear. These eyes would not gaze sympathetically on men with treasure maps, sick aunts or knives held out at threatening angles.

Hawthorn took a deep drag and exhaled, adding his own small contribution to the murky atmosphere formed by people smoking herbal concoctions more potent than the imported tobacco he favored. He quite deliberately swept his eyes around the room. Most of the incumbents developed a renewed interest in minding their own business. A group of men who sat around a table in one corner stood out in that they ignored him, carrying on with some game that involved slamming wooden counters down in front of stacks of coins. Hawthorn ignored them in return and headed for the bar.

Background sound slowly refilled the room.

"Tonk, double," Hawthorn said, flipping a quarter crown down onto the plasticized surface.

The barman put a glass on the counter and poured him a generous measure from an unlabeled bottle. He collected the quarter and dropped it into a pouch in his apron. He didn't offer change or utter a word of thanks. The Leaping Frog would not rate highly for service in any tourist guide.

Hawthorn lifted the glass with his left hand. He took a gulp of the Tonk and grimaced. God knows what they cut it with. He threw the rest down his throat in one go so he didn't have to taste the stuff.

"Again," he said to the barman, resting his empty glass on the counter.

The man filled it with another measure.

"I'm looking for a man called Bishop."

Silence, complete silence, instantly cloaked the room.

"I understand he drinks here," Hawthorn said, unperturbed by the shock he had inflicted on the locals.

The barman gave him a look of utter contempt and turned away, busying himself with something behind the bar.

"We don't like people asking questions. Maybe you'd better piss off before you get hurt."

Hawthorn turned around to locate the speaker.

One of the players had left his seat.

Hawthorn leaned back, both elbows on the bar. The speaker glared at Hawthorn truculently, waving a fist that looked as if it could be used for hammering in nails. The bully had a broken nose and a cauliflower ear suggesting boxing was not entirely foreign to his nature.

Hawthorn sighed. He considered going through the preliminary ritual of exchanging insults, but decided it would be a waste of breath. He came off the bar astonishingly quickly for such a heavyset man and threw his Tonk into the bully's eyes.

Whatever they cut Tonk with in this bar clearly stung, because the bully screamed and raised both hands to his face. This left his midriff invitingly exposed. Hawthorn was not the man to look a gift horse in the mouth. He dropped his right shoulder and punched his fist a good six centimeters into the bully's relaxed stomach muscles.

The creep folded, releasing a woomph of air like a large ruminant passing wind. In doing so he stuck his chin out at waist height. Hawthorn drew back his fist.

"Good night," he said, and struck.

He put his full one hundred and twenty kilos behind the punch. The bully's head rocked, not fast enough to stop his jaw deforming and breaking with a sharp crack. He flew across the room into a sitting customer and the two cartwheeled in a crash of breaking wood.

Hawthorn clenched and unclenched his fist to restore the blood flow. He was, he thought, getting too old for this. He sauntered over to where the gamers sat and took the vacated chair. After all, the previous owner had no further use for it.

"Who feckin' said you could sit down?" a youngish thug on his right said.

Hawthorn ignored him. He carefully observed the small man sitting opposite him. Dark hair flopped down over one eye. A small forked goatee beard without moustache lent the man a satanic appearance. Without taking his eyes off the small man Hawthorn inclined his head to indicate the thug.

"I didn't see your hands move. Are you working that dummy with your foot?" Hawthorn asked.

The thug stood up. His hand hovered in what he no doubt took to be a menacing manner over the hilt of a knife worn in a sheath fastened ostentatiously to a strap across his chest. The knife would no doubt serve to intimidate mild mannered shopkeepers and bespectacled clerks. Hawthorn worried more about weapons that he couldn't see.

The knife-bearer sat down when none of the rest of the party stood up to back him.

"What're you playing," Hawthorn asked, examining the hand of the man he had replaced.

The counters were stood up on one end so the other players couldn't see the symbols on them.

"Thrones and palaces, no limit, winner takes all," the small man replied.

Hawthorn nodded. He swept the previous player's coins onto the floor, replacing them with a handful of his own.

"You're familiar with Nortanian Rules?" the small man asked.

"I'll pick them up as we go along," Hawthorn replied.

Thrones and palaces was played in a series of rounds. Each player took it in turns to match or raise the bet of the preceding player so he could select a counter from his hand and place it face up on the table. Players tried to create combinations of tablets superior to all others by the end of round five. Rules governed what counter could be played depending on what was already displayed and what the previous player had elected to do. Nortanian rules turned out to be much the same as other versions.

The barman came round and refilled glasses, including Hawthorn's. Hawthorn played cautiously while he got the feel of the other players. Anyone who thinks a competitive gambling game is a question of luck is doomed to be fleeced. He won and lost by small amounts but generally was slightly down.

When Hawthorn judged the time right he made his strike. His hand of counters at the time was no better than others he had received in earlier rounds and worse than some.

He jacked up the bet sharply and placed a counter. A couple of players dropped out rather than match. On the next round he doubled the pot and only the small man and the young thug on his right stayed in. So far there was little advantage in the counters displayed by any of the players. It would come down to the last play.

Hawthorn doubled once again on the final round and the small man threw in his counters. He sat back, sharp eyes watching.

Hawthorn and the thug placed their last counters on the table, covering them by hands palm down while they made final bets.

Convention decreed that the challenger reveal his counter first. Hawthorn turned his hand over to reveal a diplomacy counter. The thug laughed and slowly slid his hand back still palm down to display an assassination counter. Assassination nullified diplomacy giving the thug the game.

Nobody saw Hawthorn move until the thug screamed. He seized the thug's wrist with his right hand. With his left he ripped the thug's own knife from its holster and stabbed down hard. The sharp blade point thrust through flesh into the wooden table; that was when the screaming started. The thug struggled but Hawthorn kept his hand pinned like a beetle to a board.

The small man scratched the side of his nose.

"I take it that you're not just a bad loser?" he asked Hawthorn,

"I'm not a loser at all," Hawthorn replied.

He worked the knife free of the table and used it to hold the sobbing thug's hand out revealing a raid counter pinned to the underside of the palm by the blade.

"He'd two playing pieces concealed in his hand," Hawthorn said. "I take it cheats are disqualified even under Nortanian rules?"

Without waiting for an answer he scooped up the pot and put it in his pocket. The small man sighed.

"Zitter, now you've embarrassed me. If you're going to cheat at my table then at least try not to get caught. That palm slide trick wouldn't fool my old mum."

The small man waved the injured thug away.

"Get out of my sight. We'll discuss this later."

The color drained from Zitter's face. Perhaps it was just a shock reaction to loss of blood but Hawthorn doubted it. The small man didn't raise his voice or threaten but the menace in his tone glittered like the sun on jagged glass.

Zitter stumbled away clutching his wounded hand in the other.

"I take it you are Bishop." Hawthorn said flatly. It was a statement not a question.

"You talk like a toff but you behave like a man who knows his way around. What do you want?"

"Business," Hawthorn replied. "I have some business for you."

"I suppose I'd better hear you out while I still have some men left. Not that they're much bloody use."

Bishop looked at his remaining "soldiers" with mild distaste. They dropped their eyes rather than meet his.

"You can't get quality staff these days," Hawthorn said with a cruel smile.

"You have my attention," Bishop said.

"War is coming."

"So?" Bishop asked, shrugging.

What has war got to do with me or my business? the shrug said. Wars came and went but the underworld prospered either way. Business was business and customers were customers. Who cared about the cut of their uniforms?

Hawthorn took a sip of tonk before replying.

"My principal will be taking an active participation. He will require information about his enemies' intentions which I believe you through your business contacts will be admirably placed to provide."

"And why should I do that?" asked Bishop.

"I can think of two good reasons," Hawthorn replied. "First because I will pay well for accurate, timely intelligence and secondly . . ."

Hawthorn paused and gave a humorless grin.

"You will have made a friend with a long memory who intends to be on the winning side. I always pay people back, one way or another."

Bishop looked down at the blood-stained gash in his table.

"So I see."

★ CHAPTER 9 ★

Icecube

A full whiteout blizzard obscured the landing ground by Station Forty-Three. They would never have found the place without the automatics. The station itself was an ellipsoid dome half buried in ice and snow. Two open-topped torpedo-shaped frames rather larger than the barge were already parked outside on solid skids shaped like ventral fins.

A repeller field switched on across the pad once Boswell shut down the barge's frame field. This held off the snow and offered a degree of relief from the biting wind. Even so the chill factor was far below zero. The travelers wasted no time in making a run for the tunnel that passed from the dome to the pad. Allenson had brought a heavy coat for inclement weather but this was ridiculous.

The tunnel was empty but a door slid aside when they reached the end to give access to the dome. Inside a stocky man met the party. He had several days' growth of untidy facial hair under a peaked cap.

"Good evening," Allenson said, holding out his hand. "My name is—"

"I know who you are, General Allenson," the man said curtly, ignoring the hand. "The automatics announced you. What I don't know is why you're here."

Buller snorted in amusement.

"So you're not welcome everywhere, eh, Allenson?"

Buller had not taken Allenson's lionization by the Arcadians well. Of course, neither had Allenson himself but for a rather different reason.

"I'd hoped for some hospitality for the night and a recharge for my barge's fuel cells," Allenson replied, somewhat nettled by the man's incivility. "Obviously I expect to pay my way."

"You and your party are welcome to the use of the guest room," the man said, unbending slightly. "You can buy meals in the staff canteen."

"And my barge?"

"Won't be recharged tonight," the man said with a certain relish. "You may have noticed there's a little bit of a blow on. The repeller field interferes with the charger."

"Tomorrow, then."

"Of course, right after we've recharged our own cars."

The guest room boasted but Spartan accommodation in the form of bunk beds but it was at least warm. A functional staff canteen provided basic meals that suited Allenson but caused a degree of moaning and gnashing of teeth from Buller and Redley. They also took exception that Allenson invited Boswell to eat at the same table as the gentlemen. Allenson was pleased to note that Todd kept his own council on the matter.

None of the staff or employees in the canteen showed overt hostility but there was a definite coolness towards Allenson's party that had nothing to do with Icecube's climate. He retired early to his bunk and spent some time on his datapad checking through the news on Icecube's open access net. He found nothing that he didn't already know beyond the fact that the station was a private venture by a Brasilian perfume company. He fell asleep before finding out why a perfume company would want a station on a Hinterlands snowball world.

Buller skipped breakfast the next day. After he'd eaten Allenson tracked down the unshaven manager whose name, he discovered, was Whitbee.

This morning Whitbee was all smiles, oozing what he no doubt fondly considered to be charm.

"How pleasant to see you, General Allenson. I trust you slept well?"

Allenson had slept tolerably well despite being woken in the early hours by Buller staggering into the room much the worse from a drinking session with some of the riggers. He gave an appropriate response.

Whitbee clasped his hands to his breast and put on an expression of pious rectitude.

"I regret I have some bad news, General."

"Oh?"

"Our charger has broken down. I'm sure a mechanic will quickly rectify the problem but there'll be a short delay before you can be on your way."

"I see," Allenson replied.

"We did get one of our cars recharged and the storm has passed so we'll be sending out a hunt. I thought you might wish to accompany them to pass the time?"

"What do you hunt?" Allenson asked, intrigued.

"Spirotrich."

Allenson looked blank. Whitbee hastened to explain.

"Spectacular marine organisms that filter feed on the plankton swarming around the edge of the ice sheets. The plankton congregate at the surface so we harpoon spirotrichs when they come up after them. The beasts themselves are valueless but they secrete fecal pellets in their digestive tract that are rich in a complex alcohol called ambrein. It's prized for stabilizing perfumery; so is valuable stuff back home. Terran women in particular will pay exotic prices for ambrein-based perfume."

"And the chemical can't be cheaply replicated in an industrial process?"

Whitbee shrugged.

"Sure, but the top perfumers swear that the artificial compound is too pure and lacks the necessary complex organic contaminants that give natural ambrein its unique qualities."

Allenson suspected that natural ambrein based perfumes were simply another way for the ultra-rich to display their status through luxury unobtainable to the merely wealthy. Not that it mattered. Wealth display was a valuable way to recycle money back down the social system in a form that didn't alarm the aristocracy. Redistribution of wealth without revolution was always a tricky issue in human society. Any system that had fat cats competing for the privilege of throwing cash at the proles was to be encouraged.

"I believe I would find the hunt fascinating. Thank you, Master Whitbee."

"We'll lend you a spare survival suit. I'm sure we have one somewhere that will fit you," Whitbee said measuring up Allenson's sizable frame with his eyes. "It gets pretty cold over the ocean."

The dresser finally located a suit that more or less fitted after a search in the deeper recesses of his lockers. Suitably clad, Allenson headed out to one of the cars. The air was still and clear. You could see right up to where the blue sky was so dark it was almost black.

The car had the usual retracted frame pylons but what was unusual were the heavy turbofans mounted in pairs at the bow and stern. They must be incredibly power-hungry and Allenson could not for the life of him see what use they could be. No doubt all would be revealed.

Technicians prepared the craft. They pulled covers off the open crew area to reveal a large harpoon gun on three hundred and sixty degree gimbals in the bow.

Allenson introduced himself to the hunt captain.

"I hope I won't be in the way."

"Not at all, General. Master Whitbee has made the necessary arrangements. I 've arranged for you to ride up front with the gunner where you'll get a good view."

Allenson climbed up a ladder affixed to the bow to enter the small front compartment partly filled with the harpoon gun. The only other crewman stationed there was the gunner. The captain and the other two crew members rode at the rear where the flight controls were located. The crew compartments were separated by bulky fuel cells so it was not possible to move between the two in flight.

The crew completed the final checks. They just switched on the drive when Todd hurtled out of the tunnel, still zipping up a survival suit. The captain stood up to wave him away but Todd ignored the man. He hauled himself into the crowded front compartment as the pylons extended and the field formed.

"There's only room for two up here. You'll have to get off," the gunner said, moving to intercept Todd who brushed him aside.

"Room for a smaller fellow, I think," Todd said, cheerfully, planting his back firmly against the rear bulkhead with the air of a man who would brook no argument on the matter.

The gunner gave up and sat down behind the harpoon. Allenson leaned over from the co-gunner's seat to put his head close to Todd's.

"What are you playing at, Nephew?" he asked.

"Colonel Hawthorn gave me strict instructions to remain at your side at all times, Uncle."

"Colonel Hawthorn is an old woman with a paranoiac streak."

Todd folded his arms indicating that he was immovable on the subject.

"Nevertheless, he was most insistent and I would not wish to disappoint him."

Allenson gave up.

The frame lifted and phased almost immediately into the Continuum. After a short jump it semi-dephased low over a flat gray landscape of an ice sheet. Low rounded rocks thrust through the ice behind them, rising to jagged peaks inland.

"Can you hear me, General?"

The hunt captain's voice sounded in Allenson's helmet.

"Loud and clear," Allenson replied in the time-honored response.

"The rocks mark the edge of the continent. We'll move out to the edge of the ice sheet to look for plankton blooming in the mineral-rich upwelling currents. That's where we'll find spirotrichs."

The ice sheet started to crack and break up in the heavy swell a few hundred meters from the rocks. According to Allenson's pad, the world ocean ran right around Icecube's equator so there was nothing to stop the waves building into massive proportions. After a couple of hundred meters more the sea was ice free except for chopped up fragments.

Like most people, Allenson had noticed over the years that solid water, ice, was lighter than its liquid phase. Icecubes floated in a cocktail but he had never considered the ramifications of this peculiar property before. It occurred to him that if ice sank then Icecube's ocean would soon be solid with a thin veneer of water on top. Life would never get past the bacterial phase. Presumably the same was true of Old Earth and many other worlds.

The craft turned parallel to the ice edge. It cruised slowly along, snaking out to sea and back. The gunner undid his seatbelt and stood up to look over the side so Allenson did likewise. All he saw was heaving gray sea and fragments of ice. He had no idea what a spirotrich looked like. He checked in his datapad for a picture without success. Recorded data were more concerned with the economics of spirotrich ambrein than the organisms themselves.

He ran a general search on spectacular plankton-feeding organisms. The pad came up with an extinct air-breathing fish on Old Earth called a whale. Apparently this was the largest animal ever to evolve on humanity's home world. Intrigued he wondered how a species with such a large biomass and fast metabolism could feed on tiny one-celled organisms.

The answer when he found it was blindingly obvious. The food chain was all about productivity rather than biomass. Plankton had staggeringly fast turnover rates with massive productivity compared to the population of the whales that fed on them.

He also discovered that evolution on Icecube had failed to produce anything resembling a mollusk or vertebrate so presumably spirotrichs couldn't be all that large. He prepared himself for disappointment.

The gunner shifted suddenly, bumping into Allenson in the crowded compartment. The man shaded his eyes and looked down at the ice sheet. The craft descended and moved shoreward. The blades in the turbines started up one by one, rotors whining as they came up to speed, causing the craft to vibrate. The craft fully phased into reality while in the air. Color bled into the landscape and Allenson noticed that the sea had an orange tinge.

The pilot handled the transition well from frame field to true flight with only a slight drop and wobble as he adjusted the rotors. These could swivel to provide horizontal thrust in any direction but tilted blades had to bite that bit harder to maintain lift. This required more power from the engines, causing the noise to rise to a scream that made talking difficult.

Allenson had only been in an air car once before as a child. He'd been persuaded to ride in a modern copy of an antique vehicle giving rides at fairs. His brother Todd had whooped in pleasure but Allenson had not enjoyed the experience, to say the least.

The car lurched into a tightly banked turn to the left. Allenson's stomach made a counter rotation to the right.

He put his pad away and examined the bare ice but saw nothing of note. He looked quizzically at Todd, who shrugged. Noticing the exchange the gunner pointed to where there was a moving darkness on the ice. Allenson thought it a cloud shadow but now he looked again something moved *under* the sheet.

The shadow passed the ice edge and a bulge of water formed under the waves, causing the tops to break away in wind-blown spray speckled with orange. The harpooner noticed his puzzled expression.

"The plankton are orange," the gunner said, putting his head close to Allenson's ear.

The spirotrich broke surface. Allenson found that he was not disappointed at all. The beast was massive, perhaps a hundred meters long, an orange-tinged, semi-transparent, cone-shaped worm with a long trailing tail. There were no fins that he could see and the open end of the cone was at the front. Waves of spirals descended into the mouth of the cone, turning rapidly counterclockwise such that the spirotrich rotated slowly in the opposite direction. It was a surreal sight, almost hypnotic.

The car moved closer until the individual meter-long cilia that gave the illusion of waves could be seen beating. The cilia pushed water down the gullet and out through slits near the tail. The system served for both jet-propulsion and filter feeding. There was no sign of a brain or central nervous system, indeed, little evidence of organs within the vast body at all. It seemed to be mostly jelly. Spirotrichs were huge, dumb, simple beasts.

Plankton accumulated in dense orange sacks near the water exit slits before some process pushed the material through the jelly towards the head. The plankton lent the whole organism its orange-brown shade. Modified cilia around the mouth of the cone projected outwards. No doubt they carried sense organs like simple eyes and chemo-receptors.

The gunner pulled down a large red-handled lever at the base of the harpoon gun. He took hold of the double-handed trigger grip and swung the gun left-right, up-down to check the gimbals moved freely. The spirotrich submerged and the car moved ahead to intercept at its next broach. The gunner pointed the weapon down over the starboard bow, clearly expecting the pilot to position the target on that flank. Allenson was intrigued to find out how the gun would work. It wasn't going to kill the spirotrich with a single shot. How do you "harpoon" a mass of jelly?

The spirotrich broke through the surface of the water again and fell back in a great splash of foam. The gunner fired. The electrical flash around the muzzle burned green lines on Allenson's retina. He leaned out over the side to watch. Cable spun out of a power reel with a loud whine that sounded even over the turbofans. It was the sort of nail-down-a-blackboard noise that made your teeth curl. The harpoon struck true about a third of the way down the spirotrich's body, slicing easily into the jelly.

The harpoon head expanded like an opening parachute. The power reel went into reverse, hauling in the cable until it twanged taut. The pilot increased power and the turbofans screamed. By brute force the vehicle pulled the head of the monster around to point towards the shore.

The spirotrich dived and the reel spun out more cable to prevent the car being dragged under. When the monster broached, the cable ran back in to take up the slack. The pilot played the beast like a fish on the end of a rod and line. All the time he fought to keep the spirotrich moving towards the edge of the ice sheet.

The crisis came when the spirotrich tried to dive under the ice. The pilot gave the rotors all the power he had to keep the beast's head up. The cable twanged under the strain, shaking off water which fell towards the sea in a fine spray. The beast crashed head first onto the ice sheet, which submerged and split under the impact. The monster twisted left and right, trying to roll back into the sea.

The car lurched without warning. Allenson was thrown against the side. The gunner crashed into his back, flipping him clean out of the compartment.

Allenson hung one-handed from the rail. He clawed desperately with the other to find something, anything, to grab hold of. The gunner stared down at him, frozen, not attempting to help. The moment of time lasted ten thousand years. Todd hauled the gunner out of the way and reached down to Allenson.

The car gave another lurch and Allenson's hand slipped. He had one quick glimpse of Todd's horrified expression before he fell backwards into empty space.

He hit the cable with his shoulders and bounced off. He made a wild grab that missed but managed to get one arm around the line, then the other. Initially he fell freely, the cable sliding easily through his hug. Increasingly as he dropped the cable curved, wrenching at his arms. He went into the water feet first. The shock of the chill liquid against his unprotected face made him gasp and nearly inhale but the sudden slack gave him a chance to get his hands firmly on the cable.

Allenson clutched the cable with all his strength when it dragged him under. He held his breath until the line tightened, pulling him up towards the light. He shot right out of the sea like a rabbit out of a burrow as the car fought against the weight of the spirotrich. The cable hurled him into the air until it twanged straight. He lost his grip, fired like an arrow from a bow.

Sky and sea rotated in an orange blue blur until he fell with a squelch into something mushy. He struggled in a sticky mix of goo and fibers, spitting foul-tasting muck out of his mouth. He just about managed to stand upright buried to his waist when the spirotrich lurched. He lost his footing and got another protoplasmic ducking. It was like trying to wade through blancmange. He partly crawled, partly slid, and partly swam. Another heave and he was out of the monster, rolling and falling. He hit something hard that knocked the breath from his body.

Allenson tried to stand, but slipped onto his bottom. He discovered that spirotrich goo on ice gave an almost frictionless surface. The spirotrich rolled away from him. Allenson scooted inland as fast as he could in case the creature reversed its roll. He slid on his bum until he reached a place where the ice had broken and refrozen, giving some purchase for his feet on the roughened surface.

The car swooped over him. The downdraft from its rotors became a howling gale that bowled him over once again. God he was going to have some spectacular bruises by morning. The car sank down and landed. Todd was over the side before the rotors stopped turning.

"Uncle Allen, are you okay?"

Allenson sat up and spat again, trying to clean the oily taste of spirotrich blubber from his mouth.

"I'll live."

He started shaking.

"You're cold."

"Water got in my suit," Allenson replied defensively.

Actually the water inside the insulated survival suit was warm, heated by his body. He shook with shock, not cold.

Todd assisted Allenson to his feet and helped him back to the car.

"Right, let's get you back to the station."

Allenson noticed he had drawn his ion pistol, which seemed a strange thing to do under the circumstances.

"It's all right, Nephew, I'm not a complete invalid," Allenson snapped as Todd tried to help him up the steps.

"Of course not, Uncle," Todd replied, hovering close as Allenson climbed.

Todd followed him into the larger rear compartment of the car and addressed the hunt captain.

"Get this thing back to the station immediately so we can get the general checked over."

"But we haven't cut our way into the spirotrich to check for ambrein yet," said the hunt master.

Todd pointed the pistol at the master.

"Fine, if any of you feckers want to get out on the ice that's up to you but this car is heading back right now. Am I making myself clear?"

He was.

Allenson's injuries turned out to be superficial and were soon fixed by the paramedic. The station had a decent medical facility as accidents were not uncommon given the crews' line of work. He valued the hot shower after treatment rather more than the medical aid. After he had dressed in clean clothes Todd insisted that they go out onto the landing pad to look over the barge. Redley and Buller remained in the bar.

Boswell sat stoically on the barge in a survival suit watching the Icecube riggers charge their cells.

"Everything in order, Boswell?" Todd asked.

"Yes, sar," the unflappable servant replied. "We'll be finished within an hour or two."

"Very good."

Todd steered Allenson past the barge to where they could not be overheard.

"Something bothering you?" Allenson asked mildly, although he was a little irritated at being treated like cargo.

"Yes, something's bothering me. Those bastards tried to kill you back there."

"Oh come on," Allenson replied. "Surely it was an accident. Why would these people have designs on my life?"

"Because you're about to upset the order of things and they've a nice little business here provided matters stay as they are. If the revolutionaries get in power they could all be out of a job."

Allenson thought for a moment and then shook his head.

"No one could have set up an assassination plot. No one knew we would come here. Hell, I didn't know myself until a few hours before we arrived."

"Oh, I agree. This wasn't a conspiracy, just a bit of freelance initiative on the part of the local Icecube management."

"You're beginning to sound like Hawthorn."

"Colonel Hawthorn talks a deal of sense. If I hadn't been there what do you bet you'd have never got off that ice sheet alive? They didn't turn to pick you up until I pulled my pistol."

The suggestion was preposterous but then he remembered the car's crewman looking down at him impassively while he hung by one hand.

Maybe Hawthorn had a point.

★ CHAPTER 10 ★

Trent

The barge made a further stop at a small agricultural and logging community called Sark. It could have made Port Trent in one jump by running along the smooth passage of the Great North Road. Buller pointed this out at some length. Todd was insistent that Allenson needed a day or two's rest after his accident before throwing himself into the maelstrom of Trent politics. Allenson did not argue the point

Sark's landing beacon guided them to a small guest house located on a spit of land turned into a cluster of small islands. A meandering river had burst its bank sometime in the past and cut off an oxbow. No doubt at some time in the future the old channel would silt up completely, creating a lake. For now Sark was scattered over what were known as the Channel Islands.

The guest house was simply furnished but comfortable. Allenson retired immediately and slept the sleep of the completely exhausted. He met up with Todd for a substantial breakfast of locally caught smoked fish washed down by cafay, real coffee being unobtainable.

"Where's Buller and Redley?" Allenson asked.

"Still getting their beauty sleep," Todd grinned. "We went onto a local bar, *the* local bar, after you retired for the evening."

Allenson pointed his fork at Todd before noticing he had speared a piece of fish with it.

"I see. So how come you're awake?"

Allenson pushed the fish into his mouth. It had a peppery flavor that was not unpleasant. He wondered whether the taste was a property of the fish or the wood they used to smoke it.

"Genosurgery can only do so much, Uncle. Neither Buller nor Redley are young men."

Allenson winced. "No need to rub it in, Nephew."

Todd gave a sly grin.

"And I took the precaution of taking a detox pill before going out."

They applied themselves to eating. Eventually, Allenson pushed the remains of the fish away, quite beaten by the liberality of the house's hospitality. He broke what was left of his bread in half and consumed a piece.

"You were right," Allenson said. "I feel much refreshed after a decent night's sleep. We can go on to Trent after we collect the old soaks."

Todd spluttered into his cafay.

"That's no way to talk about two senior officers of our new nation."

Allenson sighed.

"I doubt whether the Assembly on Paxton has got around to declaring independence yet so there's probably no new nation. They're no doubt still debating what color the flag should be. We are, I'm afraid, not only an army without professional soldiers but an army without a state—a somewhat original position for a captain general to be in."

"About leaving today," Todd said, carefully not looking at Allenson.

"Yeees," Allenson replied.

"We're not," Todd rushed out. "I don't think it's a good idea."

"*You* don't think it's a good idea?" Allenson asked, using a tone to remind his nephew who was the general and who the aide.

"I have hired a couple of men to sit in the barge and pedal to boost up our charge so we have a decent safety margin. Boswell's keeping an eye on them for me. I don't want us to have to pedal into Port Trent, Uncle. It's undignified. Buller and Redley would be useless so it would come down to you, me and Boswell."

"So what am I supposed to do all day?" Allenson asked.

"Ah, I've thought of that. Apparently, there is a spectacular water feature upstream, so I've also hired a boat to go and look at it. Our hostess is preparing a picnic hamper as we speak."

"You think of everything," Allenson said, not sure if he was amused or annoyed—or both at the same time.

Allenson paraded, no other word sufficed, through the tiny village down to the small quay on the river bank. Men wished to be recorded shaking his hand. Even more embarrassingly, women wished to be recorded kissing his cheek, if he was lucky, or his lips if he was not. One plucky matron with arms like tree trunks hauled him down to her level before sticking her tongue down his throat. She retreated to sustained cheers from her peers.

"For pity's sake get me out of here," Allenson whispered to Todd, all the while waving and smiling until his cheek muscles ached.

Todd cleared a way through the enthusiastic villagers to their awaiting fishing boat. It was flat bottomed and open and a tube drive clamped to the transom propelled the boat. The boatman touched his forehead upon Allenson's arrival.

He and Todd clambered in, Todd resting his legs on the hamper. The boatman unhitched the rope at the stern, threw it in and jumped in after it. The boat rocked alarmingly. Allenson gripped the sides while maintaining his politician's rictus of a grin. He hoped none of his admiring public noticed his mounting alarm. He was not keen on another ducking after Icecube.

The boatman started the engine on the end of the tube drive by vigorously pulling on a cord until it fired. The clatter suggested some sort of long-stroke single cylinder piston motor. The crowd backed away. The reason became clear when the boatman lowered the end of the drive tube until it was partly submerged. It blew air, throwing up a spray of water and mud in a wide arc as he conned the light craft away from the bank. The water must have been scant centimeters deep.

Once they moved out into deeper water the boatman lowered the tube until it pumped only water. It was then far more efficient. He throttled back the motor, reducing the noise considerably. Allenson was intrigued by the novel device.

"What do you use as a power source?" he asked, turning his head to communicate with the boatman at the stern.

"Ethanol, Sar General. We distill it from the fermentation of a native high sugar vegetable root. Makes decent fuel—and a fair tonk too if you don't mind your gums shrinking."

Allenson made a mental note to stick to plum brandy or beer while on Sark. The river was slow-flowing so they made fast progress upstream, but the waterway was so meandering that they traveled three kilometers for every kilometer closer to their destination. The banks on either side were flat. Crops grew down to the water, with small huts scattered about. No doubt the local farmers used them to store tools or even to sleep in over busy periods. These signs of habitation gradually became rarer as they went upstream until they disappeared altogether.

The sunshine was warm but not unpleasantly hot. Sark had a most agreeable climate for . . . whatever season it was. He had an impulse to look it up on his datapad but couldn't be bothered. After all, it hardly mattered.

He shut his eyes and half dozed, lulled by the rocking of the boat and the gentle play of warm air on his face.

"General," Todd said, touching him lightly on the arm to get his attention. He nodded towards the boatman.

Allenson realized that the man had been speaking.

"My apologies, master. What did you say?"

"Over there, sar, razor fish."

A shoal of narrow silver fish leapt into the air, tails thrusting vigorously but pointlessly. The fish provided a graphic lesson in the uselessness of power without traction. They measured about twenty centimeters long including the long narrow snout and forked tail. The water around the shoal boiled white, throwing a fine mist into the air. Sunlight glittered of the creature's metallic scales and filtered through the water to create an ever changing iridescent pattern of transient rainbows.

Larger torpedo shapes prowled under the water around the edge of the shoal. The silver fish jumped not for pleasure but in panic.

Refreshed and wide awake, Allenson looked around. Trees like pines with dark green needlelike leaves grew in clumps on the bank. The farther they went the more the trees replaced grassland until they lined the banks and turned the waterway into a corridor.

After another half an hour or so the boatman cut the power and drifted the boat into the left-hand bank. A couple of felled trees served as a makeshift dockside. The boatman jumped out with a mooring rope line that he tied to a convenient branch. He pulled the craft flat alongside the shore and held it so Allenson and Todd could alight safely.

Now that the motor was quiet Allenson heard a dull rumble in the distance. Otherwise the countryside was utterly silent except for the boat tapping gently at the wooden dock.

"The lookout point is dreckly reached by cutting overland to avoid the last loop of the river. I don't want to risk taking the boat too close to the Gate. The currents can be fair scary."

The boatman handed Allenson a shotgun and a couple of cartridges.

"The young gentleman and I can carry the hamper between us if you wouldn't mind holding Bessy here."

"You are expecting trouble?" Allenson asked, taking the weapon.

"Oh, no sar. The last dragon 'round here was killed years ago. Bessy is just in case, you understand."

Allenson nodded.

The boatman led them between the trees. One advantage of an evergreen wood is that the ground under the canopy is clear, so they made good progress. The path turned into a delineated animal trail, the sort of place a predator might well wait for prey. Allenson surreptitiously checked the shotgun cartridges.

The boatman saw him and smiled.

The roaring sound grew steadily louder as they walked, so the nature of the Channel Gate was not entirely a surprise. Nevertheless, its scale still impressed. A rock outcrop to the left obscured the view. It ended abruptly at the river bank and Allenson got his first look at the Gate.

The party stood on a rocky outcrop above a sheer drop into a black pool. Vertical cliffs of splintered rock curved around to the left to form a natural theatre. The river poured through the cliffs where it had cut a deep channel. It fell into the pool, making the continuous roar of sound. A single natural tower of rock guarded the right-hand side of the waterfall. The pool in its turn emptied through a sharp V-shaped channel nearby. The land flattened down-channel and was carpeted in coniferous trees. Similar forests grew thickly on the top of the plateau from which the river originated.

The tower leaned outwards from where water had undermined the base. Deep vertical cracks split it from top to bottom. Allenson thought that it would not be many years before it fell. When it did, the rubble would damn the river until the pool filled sufficiently to burst through. The likely result would be a tidal wave sweeping downstream to inundate the banks and low lying islands such as the community of Sark.

He opened his mouth to ask the guide whether the Sarklanders were aware of the potential hazard but thought better of it. What could they do even if they were aware? Setting up an early warning system and building flood barriers around the village was potentially possible but he doubted they had the resources to buy in the technology. The Sarklanders would just have to take their chances like everyone else in a dangerous galaxy.

The waterfall threw up copious amounts of spray so there was a permanent rainbow over the dark pool. Its colors danced in time to the chaotic patterns of the surging water. Waves flowed out across the pool from the fall to reflect off the steep banks, clashing in a battleground of intersecting foam.

"How deep is it?" Allenson asked, putting his mouth close to the boatman's ear.

"Terrible deep, sar, and there's a vicious undertow. Sometimes when a tree goes over the Gate it stays trapped for days. It gets pushed under at the waterfall, coming up near an edge to be pulled to the fall and shoved down again."

Allenson nodded.

The party sat on a carpet of dried conifer needles and lunched from the hamper. The noise was worth enduring to enjoy the view. Todd threw a pine cone into the pool to test the currents. It just disappeared into the foam. The scale of the place fooled the eye.

"It is so very, very beautiful," Todd said.

"I suppose so," Allenson replied, "and a source of near limitless free hydroelectric power. One day we'll clear the trees and turn this place into a great production center for the Cutter Stream. Imagine the wealth this waterfall will create."

He nodded towards the top of the plateau.

"A major industrial city will rise there. No doubt the factory owners will build villas on those downstream slopes."

"No doubt." Todd sighed. "But it seems almost a crime to destroy such a beautiful wilderness for mere gain."

Allenson looked at him in puzzlement, suddenly aware that his nephew was in many ways more Brasilian than Manzanitan.

"There's plenty of wilderness. The Hinterlands are full of little else."

The guide interrupted the conversation by standing and brushing pine needles from the seat of his trousers.

"If you've finished, gentlemen, we ought to be getting back."

Another day, another world, another hotel room—this time located in Port Trent. The trip from Sark was swift, which was just as well. They endured more long lectures from Buller on the military art interspersed with rants about unfair preferment of Brasilian chinless wonders.

Port Trent was big, the biggest commercial port this side of the Bight except for Port Brasilia, an isolated world to the galactic south beyond the Cutter Stream. Port Brasilia's wealth depended partly on its early discovery. Mostly its prosperity depended on vast natural reservoirs of an expensive to manufacture organic useful as a biochemical precursor to a vast array of valuable compounds. In short, Port Brasilia provided another raw material source, albeit one more valuable to Brasilia than all the Cutter Stream colonies together.

The commercial importance of Port Trent was obvious long before they arrived, flagged by the number of small craft moving up and down The Great North Road.

Allenson chose an unpretentious hotel close to the commercial dock. It mostly catered for ships' officers and business men. Buller selected a far grander establishment in the villa zone. Allenson could not help but wonder who would be picking up Buller's tab this time. He reproved himself for a lack of charity.

Allenson's datapad pulsed with messages as soon as they phased in on the controlled approach to one of Port Trent's frame parks. He received adverts for various products and forms of entertainment. They included women guaranteed to be friendly and welcoming to strangers, exotic but safe recreational drugs and gambling games that were impossible to lose. He set the pad's discriminator to go through and discard the lot. That left only an invitation to the luncheon reception being held in his honor the following day.

With Boswell's able assistance, Allenson donned his full dress uniform for the reception. Port Trent boasted a considerable extent of properly paved streets rather than the stabilized earth more commonly found in Stream urban zones. People and goods moved around the city in fat-wheeled, battery-powered buggies. These were so commonplace that their electric whine was the sound that woke him that morning.

The buggies popularity also meant the main thoroughfares were choked with slowly moving traffic. Allenson was familiar with the concept of a traffic jam but the reality was an unwelcome novelty. The weather was fair and his hotel close to the Commercial Exchange building at which the reception was to be held, so he elected to walk along the Front with Todd and take the sea air.

Their uniforms marked them out and they received curious glances from others on the streets. A few insisted on shaking Allenson's hand and declaring their support for an independent Cutter Stream or otherwise indicated approval by smiles and gestures. Most simply stared, expressions carefully neutral. Few showed overt hostility, the worst being a man who spat on the ground as they passed. Todd took a step forward, fist raised. Allenson held his nephew back while the man faded into an alley.

A dozen or so Continuum ships floated in the deep-water harbor. Some were tied up to jetties for convenient loading or unloading of cargo while others were moored to buoys out from the shore. Small water craft plied backwards and forwards. Todd and Allenson passed one jetty that served exclusively as a dock for pleasure craft. Tiered cabins and frame pads overloaded the plushest examples. Allenson wondered how seaworthy the boats were. Maybe they were purely floating brandy-palaces.

Some had racing lines that served no conceivable purpose other than to display their owners' wealth. Allenson suspected that many rarely left the dockside. It was a normal business day in Port Trent so few of the boats were occupied except for servants carrying out basic maintenance.

"A great deal of wealth to leave floating around," Todd said, noting Allenson's interest.

"And I suspect a number of the owners may not entirely be supportive of our political aims," Allenson replied ruefully.

A large statue of Brasilia dominated the center of the harbor front. Seats surrounded the raised semi-circular platform on which it was displayed. Allenson glanced at his datapad and discovered they had time in hand so he suggested they sit.

He contemplated the golden statue. Brasilia was the Mother of the Nation. The statue crystallized the genius, the guiding spirit, of Brasilia. She took the form of a naked woman sitting bolt upright on a world. A thin swathe of material provided her modesty. In her left hand she held an oval shield crackling with an energy field. In her right a power lance, butt down beside her foot. An ancient armored helmet tilted back on her head to show her face. Her eyes fixed the far horizon.

The weaponry was traditional, supposedly the arms of the early knights when Brasilian civilization clawed its way out of the Dark Age. Later generations used similar devices for aristocratic hunts. The social purpose of the activity was not so much to obtain food as to demonstrate the prowess of the user. Now such things were only seen on monuments or as stylized remnants on ceremonial costumes. There had been a brief resurgence of interest in dueling using knightly garb but the fashion soon died out.

Todd fidgeted with the restlessness of the young and got up to look out over the harbor. Allenson had learned to rest when he could. He shut his eyes and tilted back his head to enjoy the warmth of the sun on his face.

He must have dozed because Todd's voice sounded a long way off.

"Strewth, what the devil happened to her?"

Allenson twisted around to find Todd just behind him. His nephew bent down to observe the harbor through a pair of binoculars mounted on a pedestal. There was a loud clunk.

"Damn," Todd fished in his pocket for a small coin. He slipped it into a slot in the pedestal, eliciting another clunk. Noticing Allenson was awake, he beckoned. "Have a look at this, Uncle."

Allenson bent down and peered into the binoculars. The instrument was trained on a ship out in the harbor. He had to widen the lens distance and correct the focus for his eyes before he could clearly see it. The vessel had a twin hull, a most unusual configuration that maximized the surface area to volume ratio. Ship's architects normally considered the opposite to be best practice. The color scheme was the light gray used by the Brasilian Navy. Blast damage had trashed one of the hulls. No doubt this rather than the novel design had caught Todd's attention. Some attempt had been made to hide the wreckage with screens but a gust had blown the canvas off.

Blast-damaged ships in peacetime were not something one expected to see in a harbor. Frame ships tended to arrive in good shape or not at all, although fortunately total losses were rare. Heavy naval warships could withstand a fair battering and make port but reports of a naval battle would have been all over the news channels by now.

"Quite a mess, isn't she?" asked a voice.

Allenson straightened to find himself addressed by man in the uniform of an officer of a civilian ship's line. The officer had short brown hair that stood vertically upwards like a startled comic character.

"Indeed, which ship is she?"

The officer tapped his nose.

"Ah that's top secret. O'Brien, I'm the purser of the *Greenfields*."

He held out his hand and Allenson took it before introducing himself and Todd.

"I know who you are. Your pic is all over the vids. You're the man who's going to shake things up in the colonies," O'Brien said cheerfully. "You'll lose in the end, of course, but with a bit of luck you'll give our masters a good kick up the jacksy. God knows they could do with it."

He gestured to the ship in the harbor.

"None of the crew've been allowed ashore but our bosun reckons he's seen her before. She's known as the Twin-Arsed Bastard for obvious reasons."

"I don't suppose that's her name on the muster roll," Todd said.

O'Brien laughed.

"Her official name is the *Reggie Kray,* named after a famous twin from the mythology of Old Earth. She's a research ship. Makes you wonder what they were researching."

He lifted a hand.

"The passengers will be coming aboard the *Greenfields* soon. I for my sins have to be there to listen to their whines. Fair currents, General."

★ ★ ★

Allenson and Todd strode into the reception.

"Captain General Allenson and Lieutenant Allenson," boomed the voice of the *maître dé* at the door.

Allenson had vaguely anticipated guests wearing the somber dress of the Ascetics of Trinity. The merchants of Trent danced to a different tune. Clothes shimmered in cloth weaves that polarized and refracted light. An outfit rippled through the spectrum from red to green as its occupant rotated against the angle of the light—and that was only one of the men. The ladies sported metallic streamers in silver, gold and polished bronze from their hair and arms.

He had been concerned that he would look like a peacock in his dress uniform but he was completely upstaged. However, it was noticeable that a momentary hush fell on the hall as the guests gave him the once over. A tall man with sharp features and a thin mouth pushed through the crowd as the babble of conversation restarted. His suit was bright lemon yellow with silver piping and he wore a small pillbox hat in scarlet with silver tassels.

The man spoke with an accent Allenson could not place.

"General, I'm Venceray, your host."

Allenson knew little about the leader of the independence movement in Port Trent other than the basic details. He was rich with business interests in cross-Bight transport. Venceray guided him through the reception person by person, proffering the necessary introductions. The sea of unfamiliar names and faces flowed past Allenson leaving little trace in his memory. Not that it mattered. Conversation never got beyond social platitudes.

"When did you come to the Stream?" Allenson asked Venceray, during a pause in the circulation.

"I was born here. My father was a younger son of a Brasilian trading gens so he drew the short straw and became the colony representative. He married one of his servants and had me, so there was nothing to return home for, if you see what I mean. We were never going to inherit. The family made it clear my mother was unacceptable. Eventually we built up our own business, which prospered. My father bought an estate inland and retired to look after it, leaving me to run the family company. He's quite the country gentleman now."

Venceray chuckled.

"I see," Allenson said, and he did. Venceray's future, like his own, was bound up in the Cutter Stream because they had no home to go back to. The social extreme between his Brasilian parents explained his odd way of speaking.

"My contemporaries are at best neutral to the idea of independence. Fortunately most care little for politics. There are only a few outright Home Worlder activists but they're making waves. I think we can keep most of Trent neutral provided we keep the Trinity radicals in check. Any suggestion of redistribution of wealth to the great unwashed to drink themselves to death on will arouse fervent opposition."

Allenson nodded.

"And what are the political opinions of the, ah, great unwashed?"

Venceray shrugged.

"Who knows, who cares? I doubt they've got any opinions worth considering."

Allenson wondered if news from Paxton had overtaken him.

"I suppose there is no word of the official Declaration of Independence yet?"

Venceray shook his head.

"Pity," Allenson said. "It would help us to control the Home Worlder faction if we could use legal sanctions. We can't lock people up for treason to a state that doesn't yet exist."

He looked around and noticed a well-dressed couple slipping out through a side door.

"Is it just me or has the room thinned out?"

Venceray colored.

"I hoped you wouldn't notice. The ship carrying the new governor from Brasilia touched dock earlier this morning. He must be installed in Government House by now."

"So?" Allenson asked.

Venceray's lips compressed.

"He has asked to meet the heads of the best families in Port Trent. People will want to go and pay their respects as soon as possible so as not to be thought disloyal. There is even talk of setting up a Home Worlder Militia"

A surge of fury choked Allenson. He froze until he was sure he could maintain an outward composure.

"The governor can meet whomsoever he chooses but you will arrest him if he tries to arm our enemies."

"On whose authority?" Venceray asked.

"Mine," Allenson replied. "You will arrest him on my authority."

★ CHAPTER 11 ★

Trinity

Hawthorn came to Cambridge on the world of Trinity unannounced and in civilian clothes. He traveled on a one-man frame that had seen better days. The casual observer might be forgiven for dismissing him as another itinerant attracted to the war zone either as a potential combatant or profiteer. The careful observer would have noticed that the frame might be battered but was entirely serviceable and that the well-used hunting rifle slung over his shoulder was an expensive import from a master gunsmith of Brasilia. Fortunately there were no careful observers.

Cambridge was a college town a few kilometers out of Trinity's commercial capital, Oxford. It possessed all the refinement one associated with such lofty aspirations. It boasted a theater and a concert hall where intellectually stimulating and improving works were performed by painfully serious people. The town houses were tall three-story buildings clustered tightly together with tiny gardens given over to flowers and decorative shrubs. Once, the town had been restricted to an area inside an earth berm, but that era had long gone. Nevertheless, families clung to their prestigious town addresses, building upwards when they needed more room for servants' quarters.

College buildings rather than shops or business premises formed the focus and heart of the town. Presumably food and other goods were brought in from outlying demesnes and villages. Nothing as sordid as a bar polluted the streets of Cambridge, but there were dram shops where customers could taste expensive imported booze before making a purchase.

Hawthorn made for a dram shop called Sament's Fine Wines and Liquors. Inside, racks of bottles in a variety of colors hunched draped in cobwebs. Web-spinning spiders were uncommon in the Stream. Hawthorn assumed the webs had been sprayed on as a marketing device. Nothing so uncouth as an actual bar brought down the tone of the establishment but tables and chairs were discreetly set out in one corner of the large carpeted room. A small open kitchen off the main room contained glasses and bottle opening devices.

Two customers in the dark clothes of Ascetics sat smoking and tasting wine at one of the tables. From the glassy-eyed stare of the one facing Hawthorn, they had "tasted" for some little time. Presumably, they were having problems making up their mind what to purchase. A man in an apron bent over their table running his finger down a catalogue. After some discussion he carefully selected a bottle from low on one of the racks. He fetched two glasses from the kitchen and set them in front of the customers. With a theatrical flourish he poured an inch of purple-dark liquid into each glass.

The shopkeeper managed to ignore Hawthorn throughout the entire ritual. In return Hawthorn ignored him back, flicking through a catalogue suspended from a rack. The shopkeeper replaced the bottle slowly but was eventually forced to accept that Hawthorn was not going to go leave even when he saw the extortionate prices.

"Can I help you?" the man asked in a most perfunctory tone.

He was bald on top and the hair over his ears projected out at forty-five degrees, giving him the appearance of a nervous rabbit.

"I don't see any tonk in your catalogue," Hawthorn replied in the accent of a Port Trent dock worker.

The man froze as if Hawthorn had made an obscene suggestion involving lead piping and lubricant.

"No, we don't stock it. I don't imagine anyone in town does but there are taverns in the outlying villages that might have products more suited to your palette," the man suggested.

"Pity, oh well, one must make do," Hawthorn replied, adopting the more normal drawl typical of a Manzanitan gentleman.

He dropped the catalogue which swung on its chain.

"I'll try your Sanja Berry distillate."

The man gaped at Hawthorn.

"You do have Sanja?"

"Uh, yes sar, but it is rather expensive."

"It usually is," Hawthorn replied cynically. "Well, run along."

Hawthorn seated himself, as no one had offered him a table. He dropped the laserrifle on the top and pulled out his datapad, immersing himself in the latest scandal concerning a generously endowed socialite lady in Port Trent. He ignored the shopkeeper when he returned, forcing the man to cough discreetly to get his attention. The shopkeeper eyed the laserrifle, obviously considering asking Hawthorn to remove it but lacking the nerve. From the bottle he carried, he poured a measure.

"Wait!" Hawthorn said when the man went to leave.

Hawthorn rolled the oily liquid around in the glass, holding it up to the light to check the color. He inhaled the bouquet before taking a sip.

"This is Sanja Nouveau. Personally, I can't stand the muck. It's suitable only for clerks and politicians. Don't you have any vintage?"

"Yes, sar," the shopkeeper said, looking as if his world had turned upside down. He could not have been more surprised if his dog started quoting Cicero.

"Then get me some, at least ten years old, mind."

"Yes, sar."

The shopkeeper disappeared to locate a bottle from a back room. Hawthorn repeated the testing procedure, to the intense fascination of the two onlookers.

"Acceptable, leave the bottle."

Hawthorn returned to his pad, the perusal of which took up his attention for the next half an hour until the inebriated tasters tottered out. The shopkeeper shimmied over to Hawthorn.

"I'm afraid we're closing, sar: if you wouldn't mind settling the bill."

"You must be Master Sament."

"Indeed, sar."

"Which is odd because I thought you were called Grenvil. That was the name you gave the Paxton Proctors was it not, when they nicked you for pimping out your wife to prominent citizens before blackmailing said pillars of respectable society?"

Sament went white.

"If you think you can come in here making accusations—"

"Sit down, Sament."

Hawthorn kicked a chair towards him.

Sament sat.

"There's still a warrant out for an unpaid fine. I imagine the Proctors would love to know your new name and address."

"I have powerful friends in Paxton. You wouldn't want to cross them," Sament blustered.

"Powerful friends, no less? That knocking sound you hear is my knees," Hawthorn replied in a tone that suggested he was singularly unimpressed.

"Bishop wouldn't be one of those friends would he? He was the man who smuggled you out, as I remember, but that was surely for money rather than undying friendship. For more money he's sold you to me."

"Who are you? What do you want?" Sament asked in a whisper.

Hawthorn grinned.

"Now that is the issue. Where is your wife, by the way?"

"In Oxford, she was trapped when the Brasilian army sealed off the town."

"That is what I heard. I take it she is, ah, pursuing her old profession?"

Sament didn't answer, which was a sort of answer in itself.

"Quite an upmarket operation you and she ran. I would imagine that she would have little trouble getting intimate with Brasilian officers?"

"What do you want?" Sament repeated.

"To pay for my bottle of Sanja, of course."

Hawthorn took a hundred crown chip from his wallet. It flashed gold to indicate authenticity when he placed it on the table.

"I will have trouble finding change for that," Sament said, licking his lips

Hawthorn switched on the laserrifle and angled the weapon towards Sament, so that the red sighting dot lit up the center of the merchant's torso. His finger caressed the trigger as if it were a lover's breast.

"I want good, accurate information on Brasilian military activities and intentions. I will pay generously if what you tell me works out then. If it doesn't, well, the substantial bounty on your head back at Paxton is payable dead or alive. You really upset some important people, old son."

Hawthorn waved his free hand over the chip and the rifle

"Your choice, sunshine, I make a profit either way."

Sament picked up the chip, which flashed gold, triggered by the chemistry of his hand.

"I will make the necessary arrangements."

"Good!"

Hawthorn stood up, putting his rifle over his shoulder.

"I'll see myself out."

He picked up the bottle as he left. He'd damn well paid enough for it.

Allenson and Todd arrived in Cambridge some time later but rather more conspicuously in a limo pedaled by two chauffeurs. The beacon guided them in to one of the college buildings that had been requisitioned by the Oxford Assembly in Exile. It was late afternoon local time and gloomy. Black clouds hid the sky like portents of bad tidings.

Two men in business suits emerged from the central three-story, brick-built structure to greet them. It was the only place to show lights at the windows. Darkness draped the surrounding stabilized earth and wood chalets. Allenson was a little surprised that the welcoming committee was so low key. They were supposed to be expecting him and he was the captain general of all the colonial militias. The only pan-Colonial official in the entire Stream might have expected a little more pomp and ceremony.

He discovered from the initial introductions that the men were middle ranking clerks. His ego was not hurt but the lack of respect for his office was a matter of concern. He was shown to a waiting room and offered cafay, which from the stale taste had been reheated several times. He sat drumming his fingers for some five minutes before one of the clerks returned.

"Council Leader Inglethorpe sends his regards but regrets he is running late with important business. If you'll wait he'll try to see you as soon as he's free," the clerk said.

"Will he indeed?" Allenson asked, clamping down hard on the white fury that leapt trough his veins. "Will he really?"

He pushed past the clerk. Todd followed in his wake like a frigate in convoy with a battleship.

"Sar, sar, I really must insist—" the clerk squeaked.

Todd checked the clerk with a finger to his lips. Allenson strode down the corridor deeper into the building until he met a woman carrying a stack of papers.

"Where would I find Inglethorpe's office, mistress?" he asked, trying not to be too brusque as the woman had offered him no provocation. It would be ungentlemanly to spill some of his anger onto her.

"Up one floor and at the end of the hallway to the left," she replied automatically. "His name's on the door."

"Thank you, my good lady."

Allenson covered the ground in long strides.

"But you can't go in without an appointment . . ."

Todd winked at her and hurried after his principal. He had to half run to catch up.

Allenson found the office door without any difficulty as Inglethorpe's name was indeed upon it. The thin plastic had torn away from one of the attaching tacks so that the sign hung down on one side in a way that was wonderfully symbolic.

". . . well, I don't know what to say to him. Maybe if I keep him waiting long enough he'll go away—"

Was what Allenson heard when he flung open the door.

The man who sat at an office podium was small but possessed of an impressive girth around the middle that a well-cut jacket failed to hide despite an heroic attempt by its tailor. He had his head back, apparently talking to the ceiling. This meant he was using the network without even taking the precaution of setting the sound suppressor. Or he could be mad.

"You can't just come in here," Inglethorpe said.

"I just did."

Allenson moved to stand behind the council leader from where he could see the directional hologram depicting Inglethorpe's communicant. The man wore the uniform dress tunic of a Brasilian senior field officer. The officer's eyes widened since Allenson was now equally visible to him. The soldier moved his arm slightly and the hologram winked out leaving Allenson and Council Leader Inglethorpe together in the office.

They glared at each other, both uncertain how to proceed. The Brasilian officer was probably in Oxford. Allenson could hardly accuse Inglethorpe of consorting with the enemy because until the Assembly on Paxton declared independence they were all technically still Brasilians. Inglethorpe had left Oxford to join the Trinity Council in exile which said something. Presumably the man was simply trying to keep a foot in both camps until he saw how things panned out, a typical politician in other words.

Allenson decided to offer only gentle advice, as Inglethorpe might be useful at some future date.

"Not wanting to burn your boats is understandable but the trouble with riding two horses, Councilor, is that you tend to get splinters in the arse from sitting on the fence."

Inglethorpe gaped at him without replying. Allenson thought this ungenerous given the effort he had put into mixing an amusing metaphor. Oh well, he never had been any good at jokes.

"This is purely a courtesy visit to announce my arrival. No doubt you have many calls upon you in these trying times, so I won't detain you further. Perhaps you could tell me where to find Army Headquarters?"

"Lillian, my secretary, the office opposite the stairs, she'll help you." Inglethorpe pointed in the general direction of the door.

"Thank you."

Allenson re-joined an amused Todd in the corridor.

"You forgot the one about losing your money in mid-stream by backing two dogs," Todd said.

The Militia headquarters turned out to be located in buildings belonging to another of the colleges. The availability of so many venues with lecture theaters, offices, canteens and sleeping accommodation explained why both the army and the government in exile chose to relocate to such a small town.

Moving the barge a short hop was more trouble than it was worth so he elected to walk. Nowhere in Cambridge was very far from anywhere else. Inevitably it started to drizzle as the sun dropped below the horizon. They navigated using Allenson's pad while Todd used his as a torch to provide illumination. Lamps at the front of some houses spilled light into the street but many areas were in darkness.

The rain set in quite heavily by the time they reached their destination. This turned out to be another two-story redbrick building surrounded by one-story wooden chalets. The sentry on the door hunched miserably inside a waterproof cape.

"Where will I find the duty officer?" Allenson asked.

"First corridor to right, first door on the right," the sentry replied morosely, with a jerk of his thumb.

The movement caused water collected in a fold of the sentry's cape to run down his leg, eliciting a foul curse. The only thing that surprised Allenson about the exchange was that there was a sentry on duty at all in such inclement weather.

Once inside he shed his coat and left it draped over the back of a chair. The vestibule was empty so he followed his instructions. When he opened the first door on the right he was greeted by the sight of the soles of a pair of military boots crossed at the ankles and resting on the duty desk. Behind them a man sat hidden by the open Orders of the Day that he dutifully read.

"Good evening," Allenson said when the man showed no response.

"Can't you knock?" the man replied.

He lowered the file to peer over the top. There was nothing wrong with the soldier's reflexes. He shot to his feet at attention after one glance at Allenson's uniform. His gaze fixed firmly on a point two feet over Allenson's head before the file hit the ground.

"Chung, duty sergeant, awaiting your orders, SIR."

The last word was snapped out. Clearly Sergeant Chung hadn't always been militia. Everything about him suggested regular army.

"At ease, sar'nt."

Chung moved his feet the regulation half meter apart in a crisp stamp and put his hands behind his back.

"The duty officer is?" Allenson asked.

"Sir, Captain Frames, sir."

There was a pause.

"Would you like me to summon him, sir?"

"No, just point me in the right direction."

"Through the door to the left, sir."

Allenson noticed that a brightly colored insert had slipped from Chung's file when it hit the floor. Military documents are not normally noted for their visual splendor so it caught his eye. He reached down and picked up the file. He slipped the illustrated copy of *Brothel Big'uns* back inside The Orders Of The Day before placing it back on the sergeant's desk.

"Very good, sar'nt, you may carry on."

"Sir."

Todd opened the door to the left, which turned out to be a broom cupboard full of assorted stationary and cleaning equipment.

"My left, sir," said the sergeant, sounding desperate.

Inside, two young officers sitting around a desk playing cards came stiffly to attention.

"It seems to be my night for surprising people," Allenson said mildly. "As you were, gentleman."

"General Allenson, sir?" the one sporting captain's flashes asked tentatively.

"You were expecting someone else?"

"Ah, no sir, but we were not sure when you would arrive."

"You must be Captain Frames."

"Yes, sir."

Silence.

"And you are?" Allenson asked the other officer.

"Jingle, sir, Lieutenant Jingle," the young man squeaked.

Allenson studied him, wondering if he was old enough to shave. Militia officers were getting younger every year. At this rate they would be recruiting in the kindergarten soon. Jingle looked increasingly nervous under Allenson's gaze so he switched back to Frames.

"Is Colonel Masters on base?"

"No, General, he's away on business," Frames replied.

"I see, on business. No doubt Colonel Masters has a home located somewhere conveniently nearby as he is resident on Trinity," Allenson said to no one in particular, as if he was thinking aloud.

"Yes, sir," Jingle said, helpfully, before shutting his mouth tight after a warning look from Frames.

"I believe Colonel Masters does own such a property in a village a few kilometers from here," Frames said cautiously. "It is possible he might be there. Shall I try to find him?"

Allenson paused as if considering.

"I think not. There's no need to disturb him unnecessarily. That's an order, not a suggestion, Captain."

He didn't want Frames to tip Masters off. It might be useful to meet the other officers of the besieging army without him around.

"Yes, sir."

"My aide and I require accommodation in the base."

"Yes, sir, arrange it please, Lieutenant Jingle."

Jingle's eyes defocused as he thought hard. Space would be at a premium. A whole line of people would have to be bumped down to give Allenson a room appropriate to his rank. The most junior officer, possibly Jingle himself, could end up sleeping in a waterlogged tent.

"And my barge is over at the civilian HQ with our luggage. Please arrange to move them here."

"Yes, sir, both the barge and the luggage?" asked Jingle anxiously.

"I think that would be convenient," Allenson replied, keeping a straight face. "You will find my man, Boswell, keeping an eye on it."

Jingle hurried out, forgetting to salute. Frames closed his eyes.

"Have you and your fellow officers dined yet tonight?" Allenson asked.

"No, sir, we club together using one of the lecture theaters as a mess. There are eight of us, usually, and Lieutenant Lamborgi has a servant who is an excellent chef."

"Well, Captain, if you think the fare might extend from eight to ten, I would be pleased to join you. I have a couple of bottles of decent wine in my kit that I could contribute."

"We would be delighted to welcome you and your aide, sir."

Actually, there was no other acceptable reply that Frames could give but he did seem genuinely happy at the prospect.

The dinner was indeed rather good. Initially stilted, conversation flowed more freely in direct correlation with the consumption of alcohol. Eventually the young officers felt bold enough to give Allenson their opinion on how the war should be fought. He was pleased to see that they wanted to take the fight to the enemy with an immediate assault on Oxford. Only an idiot would take strategic advice from a junior officer, but it was right that they erred on the side of aggression. Older wiser heads could be allowed to decide how and where to direct that aggression.

The wine ran out early with Allenson limiting himself to a single glass. After that it was tonk all round. Allenson joined in but cut his tonk with water. He gently encouraged his companions to talk and listened carefully to their conversation. He heard the usual stories of bored troops getting into fights, equipment that malfunctioned, stores that never arrived or contained something completely different from the label: all the normal trials and tribulations of an army in the field.

One casual remark from a young lieutenant concerned him. It was to the effect that one third of his men had gone down with fever in the last week. The patients were responding well to a general viral suppressant but the bug was spreading through the camp and putting medical resources under strain.

Allenson eventually steered the conversation around to social matters. By the time tonk and cafay was served officers were loosening their jacket buttons and removing neck ties. The evening began to take the form of a college supper. A captain called on one of the party to sing, a cry that was soon taken up by all. The victim made a token protest before standing up.

He had a good voice and gave a creditable performance of "Bugle Calls," a marching song that probably dated back to when men trailed a pike. Each officer was prevailed in turn to contribute, irrespective of whether they possessed any discernible musical talent. Most of the songs spoke of the terrible burden of duty or the girl/boy I left behind me, two tropes never far from a soldier's mind. Some were serious while others were played for comic effect.

The revelers prevailed on the general to give them a song when suitably emboldened by liberal consumption of tonk. Frames, in his role as President of the Mess and hence technically the host, hushed them up but Allenson forestalled him by standing.

"Well, gentleman, no one has ever accused me of being able to hold a note but I see that also goes for many of the rest of you."

The assembled company laughed. When a general assayed a joke it was always funny no matter how weak or poorly delivered.

"So here is a little marching ditty that the Manzanitan Militia picked up from Brasilian regulars in the Terran War. You may not have heard it yet this far up the Stream."

He cleared his throat.

"Here's a shining crown yours for free
For all who'll volunteer with me,
To 'list and fight the foe today,
Over the stars and far away."

"When duty calls me I must go
To stand and face another foe.
But part of me will always stray
Over the stars and far away."

"If I should fall to rise no more,
As many good friends did before,
Then ask the trumpet band to play,
Over the stars and far away."

"So fall in lads behind the drum,
Our colors blazing like a sun.
Along the road to come what may.
Over the stars and far away."

There was a pause, then Frames banged his hand on the table.
"Bravo, General, bravo."
The spell broken, men applauded and called for more.
"No, no," Allenson shook his head. "The night may be young but I'm not. But don't let me spoil the evening. You carry on."
He looked at Todd.
"You stay too, Lieutenant."
"It's been a long day, sir, so I think I'll join you."
They left as the mess began to warm up. An officer began a new song whose lyrics followed them out of the building.

"I don't want to join the army
I don't want to go to war
I'd rather hang around Oxford drinking underground
Living off the earnings of a high-born lady
I don't want a bayonet up me arsehole

I don't want me bollocks shot away
I'd rather be in Oxford
Merry merry Oxford
And fornicate my feckin' life away, cor blimey."

Todd firmly shut the door, cutting off the next verse that discussed more intimate revelations about the aforesaid high-born lady's boudoir.

"The wind's changed but at least it's stopped raining," Allenson said when they got outside.

Todd lifted his face and sniffed the air.

"What the hell is that evil smell?" he asked.

"The reason there is fever in the camp," Allenson said grimly.

The next morning Allenson breakfasted in his room before attending the morning briefing. They held it in a stepped lecture theater in the main building. He arrived early and waited by the lectern down at the front. Officers drifted onto the seats in twos and threes in various combinations of civilian and military dress. A number of majors put in an appearance but Masters still didn't show. Allenson ordered the door locked dead on the appointed hour.

"Good morning, gentlemen, my name is Allenson. I hold the rank of captain-general which means I am in command of the combined Cutter Stream army. You have a question?"

The last was addressed to a major who was visibly disturbed at the situation.

"But sar Allenson, there isn't a Cutter Stream army."

"The elected political leadership of the Heilbron colonies has asked the Colonial Assembly to adopt the Heilbron militias into the army. Right now your militias *are* the field force of the army which makes me your commander in chief. As such you will address me as sir, understood?"

"Yes," said the major.

Allenson stared at the major

"I meant yes, sir."

"Good, and in future when my officers attend a meeting I expect them to be in dress uniform or combat fatigues. I expect you to look and behave like officers."

"The Heilbron militias have always had a relaxed attitude to discipline, sir."

"The Stream Army doesn't," Allenson said firmly. "Right, who's General Master's chief of staff?"

"That would be Colonel Wilson, sir. He's away on business but I'm his deputy."

"You are?"

"Major Ling, Sir."

"Well Major, it appears you are elected to come up here and brief me. I want everyone else to remain and participate in the discussion. Assume I know nothing, Ling, and start with the basics. I want us all to be singing from the same sheet."

Ling keyed a large scale holomap of the area from the lectern. The eastern half of the primary continent on Trinity drained into three major rivers which fed into a large bay called The Bowl. Two long fingers of bedrock projected out from low-lying plains into the bay. Oxford city was built on one. Its space port with hard pads for small vessels and docksides for larger ships was on the other. Bridges linked the two peninsulas.

"The map only shows roads in and around Oxford and the spaceport?" Allenson asked.

"That's pretty much all there are, sir," Ling replied. "The rivers are convenient and cheap for transporting heavy goods, and people and light stuff are moved around on frames."

Ling shrugged.

"It's never been worth the expense to build and maintain a road network."

Allenson grasped the point. Trinity was a convenient deep port all ready and waiting for the first colonists standing. It stood at the terminus of a massive waterway system suitable for concentrating goods to ship off planet and the distribution of imports. It hopelessly outclassed Manzanita's lake and transient streams and rivers. Sheer chance gave the Upper Stream colonies like Trent and Trinity an economic head start which they had never relinquished.

Ling gestured to the low plain around the landward half of the rocky fingers,

"The low ground here is methane marsh so it's unused waste ground."

He turned his attention to the peninsulas.

"Brasilian Regulars landed on the spaceport and secured the town, putting down rioters and generally imposing martial law."

"Was this unpopular with the residents?" Allenson asked.

"Well, that kinda depends on who you talk to," Ling replied, "It was unpopular with the agitators who were shot and *their* friends and relations. Many of the residents although politically for independence were none too sorry to see troublemakers dealt with firmly as there had been incidents."

Allenson nodded. Criminal elements tended to come to the fore in any urban insurrection.

Ling continued.

"Once they secured the city the regulars sent patrols out to pacify the countryside."

Allenson said, "I suppose a pattern developed of ambushes, reprisals against the civilian population leading to stronger reaction from the militia and so on."

"Yes, sir. Eventually militias from all over the Heilbron Worlds arrived and joined in until we outnumbered their patrols considerably. After we gave them a few bloody noses the Brasilians retreated back into the town. The militias fortified this rock outcrop to pen them in."

Ling pointed to a spot roughly at the shoreline.

"From there we could bombard Oxford, the Bowl and the most of the spaceport. We don't actually have any artillery but it seemed useful to grab the high ground while we could."

Such initiative and grasp of strategy pleasantly surprised Allenson.

"Excellent, Major, you have done well. We have our foot on their throat."

Ling looked uncomfortable.

"Well, we did sir, but unfortunately they mounted an attack and recaptured the outcrop. Oh, we won the fight, sir, you can be sure of that. We killed ten of them for every man of ours that fell but eventually we were forced to pull back, you see."

Allenson saw only too well. Potting men from behind fortifications was one thing but standing up to regulars in close assault was quite another. That required the confidence that comes with training and iron-hard discipline.

"So where are our lines?"

Ling's discomfort increased.

"Well, sir, we, ah, don't exactly have any. Most of our army has pulled back onto the dry ground leaving just a few scouts behind as a tripwire. It's not like they're going anywhere, General."

"Nor it seems, are we," Allenson observed.

★ CHAPTER 12 ★

The Camp

After lunch Allenson toured the encampment accompanied by Colonel Wilson, who had finally shown his face. He was flanked by various staff officers. Wilson was a nondescript sort of man with white in his hair and moustache. Allenson wondered if the hair was an affectation or whether rejuvenation treatments were failing the man. One could only cheat time for so long despite expensive genosurgery.

The camp did not impress. Tents were planted higgledy-piggledy in fields separated by low fences. Men lounged around doing nothing in particular.

"Tell me, Wilson, why do you have such a ridiculously large staff?" Allenson asked, observing the long trail behind.

"Ah well, it's so that each of the militias has a representative at headquarters," Wilson replied.

"A representative?" Allenson asked, looking at Wilson as if he had sworn in church.

"That's right," Wilson said, defensively. "Each group of men has an elected representative to present their views and opinions."

"On what?"

"Strategy, tactics, when to attack, that sort of thing."

Allenson looked at the man as if one of them was demented.

"Dear God! Well that ends right now, Colonel Wilson. The 'representatives' can stay for today so they can carry my instructions, my orders, back to the militia units."

"But—"

Allenson spoke over Wilson.

"I want the entire edifice disbanded and replaced by a streamlined, effective staff. I also want proper chains of field command so we can group units into brigades."

"But you can't do that," Wilson finally got out.

"Why not?" Allenson asked.

"Because each militia is autonomous and—"

"Each militia *was* autonomous," Allenson interrupted. "As of now they are units in the Cutter Stream Army and as such are subject to such orders and regulation as I see fit to promulgate."

A voice interjected.

"I'm not putting up with that."

Allenson turned to find a small man, pugnaciously sticking out a bearded chin.

"And you are?"

"Captain Firkin, Rostray Militia," said the small man. "We're not demesne servants to be ordered around by some jumped up Manzanitan aristo. You'll watch your manners around us, sunshine. We have rights."

"You will address me as sir, Firkin, and you are quite mistaken. You have no rights at all. You only have duties as laid down by military law."

Firken turned puce.

"That's what you think. Push it and I'll advise my comrades to debate whether we should just go home. I think I can guarantee which way the vote will go."

A small murmur of approval ran through the other representatives. Wilson nodded but said nothing. Allenson realized that he would get no support from his chief of staff. Ling froze and maintained a blank expression. This was the pivotal moment. If he backed down now then the revolution was over before it had started.

Allenson's mind raced as he considered and discarded options. Attempts to persuade would be seen as weakness and would invite further liberties. Allowing an outright refusal to obey orders would destroy his authority. He had to enforce his will. He could draw a pistol and threaten the man but when it came to it, the only person he could be sure of was Todd.

Hawthorn chose that moment to emerge from behind a tent.

"Desertion in the face of the enemy is an admission of a capital crime under military law. Should I deal with him now or do you want to go through the formality of a trial before we shoot him, General?" Hawthorn asked casually.

He was dressed in a tailored black uniform with gold piping on the cap and wrists. A badge over his left breast displayed a black shield crossed by red lightning flashes and the initials SP. A dozen men followed him, dressed in combat fatigues of the same color. They had combat helmets with the same insignia.

"This is, ah, Colonel Hawthorn, Head of . . ." Allenson said.

"Special Projects," Hawthorn prompted.

Allenson wondered where Hawthorn got the uniforms. Come to that where had he found the men? Despite the uniforms they didn't look like soldiers. In fact, they looked more like paramilitary police. They ambled rather than marched and each carried a lasercarbine on a sling over the shoulder by their side so the pistol grip was conveniently at hand height.

Firkin gaped.

"You wouldn't dare."

"Krenz," Hawthorn said, lifting a finger.

The security trooper immediately behind Hawthorn sported sergeant stripes. He barked something and the men lifted their machine pistols. Targeting sights illuminated. Flickering orange dots danced over Firkin's torso.

"You wouldn't dare," Firkin said again, his voice almost a whisper.

Allenson decided it was time he intervened.

"I have yet to find the limits on what Colonel Hawthorn dares and I have known him all my life," he said.

He raised his voice so that everyone could hear.

"Possibly Firkin misspoke. Possibly he didn't realize he was subject to military law. Possibly he would like to reconsider his position now that he has been enlightened? Well, Firkin?"

Allenson tilted his head to one side and observed the man as if he did not care much one way or the other. Actually, he did. It would be distasteful and an inauspicious start to his command to have the man killed but give the order he would. To leave the decision to Hawthorn would rightly be seen as gutless by the men. The army had to know who was in charge. The death of one man now could save a great deal of blood later.

Fortunately Firkin grasped the lifebelt he had been thrown.

"Yes, General, sir, that's it exactly."

"Excellent," Allenson said heartily. "Your men can stand down, Colonel."

Hawthorn raised the finger again and the orange spots switched off, although his troopers kept their hands on the pistol grips.

Wilson gaped, looking as if his world had been turned upside down.

Hawthorn ignored him.

"Krenz, I want two of your men within a meter of General Allenson at all times with two more to provide door security on any room he occupies."

"Yes, boss," Krenz replied.

Hawthorn frowned.

"Yes, sir; you're in the army now. And they had better be bloody alert because if anything happens to the general, anything at all, then you're dead meat."

"Got you, boss, I'll keep the boys on their toes."

Krenz glowered at his squad, who didn't seem too worried. They didn't look at Allenson but at the people around him.

"The lads know to shoot first if they are in any doubt and leave the lawyers to clear up the mess; simpler that way."

Allenson wondered where Allenson found Krenz. He was definitely neither militia nor regular army, that was for sure.

The overwhelming smell of sewage and general human waste reminded Allenson of his next priority.

"Gentlemen, this camp stinks. It's a bloody disgrace, nothing but a breeding ground for pestilence. Even Riders don't live like this and they take the precaution of moving on after a few days. Tomorrow morning at dawn the whole camp will move to a new location. Tents will be erected in rows and latrines will be constructed at a safe distance from the living accommodation. They will be inspected by your staff, Colonel Wilson, to ensure they meet the requirements necessary for decent sanitation."

"You expect my men to oversee the latrines?" Wilson asked.

"Indeed, Colonel, furthermore I expect you to lead such inspections to ensure they are carried out properly. In future any man who fouls the camp will be on a charge. No doubt you can invent some suitable punishment, Colonel Hawthorn."

"Latrines will need to be filled in and new ones dug at regular intervals," Hawthorn said. "The punishment can fit the crime."

"I'm damned if I'll let you turn me and my officers into janitors," Wilson said, finding his voice. "Who the hell do you think you are, Allenson?"

"I think I'm your superior officer," said Allenson. "I also think I shall dispense with your services. Thank you for your contribution to defending the Stream. Be assured if we need you again I shall let you know."

"I don't understand. What do you want me to do?"

"I want you to go home, Sar Wilson, and enjoy a well-earned retirement."

Wilson visibly shrank under Allenson's gaze, aging twenty years in a second. Suddenly he didn't look like a senior officer but a tired old man in borrowed clothes. Allenson felt a complete and utter shit but he hardened his heart. Battle was too unforgiving for misplaced compassion. He had to establish discipline and quickly if the army and the new state were to survive. Wilson offered himself up as a sacrificial lamb—or more properly a scapegoat. The story of how Firkin was brought to heel and the ruthless disposal of Wilson would spread like wildfire through the army.

"Major Ling," Allenson said

"Sir?"

"As of now you are chief of staff with the acting rank of colonel."

"Sir."

"Do you anticipate any difficulty carrying out my orders?"

"No sir."

Allenson nodded. Ling would do.

"But do you understand why we must ruthlessly enforce sanitation?" Allenson asked.

"Well, I suppose we have to look the part of army regulars, sir, but it won't be easy." Ling said tentatively.

"Go on, I need my chief of staff to speak his mind."

"Well, it's just that the men are not used to regimentation so I expect we will have to make examples of a few recalcitrants. Your policy won't be popular, sir."

"I really don't expect to be popular, Ling."

"No, sir."

Ling wasn't stupid so why couldn't he see the obvious? The answer came to Allenson as a revelation. Manzanita City had long stopped dumping raw sewage offshore after the Big Stink when Lake Clearwater became anything but. The waters around the island turned anoxic. Vile-smelling vapors wafted into the air. Since the people who lived along the shore were the wealthy villa owners this created a political stink of equivalent proportions to the chemistry.

The large cities of the Heilbron colonies, in contrast, were built on continental sized rivers—usually at the point where they opened into an ocean. All they had to do was channel rainfall through the sewers and the waste just washed away and diluted into the oceans.

Similar forces operated in the countryside. In the southern Stream, large demesnes carried out most of the agricultural activity. Manzanita land owners might not be all that concerned over creature comforts in their servants' barracklike quarters but they sure as hell were willing to spend money on sewage systems. Labor was always in short supply and one just couldn't afford to have half your servants down with some loathsome disease at harvest time. Beside, loathsome disease didn't always stay in the servants' quarters.

In contrast, the Heilbron practiced farming on smaller scales presided over by single family units living on their own land. The opportunity for contagious disease to spread was limited.

Allenson decided to have one more try.

"More soldier casualties are caused by disease throughout history than ever through enemy action. I reckon we were two weeks away from a major outbreak here at most, Colonel."

Ling looked shocked.

"I'll get right on the matter at once, General, as soon as we are finished here."

"Good, in that case we shall proceed to inspect the camp without delay, after you, Colonel Ling."

The crocodile of officers wound through the camp. Hawthorn's party attached itself to the rear of the retinue. Ling pointed out the camps of the various militia units. The procession elicited cheery greeting from troops. The better trained occasionally saluted. A courtesy Allenson returned. He stopped every so often to exchange a few words with a man chosen at random.

The results both pleased and depressed him. Morale was high and the physical condition of the troops was generally still good despite the poor hygiene but the place had the feel of a holiday camp. An air of relaxation pervaded that had no place in a combat zone.

Outside one tent an elderly man cut the hair of another soldier. From his kit and competence at the task it was clear that he was a tradesman.

"I see we have all the comforts of home," Allenson said to Ling. "I'm surprised you can get a barber to come out to the camp."

The barber smiled.

"Bless you, General, I'm here anyway. I'm the commander of the Treeline Militia. I think they only elected me so they could get a decent trim."

The barber laughed, clearly having made the joke often. Ling looked embarrassed, an emotion that was becoming his stock expression.

"I set great store by a proper cut myself," Allenson said, lying.

Trina had to tie him down to a chair when she summoned the demesne barber.

"However you do present me with a certain problem since barbering is a corporal's job," Allenson said with a straight face. "So I think we will have to bust you down and promote your second in command. Make a note, Mister Ling."

"Yes, General."

They proceeded to the next group of tents. A half dozen men sat outside one tent playing dice and, from the flashes on his sleeve, one of them was the major commanding. They watched Allenson approach with some interest but without letting his presence disturb their game.

"Attention," Ling yelled, red faced.

"You can't tell my men what to do," the sitting officer said.

"Oh, yes, Colonel Ling can," Allenson said. "I am Captain General Allenson. Now get on your feet before I bust you down to private, soldier."

The officer jerked to his feet and saluted.

"This is Major Vaun. His unit has performed better than most," Ling said.

Allenson sniffed.

"Indeed, so what are you doing gambling with the other ranks?"

"No excuse, sir," Vaun said, showing remarkable quickness on the uptake.

Unfortunately this was not shared by all his comrades.

"Now wait a damned moment," said a large solid man opposite Vaun said, climbing to his feet. "We're not your feckin' servants and you're not on your sodding estate out on some southern mudball. Here in Heilbron we do things democratically."

Hawthorn took two steps forward and punched the man on the point of his chin. He went down like a felled log.

"Anyone else have a comment to make?" Hawthorn looked around. "No? Excellent."

There was one of those tricky silences. Allenson looked around for inspiration on how to defuse the situation. He pointed to a large block of stone beside the tent.

"What do you use that for, Major Vaun?"

"Some of the fellows and I have been throwing for distance: a sort of test of strength and skill, General."

"I wondered if that was the case. I used to enter similar contests myself. Do you remember, Colonel Hawthorn?"

"I do. I also seem to recall that you usually won. Of course, we were all a lot younger and fitter then," Hawthorn said.

Allenson laughed.

"I suspect you are being diplomatic. What you mean is that I was a lot younger and fitter in those days. Well let's see if I have retained any of my talent."

Allenson picked up the stone, swaying slightly under the weight as he maneuvered his hands underneath. Men from other tents gathered around to watch. The sight of a general playing "toss the stone" must be a remarkable novelty. Allenson pointedly didn't notice money being produced among the men as bets were laid.

"Is that the mark, Major Vaun?"

"Yes, sir, and that peg marks the furthest throw yet," Vaun said, pointing to a stick hammered into the ground a couple of meters beyond.

Allenson stood behind the line and inhaled deeply. Taking one step forward he thrust the stone up with both hands. It curved in a parabola and hit the ground just behind the peg, bouncing so it ended up some ten centimeters in front.

Allenson laughed again.

"It seems you are right, Colonel Hawthorn. I'm not the man I was."

"No, General," a soldier said, while collecting from his fellows. "We take the mark to be the furthest distance reached by the rock, not its first contact with the ground. You win squarely."

"Well let's give the previous record holder a chance to regain his crown with the best of three," Allenson said. "Who is he?"

"Macreedy, sir" said the soldier, chuckling. "'You'll have to wait until he wakes up 'cause that colonel of yours has laid him out."

There was a general burst of laughter. Even the men who had lost money seemed not entirely displeased to see Macreedy knocked off his throne. Possibly he was not the most popular man in the unit.

"Well, well, he obviously needs a bit more practice, as do I. Major Vaun?"

"Sir?"

"Tell Macreedy to come up to the headquarters when he's recovered and we'll do a bit of toss-the-stone training together. Carry on, Major."

Allenson returned Vaun's salute and resumed his tour.

"Tell me, Colonel Ling, is it normal practice for the officers to share a tent with their men?" Allenson asked when they were out of earshot.

"Yes, sir."

"That stops now. I want the officers to mess together to create an army esprit de corps. We need to separate them from the men they command. The officers will endure the same conditions as their men, eat the same food and undergo the same dangers but they will not fraternize. When they give an order it must be obeyed without question or argument. That won't happen if they are seen as one of the boys."

"Very good sir, I'll arrange it," said the unflappable Ling.

Allenson hid a smile. Ling was going to be very busy in the next few days, but if he survived this challenge he would make an excellent staff officer.

The raucous sound of a badly silenced internal combustion engine drew Allenson's attention. An agricultural tractor pulled a trailer from the direction of the siege lines.

Ling anticipated Allenson's question.

"Frames near the shoreline attract Brasilian lasercannon fire if they rise above the skyline. We tend to use ground vehicles to shuttle backward and forward. They're not much slower than a frame crawling along at ground height, particularly if it's got metal on board," Ling said.

"Damn sight noisier though," Hawthorn observed.

The trailer contained a number of soldiers, presumably the relieved shift. A man stood at the front of the trailer where he could hold on to the slatted bulkhead. His considerable silhouette seemed familiar so Allenson shaded his eyes for a better look. One of Ling's aides materialized at his side with a pair of binoculars. Allenson adjusted the fit until a three-dimensional holographic image was focused into his eyes such that the trailer appeared to be just in front of him.

"Ah," Allenson said. "I see Colonel Buller has arrived. Perhaps we should wait for him."

The tractor bounced across the field at a respectable lick. Men dropped off the trailer on the move as it went through the camp. It stopped only for Buller to dismount.

"*That* is Colonel Buller?" Hawthorn asked quietly.

Ling suddenly acquired diplomatic temporary deafness which was a useful attribute in a chief of staff. The man was recommending himself for permanent promotion in Allenson's eyes.

"Allenson, I see you've been inspecting the camp. Rather you than me. Place is a bloody cesspit, troops a disgrace."

Ling winced and several of the militia representatives glowered at Buller.

"You really should call me General, you know," Allenson said gently.

Buller didn't do tact. It was a warm day so his jacket was unbuttoned. His shirt was done up one button askew so there was a spare button thrust under his left ear and a spare hole above his belt giving a view of an expansive hairy stomach.

"I've been down to have a look at the siege lines. I use the words advisedly because there bloody aren't any. All I found were a few bunkers and they aren't even much damn use for observing the city. Most of them are on reverse slopes."

"We tried siting them more prominently but the Brasilians have lasercannon," Ling said pointedly. "The bunkers were soon discovered and then you could measure their survival time in minutes."

"You've heard of camouflage, I suppose?" Buller asked

"Sometimes we didn't even finish construction before they were destroyed," Ling replied.

"For Satan's sake man, you dig through from the reverse side." Buller said. "All it needs is work and a modicum of military skill."

He turned to Allenson.

"There is nothing to stop the Brasilians mounting a sortie any time they damn well please with every expectation of surprising the camp. Can you imagine how a couple of units of Brasilian light infantry would sweep through this rabble?"

Buller waved his arm to encompass the camp, his voice pitched to carry.

"I think you underestimate the resolution and bravery of our soldiers," Allenson said to forestall a riot. "Nevertheless, you make a valid point. We need containment lines strong enough to hold up any attack until we can reinforce the defenses from the camp."

Allenson raised his voice to address the entire entourage.

"Colonel Buller is one of the foremost authorities on modern siege tactics. Indeed, I hope I do not embarrass him if I say he probably has more experience of this military art than any man alive."

"True," Buller said smugly, clearly not embarrassed at all.

"We would be foolish not to avail ourselves of that knowledge. I propose to put Colonel Buller in command of the siege lines. Arrange with Colonel Ling to co-opt what resources you need, Colonel, but rotate the men as I propose to start intensive training of the reserves here."

"Excellent, Allenson, nothing wrong with an amateur gentleman figure-heading the operation when he knows when to hand over to the professionals. I'll make out a list for Ling."

Buller stomped off.

"At least down at the siege lines the damn man'll be out of our hair," Ling said to one of his aides.

Allenson ignored the remark. Knowing when to be afflicted with temporary deafness was one of the virtues good generals shared with good chiefs of staff.

★ ★ ★

The next day Allenson's pad relayed a message from Ling asking for a meeting in the engineering workshops. Ling being Ling, there was a map added giving direction. Allenson walked through Cambridge on his own so he could collect his thoughts. Alone of course, meant being closely trailed by two of Krenz's goons. By now he regarded them as part of the woodwork. The road was quiet; not even his boots made much in the way of noise on the partly stabilized mud surface.

Small creatures in the undergrowth called to each other with mournful whoop noises. He didn't know enough about the fauna of Trinity to know whether these were alarm calls notifying others of his presence or mating cries. For all he knew, they just made noises for the fun of it. He made a mental note to discuss the matter with Destry next time he saw him. Then he remembered Destry was gone.

While he walked, he thought through the situation. It seemed to him that they were at stalemate with the Brasilians. Oxford's location had been chosen by the original colonists partly because of its defensive possibilities. The Stream Army was now paying the price for the stupidity of the Trinity mob. They had done just enough to arouse the Brasilians without doing enough to secure the city.

The Brasilians acquired Oxford on the cheap. It would be the devil's own job to dislodge them now that they were dug in. The question was, who benefitted from a stalemate? He told the Assembly that the colonies did not have to win the war but merely had to survive to achieve independence. Now he was beginning to wonder whether that was entirely true.

He worried that he may have misjudged matters. He tried to see the situation from a Brasilian perspective. They might be entirely satisfied with hanging on to a few key cities like Oxford and Port Trent while ignoring the rebellion until it fizzled out through logistical decay and exhaustion. That way Brasilia could claim victory in so far as was required for Home World propaganda. But they avoided the cost of a long distance war of attrition for territory that they undoubtedly regarded as next to useless. After all, they lost interest in the Hinterlands after the last war the moment the Terrans had been evicted.

The city ports would also be springboards for any future

campaigns should political events make further Brasilian intervention necessary. Dammit, that's what Allenson would do if he were the Brasilian commander. Grab the ports while the grabbing was good and ignore the rest. It was a moot point who was besieging whom at Oxford. Allenson had read enough military history to know that sometimes the besiegers "starved" before the besieged.

His pad beeped, letting him know he had arrived. He extracted himself from his thoughts with an almost physical effort. The army's engineers were based in a requisitioned college of technology. Ling was waiting for him at the entrance.

"If you'd like to come through, sir, Major Kiesche has a demonstration arranged," Ling said mysteriously.

Ling, Allenson, his bodyguards and a small tail of mechanics snaked through corridors. They went down a flight of narrow stairs and into a scullery with a stone floor that rang under their military boots. A door opened into a yard.

Kiesche stood proudly by a pile of equipment that looked like a miscellaneous heap of plumbing. It resembled a modernist sculpture bolted together by an *avant-garde* artist abusing some pretty potent mind expanding substances.

"I know it looks a bit like an exploded diagram of a ruminant's gut structure," Kiesche said.

"Yes," Allenson replied, firmly suppressing that vision.

"But it's a hydraulic pump that I've stripped out of a canal lock gate and converted into a ram."

"I see," Allenson said, patiently. "And why would you want to do that?"

"To make artillery, sir, to supplement our lasercannon."

Allenson must have still looked blank because Kiesche elucidated further.

"Like battleship guns, General."

The penny dropped. Heavy naval assets employed hydraulic-power rams to throw ceramic kinetic projectiles out through their fields into the Continuum. These weren't the most powerful weapons in existence but they generated little heat or toxic fumes compared to railguns or explosive weapons.

Kiesche said helpfully, "The power and recycle speed of a naval cannon depends on the pumping rate. Almost any pump will do for any sized gun within reason if you can wait long enough between shots."

Allenson looked at the man, wondering what to say. No one in their right mind would use hydraulic cannon if there was anything else available. Continuum combat was a very special case. However, he didn't want to insult the engineer or curb his enthusiasm so he replied noncommittedly.

Kiesche insisted on demonstrating his spaghetti-weapon. It lobbed a ceramic bolt a surprisingly long way but the chamber took forever to repressure. Kiesche tried to speed it up but something inside broke. It sprayed the engineer with oil as he struggled to stem the leak

Allenson retreated to a safe distance as he only had one decent dress uniform and he was wearing it.

"Perhaps it needs a little more work, Kiesche?"

"Yes, sir," Kiesche said, a little crestfallen.

"Keep up the good work," Allenson added.

★ CHAPTER 13 ★

Home World High Jinks

"Marshal Ovaki will see you now," the secretary said.

General Brine paused at the door to watch her sashay back to her podium. Long flowing lilac and indigo hair cascading down onto a very pert bottom made her worth a look. Her metallic *purpurrot* dress in a crushed velvety cloth unfortunately retained imprints. These included a distinct outline of a large male hand on her right buttock.

Brine knocked and walked in without waiting for a reply.

"Ah, Petrov, thanks for popping over, have a seat," Ovaki said.

"Your secretary's looking a little flushed, Sam," Brine replied.

"She's a charming girl but a bit forgetful. She mislaid a file so I had to admonish her."

"So I saw."

"Scotch?"

The marshal produced a bottle and two glasses.

"Plum brandy for me, if you have it."

Nancy-boy's drink, Brine correctly predicted the marshal's next sally.

They went through this ritual every time Brine was summoned to the marshal's office. Why Ovaki couldn't just get on with it and pour him a plum brandy was beyond Brine's comprehension. Possibly it was some sort of psychological dominance display. Maybe Ovaki actually liked scotch and really couldn't understand why no one else did. God knows, he drank enough of the filthy stuff.

Brine asked, "Well, what was so urgent and confidential that I had to rush over in person?"

"It's about the damned Bight colonies."

Brine groaned and took a gulp of the brandy.

"Not again. Haven't we wasted enough energy, not to say money on those mudballs. Don't tell me some idiot politician on the Council has decided to make the little coup the colonials are cooking up a *cause célèbre.*"

Ovaki tried to reply but Brine was in full rant mode.

"It's not as if we want the Bight colonies particularly. They're an economic sinkhole of no strategic value. The only reason we fought a war there last time was to stop Terra getting them. That was purely for reasons of national prestige. Surely it's not beyond the wit of even our politicians to come up with some face-saving form of words that will give the colonials independence in practice while maintaining Brasilia's prestige among the Home Worlds?"

He finally ran down and glowered into his glass. Ovaki took the opportunity to get a word in edgeways.

"That was the plan. However, it's not some politician who's dropped a grenade at the mess dinner this time but the poxy academics."

Brine was genuinely astonished.

"What? Who cares what academics think?"

In Brasilia's socio-economic structure academics ranked somewhere between poets and classical dancers in that they were decorative items.

Ovaki continued. "It's not what they think, it's what they've discovered. Have you heard of unbihexium?"

"No," Brine replied.

"It's element 126, a super-actinide," Ovaki said helpfully.

Brine didn't bother to reply. The marshal knew very well he hadn't a clue what that meant. He doubted Ovaki had heard of unbi-whatever until he read the plastic file lying on the desk.

Plastic files were secure isolated datapads disconnected from any outside communication system and code-locked. They could only be read when activated by someone whose DNA, epigenetics and proteomic patterns matched the lock. In this case that was probably only Ovaki and possibly his secretary.

"Super-actinides are transuranic stable elements," Ovaki said didactically. "Except this one becomes unstable in the presence of a continuum field."

Brine shrugged.

"So it's another explosive, so what?"

Ovaki explained.

"It doesn't explode it implodes, sucking in energy."

"And that makes it important enough to fight a war over because . . ."

"Because tiny amounts can be used to refreeze a ship's heat sinks while in transit."

"I can see that more efficient ships would be useful—" Brine began.

Ovaki silenced him with a gesture.

"No you don't see. This stuff makes possible massive battleships with near infinite range at full speed. We can build fast armored transports that carry huge loads—including metals. In short, we could build an invasion fleet that could conquer a Home World. All it takes is a few kilos of unbihexium. Right now no one knows how to make the stuff in usable quantities, but the navy found a source in the Bight Hinterland with shiploads just waiting to be mined."

"Oh dear God," Brine said finally catching on. "If the Terrans get their hands on it . . ."

"Quite! I want you to plan for a major invasion across the Bight. I know," Ovaki held up a hand to forestall a list of reasons why that was next to logistically impossible.

Brine considered. "Our army is already overcommitted in a dozen brushfire conflicts with Terran proxies this side of the Bight. It will take time to recruit, train and equip new formations."

"Time is what we don't have, so hire mercenaries." Ovaki said. "I have a near unlimited budget for this operation. That is how seriously element 126 has rattled the Standing Security Committee. For once the political parties are in tight agreement. The politicos see their personal cozy little universes threatened."

A hologram marker winked over Ovaki's desk. He waved a hand and it disappeared.

"Just my secretary telling me she is going to lunch," Ovaki said, in answer to Brine's unspoken question.

"She's quite a babe even by your standards." Brine said, recalling the pert bottom. "Where did you find her?"

"She came highly recommended by a colleague in Security." Ovaki replied. "He had to unload her in a hurry. His wife bumped into her at a reception and discovered she wasn't as homely as my colleague had implied."

"I can imagine the scene," Brine said, chuckling. He raised his glass, "To our wives and loved ones; may they never meet."

The babe in question often lunched outside the Department of War building. Today was no exception. She hurried across the open square into the warren of alleyways housing cafes and shops that serviced the staff who worked in the various government offices around the plaza. Her gait was a little stiff. Her bottom still smarted from the spanking administered earlier by the marshal.

He enjoyed catching her out in little errors because it gave him an excuse to indulge his obsession with pert bottoms. In this case, she thought, the filthy old perv's habits were useful as they distracted him from wondering why the unbihexium file had gone missing. It was sheer bad luck he asked for it while she had it linked to her pad.

She sat down somewhat gingerly on a bench outside a small restaurant specializing in spiced food from Rautmala, an unimportant Home World in the Terran sphere of influence. She opened her bag to find the sandwich she had purchased earlier. She also took her pad out of her bag and watched a catch-up program about a popular soap opera as she ate.

She blinked back tears. The food aromas and restaurant music reminded her of the Rautmalan boyfriend she had met on holiday and with whom she had fallen deeply in love. She hadn't seen him in months, not since he had been picked up by the Rautmalan Social Protection Guards for ownership of proscribed texts.

Terran Security had promised to use their influence with the Rautmalan authorities to free her beloved if she did the odd favor for them occasionally. Favors like copying high security files using one of a suite of apps they had added to her pad.

The catch-up show was a Terran app with special features marked only by an inconspicuous green light in one corner. After a few minutes the light turned yellow and disappeared, indicating that the unbihexium file had successfully downloaded into the restaurant's espionage equipment.

She finished her sandwich and returned to work.

General Brine worked late that evening in his office. He often did but rarely on something as important as planning a war. At the moment however, exhaustion had set in and further action would be counterproductive. He buzzed his secretary, who had stayed to access necessary files and send out the streams of orders that would start the slow and ponderous wheels of the Brasilian military spinning.

"We'll call it a day, Trixie. Thanks for working late."

"My pleasure, sir, is there anything else before I go."

"Yes, we will need to start again at eight. It's hardly worth me going all the way home and back. I think I'll stay in town tonight. Would you let my wife know?"

After a moment's thought he opened the link to his secretary's office again.

"And send a message to Mistress Fairhead asking if she wants to meet me for dinner at nine."

"Of course, General, at your club?"

"Correct, goodbye, Trixie. Get a good night's sleep as we have a busy day tomorrow."

"You too, sir."

"Oh, I intend to."

The advantage of the reverse cowboy position, thought Reeva Fairhead, is that you can feign passion with just a few theatrical moans without the tedious business of also having to simulate an expression of ecstasy. The disadvantage is that it is hard work involving bouncing up and down, especially when your protector is elderly and tired. By the time Grimes climaxed she was exhausted. She leaned forward for a few moments to catch her breath.

Pointing down the bed, she had a good view of herself in the mirror. She examined her reflection with a professional eye. By most standards she was beautiful but the competition from younger hetaerae grew ever fiercer. Her breasts were sagging just a little and lines were showing in the skin around her neck. She was, she thought, getting too old for all this exercise.

Reeva was a great deal older than she looked. As the years passed the degree of rejuvenation treatment required to give her the right appearance of bubble-headed youth became more costly and uncomfortable.

It would be nice to retire. She had built up a decent little nest egg by the simple expedient of running a number of protectors simultaneously. Each paid the rent on her villa unaware of the others' existence. Additional revenue accrued to her pension fund by getting each protector to buy her identical presents such as clothes and jewelry and then selling off the surplus. She only needed one of each item to wear for each doting admirer in turn.

Nevertheless prices never came down. One's nest egg could never be too well padded. There were too many horror stories of elderly courtesans who had overlooked the effect of inflation forced out of retirement in their dotage. Reeva did not intend to be reduced to hanging around docks doing favors for sailors for the price of a hot meal. She shuddered at the thought.

At one time she had hopes of marrying a suitable financially endowed protector. Somehow no offer ever seemed good enough when she was younger and they had dried up as she aged. Reeva was enough of a realist to grasp that this situation was unlikely to change now.

A snore behind her back indicated that Grimes had gone to sleep. Charming, she thought, not even a thank you for her efforts. She carefully lifted herself off but she needn't have bothered. Alcohol and sex had worked their usual magic on the male body.

Reeva wore clothes that could be donned as well as removed easily. One of the attractions of a professional companion to gentlemen is that unlike a wife they leave without fuss when the business is concluded and let a chap sleep in peace. She forced herself to dress quietly even though her mind was racing.

Grimes, like many men, had the urge to try to impress the woman he was about to screw. That was wasted energy as far as hetaerae were concerned. She regarded him in much the same way a farmer considered a dairy cow. To wit, it was only as valuable as its milk supply. In Grimes's case said attempts to impress took the form of boasts about the importance of his work projects. He recounted these in tedious detail despite his patronizingly expressed view that she wouldn't really understand.

Actually Reeva understood far more than he gave her credit for. Her wide-eyed expression of awed stupidity was purely professional courtesy. Hetaerae entertained by massaging egos as well as bodies. She understood that what she had heard tonight was probably worth a great deal of money to someone. On the taxi ride home she thought long and hard about her future and how it could be best secured.

Suntalaw tapped his fingers on the blank surface of a switched off desk while keeping a subordinate called Preson waiting outside his office.

His official title was Director General of the Terran Commonwealth Social Welfare Directorate, in which role he chaired the Committee for Public Security that was his true powerbase. Public Security covered a wide remit including counterinsurgency, counterespionage, and public morality. The counterinsurgency hat gave Suntalaw control of the internal security troops but his public morality brief was even more valuable. In the final resort everyone was immoral in some way or other. A case could be made against any person whom he decided needed removing. He kept files on anyone who mattered in the Terran power structure and many who did not but might someday become important.

The only individual more powerful than Suntalaw was the advocate general himself. He perched atop the various silos of state, playing off one DG against another.

Suntalaw drummed his fingers, impatient to hear Preson's news, but it wouldn't do to let an underling think he was important. Always make 'em wait outside the door to establish the pecking order.

Finally he keyed the desk on and said, "Come."

Preson oozed in, oilier than a seabird caught in a petroleum disaster.

"Well, what is it?" Suntalaw asked, injecting just the right amount of boredom into his tone. "You claimed that you had to report something to me personally."

"Important intelligence from the Exoworld Directorate spooks, sir."

Preson placed a plastic file on Suntalaw's desk with exaggerated care.

Suntalaw gave it a sneer but refrained from opening it. Preson claimed to have a snout, an informer, in the Exoworld Directorate that among other things ran Terra's outworld spy networks.

"I don't have all day so summarize the salient points."

Preson did as he was bid and when the man finished Suntalaw sat back in his seat.

"And Exoworld buy into this fanciful tale of magic Hinterland colony metal that will revolutionize naval warfare."

"They have independent verification from two separate sources. The first is a secretary that they turned using a honey trap. She thinks her beloved an imprisoned Rautmalan dissident," Preson said.

Suntalaw sniggered.

"I presume the boyfriend is an Exoworld operative."

Preson nodded.

"The other source is a mistress of a Brasilian general."

Suntalaw wondered how this could be worked to his advantage. His mind plodded carefully through the various possibilities, each scenario more paranoiac than the last. Should he sit on the information, pretend he'd never seen it, or report the matter to the advocate general. What spin should he apply if he decided to pass it on?

His first reaction was to ignore the whole affair and let matters take their course. He would have to impress upon Preson the need to keep his mouth shut if he chose that option. The advocate general undoubtedly had spies within every DG including Home Security. Could he trust Preson? Now that was a stupid question.

An unfortunate fatal accident could be arranged, of course, but suppose Preson was the advocate general's spy in Suntalaw's directorate. Terminating him might seem like an attack on the advocate general himself. That thought brought Suntalaw out in a cold sweat.

He forced himself to think through the logical possibilities. It was of little concern whether this magic metal actually existed but who thought it existed. Could this be an elaborate and convoluted scam by Brasilian Security to discredit Exoworld? In that case it would be better for Suntalaw to lie low and let events take their course.

Suppose it was a plot by Exoworld to discredit Social Welfare and hence him? If he misled the advocate general with false information it could be construed as treason. The AG had a swift way with traitors, real or imagined.

Suntalaw examined Preson carefully, trying to read his mind. Life would be so much easier if he could read his subordinates' minds. Preson was supposed to be his pipe line into Exoworld but it often occurred that Preson could just as easily be Exoworld's pipe line into Social Welfare.

An even more horrendous idea erupted into his consciousness like a gas bubble from a swamp. Suppose the advocate general himself had set up the scam to test the loyalty of his director generals? In that case not reporting the information could be construed as treason.

The more he thought about the matter the more Suntalaw convinced himself that it didn't matter whether the information was true or untrue. The only issue was whether the advocate general believed it might be true. *He* had developed paranoia into a high art form. The AG was likely to believe any tale no matter how fanciful where his own personal safety was threatened.

He would prepare a report for the AG. If it all blew up he would just have to find a scapegoat. Suntalaw smiled at Preson, deciding to let him live a little longer. The man might yet be useful.

★ CHAPTER 14 ★

Siege Lines

Allenson spent the next few weeks reorganizing his army. He set up a rigorous training schedule. He busted down some officers and NCOs and promoted others. Slowly but surely the army changed from a ragbag collection of militia into a professional fighting force. He created uniform regiments by merging understrength units. He grouped the regiments into brigades until he had a field army of interchangeable units with predictable reactions.

He pitched brigades and battalions against each other in competition. The winner was excused fatigues. The losers got the winners' duties in addition to their own. Men lounging who had been catcalling and uttering unsubtle jokes to colleagues found themselves digging ditches instead. Allenson's universal reply to any complaints: "It pays to be a winner."

He was cordially hated by all and sundry but they sweated and they worked nonetheless. Allenson consoled himself by the thought that being popular was not in his job description.

He set up an event and was cheering on the contestants when the intruder alarm sounded. Companies were competing to dig and occupy a trench line before an automatic defense laser cannon raked the air space above one meter off the ground.

There was in theory no danger. One meter was easily sufficient for someone to survive simply by lying down on the surface, never mind in a trench. Regrettably, some idiot always ran too slow or cut it too fine when the warning klaxon sounded. Live fire casualties inevitably happened in training. Each one lay on Allenson's already burdened conscience, but a little bloodshed now could save rivers of gore when the army had to do the business for real.

This time the klaxon went off early before either of the trenches was ready. The troops flung themselves at the ground without waiting for an explanation, but the lasercannon unaccountably failed to fire. It wasn't even pointing in the right direction. The barrels stuck fast in the rest position. The weapon's crew gawped at it in astonishment. They prodded a few buttons experimentally, but the machine continued to sulk like a teenager at an aged relative's birthday party.

The other defense cannon positioned around the perimeter of the camp also went on strike. They failed to react even when a swarm of one and two-man frames phased in directly overhead. The intruder alarm successfully detected intruders, but that wasn't all that helpful if the defense cannon failed to respond.

Allenson pulled his ion pistol out and shot it uselessly into the air. He had enough trouble hitting anything with a rifle. With a pistol he could barely target the sky. His action was more in the way of a warning to the camp. Krenz's men closed up on each side of him, carbines at the ready. They, sensibly, did not try to target small fast-moving objects at extreme range.

The klaxon continued to wail, signaling an air attack. Soldiers tumbled out of tents. Some, those who had both remembered to grab their rifles and managed to switch them on, fired at the frames—mostly without effect. A rare hit caused a two-man frame to sideslip towards the ground, trailing smoke. The front rider slumped forward over the controls while the man behind pedaled furiously.

The frames scattered, some rephrasing back into the Continuum. Others dropped swiftly to the ground, braking only just in time to effect a soft landing. The crews dived off their machines as soon as they were down. They hid in the half-finished trenches or lay flat with their arms over their heads. If this was an attack then the enemy were a right bunch of pacifists.

Allenson keyed an all ranks channel. "Cease fire. The newcomers are friendly, cease fire immediately."

Rather to his surprise his men obeyed and the shooting died away. Allenson shrugged off the restraining hands of his minders and bounded over to the half-finished defenses.

A young man wearing a cheeky grin and an unfamiliar canary-yellow uniform climbed out of a trench with his hand extended.

"Who the hell are you?" Allenson demanded, ignoring the proffered limb.

"Captain Reese Morton, sir, Morton's Marauders. I guess you must be our new general," the young man said, saluting with a flourish.

At that point the klaxon sounded again. Allenson turned and was horrified to see the exercise lasercannon swiveling on its gimbals. The damn thing was still obeying its preprogramed fire pattern instructions.

Some things are so burned into one's body that they override the conscious mind. Allenson's old combat reactions kicked in. He was the first into the trench. The others landed on top of him.

Allenson felt the back of his neck gingerly. Some damned squaddie had planted a combat boot on one of his upper vertebra.

"I'm terribly sorry, sir. I didn't think," Morton said.

"No, sir, you bloody well didn't," Allenson replied. "You are damned lucky half your command wasn't flamed by our lasercannon. Never ever try to beat up my command like that again or I will shoot you personally if the autos don't do it for me."

He turned to Ling.

"And why is Morton still alive, Colonel? Why didn't our autos fire? What if it had been the Brasilians and not some damn fool from our own side."

Allenson glowered at Morton, who was not noticeably crushed.

Ling said, "I anticipated you would want to know what went wrong so I've had the engineering officer check the equipment over. It seems there's a flaw in our control system."

"A flaw that could get us all killed," Allenson snarled.

Ling nodded seriously.

"Yes, sir, taking one cannon off line for the exercise shut down the entire system. Apparently, it's a health and safety measure to render the equipment safe in the event of a malfunction."

"Safe?" Allenson asked, pronouncing the word as if it described an obscene act involving rubber trousers and an electric prod. "I see we are using a novel definition of the word safe. Safe to me means having a working bloody air defense system."

"Yes, sir, I agree. I have instructed Major Kiesche to disable the, ah, safety feature."

"I suppose you actually did us a favor, Morton. Just don't do it again," Allenson said, rubbing his neck.

"Do you want the doctor to have a look at that?" Ling asked.

"I've had worse. A plum brandy will put me right."

Taking the hint, Morton caught the waiter's eye and ordered drinks.

"Remind me, what are Morton's Marauders?" Allenson asked.

"A small detached commando operating independently in the Hinterland," Ling replied.

"We've been hitting isolated Brasilian outposts and their supply routes," Morton replied proudly.

"Pin-pricks only, I'm afraid, sir," Ling said. "I doubt the Brasilians care overmuch, but Morton's raids do show the flag around the mudball colonies and dissuade Brasilian loyalists from trying to raise an army in our rear."

"I think I do rather more than that," Morton said, a trifle stiffly. "On this raid we captured Fort Champlain, slighted the defenses and burned the building to the ground."

"Indeed," Allenson said, impressed.

"Fort Champlain was a weapon store. We've brought back some useful captured equipment," Morton said.

"Like what?" asked Allenson.

"Mortars, sir! Ceramic tubes and a supply of shells."

"Now that is truly useful," Allenson replied, delighted.

With mortars in support, an infantry assault on Oxford might become a viable proposition. Allenson would prefer the Brasilians to be the ones to launch an attack. It was true that modern troops were so tactically mobile that the attacker had all the strategic advantages of tempo. He who chose the time and place and could easily concentrate overwhelming force on the point of contact before the defender could reinforce. Nevertheless the defense was always tactically stronger. This was especially true if the defenders were aided by the force multiplier of a prepared position. Green troops in particular found it easier to defend fortified positions than to attack them.

"How did you storm Fort Champlain with only light infantry?" Allenson asked.

"Truth to tell it wasn't as difficult as it sounds," Morton replied with disarming honesty. "The walls were in a parlous state. The fort was undermanned with demoralized garrison troops. They fired a few volleys for effect then legged it."

Allenson thought Morton underrated his achievement.

"Nevertheless, a successful *coup de main* requires boldness and skill. Well done."

He noticed that Morton visibly preened under the praise. The young man wasn't overly modest at all. In fact he was incorrigibly vain but it was difficult not to like him.

"The choice of uniform for your unit surprises me. Isn't bright yellow a little, well, visible?"

"You are not the first to express that view," Ling added.

"There was talk of a combat uniform in some peasant shade like earth brown or olive green but I soon put a stop to that," Morton replied, loftily. "I want my men to be seen and recognized as an elite fighting force. Besides, no gentleman should be asked to go to war looking as if he has just rolled in a swamp."

"So how are you getting on with your new minders?" Hawthorn asked, easing himself into a chair in Allenson's office and sinking half a glass of brandy.

Allenson glowered at him.

"Not well, the bastards follow me around like randy youths after a girl with a reputation. I had to physically dissuade some of the more enthusiastic from accompanying me to the bathroom."

Hawthorn snorted into his drink, shooting a fine spray across Allenson's desk.

"Excellent. I must organize a suitable bonus for Krenz."

Allenson glowered.

"Pleasurable as it is to offer myself up as the butt for your peculiar sense of humor, was there something else you wanted to discuss?"

"Information!" Hawthorn said succinctly. "I take it you are interested in what is going on in Oxford?"

"Very much," Allenson replied, refilling Hawthorn's glass.

"The short answer is not a lot. The Brasilian military have hunkered down and are playing a waiting game. The troopers are getting bored. There have already been one or two incidents. Some of the licentious soldiery caused trouble and one or two local hotheads picked fights in retaliation. The general in charge, one Moffat, is old school. He may not be the shiniest cog in the Brasilian military machine intellect-wise but he does have a grasp of discipline. He hung a few malcontents from both sides and publically flogged others as an example and so is keeping a tight lid on things. Shame really, a good insurrection and blood bath might have been useful propaganda."

Allenson winced.

"I suppose it might have given us opportunities in the short term but I'm rather glad Moffat is competent to that degree. I don't want a civilian massacre on my conscience. The key question is whether they have enough supplies to withstand a siege? Oxford must have depended heavily on a continuous supply of fresh agricultural produce from the surrounding farms. I doubt if they had much in the way of sterile long-term food storage."

Hawthorn shook his head.

"My informants tell me that the city's on short rations but there's not much chance of starving them out. They're getting a constant supply of material from tramp ships running in from nearby worlds and even some of the outlying areas of Trinity. The price of food in Oxford has doubled and some of our dear, patriotic countrymen can't resist making a fast crown or three."

"It's difficult to blockade a port when you have no navy," Allenson said. "Of course many ship owners support the status quo rather than the rebellion and many others won't care much one way or the other. After all, business is business."

Hawthorn tapped his glass.

"We could turn Morton's men loose on the food supplies and ship owners, I suppose."

"We could but that might do us more harm than good in the long run," Allenson replied. "We'll eventually need those people for our own purposes, if not during the war then certainly after it. In any case the Brasilians could ship supplies in on military transports if necessary."

"If we lose I suspect we won't have to worry too much about what comes after," Hawthorn said with his usual cynical detachment.

"How long have we got before the Brasilians attack?" Allenson asked.

"What makes you think they intend to? My information is that they intend to sit out the siege until we die of boredom, dysentery or old age. There seems to be some debate as to whether we'll attempt to take the town by storm."

"Indeed, does the thought bother them?" Allenson asked.

"The junior officers positively salivate at the thought," Hawthorn replied. "Anything to relieve the tedium. They foresee promotion and honors all round."

"Not a morale problem then."

"No so's you'd notice, no."

"How about the senior officers, what's their opinion?" Allenson asked.

"Publicly they seem confident of being able to resist any assault we might mount."

"Well they would say that, wouldn't they? I wonder what they really think?"

Hawthorn shrugged.

"I don't yet have an agent in place who is privy to the command staff's private discussions. One of my agents is laying the colonel of artillery. He boasts that he had enough multibarreled lasercannon to weave an impenetrable shield over both port and the town and still have guns left over to sweep both causeways clear of any attackers on foot."

Allenson's heart sank. Fond ideas of using Morton's light mortars to overcome the defenses melted like summer hail.

"I see. Was he exaggerating to impress his girlfriend?"

"Possibly."

Hawthorn shrugged again.

"I am going to need some more Brasilian crowns. I've spent my own money up to now and I'm running short of ready cash. My agents refuse to accept the Heilbron paper Thalers we pay our troops in."

"I see your people are not optimistic about our chances," Allenson said dryly.

He made a note on his pad.

"I'll make sure you get a plentiful supply of hard currency. Pay yourself back whatever the treasury owes your personal account as well."

"There was one other point," Hawthorn said. "A youth in my

employ was part of a group hired to entertain naval officers and overheard a rather odd remark."

"Oh?" Allenson looked up from the pad.

Hawthorn said, "An off-color joke about the size of an officer's personal weapon involved comparing it to a new *über*-powerful secret device being developed for the Brasilian Navy. Apparently it's going to crush us rebel scum."

"A war-winning secret weapon?" Allenson asked, raising both eyebrows. "And how much credence do you put on that information?"

"The same as you: as next to none as makes no difference," Hawthorn replied with a grin. "But if I start filtering information before you get it then we might miss something important."

Allenson nodded agreement.

"Historically, that's always the problem with intelligence. Everyone always gets accurate information about the enemy's intentions but it's usually a lone straw hidden in a hayrick of crap. Okay, secret weapon, Brasilian Navy, for the use of. We'll make a note and file under *Doubtful*."

"Only a bloody fool would send troops along that causeway. You might as well line them up and shoot them yourself. Save a lot of time and the result will be the same," Buller said, jabbing his finger in the direction of Oxford.

Buller might be short changed on many of the qualities needed to make a gentleman but he knew how to conduct a siege. Allenson lay on his stomach in a dugout on the reverse side of the slope overlooking Oxford. He surveyed the town through a scope mounted in a camouflaged port drilled through the crown of the ridge. Buller and Todd squatted behind him.

The Brasilians rigged gun towers to give clear fields of fire over the town buildings onto the open causeways leading to the mainland and the Streamer lines.

"The cannon will have excellent low light sensors. I hope no one is under any illusions that a night attack would be any less of a slaughter," Buller said.

Allenson assumed that to be the case and hardly needed the obvious to be pointed out. That never stopped Buller. What the besiegers needed was heavy artillery to smash up and breach the defenses and keep the defenders' heads down during the assault. Allenson may as well wish for immortality while he was at it—and a plate of warm muffins.

Heavy artillery tended to be metal based and so was incredibly difficult to transport across the Bight. Perhaps that was fortunate as otherwise the Brasilians would have entire batteries at their disposal. None of the Stream colonies had the industrial base to make their own.

Lasercannon were mostly ceramic and silicon crystal-based devices. They were horribly expensive to manufacture but easy to transport through the Continuum, not least because they didn't require metal ammunition. But their properties caused certain tactical limitations, notably direct line of sight fire restrictions. The Stream Army ideally needed weapons that could be mounted safely in artillery pits. Guns capable of lobbing indirect fire at the enemy.

Many of the old militia regiments had lasercannon, which were now coopted into the Army. But Allenson was under no illusion about the end result of a war of attrition between direct-fire lasercannon batteries should he choose to start one. The Brasilians could simply ship in more to replace losses. The colonials couldn't. They couldn't manufacture new ones either or even carry out any but the simplest repairs.

"How about the mortars captured by Morton," Todd said. "We can manufacture mortar shells easily enough. Couldn't the tubes knock out the gun towers long enough for our infantry to carry the city by storm?" Todd asked.

"I thought some idiot would suggest that so I have arranged a little demonstration," Buller replied. "Seeing is believing, so I'm told."

He tapped the small datapad strapped to his wrist. Artillery crews must have been on standby because the blunt cough of the mortars started up within seconds. The laser cannon in Oxford responded with the same alacrity, no doubt on automatic. The light beams were theoretically invisible unless they were aimed directly at an observer's eyes, in which case the hypothetical observer would soon need a new head. In practice atmospheric dust and water vapor compromised light coherence such that the laser pulses left streaks of incoherent light across the sky.

The first mortar bombs exploded over the edge of the siege lines.

The lasercannon picked them off but the fast rate of fire from the simple artillery weapons moved the intercept barrier closer and closer to the town. The centralized fire control of the lasercannon prioritized which targets to defend once the defenses started to be overwhelmed. The selection chosen by the weapons defending Oxford suggested that these priorities included the gun towers themselves and certain strategic assets but not civilian property.

The rain of fire continued until hits registered on Oxford roof tops and in the streets. The light bombs caused but slight damage. A single hit on the side of a tower chipped off small fragments of syncrete.

"Cease fire, we're just wasting ammunition," Allenson said. "Even when we get a strike we barely scratch their paintwork."

Buller tapped his pad and the mortars wound down.

Todd said hesitantly, "I suppose we could make larger rocket-fired guided missiles with armor piercing warheads."

Buller dismissed the idea.

"We could but it might be more useful to set up a catapult and throw rocks at them. At least rocks would take more than one laser pulse hit to knock out, unlike your rockets, and we have plenty of stone. Bloody fool suggestion."

Todd's face reddened. Allenson wasn't sure whether it indicated embarrassment or anger. Perhaps fortunately the Brasilians chose that moment to switch their cannons to manual and sweep the ridge with laser fire. Impacts washed over the siege lines like dragon's breath. Earth fused into glass. Ground water converted into superheated steam exploded the heat-crystals like a firework display. Allenson might have found it rather beautiful if his face were not pressed into the ground.

Fortunately Buller's besieging units were so well·dug in that the laser cannon barrage was little more than a gesture of defiance. A few bits of vegetation not yet completely scorched by earlier attacks caught fire. Greasy black smoke drifted into the air.

Allenson noticed an odd phenomenon when laser bursts overshot the peninsula into the marsh. The pulses flashed bright green and created rods of thick green vapor in the air like giant fingers pushed into blancmange. The laser fire penetrated only a few meters as if fired into fog.

Crushing his curiosity he examined the town through the scope.

Bodies lay scattered amongst the wreckage where a mortar bomb had hit a market stall in a square. He noticed the bright colors of women's and children's clothes among the fallen.

"There are to be no more artillery demonstrations without my written permission," Allenson said.

Two weeks later and nothing had changed. The Brasilians settled into a garrison force. Allenson's concern that he would have to be the one to break the strategic log jam hardened into certainty. The Stream Army was at the peak of its preparation for battle. The only direction for the army's efficiency now was down. People began to lose interest as marked by a rise in the desertion rate. He was required to demonstrate that service was not voluntary by making examples.

Bored men rapidly become malefactors of one sort or another. The root of the problem often involved alcohol. He considered declaring the army dry but Hawthorn strongly advised against such a course.

In desperation he called an open meeting of all officers for a brainstorming session. The junior officers expressed enthusiasm for a simultaneous dawn assault by foot along both causeways coupled with a low altitude frame attack to the flanks. Morton was the prime mover of this plan. He spoke most eloquently in its support.

Buller heaved himself to his feet and repeated his objections to an assault with his usual pithy tact. Allenson noted the detrimental effect Buller's comments had on the other officers and intervened.

"Thank you, Colonel Buller, for your contribution," Allenson said.

Unfortunately, Buller carried on as if Allenson hadn't spoken.

"And our green army of amateurs is not going to be able to take casualties. They'll break and run and they won't stop until they reach home."

The fact that the comment was possibly true made it all the more unwise, particularly when garnished with Buller's normal contemptuous sneer.

"Sit down, Colonel Buller," Allenson said curtly.

Mouth dropping open, Buller sat. Army to his core he obeyed the voice of command before remembering that he didn't respect amateur generals.

"If I have understood the intelligence reports properly," Ling said, inclining his head respectfully in Hawthorn's direction, "the issue is the naval lifeline into Oxford. Cut that and we have the strategic initiative."

Allenson could have kissed him. The intervention came just in time to stop Buller from saying something stupid.

Morton piped up. "My unit could attack the ships out in the Continuum, General. We could do to the Brasilians what you did to the Terrans in the last war."

Allenson shook his head reluctantly.

"I only had to deal with a single slow moving convoy of lighters moving down a chasm. I knew exactly where to find them and could attack any time I liked. We didn't have to destroy the convoy, just slow it down. Even then it was a close-run thing who collapsed with exhaustion first. You'd have to maintain standing patrols around a hostile base and engage purpose-built gunships. The Brasilians could hit your patrols at times of their own choosing until they wore you down. I have better uses for your men, Morton."

"What about using artillery?" asked a captain who clearly hadn't watched Buller's demonstration. "Landed ships would be sitting ducks."

"Won't work," a major said.

"Major Pynchon, commander of artillery," Ling said quietly to Allenson.

"Our mortars are too light and we don't have enough," Pynchon said.

"Surely the lasercannon—"

"Only if you want them smashed by direct line of sight counterbattery fire," Pynchon said, patiently stating the sheer bloody obvious.

The captain sat down red-faced.

Hawthorn rose and walked to the situation hologram in the center of the horseshoe-shaped amphitheater. The display lit up in yellow and green, giving him a ghostly appearance. He pointed to a third peninsula that jutted into the bay. It was considerably lower and shorter than the other two, terminating in the marsh well before the open water.

"How about we dig in here and put lasercannon in fire pits deep enough to keep them out of line of sight to counterbattery fire but just shallow enough to light up incoming ships. The end of this peninsula should be close enough to the open water to give us a working angle of fire."

There was dead silence and Ling inspected the ceiling as if it had been painted by an artist of singular talent.

"Look, I know lasercannon are ineffectual against military transports and large ships but they could scare off the tramp ship captains," Hawthorn said, clearly surprised at the lack of response.

"I can see why you might think so," Ling said carefully "but it won't work."

Hawthorn showed his exasperation. "Why the hell not?"

Ling explained. "The marsh, you see, surrounding the peninsula, has a peculiar biochemistry. Vapors given off by the mud ignite from laser shots. The resulting hydrofluoric acid steam mix is highly corrosive. You'd be lucky to get off three or four shots and the pulses wouldn't get out of the swampy area before dissipating into heat."

"So that's what I saw down on the siege lines," Allenson said, recalling the laser pulses ending in bright green flashes. Now that he thought about it, they hadn't actually made contact with the sediment but ended in the air.

"So how come these vapors aren't a problem for people on the causeways to Oxford and the port complex?" Hawthorn asked.

"It's a matter of height, the gasses being heavier than air. Occasionally conditions coincide to cause the causeways to be submerged but that's hardly much of a problem. People just hop over the top using frames or wear a 'breather.' The vapors aren't dangerous unless you inhale them or ignite them with a spark or some such."

"Have you never thought of draining the marsh?" Allenson asked, curious as to why Oxford allowed itself to be almost cut off by useless and potentially dangerous swamps.

Ling shrugged. "People have thought about it and even tried to raise money for land reclamation projects. Nothing has ever got very far. Sooner or later there's an accident taking out the pumping gear and, well, land's cheap around Oxford."

"So we just sit here until the Brasilians have stockpiled sufficient materiel to attack us," Hawthorn said impatiently.

"Unless you have a better idea, Colonel," Ling replied.

★ CHAPTER 15 ★

The Indirect Approach

A few days later Allenson slumped in his office, wrestling with the endless and insoluble problems associated with logistics, when there was a knock at the door. Military historians like to write about battles and stories of great derring-do. Real soldiers spend most of their time organizing supplies and trying to prevent their men dying of various foul diseases, malnutrition or boredom-induced accidents.

"Yes," Allenson snarled, irritated at the interruption when he had almost worked out why the camp bakery was churning out loaves wholesale but no one had any fresh bread. Apparently the quartermasters demanded that the old stale bread be eaten up first. The end result was that the troops' bread was always stale no matter how much fresh bread was baked.

One of Krenz's men cautiously put his head around the door.

"There's a lady to see you, boss. I told her you'd ordered not to be disturbed but she was pretty damn rude about it."

Krenz's goon had a nose that had been broken at least twice and a vivid-white knife scar that ran across his left cheek. Allenson's imagination balked at imagining what he would consider rude.

"You had better show her in," Allenson said, intrigued.

"Yes, gov, but she also refuses to be searched," the goon said plaintively, "in fact she told me to stick my detector up my—"

"I get the picture," Allenson replied.

The goon momentarily retracted his head. It reappeared on the right-hand side of a lady in traveling clothes consisting of a lined green cloak and boots. His associate goon on her left-hand side fingered his lasercarbine as if escorting a ferocious carnivore who might turn on them without provocation.

"Stand down, men," Allenson said. "Although undoubtedly highly dangerous, the lady has had plenty of opportunities over the years to assassinate me at her leisure. Hello Trina, what are you doing here?"

Trina waited for the honor guard departure before replying.

"Really, husband, getting a little paranoiac aren't we?"

"Um, well, it's not me. My Head of Security is overzealous."

"Yes, I heard Hawthorn was back," Trina said neutrally.

"So what are you doing here?" Allenson asked. "Not that I'm not delighted to see you," he added hastily, getting up to hug her in case she got the wrong impression.

"Yes, well, you should be flattered that I bothered," she said, mollified. "You know how I hate traveling."

Allenson pulled up a chair for her and, after a suitable inspection of its cleanliness, she sat.

"There are stories circulating that morale in the army is not all it might be."

"There are always moaners," Allenson replied, somewhat defensively.

"Yes, but the complaints are increasing in letters home and not just from the usual suspects. I decided to bring a deputation of officer's Wags to boost them out of it."

"Wags?" Allenson asked.

"Wives and girlfriends: we've formed a club"

"What? How many? What am I going to do with them?"

Trina raised an eyebrow.

"Do? You? With them? Nothing I should hope, husband. No doubt we can leave the various couples to sort out their own arrangements to everyone's satisfaction."

Allenson blushed. Trina looked stunning. No, she looked like Trina but she behaved with more energy than she had shown for years. Being thrown back on her own resources to run their demesne obviously agreed with her. He had tried to take the weight off her shoulders after they had married, perhaps too much. He knew he had an unfortunate tendency to take over down to the smallest detail. Had he stifled her? She smiled at him and he forgot about the self-obsession.

He opened the office door and yelled out.

"I'm in conference if anyone asks and I do not expect to be disturbed by anything short of a Brasilian major assault."

He slammed the door, walked back to his desk and touched an icon that sealed his office suite from prying. He lifted Trina's hand and touched it to his lips.

"You must be very tired after your long journey and there is a comfortable couch in my private room. Why don't I show it to you? You may want to lie down or something."

He ushered her into the back room with an urgency that he hadn't shown for some time.

"Did I teach you nothing about project management?" Trina asked rhetorically. "What do you think you have a staff for? Hmmm? I leave you alone for five minutes and you're back to your old habit of letting your juniors pass their problems upwards."

Allenson mumbled something about duty that didn't sound very convincing even to him.

"You must be the only general in the world who tries to micromanage the bread ration."

"An army marches on its stomach," Allenson countered, trying to remember where he had heard the cliché.

"This army won't be doing much marching anywhere if their commander continues to confuse his role with the chef. Pass the order down the line that you expect the men to have freshly baked bread each day and that you'll be carrying out snap inspections with a view to making an example of someone. Better still, send Hawthorn. That should spread some fear and loathing where it will do most good."

"It might at that," Allenson said feebly.

Trina ignored him.

"Come on, get the files open and let's go through them to decide who's going to get dumped on—I mean delegated to."

For the next two hours Trina reorganized his workload. She used a mixture of blackmail, threats and flattery to parcel tasks out amongst various officers. After a token protest or two he let her get on with it and by the end his burden had been significantly reduced.

"There, now you have time to think," Trina said with some satisfaction.

"That will be something of a novelty," Allenson replied.

He buzzed for Boswell, who appeared in the doorway within seconds, which suggested he had been expecting a summons. Trina did a double take at the servant, possibly because of his attire. Today it involved fluorescent orange shorts down to the knees and a shirt decorated with hypnotic whirlpools.

Allenson didn't turn a hair. He'd seen it all before.

"See if you can find two tolerably clean cups and make us some cafay, please."

"Yes, sar, or I can make tea if Lady Allenson would prefer it."

"Where did you get hold of tea?" Allenson asked.

"Oh, well you know, contacts," Boswell said vaguely.

"Tea would be most welcome," Trina replied.

"Right you are, ma'am."

Boswell disappeared.

"Does he always dress like that?" Trina asked faintly.

"No, sometimes the colors clash horribly," Allenson replied. He thought for a moment. "How did he know who you were?"

Trina laughed. "If you want to know what's really going on in a house you visit the servants' hall. Their intelligence service is second to none."

Boswell reappeared almost immediately with a silver tray holding a rather decent tea service including an ornate tea pot. A small plate of Garibaldi biscuits accompanied the refreshments.

"I thought the dons had locked away their private possessions to protect them from us coarse soldiery," Allenson said, noting the college coat of arms decorating the china.

"Did they, sar?" Boswell asked. "The lock on the senior common room door must have been faulty because it opened with just a little push."

Trina covered her mouth but Allenson knew she was grinning from the sparkle in her eyes.

"You can put the tray down. I'll ring if I need you," Allenson said, wishing he hadn't asked.

"I enjoyed helping you, quite like old times," Trina said, sipping her tea. "You know, I'm glad Hawthorn has turned up."

"Really?" Allenson asked skeptically.

Trina waved a hand.

"I've never pretended to like the man. I admit I was not unhappy when he took himself off. Where did he go, incidentally?"

"Apparently he was running a Rider trading station deep in the Hinterlands."

Trina nodded.

"I assumed it would be something like that. Imprisoned in a labor camp under an assumed name was the other possibility."

"I thought he was dead," Allenson said.

"I never did," Trina replied. "The Hawthorns of this universe aren't so easy to kill. As I said, he was never my favorite but I'm glad he's back. He's devious, violent, ruthless and suspicious to the point of paranoia. He's also utterly loyal to you. I can't think of a better man to watch your back."

"He's running a spy network inside Oxford."

"Really, I would love to see what he's found out."

Allenson unlocked the file and let her flip through it.

"Astonishing," she said. "Where'd he get all this?"

"Well . . ."

"On second thought, don't tell me. I suspect I don't want to know the sordid details."

"What do you think?" Allenson asked, pouring her another cup of tea.

"The same as you I expect," Trina said neutrally.

"Humor me; I would value a second opinion."

She grimaced.

"If these reports of the Brasilian build up in Oxford are true, I suspect we are losing the logistic war. The balance of power is inexorably shifting in their direction."

Allenson sighed. "I agree."

"Presumably they'll attack out of the city when they have a sufficiently favorable force ratio."

"I would in their position but they may be content simply to make the city impregnable while letting us stew."

Trina thought about that while she sipped her tea.

Finally, she said, "Yes, that makes sense, so why would you attack if you were the Brasilian commander?"

"Because the new pan-Colonial state consists of just two institutions, the Assembly and the army. Of these the army is by far the most important. The Assembly hasn't even managed to decide on a Declaration of Independence. They could never hold things together without the army. Brasilia can stop the revolt dead in its tracks by destroying the field army. It's a hostage to fortune pinned down here outside Oxford. The Assembly by contrast is a shambles."

"Then you have to break the log-jam immediately, Allen. Your situation isn't going to improve."

"You think I don't know that?" Allenson replied sharply. "Sorry Trina, I'm angry at my own lack of foresight, not you."

"Look," she said, "have you tried making a list of your assets and liabilities in the hope it might stimulate something. Come on, I'll help."

"Very well."

He slipped his notebook out of a pocket and fished around until he found a pencil.

"Your notebook? This *is* getting serious," Trina said.

"Somehow the act of physically writing on organic material rather than dictating at a hologram fires my imagination. I used to use it to write poetry."

He laughed.

"Very, very bad poetry."

"I know," Trina replied. "I sneaked a look at it when you weren't around. So what are your assets?"

Allenson jotted down notes as he went along.

"Okay, let's see, I outnumber them in light infantry, my troops are reasonably trained and enthusiastic, I've a few mortars and lasercannon, my logistical tail is uncutable and I also have some hydraulic pumps for what they're worth."

"Liabilities?"

"My army is green, brittle and I'm desperately short of heavy weapons."

"And their assets?"

"Professional troops who will withstand losses, a position damn near impregnable to light infantry behind a poisonous marsh, and a major port facility for shipping in supplies and reinforcements."

"Their liabilities?"

"Everything has to be transported in through the Continuum but as I can't stop them . . ."

He shrugged.

"I'm not sure this is helping."

"Give your mind time to dwell on the matter," Trina said. "You made your reputation in the Terran wars by not doing things the proper way. We can't defeat a Home World by playing the game according to their rules. You showed how to beat them by changing the rules and doing the unexpected."

She looked him directly in the eyes.

"It seems to me, Allen, that you need to stop wallowing in self-pity and start thinking around the problem. You have to find an indirect approach."

Hawthorn drank on his own at the end of a rough bar in a small village outside Cambridge. He was not exactly a social drinker; actually he was not exactly social under most conditions. The bar was almost empty. It had more patrons when Hawthorn arrived but the clientele drifted away as the evening progressed. The barman made an attempt or two at conversation with Hawthorn but gave up after repeated rebuffs. He moodily wiped a glass with a dirty cloth that probably added more smears than it removed. He approached Hawthorn.

"Anything you require, master?" the barman asked, tentatively.

"Another bottle."

"Will you be drinking it here or shall I wrap it to go?"

Hawthorn fixed him with piercing blue eyes but didn't answer. The barman placed the container carefully on the bar and found something to do elsewhere. Hawthorn poured himself another slug from a bottle of tonk sporting a brand that was new to him. He took a pull. It was no better or worse than any other but then he hadn't expected it would be.

The pub door opened. Hawthorn had his back to it but was able to monitor who came in or out in a mirror hung behind the bar.

The newcomer paused to check out the room as if looking for someone. He was splendidly attired in voluminous purple pantaloons and an electric blue cape. The man came and stood by Hawthorn.

"If you're here to keep me company then you can bugger off, Boswell," Hawthorn said, without turning round.

Boswell signaled the barman with a raised finger and ordered a plum cider. He said nothing until the barman provided the requested beverage and departed.

"No offense, Colonel, but drinking with you is not my idea of a relaxing night out."

Hawthorn grunted, amused.

"I need to tell you something and I wanted to do it where we couldn't be overheard. In fact I didn't even want anyone to know we had a private conversation."

Hawthorn put his glass down and looked directly at the servant for the first time.

"Now you interest me. Let's sit over there."

Hawthorn pointed to a table in a quiet corner. He walked around the table to take the chair with his back to the wall.

"I was in a bar in Cambridge when this bloke started up a conversation about the cider," Boswell said when they were seated.

"You knew him?" Hawthorn asked.

Boswell shook his head.

"He kept trying to steer the conversation around to the general."

"Really, what did you tell him?"

Boswell lifted his head and looked Hawthorn in the eye.

"Nothing. I don't discuss my clients."

"A good policy," Hawthorn observed.

"I didn't think much of it at the time but I found out later that this bloke was in the habit of buying the soldiers drinks and talking about the general. Apparently, one of them had pointed me out as the general's servant. I dunno, it just seemed odd when I thought about it so I decided to report the thing. Anyway, I have so I'll bugger off."

Hawthorn stopped him by gripping his arm. He laughed as if Boswell had said something funny.

"Some plum brandy for my friend, here," Hawthorn said loudly to the barman.

Hawthorn started a monologue about a girl he'd known who ran a burlesque show until the barman had finished serving them.

"I don't suppose you took any pics of our curious friend?" Hawthorn asked.

"No sorry, but I would recognize him again," Boswell said eagerly. "He had an unusual orange tint to his eyes and a mass of scar tissue on his neck."

Hawthorn smiled and inwardly cursed. There was nothing better at disguising a face than a few hideous defects to distract attention from everything else.

"No matter, I will arrange a hard cash payment for you in a way that doesn't look as if it comes from me."

"There's no need for that, sar, I don't need bribing. I pride myself on my loyalty to my clients."

"If I had any doubts about your loyalty, Boswell, I would have removed you long ago," Hawthorn said, pleasantly enough, but something about his smile seemed to bother the servant. "It's not a bribe but a bonus for services outside the normal expectation of your duties."

"Oh, a bonus," Boswell said, brightening. "In that case I gladly accept, sar."

The way people divided simple acts into classes according to complex social rules had always puzzled Hawthorn. Especially with women. Some ladies had fixed fees for their favors while others required flattery and presents. It was all the same to Hawthorn, but apparently the difference was a matter of great importance to the women.

And with people like Boswell, a bribe was an insult but a bonus was a compliment. It was still just money, something whose only value was in its usefulness to achieving one's goals. No matter, Hawthorn learned society's rules and how to game them.

He had a rapid change of mind and insisted that Boswell keep him company for the rest of the evening's entertainment. Boswell had chosen his moment wisely. It was very unlikely that anyone who mattered would ever hear of their meeting, but Hawthorn liked to play the odds. He wanted to leave memories of only a couple of pals enjoying a jolly evening. The best place to hide something was in plain sight. Hawthorn was a good raconteur and worked to keep Boswell in stitches. He left a decent tip for the barman when he finally paid up and they staggered off into the night.

Actually Hawthorn was nowhere near as smashed as he looked. He came to a decision. Allenson's security would have to move up a gear from a defensive reactive posture to a more aggressive proactive strategy. He was going to have to kick arse and get answers.

★ ★ ★

It turned out that Trina had traveled with a number of cases of wine, plum brandy, and assorted sweetmeats in vacuum packs. Dinner in the officers' mess that evening was a great success and not just because of the novel varieties of food. The leavening effect of the ladies transformed the mood. Allenson did his best to join in but he was not by nature a party animal and at the moment his responsibilities lay heavy on his shoulders.

Sleep came slowly that night. He lay for what seemed a lifetime listening to Trina's fluttering breath. When he did sleep it was fitful and much disturbed by dreams. Sari Destry danced in front of him singing a bawdy ditty about the indirect approach. She waved a document but danced out of reach whenever he tried to grab it.

"Too slow, Allen, too slow," she trilled.

Somehow she disappeared to be replaced by Hawthorn, who balanced an impossibly heavy hydraulic pump on his shoulder.

"Can't wait for you to catch up, old son, I've got a battleship to build," Hawthorn said.

Allenson stood on the causeway above Oxford. Laser pulses reached slowly out for him like colored marbles rolling down the channels in a children's toy. He soared into the air avoiding the fingers of light. His flight path went over Oxford.

"Look that man's got no clothes on," yelled a small child pointing up at the sky.

Women and girls laughed and pointed. He tried to cover his nakedness with his hands, which caused them to laugh all the more. In desperation he threw himself away from the city, trying to hide amongst the vapors over the marsh.

Trina leaned out of her carriage and shook her head sadly to see him.

"You're not going to find the indirect approach by rolling around in the mud stark naked are you?"

His stepmother sat next to Trina.

"He's always such a disappointment," his mother said to his wife. "The wrong brother died."

Allenson flushed. He tried to defend himself but the words wouldn't come out of his mouth. He sank deeper into the mud. When he tried to climb out his legs wouldn't work. Hawthorn sat on a stone pier fiddling with his pump.

"Look it works fine even in the vapors," Hawthorn said. "I could drain the swamp."

Kiesche appeared beside him.

"It wasn't the pumps that blew but something else. Some idiot always disobeys the rules and brings in an unauthorized bit of kit sooner or later. Kaboom!"

Allenson tried to yell for help but his mouth filled with vile-tasting ooze. A strangled scream was all he could manage before the filthy stuff filled his lungs.

He woke and sat up with a jerk.

"What?" Trina said, dozily.

"Just a nightmare, go back to sleep," Allenson said.

Eventually, he took his own advice. When he woke in the morning he knew just how he was going to capture Oxford.

★ CHAPTER 16 ★

The Battle of Oxford

Allenson adjusted the mask over his face until it covered his mouth, eyes and nose. It supplied metallic air that tasted like an iron-based tonic wine. A thick cable ran to a box strapped over his left hip that acted as an artificial lung. It filtered out undesirable vapors and pumped in nitrogen and oxygen. Exhaled air evacuated through a valve in front. Something in his humid breath reacted with the marsh vapors to create a white smoke that strung slowly into streamers in the light breeze.

The mask design assumed the limited oxygen requirements of a man doing no more exercise than he would taking a gentle stroll. Unfortunately Allenson was helping to pull a line attached to a sledge loaded with hydraulic equipment.

The sticky ooze sucked at his feet, making each step a struggle. He tried to remember which idiot had decided that it would be easier to drag sledges through the mud at the side of the peninsula rather than manhandle the loads along the rocky high ground. He couldn't recall but he did remember which idiot had approved the idea—him.

Not that he'd had much choice. He had explored the concept of modifying various vehicles to run along the peninsula but it was full of jagged stones. Sooner or later there would be a catastrophe letting explosive fumes into the motor.

He took another deep breath, sucking in air against the resistance of the equipment and exhaling so hard that pressure built up in the mask. The mask lifted slightly. When it snapped back into position the merest trace of acidic vapor entered around the edge, stinging his eyes and nose. He resisted the urge to cough. The pressure pulse would probably let in more of the toxic whiff and crease his eyeballs for good measure.

Steadying his breathing he took another step and heaved on the line. Something under his foot squirmed. The locals assured him that nothing bigger than a bacterium lived in the swamp, so the movement must be a release of gas. An unconvinced part of his mind toyed with pictures of large amorphous things with tentacles and parrot beaks. *Get a grip, man,* he thought, forcing his imagination back to sleep.

The officer in front of him was on a rest period. He held a nightscope, one of the handful of devices that Kiesche approved for use in the swamp. Hawthorn ruthlessly strip-searched each soldier before they started, discarding anything with a power source that just might create a spark if it malfunctioned. Allenson insisted on being publically searched first to set an example.

Guns were the first to go. Hawthorn personally chose each person for the security detail and muscle part of the expedition but it was still astonishing how many tried to smuggle in a pistol. Each one assured Hawthorn that he only had it as a safeguard for unforeseen circumstances. Hawthorn ignored it all.

He encouraged the troopers provide themselves with a variety of sharp-edged and blunt instruments as personal choice dictated. Allenson could not imagine any circumstances where they might prove useful but such primitive weapons could do no harm and were a sop to morale. Many of the people Hawthorn selected were from the ranks of his security group rather than the line soldiery. This no doubt explained their attachment to clubs and the like.

"About a hundred and fifty meters to go," the officer with the scope said breaking into Allenson's thought processes.

The small speaker in his mask made his voice squeaky, like someone who inhaled helium as a party trick. Allenson nodded to save his breath for sledge pulling. There was enough ambient light cast across the swamp from the port and the city for Allenson to see the officer as a dark outline. Theoretically anyone training a scope on the swamp from Oxford could spot Allenson's small expedition, but why would they bother? There was little they could do about it anyway.

The expedition pulled five sledges in all, three carrying equipment and the other two supplies. It took another hour to cross the last one hundred and fifty meters as everyone was close to exhaustion. One man fell face down in the slime. Unfortunately he panicked and pulled off his mask when sediment blocked its valves. One breath was all it took. His companions got the mask back on him but by then he was still. They piled him on a sledge but Allenson suspected that the trooper was already dead.

The soldiers were so knackered when they reached their destination that Allenson told them to climb up on the low jumble of rocks and wait for dawn before unloading. He sent back a coded message signaling the party's safe arrival before wedging himself uncomfortably between two boulders. Rather to his surprise, he dozed off almost immediately.

Trina and Ling watched the operation from Allenson's office via a secure line to a nightscope positioned in the siege lines. Trina's hands clenched when the trooper slipped into the ooze but she showed no other sign of the stress she was under.

"That's not the general," Ling said confidently. "I can see him quite clearly at the front."

"I believe you are right," Trina replied.

They both lied. All the scope showed were struggling silhouettes barely distinguishable from the background. Her knuckles stayed white until the signal arrived, the precise form of the message indicating that all essential personnel were in place which must of necessity include Allenson. In her relief she talked more than she would normally have considered necessary.

"I don't understand why Allen had to personally undertake this operation," she said. "It's not like he knows anything about engineering."

"Strictly speaking that is true," Ling said carefully. "But the strike is critical so I expect he wanted to be on hand in case unexpected developments required an immediate response from him personally."

"Like what?" Trina asked.

"Well, anything I suppose," Ling replied, evasively.

Trina glared at the chief of staff.

"Give me an example?" she asked, remorselessly pressing the point.

"The Brasilians might, well . . . suppose . . ."

His voice trailed off.

"That's what I thought," Trina said crushingly. "There is no good reason for my husband to hazard himself."

"It's the first offensive move by the army so I expect he wanted to set an example by leading from the front," Ling said loyally.

"Ridiculous, and you know it," Trina snapped. "Generals make plans but their combat officers carry them out. He's just being irresponsible because he can't bear to stay away from the sharp end. It never seems to occur to him that he is as mortal as anyone else. What will happen to his precious army if he gets himself killed? Answer me that? People die in wars. They die stupidly, pointlessly by sheer chance."

Ling stayed silent.

"Sorry, Colonel Ling, I'm just worried about him. I shouldn't embarrass a gentleman by inviting him to criticize his superior officer's ludicrous behavior even if it is just privately to the man's wife."

Ling muttered something

"What?"

"I said it will soon be light."

"Really? I thought you said: especially to his wife."

"The difficult part is over. There's nothing now the Brasilians can do," Ling said reassuringly.

Trina would have none of it.

"I don't pretend to know anything about war, Colonel, but I do understand business. It's exactly when you know your competitor can't counter your move that he does so anyway."

"Colonel Hawthorn is in charge of the operation and I'm sure he will take good care of the general. From what I've seen I would say the colonel is a most effective officer."

"Oh, he has many competencies," Trina said tonelessly.

Ling glanced at her sharply but her mouth was set in a hard line as she watched the scope. She clearly didn't intend to expand upon the point.

A figure danced in the flames, his head thrown back, his mouth open, soundlessly screaming. His hair blazed like molten lava. Allenson reached out to try to pull him from the flames but the figure shook him off. The shaking went on and on.

"Rise and shine, General," Hawthorn said, and shook him again.

Allenson licked his lips inside the mask. He put his head close to Hawthorn's so he could speak quietly.

"I wasn't, you know, saying anything odd, was I?"

Hawthorn looked at him sharply.

"Have the nightmares started again?"

Allenson shook his head. The mask disguised his features. It was easier to lie just by body language although he doubted if Hawthorn was fooled. He levered himself awkwardly to his feet. One of his knees had frozen and his back felt as if a regiment had marched up and down it.

"Too many nights sleeping in a soft bed," Hawthorn said with a grin.

Allenson told him to commit an act that a double jointed teenage acrobat would have found demanding and surveyed their surroundings. Rosy light filtered over the horizon, flooding the green tinge of the marsh with a pastel pink. The first flicker of the sun gleamed where the sea met the sky.

Breakfast consisted of a tube of nutrient fluid with added stimulants squirted through a valve in the mask. It tasted like salted baby food. Kiesche was already up with his engineering crew to supervise the assembly of his apparatus. He hopped from installation to installation like an overworked midwife dealing with three simultaneous births.

The heavy duty pipes that linked the machinery had to be bolted on manually as the use of power tools constituted too great a hazard. Each of the three engines consisted of three separate modules: a power supply, a hydraulic pump, and a catapult with twisted steel torsion bars. Connecting the modules involved a great deal of sweat and general cursing. Kiesche constructed the gear in situ on any available bit of flat surface so each installation was laid out differently. Heavy steel cables attached to pylons driven into crevices in the rocks by sledge hammers locked down the catapult sections.

Allenson and Hawthorn had little to do but stay out of Kiesche and Pynchon's way. Allenson amused himself by observing the port and city. The port was already awake. A trans-Bight civilian freighter had landed during the night on the waters of the bay. Tugs pushed and pulled the vessel up against the dockside where laborers waited by the unloading chutes and cranes. A couple of smaller tramps sat on the concrete aprons.

Over in the town it was still quiet. One or two early birds hurried through the streets but the majority of the citizenry snored on. He examined the lasercannon towers carefully. From his vantage point in the swamp he could see they were made from preassembled modules like giant scaffolding, which explained how the Brasilians had erected them quickly. He had wondered whether they could be toppled, but the lattice arrangement of supports would be difficult to hit. Knocking out just one or two struts would have little impact on the integrity of the structures.

A flash of reflected sunlight from one of the towers caught his eye. He jacked up the magnification on the scope as high as he could go without losing all detail in hand-shake. The scope's stabilization function helped enormously. A figure hunched over an observation device that was pointed in the direction of the expedition.

He nudged Hawthorn.

"We've been spotted."

"They were bound to clock us sooner or later," Hawthorn replied.

"I suppose so." Allenson chuckled. "They must wonder what the hell we're up to."

After another hour Kiesche approached Allenson, rubbing his hands together in satisfaction like an excited schoolboy.

"They're done and I've dry tested the systems. The power supplies discharged a little overnight but I've got men replacing the lost energy."

"So I see," Allenson replied.

A man stood over each of the three power supplies pumping backwards and forwards on a lever. Manual recharging was the only sure way to replenish power into the sealed batteries without risking an explosion.

"We'll have to set up a rota with a frequent changeover. The men won't be able to stand that level of work for long in these damn masks."

Allenson walked gingerly across the rocks, which were slippery with some disgusting slime-mold like growth. He was naturally clumsy at the best of times. On this surface a fall could damage more than just his dignity. Pynchon bent over one of the pumping modules, intently watching a pressure gauge crudely welded onto the case. He looked up when Allenson approached and switched off the pump.

"Morning, sir, just powering up one of the engines. I intend to try a few shots to calibrate tension against range before we open up with the full battery. Do you have any particular mark you'd like me to try to hit?"

Oddly enough, Allenson's attention had been so fixed on getting their homemade artillery into position that he hadn't given the matter much thought. He looked across the bay allowing himself the luxury of choosing a target.

"You see that big bugger tied up against the dock?" Allenson said, pointing to the newly arrived freighter.

"Yes, sir," Pynchon replied with a grin.

"That's your mark."

Pynchon measured the range with his datapad. He carried out a quick calculation before running the pump for another five minutes or so. The torsion bars on the third module imperceptibly tightened, causing the engine to make sharp clicking noises as various components took up the load.

Pynchon adjusted the rake of the carbon fiber and steel tube that served as a barrel, before signaling to the loaders. Two men carried a heavy iron ball to the muzzle and rolled it down the barrel where it lay on a striker connected to the torsion bars.

"Stand clear," Pynchon said, testing the various cables anchoring the module to the rock one last time.

The artilleryman fired the piece by flipping a lever, because they didn't want to risk a remote. A mechanical delay gave Pynchon a valuable half second to put a couple of meters between himself and the device before it released. The catapult emitted a great clang and thumped against the ground. It bounced a few millimeters into the air before being caught on the cables. Allenson winced, thinking of the strain on the pressurized pipes connecting the pump.

"Would you look at that," Hawthorn said in wonder.

The ball soared majestically into the air, clearly visible to the naked eye. It described a high parabolic curve before dropping into the bay with a visible splash. Unfortunately it fell well short of the ship.

"I was concerned that we wouldn't be able to see the fall of shot,"

Pynchon said, half to himself, "but that isn't going to be a problem. The equipment is less efficient than our initial tests suggested. No matter, we'll try another round with ten percent more pressure."

The last was directed at a technician on the pump who pressed a large red button to reset the safety and switch on the apparatus. It took ten minutes to re-tension the catapult. Not a devastatingly fast rate of fire, Allenson reflected, but the targets weren't going anywhere. No one in the port appeared to have noticed the attack.

Pynchon fired again. This time the ball sailed clean over the ship and kicked a chip from the tough material of the syncrete. They certainly noticed that in the port but didn't connect it with Allenson's little band. Dockers stood curiously around the crater, alternating between peering down at the damage and gazing up at the sky.

Pynchon's third shot hit the water just in front of the floating ship and bounced into the hull with a crack that could be heard across the bay.

"Skipping stones," Allenson said delightedly, imitating throwing a stone across the water with a flick of his wrist.

"I remember your brother Todd was a demon at that," Hawthorn said with a grin.

"Happier times," Allenson replied, regretfully.

He turned to the engineering officer.

"That completes your part in our enterprise, Major Kiesche. You and your technicians may as well walk back and get a decent meal and rest. I expect you'll be glad to get these damned masks off and enjoy a hot shower."

"I'll send my men back, sir, but with your permission I think I should stay just in case a problem arises with the equipment."

Allenson grinned within his mask. Kiesche didn't fool him for a moment. The man wouldn't miss seeing his inventions in action for anything.

The artillery proved to be horribly inaccurate. Only one in three shots managed to hit even such a large target as the freighter but they had plenty of time and plenty of iron. The solid shot inflicted limited damage but you can erode granite if you flick enough water drops at it.

It didn't take the Brasilians long to join up the dots and work out the source of the bombardment. They reacted by raking the area with lasercannon fire. Fingers of green punched into the air in front, generating opaque clouds. Acid rain fell into the swamp in heavy drips. When they realized that they weren't getting results, the enemy's next tried focusing a group of lasercannon on a single spot.

Boiling enemy reached deep into the vapor but the extra power was counterproductive. All it did was spawn a massive chemical reaction that completely shielded the rocky outcrop. None of this affected Pynchon's bombardment. Not being able to see the target was little disadvantage as the catapults didn't exactly have sights anyway.

The green fog slowly dissipated over half an hour, finally allowing Allenson to see the fruits of their efforts. A dockside crane jib hung over at a crazy angle, swaying from side to side. The container being unloaded had half slipped out of the lifting cables so that one corner was smashed on the ground. Dockers swarmed around the wreckage trying to make it safe before the whole thing collapsed.

The Port defenses were on automatic, firing at each iron ball as it left the protective screen of marsh vapors. The Brasilian lasercannon were quality kit and the artillery rate of fire glacial so the energy pulses repeatedly hit and lit up the shot. Defenses like these easily destroyed artillery shells and missiles. Lasers wrecked their delicate fuses and thrusters and set off the various unstable chemicals in the warheads. On the other hand, heating a lump of iron white hot before it smashed into you was not an advantage. The Brasilians eventually worked this out and shut down their lasercannons. The civilian laborers, not unreasonably, took this as a sign to abandon work.

The captain of the freighter inevitably lost patience with the situation. The freighter was valuable private property and he was responsible to the owners for its safety. Tugs maneuvered the ship away from the dockside. As soon as it was clear, the ship extended pylons and lifted off. The artillerymen raised a cheer, which sounded like more of a squawk because of the masks. Nevertheless, the sentiment was clear.

All through the afternoon they intermittently bombarded the port, mostly achieving little more than chipping tiny fragments of syncrete out of the aprons. One of the tramps lifted off but the other stayed, perhaps rendered inoperable. Pynchon didn't manage to hit it but he did smash holes in a number of the port buildings and facilities.

Allenson buttonholed the man in a short break in the bombardment while his men recharged the batteries.

"Major Pynchon, I believe we will rotate the artillery crews this afternoon before it gets dark. I don't want to lose any more men in that damn mud. With the benefit of hindsight, moving the equipment at night was overly cautious. There's not a damn thing the Brasilians can do to stop us short of attacking through our siege lines and sealing off our supplies from the land. Colonel Buller would love them to try that."

"Very good, General."

"You may as well take your people back as well, Hawthorn. There's no need for a security detail here."

"Oh, I think we'll hang around for a mite longer, Allenson," Hawthorn replied with a cheery disregard for military lines of command.

"As you wish," Allenson replied, avoiding giving a direct order that would not be obeyed.

Allenson slept badly again that night. Hawthorn silently observed him in the morning drumming his fingers in an irritating manner on a power supply casing.

"Okay," Allenson said, conceding the unspoken point. "I'll go back with this afternoon's shift."

A civilian freighter phased in over the sea and started its descent into the bay. Pynchon opened the bombardment as soon as he had the ship in range. By chance he scored a lucky hit on the hull not long after it settled into the water to wait for the tugs. This captain didn't attempt to unload but simply relifted and reversed course.

A few tramp ships made fast blockade-runs into the port, dumping boxed and barrels on the syncrete before scuttling out. Pynchon failed to hit any of the relatively small targets but it was not for want of trying.

"You know something, I think we've done it," Allenson said to Hawthorn, resisting the urge to destroy his credibility by dancing a jig. It was damn difficult keeping the *gravitas* of a general when matters went well, easier somehow in the midst of catastrophe.

"The Brasilians can't survive on anything like that level of supply. There's not enough there to support the civilian population let alone the army. We've damn well cut their logistic line. Now they'll have to break the stalemate by attacking our siege lines and we'll have all the advantages of a dug-in position. Their only other choice is to ask for terms."

"If I was the Brasilian general I would think about driving unnecessary mouths out of the city," Hawthorn said thoughtfully. "We should of course refuse to let them pass our siege lines. It's not in our interests to lessen the pressure."

Allenson sighed.

"That's logical but we couldn't do it. Suppose the Brasilians simply barred the city to refugees, leaving them to starve on the peninsulas? Think of the message it would send to other colonial communities and the legacy of bitterness and hatred it would incur down the generations."

He shook his head firmly.

"No in the event of an expulsion we'll take in anyone who asks. We'll find them food and accommodation and we'll make sure everything is publicized here and back in the Home Worlds. If nothing else we should be able to claim the moral high ground and get some propaganda use out of the situation."

Hawthorn shrugged.

"I suppose you're right. It wouldn't concern me, but lots of things upset other people that don't bother me much."

Allenson reflected on the old saying that when you force the enemy into a corner where he has only two possible choices, the sensible one or the stupid alternative, then you can rely on him choosing the third option that you've failed to consider. So it was at Oxford.

Pynchon kept up an intermittent bombardment of the port more to remind the Brasilians that the Stream artillery was still there than with the hope of hitting anything vulnerable. Allenson took a rest on a rock on the side of the peninsula facing the port so he could observe events.

While he cogitated, a man rushed up, breathing heavily through his mask. He stumbled over a jagged projection until Allenson caught him.

"Steady son, this has been a near bloodless operation so far and I've a mind to keep it that way," Allenson said

"The guvnor says you should come quick, boss," the man got out.

Allenson translated guvnor as Hawthorn, whose security men had a cavalier attitude to military terminology.

"I'm to tell you that the bastards in the town are up to something."

Having discharged his duty, the trooper sat down hard and bent over to catch his breath.

Allenson gingerly threaded his way over the treacherous slippery jagged stone to the Oxford side of the peninsula. Hawthorn studied something intently through a scope.

"What's up?" Allenson asked.

"Not sure, three boats have put out from behind a pier below Oxford. Have a look yourself."

Hawthorn handed Allenson the scope.

It took a moment for Allenson to adjust the binocular to his eye width—Hawthorn had a narrower face—then another half second to find the boats and up the magnification.

Small launches bounced over the waves in ragged line-astern formation. They had squared off bows and flat bottoms, judging from the manner in which they flopped over a swell. Strangest of all, large air fans at the rear pushed the launches forward. Boxlike rudders behind the blades controlled steering. It all seemed incredibly inefficient.

"What the hell are they?" Allenson asked.

"I've been asking myself that," Hawthorn said faithfully. "Never seen anything like them before, but I suppose they would be useful in shallow water."

"They're crammed with men," Allenson said.

"Yeah, I noticed that," Hawthorn replied, dryly. "I suspect the boats are bigger than they look in the scope. The bloody thing tends to foreshorten shapes. I reckon they could have a dozen or more men in each hull."

"That's damn near thrice our strength but surely they can't get to us. Flat-bottomed or no they still would get stuck out in the marsh where it's mostly liquid."

"Yeah, I agree, but they don't look like a fishing expedition. Perhaps the Brasilians are treating their men to trips around the bay. Can you see ice creams or amusing hats?"

"No," Allenson replied curtly.

Hawthorn's sense of humor could be ill placed.

The launches turned in line, sliding sideways in wide arcs that suggested they had no keels at all.

"Shit!" Hawthorn said. "Come on."

The boats began to run in towards the marsh. Allenson and Hawthorn scrambled back up to the artillery modules.

"Krenz, where the hell are you?" Hawthorn shouted.

"Here, gov," replied an anonymously masked man.

"Get tooled up. We're about to be attacked."

"Righto, gov," Krenz replied emotionlessly.

Hawthorn might have asked him to fetch lunch for all his reaction.

"I don't understand," Kiesche said, shaking his head. "How do they expect to get through all that liquid mud?"

"I don't understand either, but I know an attack run when I see it," Allenson replied.

Hawthorn produced a wicked looking dagger with a curved point and a serrated edge from a pocket in his suit. From another he extracted a similar blade which he offered to Allenson.

"Thanks. I didn't bother to bring a weapon," Allenson said.

"I guessed," Hawthorn replied.

Various unpleasant devices appeared as if by magic in the hands of Hawthorn's security detail. Kiesche removed one of the recharging levers from a power model and swung the heavy object, presumably to test its utility as a club. Pynchon chose a heavy wrench used to tighten the bolts on the hydraulics.

At the edge of the marsh muddy water transformed imperceptibly into watery mud. When they reached it the launches kept going.

"They'll bog down soon," Kiesche said, in disbelief.

But they didn't. They didn't even slow down. The launches penetrated deeper into the marsh until they reached the first mud flat, whereupon the front runner rode over the bank, spraying ooze in all directions as it came down.

"Shit," Kiesche said. "They're hovercraft."

"What?" Hawthorn asked.

"Hovercraft, they ride over land or water on a cushion of air."

"Terrific," Hawthorn replied. He raised his voice. "Stand by to repel boarders. Stay up where we have the advantage of height, stay close, and keep them off the guns."

"I guess we aren't the only ones with inventive engineers," Allenson said.

He was furious with himself because he should have anticipated something like this. Thank heaven for Hawthorn's instinctive paranoia and indiscipline. At least they still had his security detachment with them.

The launches spread out. The lead vehicle headed straight for the guns on the peninsula while the other two swerved to the right and left to enfilade. This was normally good tactics if you were equipped with guns, but Allenson couldn't imagine how splitting one's force could help in a brawl. Soldiers, like ordinary people, tended to revert to what they knew under extreme stress when the forebrain shut down. That was why you trained troops hard so the right reactions would be instinctive. The problems were that standard reactions were designed to cope with standard situations and this was anything but.

The rudders on the lead launch went hard over when it was a few meters off the rocks. The craft spun on its axis, sliding sideways towards the promontory on its cushion of air.

★ CHAPTER 17 ★

Cut and Trust

Allenson's body went into that surreal zone he thought of as combat mode. Time slowed down and consciousness narrowed like turning up the magnification on a powerful microscope.

He saw the hovercraft in intimate detail. He noticed a spot where the carbon crystal skirt had been holed and patched with a material of a slightly different shade of light gray. The vehicle engine throbbed arrhythmically as it drove the rotor. A detached part of his mind speculated that one of the blades on the prop must be slightly out of balance.

The driver controlled the hovercraft from a small cabin in the center. He stretched one arm out towards the side of the cockpit. The hovercraft hit the boulder still traveling sideways at some speed and the skirt tore with a sound like ripping cloth. The subsequent deep gash was going to need more than a patch to fix.

Forewarned, the pilot managed to keep his feet but many of his passengers were not so lucky. They tumbled about the hull like children on a funfair ride. One unlucky soul shot head first out of the hovercraft in a high arc. He crashed onto the rocks and lay like a crumpled paper model.

The driver had tried to do something clever. He turned the launch at the last moment intending it to slide gently into the bank sideways so that the assault troops could get over the gunwale onto the rocks as a single group. His instincts were sound. It would have been a more effective tactic in a contested landing than debussing a few at a time over the front or exiting at the sides and having to wade through the ooze.

But it hadn't worked.

Maybe the driver was more used to boats than hovercraft. The greater viscosity of water compared to air would have slowed a boat for a perfect stop. Maybe, he just got it wrong in the heat of the moment. No matter, the result was chaos whatever the driver had intended.

"Take them before they can regroup," Hawthorn yelled, projecting his voice through the mask. "Follow me!"

Despite his limp, Hawthorn made good time down the slime-covered rocks. He headed straight for the crippled hovercraft. Allenson did his best to emulate but he lacked Hawthorn's balance. The younger men overtook him. A Streamer reached down and cut the throat of the Brasilian ejected from the hovercraft.

The act wasn't nice and it wasn't fair but it had to be done. It would be insane to leave an enemy behind them. Just because he was down now didn't mean the soldier couldn't get up. It wasn't worth the risk of a knife in the back.

The first man over the side of the hovercraft stabbed at Hawthorn when he jumped down into the hull. Hawthorn deflected the Brasilian's strike with his left arm and stabbed the man under his mask. He drove his blade brutally upwards through the victim's neck into his skull. The Brasilian dropped back into the hovercraft. Before he hit the deck Hawthorn turned to engage another target.

Allenson slipped on some goo. He put down his left hand on the ground to recover.

Brasilians jumped out of the crippled launch only to slip and slide on the rocks. One went down on both knees. He held up a knife to scare off a large Streamer who threatened him with an iron bar. The Streamer swung the lever down with both hands. Muscles bulged under his jacket with the power of the blow. The Brasilian's arm broke with an audible crack and he dropped his knife. He screamed, cradling his broken arm with his remaining hand. It was an understandable if suicidal reaction.

The Streamer struck again, catching the soldier's helmet. It deformed under the blow, pitching the soldier forward on his face. The Streamer hit him repeatedly across the back and neck until he stopped moving.

A Streamer went down from a knife thrust to the chest. Allenson tried to catch him but he was beyond help. Bloody froth bubbled on the inside of his mask. The badges on his uniform identified the stricken figure as one of Pynchon's artillery men.

Allenson charged the artilleryman's attacker. He mistimed his knife thrust and they crashed together. Allenson knocked the smaller man over and he rolled down the bank. One of Krenz's men dropped on the Brasilian with both knees and thrust a knife through his mask. The man's scream turned into a gurgle when toxic fumes filled his lungs.

A Streamer threatened a Brasilian soldier with a knife to hold his attention while a comrade swung a hammer from behind. A blow to the back of the knee brought the soldier down and the two troopers fell on him like wolves. They got up covered in blood.

Allenson reached the hovercraft. Two of Krenz's men materialized at each side to assist him over the gunwale. This bodyguarding lark was getting bloody ridiculous.

The fight was almost over by the time he jumped into the hull. The driver held both arms outstretched, hands open to show he had no weapons. He appeared to be trying to surrender.

"Too late now, chum," said a Streamer wearing a security badge.

A vicious blow knocked the pilot out of the launch. He fell into the ooze on the offside. Allenson leaned over to pull him back on board but the mud had closed over.

"Defend the guns!" Hawthorn said.

Allenson took stock.

Streamer casualties were mercifully light. They'd wiped out the first unit of attackers. Few wounded survived, as a damaged mask meant a death sentence. A Streamer lay back against a boulder, clutching his stomach. Blood seeped between his fingers. He would have to look after himself as nobody had time for first aid.

Brasilians scrambled towards the artillery from the hovercraft that had stopped to seaward. The one that had split formation to get inland behind the Streamers had farther to go so was still maneuvering. Climbing back up the slippery scree was easier than going down. Hawthorn's small force soon assembled in front of the artillery modules. The enemy came on in a disorganized group.

"Stand, wait for my command," Hawthorn said, spreading out both arms as if to physically hold his men back.

The Brasilians lost further cohesion as they ran across the rocks. They looked more like a cross country run than a military unit. The first few to reach the colonial position slowed and looked nervously behind for support.

"Get them," Hawthorn yelled, charging forwards.

The Streamers rolled over the Brasilian vanguard without breaking stride. They left a trail of broken bodies in their wake. The charge slowed as it plowed into thicker clumps of enemy soldiers, until it halted in chaotic melee. Allenson hacked and stabbed as targets crossed his path. He lost his knife when it snagged on a Brasilian's clothing. Cursing, he picked the man up and threw him bodily at a fellow. Both Brasilians went over. He lost sight of them when he had to defend himself against an enemy stabbing at his chest.

The Brasilians melted away suddenly. One moment Allenson was surrounded by struggling figures, the next there were only enemy corpses. Some of the Brasilian rearguard never got as far as the colonial position. Upon seeing how the battle was going, they dropped their weapons and made a run back to their hovercraft.

A Streamer whooped and started to follow. Hawthorn backhanded him head over heels.

"Nobody pursues except on my order, Krenz!"

"You heard the guvnor," Krenz said, to no one in particular.

"We walk back to the guns and we wait," Hawthorn said.

The third party of attackers halted twenty meters from the guns. They appeared to be holding a conference. Many of the soldiers displayed a reluctance to close. The fate of the first two groups probably did nothing for their confidence. Brasilian morale probably wasn't helped by the various obscene gestures directed at them by the rude colonials.

An officer waved his arms. Sergeants physically shoved men into a skirmish line. Then the group advanced slowly and carefully.

Hawthorn ordered a charge when the Brasilians closed to just a few meters. The Streamers had their tails up. They pounded into the Brasilian line despite their fatigue, bowling over soldiers with the ferocity of their attack. Allenson's attention focused tightly on the opponent directly in front. A shock of orange hair projected out from under his mask like tangled fibers from a particularly revolting fungus.

The soldier lunged with a knife large enough to be an ancient short sword. He feinted, then slashed at Allenson's neck.

Allenson caught the knife hand by the wrist but another Brasilian dropped his weapon and grabbed Allenson's free arm. He hung on with both hands, preventing Allenson from using his weapon.

The three of them struggled like some sort of perverted love triangle. A small Brasilian hovered nervously at the edge of the melee waiting for a safe opportunity to sneak in and stab. Allenson must have seemed a sitting duck. The small man jumped forward, knife-arm outstretched. Now would have been a good time for Allenson's minders to intervene but they had unaccountably vanished in the confusion—sod's bloody law.

Allenson had only his own personal resources to draw on. It was not enough for him to merely push at his attackers. Something so feeble would end with a blade in his gut. He had to overpower them, to deal them such a crack that they never got to exploit the advantage of their numbers.

He dropped his knife and took a firm grip on the two men clinging to him. He reached deep within himself as if to toss a rock for the winning throw. Allenson lifted his attackers off their feet. He clapped their bodies together like a cymbal player marking the final of a particularly energetic concert.

The men bounced off each other. Allenson released his hold, allowing them to drop. The little man stared at Allenson goggle-eyed. He'd lost his knife. He raised both hands ineffectually as if trying to swat a fly.

Allenson was fresh out of pity. This little bastard tried to gut him like a fish, thinking him helpless. Some fish. He seized the soldier by the back of his neck with his left hand and pulled him in. Putting the heel of his right hand under the man's chin, he thrust upwards with a powerful rotating motion. The scrawny neck broke with an audible crack.

Allenson looked around for his other two assailants. The one on his right lay face down with the hilt of the small man's weapon jutting from his back. That explained where the knife had gone.

The one on the left scrabbled on his hands and knees in the process of climbing to his feet. Allenson kicked him hard in the face like a footballer making a strike for goal. The soldier rolled down the slope and disappeared.

Just for a moment Allenson was clear. He did a quick three-sixty to gauge the tactical situation. The Brasilians were brave and determined, but they were soldiers. Krenz's men were street fighting thugs. This was no place for a soldier used to wielding a laserrifle at two hundred meters. This was a brawl for men who weren't afraid of sharp edges and who were willing to shed blood, their own or someone else's. A fight for men who had no compunction about ganging up on an opponent and hitting him from behind, men who were willing to put the boot in. Hawthorn's type of men.

A clang of metal against metal drew Allenson's attention. A Brasilian officer somehow broke free of the ruck and made it to the nearest artillery piece. He swung an iron bar vigorously and there was another clang.

Allenson ran back across the slippery rocks, leaping from ridge to ridge. Momentum kept him going when his fleet slipped. It was madness but he had no choice.

The Brasilian officer got in two more heavy blows. Then Allenson reached over the officer's shoulder and ripped the mask from his face.

The officer reacted automatically by sucking in a lungful of the polluted air. He coughed and retched, gasping and twitching. Blood-flecked foam sprayed from his mouth. Appalled, Allenson tried to get the man's mask back on. The officer panicked and fought to keep it off his face.

The man bled from his eyes, nose, and mouth. Mercifully it was quick. Allenson struggled to avoid throwing up in his mask. That really wouldn't be a good idea. He wiped his forehead with his sleeve while examining the equipment.

Fortunately the officer had attacked the catapult module. It might seem the most important part of the gear but it was also the strongest. It had to withstand the dynamics of throwing heavy iron balls. The beating this one received put a few dents in the casing but it seemed operational.

He had a sudden suspicion. Surely the Brasilians wouldn't have put in such a determined attempt merely to belt the gear with iron bars? He checked the hydraulic module but found nothing, so he moved on to the power supply.

Taped to the side of the module was a round can with a screw top. It looked like a perfectly ordinary confectionary tin. Allenson doubted there was anything sweet inside. He dug his nails under the tape and ripped the can off the power supply. As it came free a small voice in his head chided with the words "trembler switch." Oh well, too late now.

Throwing back his arm he bowled the tin as smoothly as he could out over the marsh. It plopped into the ooze, creating a small crater that immediately filled with brown liquid.

The surviving Streamers mopped up, slitting the throats of wounded enemies and tending to wounded comrades. There were few enough of the last.

He gestured, trying to get Hawthorn's attention, to warn him that some of the Brasilians were carrying bombs, but a large bang from the swamp deluged him in stinking mud.

"What is it with you and mud?" Hawthorn asked, not entirely facetiously while helping to scrape Allenson off. "We dress you up in nice uniforms and you ruin them. Why can't you just stay in your office and make fancy speeches like other generals?"

Allenson didn't deign to answer the question.

"As I am the general, perhaps you wouldn't mind giving me a situation report, Colonel."

"Certainly, sir," Hawthorn replied, throwing a punctilious salute.

Allenson just knew that behind the mask his friend was grinning.

"One of the hovercraft got away with a few survivors. One lies wrecked, as you can see, and we have captured the other in full working order."

"That will be useful as a ferry for the artillery shifts," Allenson said. He turned to Pynchon who stood listening to the interplay between the old comrades. "What about the guns . . . I mean catapults?"

"Major Kiesche is checking them over."

"Major Pynchon, I want the full battery to open up again immediately."

"Sir . . ." Pynchon looked as if he was about to ask something but decided against it.

Allenson pointed to the escaped hovercraft, which was making all speed back to Oxford across the bay.

"Those people will hardly admit that they fled without facing us. They will have great stories to tell of their daring and achievements that might raise hopes in the minds of the Brasilian command. I want to kill any such optimism, not least because it might discourage a repeat attempt. Commence the bombardment immediately: maximum effort."

Allenson was not required to explain his orders. Often it would not be useful to so, but he needed the enthusiastic cooperation of men like Pynchon. They were not regulars in a Home World army. They would perform better if they knew why he insisted on an apparently dangerous order.

"The target, sir?"

"Anything that catches your eye, Colonel Pynchon, it doesn't really matter as long as the battery is seen to be in full operation."

Iron balls bombarded the port, most falling once again on the syncrete apron. The odd lucky hit struck an installation. Kiesche hovered over his babies anxiously.

Allenson began to relax. A sharp twang like a shotgun fired from inside a metal drum jolted him out of his complacency. One of the thick metallic stays holding a recoiling catapult parted under tension. The cable recoiled like a cracked whip.

The stay slapped Kiesche across the head with a noise like an egg struck by a hammer. He spun around and flopped onto his front. The cable expended its final energy by smacking against the rock between Hawthorn and Allenson. It struck hard enough to break off a chip.

Allenson reached Kiesche in three giant steps and gently turned him over. The engineer's mask had gone. Worse, his face had gone. The front of his head was a bloody ruin exposing brain and skull fragments.

Allenson rose.

"That's not your fault," Hawthorn said.

"I know," Allenson replied.

"That's not even the catapult that was damaged," Hawthorn said.

"True," Allenson replied.

"That could have happened at any time to any of us," Hawthorn said.

"Indeed," Allenson replied.

The battery was still. The men had stopped firing. Allenson walked slowly and carefully over to the damaged catapult. He casually rested his foot on one of the stays.

"Recommence shooting with our two remaining machines, Major Pynchon," he said.

Allenson stayed with the catapults until the men's nerves settled, then he and Hawthorn departed with the shift change as planned. He slept like a log that night and most of the rest of the next morning. After a substantial brunch, he felt almost human.

A note from Ling awaited him on his datapad inviting, General and Lady Allenson to dine at his villa outside Oxford. Allenson was tempted to refuse, citing the work that had built up in his absence but, in truth Trina, Todd and his staff had handled most of it already. The rest would keep. Trina had taught him the importance of seemingly pointless social conventions. If Ling wanted to meet privately in an informal setting, it probably indicated that he wished to convey some informal message. That evening Allenson and Trina duly set out in their finery in a tolerably functional frame carriage that Boswell had scrounged from somewhere.

Boswell had been vague about the carriage's provenance and Allenson thought it best not to inquire too closely. He strongly suspected that somewhere in Oxford was a garage with an insecure lock, a lock that may or may not have been insecure before Boswell discovered it.

Ling lived in a small comfortable home on the outskirts of a village that served the local agricultural community. His villa looked as if it had been converted from a farmhouse, since it was structured around a central two-story building with bedrooms on the top floor above functional rooms at ground level.

A one-story wing at right angles to the main structure may once have served for animal husbandry and equipment storage. Now it made a pleasant suite for guests and entertainment. A low wall from wing to building enclosed a triangular frame park and small formal garden. Allenson suspected that the wall had once been much higher. What remained was far too substantial to be a mere ornament. He also noticed that none of the buildings had ground floor windows onto the outside.

In less settled times the farmhouse would have doubled as a castle. Now it was a gentleman's residence.

A log fire warmed the interior of the dining room. The meal

commenced after the usual convention of welcoming drinks in front of the flickering flames.

Ling's wife, Alphena, was a willowy lady who overtopped her husband by at least ten centimeters, although she wore flat-heeled shoes to disguise the height differential. She said little through the formal dinner but listened intently.

After dinner, Ling escorted Trina into the formal garden beside his villa to show her some exotic blooms he had been cultivating in controlled environment greenhouses. Allenson was left alone with Alphena. They settled into comfortable chairs and Alphena kicked off her shoes and tucked her legs under her.

"Bring us some tea, Lily," she instructed the maid, who appeared to be the only servant in the house.

Allenson wondered what the purpose was behind the evening, pleasant though it was. Chiefs of staff commonly invited their commanders to dinner, but the way he had been separated from Trina seemed a little contrived. Trina had clearly thought so too, as she indicated by a raised eyebrow to Allenson when Ling ushered her out. Allenson had expected the ladies to retire, leaving him alone with Ling. Clearly this conversation was to be very informal.

Alphena made small talk about the price of tea and the merits of various suppliers until the maid left the room. That was unusual in itself. Normally the maid stood unobtrusively against one of the walls in case further service was required. She had obviously been given prior instructions.

Allenson waited patiently, making polite conversation while sipping his tea. Something sensitive was about to be touched on. Prodding the lady would not expedite matters. No doubt she would get around to the matter in her own time.

"You are not quite what I expected, General," Alphena finally said.

"Indeed, what were you anticipating?" Allenson asked.

Alphena smiled.

"I'm not sure. Someone more . . ." she paused, selecting her next words carefully, ". . . authoritarian and ambitious perhaps. Someone more interested in politics and less involved with his family and farm."

"We call them demesnes," Allenson said.

He smiled, "Although they are just farms, albeit on a large scale."

"That's it exactly, that self-deprecating humor. *That* was not what I expected."

"I'm afraid that I'm poor martinet material," Allenson replied.

"Yes," Alphena said seriously.

There was a pause in the conversation.

"What made you imagine I might be?" Allenson eventually, asking an open-ended question to get her talking.

"You came to us with a great reputation, Sar Allenson, not just your record as a war hero but as a powerful businessman and a key player in Manzanitan and Stream politics. It's difficult to reconcile that image with the man. People who have never met you have some strange fancies."

"Really?" Allenson replied, merely to keep the conversation going.

She chose her next words carefully, like a lawyer recalling the terms of a verbal contract.

"Many of the radicals, particularly the younger men, and some of the army officers, are frustrated at the slow progress of the Assembly and their inability to come to any decision. There is talk in such quarters that we would be better off with a strong-man in charge. Someone who gets things done . . ."

". . . and makes the frames run on time." Allenson interrupted.

She laughed.

"Precisely!"

"And these hotheads imagine me in the role of captain general, dictator and all-round grand supremo of the Cutter Stream?" asked Allenson, shaking his head in amusement.

Alphena looked serious.

"Put like that the idea is ridiculous to anyone who's met you or bothered to take a close look at your decisions. You don't act like a supremo and your actions are hardly calculated to set up a military dictatorship."

"But there is still a problem," Allenson said flatly.

"These're troubled times. Many people have not met you and are too frightened or ignorant to analyze the situation logically. There are several people horrified at the idea of a military dictator for every individual who likes the idea."

"A view I share, Lady Ling. I assure you that my only intention is to get this unpleasant business over as soon as is practical. I'm impatient to return to my demesne on Manzanita and get on with my life. My personal plans have no room for ridiculous coups."

"I believe you, Sar Allenson, but not everyone will. Not all your enemies are on the Brasilian side. I urge you to watch your back."

From there the conversation returned to trivial matters.

Allenson was inclined to dismiss Alphena's warning as understandable paranoia. Everyone was nervous and inclined to see plots behind any chance remark. There would be losers whoever won the confrontation with Brasilia. Some people were going to be labelled loyal patriots and others traitors, but at this stage it was not clear which was which.

The trooper reeled and waved a glass of plum brandy.

"Another bol, barkeep. Plum brandy, only the best for me and my mate. If it's good enough for the bloody nobs it's good enough for us."

He turned to his drinking companion, waving an arm for emphasis.

"Whatdaya say your name was again?"

"You don't like nobs much then," said his companion, deftly putting out an arm to steady the drunken trooper before his expansive gesture caused him to overbalance.

The bartender opened a fresh bottle of branded plum brandy and poured the first glass. The drunk tossed a Brasilian twenty crown onto the bar. He used far too much force so the coin skated off the other side. The barman, who was used to dealing with drunks, caught it one-handed.

"Keepsh the change, my good man," said the drunk waving his hand in what he clearly fondly imagined was a display of liberality to the lower orders.

The barman examined the coin carefully. In his considerable experience drunken troopers rarely owned twenty crown pieces, let alone threw them around. The coin must have passed the barman's expert scrutiny because he put it in the till.

"You don't like nobs," repeated the drunk's companion.

"Feckin' Manzanitan snobs," the drunk said reflectively. "Come here to a civilized world like some cock o' the walk. Captain of Militia I was, properly 'lected by my peers."

He thrust his chin out and raised his voice.

"Wasnae good enough for *Him* though was I? Busted me he did for being more popular with my men than he was."

"Bloody liberty," said his companion, raising his refilled glass to his lips.

An observant person might have noted that the level in the glass had not perceptibly changed when he set it back down on the bar. The drunk was far too deep in his cups for such levels of perception.

"Liberty, yeah, liberty's coming mate," said the drunk. "Feckin' snob's turn will come. Gonna be a reckoning, though, or my name's not Prat."

"A reckoning! What are you going to do."

The drunk tapped his nose conspiratorially.

"Wait and see, mate, wait and see. Gonna be a reckoning soon. Whatya say your name was again?"

His companion looked at something over the drunk's shoulder.

"Krenz, my name is Krenz," his companion said.

"This the man?" drawled an upper-class voice from behind the drunk.

"Yes, gov, he's come into money suddenly and been making threats against the boss."

The drunk frowned, his fuddled brain processing the information slowly that a third party had joined the conversation. When it did, he turned.

"You're a feckin' snob as well."

The drunk threw a sudden swinging punch. Hawthorn leaned his head back three inches, so the blow expended on empty air. This time Krenz made no effort to effect a catch, so the drunk crashed to the floor.

Hawthorn looked down at the drunk dispassionately, like a taxonomist who had discovered yet another new species of parasitic roundworm doing all the usual things one expects such creatures to do.

"Hose him down and detox him until he's reasonably sober, then we can have a little chat. You recorded the conversation?"

"Yes, Gov."

Krenz's face showed an unusual expression. Actually any expression was unusual for Krenz.

"Something on your mind?" Hawthorn asked.

"Well, Gov, you know recordings can't be used in trials," Krenz asked, adopting the tone one uses when a normally reliable superior appears to have overlooked the obvious.

Krenz and the criminal justice system of the Stream were old acquaintances. He had a working knowledge of court procedure that would not have disgraced a professional advocate.

"Trial?" Hawthorn asked, genuinely astonished. "This man's not going anywhere near a court."

"Good of you to see me, Jem. I realize that you have many calls upon your time," Trina said.

"Not at all," Hawthorn replied.

In truth he was curious why Trina should suddenly demand his attention. They were hardly intimates, so why did she want a private meeting?

"Would you care to take tea?" Hawthorn asked politely.

"As you are busy, I will get right to the point," Trina said, showing a most unnatural directness for a Manzanitan lady.

"That would probably be for the best," Hawthorn replied neutrally.

"I understand that you have arrested a man for threatening the life of my husband."

Hawthorn blinked.

"Possibly you should be running security rather than me, Trina. We only picked him up a couple of hours ago. The matter is not supposed to be public knowledge. I would be curious to know your source of information."

"Oh, one hears things," Trina replied vaguely.

Hawthorn wondered who inside his organization was spying for her. It didn't really matter that Trina had a pipeline into Special Security, but he was concerned that he hadn't known. It was professionally annoying and it raised the possibility that other more unfriendly principals had planted double agents on him. He resolved to have a purge. No one had yet adequately resolved the conundrum of "who will watch the watchers?"

"Was it a serious threat or just a drunken blowhard?" she asked.

Hawthorn regarded her curiously.

"I have reason to believe that we should regard it as serious."

"Have you told Allen yet?"

"That we have made an arrest? Not yet."

"Then don't," Trina said firmly.

Now she really had surprised him.

"Why ever not? He should be warned to be on his guard."

"You will question this would-be assassin to establish who his principals are." Trina made a statement. She hadn't asked a question.

"Of course, my people are sobering him up and putting on the frighteners to prepare him."

Trina nodded.

"Quite so. If you tell Allen he will insist on the matter being done by the book with a proper trial."

"That would certainly impede my investigation," Hawthorn said thoughtfully.

Trina leaned forward and her eyes blazed.

"Let me make myself clear, Jem. Some bastard is plotting to murder my husband and I want this person found and permanently neutralized by whatever means you find necessary."

Hawthorn threw one of his dazzling innocent smiles.

"Then we are of one mind, Trina."

He paused to reflect.

"It hadn't occurred to me that Allen would be squeamish about this but you're right. He'd do anything to protect his friends, but would regard it as ungentlemanly to do the same for his own welfare. Sometimes I forget how bothered other people can be by abstract ideas of conscience."

He shook his head, ever puzzled how seemingly intelligent people failed to grasp simple truths.

"You can rely on me, Trina. I will squeeze this oik like a soft fruit in a vise. I will get to the next link in the chain and so on until I find the head of the conspiracy."

He looked her firmly in the eyes.

"Then I will decapitate it," he said without special emphasis as if stating a simple fact.

Trina visibly relaxed.

"I knew I could rely on you, Jem. I believe I will take that tea now."

Hawthorn called in an orderly and gave the order. They made small talk while they waited for their tea to brew. Trina finally raised something that was clearly on her mind.

"You haven't told Allen that it was me who sent you away all those years ago," she said, somewhat diffidently. "Why is that?"

"It would upset him," Hawthorn replied.

He grinned.

"Beside you didn't send me away. You merely pointed out to me how much damage I was causing my friends and suggested a solution. As it happened, I agreed once the matter had been explained to me. Sometimes I overlook how people react. So you see, I sent myself away."

"I'm glad you don't hold a grudge."

"I make my own decisions about what I do or not do, Trina, and I blame no one but myself for the consequences."

At that point the orderly came back and the conversation shifted to safer ground.

Allenson was not quite as naïve as his nearest and dearest assumed, but in this case he was far too busy to notice that Trina and Hawthorn were unusually close. An urgent message summoned him to the control room in his headquarters. He erupted from his office, pulling on his jacket, as warning sirens sounded all over the camp.

He burst into the control room to find Todd and Ling already present. Ling stood behind the main hologram, conferring with the operators. Allenson didn't want to distract his chief of staff so he grabbed Todd and pulled him to one side.

"What's happening? An attack?"

"It could be, Uncle. Our instruments have detected significant wash in the Continuum from a sizable inbound tonnage."

A new hologram opened in the room, showing a visual of the air above Oxford Bay. It shimmered and distorted, then three large structures appeared. The picture sharpened and they clarified into ovoids with shimmering pylons that slid from red to blue as the ships turned and descended onto the Port's hardstands.

"That's precision navigation," an operator said. "To dephase in formation like that right above the target is bloody impressive."

"Brasilian Navy pilots," said another operator. "Flying like that means they have to be regular navy."

"Surely Port Oxford hard stands aren't big enough or strong enough for ships of that size," Todd said, shaking his head.

The ovoids deployed dozens of ground skids under their hulls and settled down. The hard stands weren't nearly big enough but the ovoids landed mostly on the grass surrounds. The ships rocked gently as the skids took the weight and self-levelled when their pads pushed deep into the soil.

"Those are specialized assault ships," Allenson said. "They can land regiments damn near anywhere reasonably flat and cost as much as a battleship. I doubt if there are more than a dozen in the whole Brasilian Navy. Why the hell are they using them here?"

"How do we fight that?" Todd asked in wonder.

"We don't," Allenson said bleakly.

★ CHAPTER 18 ★

Commandos

A small disorganized flotilla of tramp ships followed one at a time after the assault ships. They landed wherever they could find a space. The navy ships fired warning shots from their defense lasers at any tramp venturing too close. One tramp captain panicked and set his frame down on a soft spot. It promptly overturned and broke its back.

Landing ramps lowered from the ovoid hulls as soon as the frame fields were completely switched off. A few security ratings debussed and set up heavy weapon points around the ships, but apart from that they were quiescent.

"That's odd," Ling said.

"What?" asked Allenson.

"They've offloaded nothing, no troops or equipment."

"Maybe they're not ready," Todd hazarded.

"Those ships are designed to come in on hot landing grounds and dump a regiment in minutes," Allenson said.

He had an idea.

"Colonel Ling, could your operators focus on the city and the bridge?"

The hologram blurred and shifted. Allenson felt a surge of seasickness as his eyes and ears sent contradictory messages to his brain. He shut his eyes until the vertigo disappeared. Cautiously he waited a few more moments for the hologram to stabilize before looking at it again.

The city looked like an ant hill poked with a stick. It heaved and spat vehicles and pedestrians out over the bridge.

"What the hell?" Todd asked.

"Those ships haven't landed to reinforce the garrison, but to evacuate it," Allenson said flatly.

"But that means . . ." Ling's voice trailed off.

"That we've won," Todd said quietly, then repeated himself more loudly. "Victory, Uncle, your stratagem has given us victory."

Operators began to cheer and clap.

"Silence, silence," an NCO said but gave up when he was ignored.

Allenson had to fight off an attempt to lift him shoulder high. Apart from the embarrassment, he was in a room with a low ceiling. He excused himself and slipped away followed by Todd.

The air outside was clean, or at least it was until Todd lit up a cigarette.

"I didn't know you smoked," Allenson said.

"My mother thinks the habit coarse, so I've given up," Todd replied with a grin. "But I don't think she would mind under the circumstances."

"Well, she isn't here to complain," Allenson said, ever practical.

A rumble sounded from the camp, swelling into a tidal wave of sound.

"Good news travels almost as fast as bad," Todd observed. "You may yet be marched around shoulder high."

Allenson managed to avoid the circus by calling an immediate council of war of his senior officers and staff.

Buller opened the discussion without being invited to speak.

"I've got my people organizing assault groups to hit the Brasilian rearguard. An army is always vulnerable in retreat."

"No," Allenson said firmly.

"A few decent blows and they'll panic, then we'll slaughter the bastards. Teach them a lesson, what?"

"You will do no such thing."

"But why," Buller asked in astonishment.

"For a number of reasons, first, because I don't believe Brasilian regulars will panic. They have their weaknesses, notably their inflexibility, but they don't panic. On the contrary, they'll stand."

Allenson paused to pour a glass of water from the jug at his side. He made the company wait while he took a sip. He wasn't thirsty. This was just a cheap rhetorical trick to focus everyone's attention. He hated himself for playing such games, but it was necessary.

"If—when—they stand we'd have a serious urban fire-fight on our hands. I have no doubts at all that our troops would prevail . . ."

He lied, having many doubts about whether his citizen army could withstand professional soldiers in the bloody business of urban combat.

". . . but casualties on both sides, including civilians, will be heavy. That is decidedly not in our long term interest."

"You're a bloody fool, Allenson," Buller said. "You think you can win a war without destroying the enemy army? Ridiculous!"

Hawthorn's eyes were like chips of glacial ice bathed in ultraviolet radiation. Allenson cut in before the situation escalated.

"Perhaps so, *Colonel* Buller, but I am your commanding officer and you will obey my orders. This's not yet a total war. I don't intend to escalate matters."

"Have it your own way," Buller said.

"Thank you, I will," Allenson replied politely. "Gentlemen, Colonel Buller's time has not been entirely wasted. I want sections of reliable men to enter the city close on the heels of the departing Brasilians to maintain order. I intend to proclaim martial law until such time as civilian authority can be reinstated. If you will assist with this, Colonel Ling."

"There'll be looters," Buller said sourly. "What do you want my men to do with them?"

"Take them alive if possible and hand them over to Special Projects."

He turned to Hawthorn.

"Colonel, find somewhere to lock up minor transgressors. We'll hand them over to the civilian government for punishment in due course. Then they're SEP."

Todd looked puzzled, "SEP?"

"Someone else's problem," Ling translated

"And the hard cases?" Hawthorn asked.

Allenson sighed.

"I suppose the criminal element is bound to try it on. We'll need to make an example or two to show who's in charge. Convene an immediate court-martial for people accused of serious violent disorder such as murder, rape or large-scale property destruction. Give them a fair trial and publically execute any found guilty. I doubt you'll have to do it very often."

"No problem," Hawthorn said with a nod.

"Captain Morton, I want your men to shadow the Brasilian force after it leaves. I want to be reassured that they have really given up and this isn't some sort of elaborate ruse. I am confident it's not but it never hurts to make sure."

"Any questions? Very well, gentlemen, you have your orders."

Hawthorn walked down a long underground corridor inadequately lit by open emitters devoid of any light diffusion baffles. His face was bathed in harsh artificial light as he approached each emitter, only to be draped in shadows as he passed. Somewhere water dripped with a steady slow rhythm. The air smelt of damp and musty boxes.

He reflected that interrogation rooms were traditionally located off passageways like this. People would no doubt argue that it was because the interrogators could work undisturbed without offending the sensibilities of more delicate souls. Hawthorn suspected that there was a much simpler explanation. It was all part of the softening up process.

The corridor would prey on even the mind of a perp dragged along it by a couple of goons. Even the meanest and most stolid imagination could picture the divers horrors that might await beyond the door at the far end.

He reached the aforesaid door, opened it and went inside. The drunken trooper had sobered up. It hadn't noticeably improved his appearance. Blood and vomit stained clothes that had been none too clean to start with.

They'd tied him to a chair in the middle of the bare concrete room under the single emitter. Harsh white light illuminated him while everything else was in shadow. Two of Krenz's larger and uglier men stood each side of the door.

The man looked up when Hawthorn entered the pool of light around the chair.

"Whadya want?" the man asked querulously in a pathetic attempt at bravado.

The display would have been more convincing if his lower lip stopped shaking and he hid the terror in his eyes. Not that Hawthorn felt any pity. He subscribed to the motto of the Streamer underworld: "Don't do the crime if you can't do the time."

The little runt put himself in harm's way when he accepted money to assassinate Hawthorn's friend. It was his tough luck if he hadn't grasped that point before taking the dosh. Hawthorn had few friends but the universe was full of little runts. The loss of one more was hardly of consequence.

Hawthorn removed his jacket and handed it back to one of Krenz's men without taking his eyes off the prisoner. He slowly and carefully rolled up his sleeves into neat folds just above the elbow. Without comment Hawthorn held out a hand and Krenz's other man handed him a large spiked knuckle-duster. Hawthorn carefully placed it on his right fist and adjusted it for fit.

It was all theater of course, but only up to a point. It would be more convenient for everyone, not least the prisoner, if he could be convinced that Hawthorn was not bluffing.

"Let me make something clear," Hawthorn said in an exaggerated upper-class drawl. "I don't give a tinker's fart about you, your name, your ancestry or your future. The only thing I care about is finding the name of the man who ordered the hit."

The runt opened his mouth, but closed it again when Hawthorn held up his left hand in negation.

"I don't suppose he gave you his real name and credit account details, but you had more than one meeting. Money changed hands, so there is a chain. You are going to help me climb that chain before you leave this room. One way or the other you will cooperate."

There is honor amongst denizens of the underworld, but it runs monomolecular thin and was never intended to withstand the sort of pressures that Hawthorn was applying.

"I'll squeal, gov," the runt said. "To start with this geezer had a Nortanian accent . . ."

In the event, Special Projects only had to shoot one criminal. It seemed that Hawthorn's name was not entirely unknown to the

Oxford underworld. The well-publicized news that he would be enforcing law and order had a salutary effect. Somehow they had already taken the measure of Jem Hawthorn and considered it unnecessary to test his resolve further. How or why this had happened was something of a mystery to Allenson but he was nonetheless grateful.

The perp they were obliged to execute was the sort of messianic nutter who wouldn't be dissuaded by anyone's reputation. He raped and killed a child in the confusion surrounding the handover of power. Easily detected by a DNA trail he hadn't attempted to conceal, his trial lasted ten minutes. Allenson attended the punishment, but this was one death that would not disturb his conscience.

Hawthorn's security people had to be present to keep order. Allenson didn't want the perp lynched before he could be properly killed according to military law. Utterly irrational, of course, but human beings were irrational on some matters. Order, law, and a respect for civilized behavior must be maintained or they were all lost.

"By the way, I intend to put in a request for leave," Hawthorn said at the execution.

"Really, what for?" Allenson asked.

"I thought now that matters have quietened down that I might take a short holiday break."

"A holiday break?" Allenson echoed, wondering if he had fallen down the rabbit hole.

"Quite, a week chillaxing in the sun with an improving book and a cold drink will do me the power of good. Maybe you should try it yourself, Allenson. We are none of us getting any younger, you know," Hawthorn said piously.

"I see," said Allenson, who didn't see at all.

Realizing that he was gaping at Hawthorn as if he had announced an intention to take holy vows and join a monastery of castrates, Allenson searched for something to say.

"Where will you go?"

"Mogadosh on Nortania sounds charming. I hear they have astonishing cultural centers with an exciting line in experimental theater."

"Indeed," Allenson replied, checking around surreptitiously for a white rabbit.

It was such a strange conversation that it preyed on his mind. He raised it with Trina that night.

"It's not that I begrudge him some leave, Lord knows he's earned it. I'm just a bit surprised, that's all. Hawthorn was never the holidaying type, let alone a devotee of experimental theater."

"People change," Trina replied, "and, as you've said, he's earned a break. I think it's an excellent idea. He will return to his duties refreshed and reenergized; good for Hawthorn. You should take notice and emulate his example sometimes."

Allenson looked at his wife as if she'd expressed an interest in boll weevil soup.

"Forgive me, my dear, but I have always had the impression that you and my friend were not exactly soul mates."

"He's been growing on me lately," Trina replied.

Allenson sat in his office a few days later struggling with endless correspondence from people needing his authority to do things. Todd had sorted the files into those that he could "rubber stamp"—did people once really stamp things with rubber?—and those that actually needed his attention.

A third group consisted of demands that Todd thought could be rejected out of hand. Allenson's sense of duty forced him to at least skim through this category before canning them. He would be extremely pleased when the civilian administration finished decamping back from Cambridge. For some reason this simple task was absorbing more time and resources than the siege itself.

His door burst open and Reese Morton exploded into the room.

"General, we've found the Brasilians!"

Todd followed him in.

"Captain Morton would like to see you when it is convenient," Todd said pointedly.

"So I see," Allenson said, trying to keep a straight face.

"Haven't got time for all that protocol malarkey," Morton said. "The general'll want to hear this."

Allenson gratefully closed the file.

"Perhaps you'd better sit down and compose yourself, captain. See we're not disturbed, Todd."

"Yes, sir," Todd said, closing the door.

"He only calls me sir when he disapproves," Allenson said.

"Oh he's a good lad, your nephew, just a bit Brasilian, that's all. We'll soon knock the stuffed shirt out of him in the Stream. You see if we don't, General," Reese said, taking a seat.

"So you've found the Brasilian army. I hadn't known you'd lost them."

Reese colored.

"Ah well, it didn't seem necessary to worry you with every detail, sir. We sort of mislaid them, temporarily. They fooled us by doubling back."

A cold chill went up Allenson's spine.

"Doubling back to where?"

"Here, General, they've landed back on Trent."

"Where?"

"Insubran."

The name meant nothing to Allenson, so he called up a map. Insubran was a small continent, large island really, to the north and east of Trent; both the world and its main continent had the same name. He flicked through a brief description of the place. Desolate, was the word most used in the briefings. A small community on the east coast serviced a harvesting fleet and scattered farming communities operating at little more than subsistence level. Barren soil and water shortages prevented profitable exploitation.

"Why would the Brasilians go there?" Allenson asked, thinking out loud.

"It's a useful isolated place for a base," Morton said confidently.

"I doubt the Brasilians would see it like that," Allenson replied. "From their perspective, Insubran is a lousy place for a base. It has no local supplies and no port capable of taking anything bigger than a tramp. Sure the assault ships can land anywhere but they would need somewhere to unload decent sized freighters to supply their army."

"Perhaps they intend to build a port," Morton said.

Allenson considered the suggestion, but rejected it almost immediately. He shook his head.

"Not possible."

"Why," Morton asked, clearly not comprehending.

The remark reminded Allenson how young and inexperienced Morton was.

"With what, and how, would they move heavy building gear in starting from such a low infrastructure? The cost would be prohibitive and take months, maybe years, and what an easy target they would give us for raids and sabotage."

Another thought occurred.

"They would have to bring in construction teams, feed them, and provide security. It would be a logistical nightmare."

Morton looked exasperated. "So what else could they be doing?"

Allenson spread his hands.

"Any number of things. They might be carrying out repairs. They did take a few hits from our improvised artillery."

"But are you so certain that we can afford to ignore them?" Morton asked.

That was the rub, of course. Morton deftly fed the worm of doubt that gnawed at Allenson's confidence. Was he really so sure of his logic that he was willing to bet the future of the new state on his decision? Put like that the answer was obvious.

"No, I'll have to find out exactly what the situation is. Put together a reconnaissance team from your people."

Morton didn't move.

"Well?" Allenson asked.

"Do I take it that you intend to come as well?"

"You do," Allenson said, lifting his chin in a "so what" gesture.

"Colonel Hawthorn might have some thoughts on that," Morton said, choosing his words with care.

"Colonel Hawthorn is on holiday," Allenson said.

They grinned at each other like a couple of schoolboys let off the leash.

Allenson reveled in the freedom of riding a one-man frame. How long had it been, two years, three, maybe more? Morton led, then Allenson and finally three of Morton's canary-clothed commandos. Allenson kept close to the others as he was quite out of practice at pinpoint navigation.

They slipped in and out of the Continuum in a series of short bunny hops a klick at a time so they could safely navigate a bare hundred meters above the ocean. It was impossible to judge orientation properly so deep in Trent's gravity well, so they needed a twenty- or thirty-meter safety cushion in height even over so short a distance.

At least the ocean was reasonably flat. Over land they would have needed four or five hundred meters clearance. It took three hours of hard work to reach Insubran but there really was no acceptable alternative strategy. Sure the journey could have been done in ten minutes in a single hop but they would have had to partially dephase high overhead. The sophisticated sensors on the assault ships would have instantly detected their arrival.

They covered the last kilometer almost completely dephased at an over-land speed of barely two hundred kph. The Insubran western shoreline rose steeply out of the water, waves pounding on yellow-red rock formations. Their passage disturbed large scaly creatures twice the size of a man sunning themselves on the rocks. Some bull-males lifted their heads as the frames soared overhead. They snarled soundlessly, showing rows of needle teeth optimized for catching fish. The females and cubs slid into the sea, wriggling from side to side to get purchase for flipperlike limbs.

Once they reached the sea, they disappeared under with barely a ripple. Moving from land to water transferred them from helplessly clumsy beasts to sleek, well-adapted organisms. Allenson wondered why the passage of the frames triggered the beasts' flight. What could possibly threaten them in this barren place?

He glanced uneasily at the sky and wished he had thought to research the local wildlife before leaving. He was tempted to get out his datapad and search for flight-capable Insubran macro-predators but thought better of it. Flying safely in close formation at low level took all of his concentration.

The frames climbed up towards the mountainous ridge immediately behind the shoreline. The terrain was a badland of broken rocks and wadis with no soil and so no plants. Flashes in a dark area higher in the peaks indicated an electrical storm. Morton altered course to give it a wide berth. Lightning played havoc with frame fields. On the plus side it would also confuse Brasilian detection equipment.

Morton slowed down to twenty kph or thereabouts when they reached the summit of the ridge so that they could follow the gullies and keep below the skyline. He dephased and landed on a ledge where they could look out over the plain below. The mountains sloped more gently on this side and scrubby vegetation had taken hold in hollows where there was a modicum of sediment and, Allenson surmised, moisture. Insubran was a desert.

The weather came in from the west. The mountains forced the airstream up. It cooled, depositing rain primarily on the barren western slopes. Heavy sheets of precipitation tumbled straight back into the ocean, washing away soil and carving out the badlands. The eastern plain was in rainshadow, baked dry under cloudless skies.

Allenson wondered how the locals farmed at all. They clearly did, as he observed tiny hamlets of square, yellow mud brick houses scattered about amid plots of desiccated vegetation. The Brasilians had landed close to the edge of the mountain slope. Using the resolution of his datapad as a passive telescope Allenson could see movement between the three assault ships and various tramps. Vehicles kicked up clouds of dust so it was impossible to work out exactly what they were doing.

"We need to get in closer," Allenson said.

Morton shaded his eyes and pointed.

"We can follow that wadi down close to the plain without being seen. 'Fraid it will be shank's pony from here on, General. It will be hotter down there."

"The hike will no doubt do me good. Sweat off a few kilos," Allenson said, unconvincingly.

When they got closer to the plain, Allenson noticed perfect circles where the soil was a deeper red ochre than the yellow brown of the plain. He estimated that the circles were quite small, perhaps a meter across, although it was difficult to judge scale. The circles must be artificial, as they ran in perfect straight lines away from the mountains, each one about a hundred meters apart. Sometimes the lines bifurcated. Sometimes right-angled cross links connected the main lines.

The descent went smoothly enough. The reconnaissance team left their frames hidden in a jumble of rocks. A large plant clinging to one of the boulders marked the place. It dropped long thick fibrous roots that disappeared into the thin sandy soil.

The plant resembled a squat bulb with a woody outer integument. Straggly branches erupted from the top and flat leathery yellow leaves dangled. The dried up remains of purple flowers clung to the leaves.

Allenson ran a finger down a leaf, to find it dry and leathery.

"Curious texture, I guess that the plants are quiescent for most of the year, coming into bloom only after rainfall."

"Suppose so," Morton replied, looking quizzically at Allenson.

He clearly wondered why Allenson was interested in obscure botanical observations. Destry would have been fascinated. Morton didn't give a damn.

It took the best part of an hour to walk the half kilometer to the plain through the broken landscape. The air was bloody hot but at least dry. Hot humid climates were one of Allenson's pet hates.

Every fifty meters Morton chipped a rock with a small hand axe to mark their way back. Allenson had already locked the location of the frames into his datapad's inertial navigation, but it never hurt not to have to rely on technology. Datapads were famously robust and foolproof, but even the best gear had a nasty habit of letting you down at the worst possible time.

Allenson noted that the chips showed as dull red against the yellow sandstone just like the mysterious circles. He nearly drew Morton's attention to the anomaly, but decided not to bother.

The wind rose until it swirled in little eddies through the stone. Fine red dust lifted in dancing whirlpools. When they finally stood on the plain, the particles in the air were dense enough to sting their eyes.

"That's torn it," Morton said. "I don't know about you but I can't see a bloody thing. What now?"

"If we can't see them then they can't see us. We go on."

Morton groaned theatrically.

"I just knew you would say that. I hate walking. Okay, men, more yomping."

His loyal band catcalled but they followed.

"Hey don't blame me, thank our gung-ho general. All officers above the rank of captain are mad, you know that."

He continued sotto voice.

"You aren't going to be out-hiked by an old man are you?"

Allenson closed his ears. Morton had an easy attitude to discipline and command but his men followed him willingly enough. Ironically, the canary yellow uniforms blended in quite well with the sand storm.

Allenson used the inertial navigation built into his datapad to plot their way towards the Brasilians.

They stumbled across one of the hamlets. Doors were closed on the houses and windows had shutters fastened tight. There was no evidence anyone lived there. Nevertheless Allenson had the feeling of eyes watching between the slats. He ostentatiously switched on his carbine and checked the load and diagnostics. Morton noticed and signaled to his men to do likewise with their laserrifles.

Allenson preferred the carbine because he could get off a fusillade quickly. The burst would be largely undirected but careful aiming had never worked that well for him anyway.

There probably was no one watching and if there were they probably had no aggressive intent. However, displaying that the small group was heavily armed did no harm.

Just outside the hamlet was one of the red circles. Curious, Allenson scraped away the covering of dust with his boot. Underneath the stone was amber. Red dust blown by the wind stuck immediately by some sort of static charge. It hid the yellow layer in a matter of seconds.

Morton watched and raised an eyebrow. Allenson signaled that they should press on, unwilling to try to explain when all he would get was a mouth full of grit for his pains. It wasn't like Morton would care anyway.

After half an hour the wind eased and the dust settled. Morton led them into a crop to give cover in the clear air. The plants were a little like chest-high mushrooms. Fruiting bodies hung in clusters under the domes. A semi-translucent cellulose shield across the top of the dome let in light for photosynthesis but gave protection from erosion and desiccation by the dry, dust-filled wind.

They walked crouched over to the edge of the crop. Allenson's back protested at the unusual exercise. He really was out of shape for playing commando. Morton appeared to be enjoying himself. He stopped behind a hedge of some dried out plant material that acted as a windbreak and motioned Allenson over. The Brasilian ships were parked about half a klick away. Allenson glared at the ovoids with envy. To have command of such resources!

Small tractors dragged sleds around the parked ships. After a while Allenson discerned a pattern of movement between the small tramps and the assault ships. He used his datapad to create an image and magnify it, not daring to use anything other than a passive system for fear of alerting the Brasilians.

The sleds from the tramps to the ovoids were loaded with gear but they came back empty. Some tractors moved material out of the assault ships into stockpiles while others transported it back again. No troops occupied the ground apart from small security details grouped around single barreled lasercannons on tripods and other less recognizable equipment. Now that he could watch the activity in detail it was obvious what the Brasilians were up to.

He never knew what gave the reconnaissance team away, maybe leaking emissions from his datapad. The Brasilians knew the locals had no device more sophisticated than a garden hoe.

Maybe the enemy had some other sort of sensor that could pick up living bodies in a field. He should have anticipated that Brasilian state of the art military gear might have unusually sensitive properties. Whatever triggered the alarm, a security point suddenly came alive.

A trooper swung the cannon and loosed off a short burst. It wasn't a bad shot considering that he was probably firing indirectly on estimated coordinates. The burst walked through the mushroom crop to Allenson's right in a series of explosions. Mushrooms blazed, releasing white smoke that rolled across the plot.

"Shit," Morton said, pithily. "Run for it."

Allenson was already on his feet and moving. Tripod-mounted lasercannon required time for the focusing optics to cool and the capacitors to recharge. Exactly how long depended on the sophistication of the engineering. Allenson counted off the seconds in his head as he ran. He had got to three when the next shot raked through the mushrooms.

Smoke concealed the reconnaissance team, so the gun aimer fired blind. He swiveled his weapon transversely, shooting short bursts. This time he was short. Exploding mushrooms sprayed fragments that trailed white smoke trails in the air like flatulent fireworks.

Allenson ran flat out. His breath came in gasps. Acrid chemicals in the smoke seared his throat. He was probably breathing in carcinogens. He made a note to get a check-up by a genosurgeon when he got home—if he got home. It must be a sign of age to worry about your long-term health while someone was trying to kill you with a bloody big gun.

After a couple more bursts, the gunfire ceased. By then the field was a sea of fire. Everything was dry and inflammable. Fortunately the worst of the inferno raged behind them. Another minute and they reached the edge of the crop. Morton stopped and looked around wildly. In front of them open semi-desert stretched all the way back to the ridge.

"What now, the fire'll burn out quickly. We'll never make it to the rocks before the smoke clears. We'll stand out on the plain like a dog's balls and they'll pick us off easy with a lasercannon."

A mushroom exploded, showering the men with burning fragments. They cursed and beat at their clothes. Allenson hadn't seen a laser impact so the plants must be spontaneously combusting with the heat.

"Follow me," Allenson said, setting out across the open ground at the run.

He angled to the left while keeping the smoke between his small force and the Brasilian guns until he came to where a line of red circles tracked towards the ridge. There he changed course and sprinted towards the nearest circle.

When he reached it he brushed away the red dust deposits from around the edge to reveal an amber stone cover. He pulled at the circle but it stuck fast. Cursing, Allenson felt around under the lip, shuffling around the circular structure on his knees.

"No doubt, you have a plan?" Morton asked hopefully.

"I find curious phenomena interesting and like to explore," Allenson replied. "You should try it sometime. You might be surprised."

"Indeed," Morton said, after a pregnant pause.

"The wind's started again, sir," said one of Morton's canary commandos, biting his lower lip with anxiety.

"Which will blow away the smoke all the faster," Morton said, looking meaningfully at Allenson.

"Then we had better find somewhere to hide," Allenson said with a grin as he flipped the lever his questing fingers had located.

The hatch popped. Allenson tried to lift it open but the ceramic was heavy and he was not well balanced. Two of Morton's men helped him.

"Down you go," Allenson said, pointing to a wooden ladder lashed to metal rods hammered into the sides of the tunnel.

Morton led the way and Allenson went last so he could affix the hatch back in position. The erratic wind was a two-edged sword. It might blow away the smoke but it would also blow red dust back over the hatch. That mightn't fool the Brasilians for long but he was willing to take any advantage going. He hurried down the ladder, hoping to God it would take the weight of six men.

After only a few meters he trod on the hand of the man immediately below. The Canary responded with an imaginative curse that broke several military regulations when addressed to a general.

"What's the hold up?" Allenson asked, impatiently.

"This is a well," Morton's voice floated out of the darkness below. "I've reached water."

"It's not a well—it's a *karaz*," Allenson replied. "Get into the water. It won't be deep. Shine some light around to look for a tunnel."

There was a splash and the queue on the ladder started moving again. The water was less than half a meter deep but very cold. The men pressed together, leaving just enough room for him by the end of the ladder. Morton produced a pocket lamp. He flipped it on, adjusting the beam so it gave a gentle all round blue-tinted light.

"Would you look at that," Morton said, nodding towards an open tunnel leading into blackness.

"Wrong way," Allenson said. "We need to walk upstream— towards the mountain ridge. Come on."

"And a *karaz* is . . . ?" Morton asked, falling in beside him.

"An underground irrigation channel," Allenson replied. "I bet it only rains in the mountains so the indigs have to get water out onto the alluvial plain to farm."

"So why don't they run channels above ground?" Moron asked. "Look at the work to build something like this by hand, let alone the maintenance required to keep it going."

Allenson said, "I guess they have plenty of hands with not so much to do outside of the planting and harvesting times. It's cool down here so less of the water will evaporate."

They walked on in silence.

"Now I come to think on the problem I suspect there is another good reason for underground channels," Allenson observed.

"Oh?" Morton asked with a distinct lack of interest.

"Irrigation salinity, I seem to recall reading that evaporation concentrates minerals in the water. Over time soil salinity rises until the land is sterile. The *karaz* system must control that."

"Fancy," Morton said politely.

Allenson stopped flogging the dead quadruped. He was used to fellow gentlemen not sharing his curiosity about the universe. Destry would have been fascinated. His friend had the true academics' love of knowledge for its own sake.

Allenson wouldn't go quite that far, but understanding how the natural world worked was often useful. No one could have predicted that knowing the difference between a simple well and a *karaz* would one day save his life. He wondered how Destry was faring back in Brasilia.

He was still mulling that over when the bomb went off.

★ CHAPTER 19 ★

Intelligence Gathering

A second, much louder explosion drowned out the first. A mighty hand of water thumped into the small of Allenson's back and he was thrown into silent darkness.

Someone hauled on Allenson's arm. Freezing cold water covered his head. He shook the person off and climbed onto his hands and knees. A voice mumbled into his face. The lamp came back on. Morton was the irritating person. He mouthed something but all Allenson could hear was a blurred murmur like a distant conversation heard while dozing.

He held his nose and blew hard until his ears popped with a sharp crack.

"Are you all right, General?" Morton said.

"Yes, yes." Allenson waved him off. "What about the men?"

"A bit shocked but okay, apart from cuts and bruises. The pressure wave from the bomb knocked us over."

"What bloody bomb?" Allenson asked.

"The Brasilians must have worked out where we'd gone and blown the well entrance. They no doubt think we're dead."

Morton paused, thinking.

"We would be if this really had been just a well. Looks like they don't know what a *karaz* is either."

Allenson's head still rang.

"What the hell did they use, a plasma shell?" he asked.

He poked at his ears with his little fingers but that didn't help. He suspected he had impacted wax against the ear drums. He would have to get Trina to look at it. He was damned if he was going anywhere near an army medic.

Morton shook his head. The motion looked abnormal in the dim light.

"No, I heard two distinct explosions. I suspect they blew us up with a *stereophonic*. I've used them myself to clear caves and bunker tunnels."

"Stereophonic?" Allenson asked.

"It's a homemade bodge but it does the biz," Morton replied, clearly pleased to know something that his general didn't. "You lower two charges into, say, the well where you suspect insurgents are hiding. The top one is a standard explosive device but a few meters below you have a fuel-air explosive mix."

Morton used his hands to outline the shape of the device.

"A charge taped to a bottle of alcohol will do the trick if you have nothing more sophisticated. The charges are rigged so that the top one explodes first, collapsing the tunnel. The thermobaric goes off a few microseconds later. The blast is directed downwards by the overpressure of the first bomb. Anyone in the well is smashed by blast or incinerated by the flame front. With a bit of luck the whole tunnel collapses. In any case oxygen deprivation usually takes out any survivors."

Morton looked thoughtful.

"I guess we survived because the blast dissipated along the long irrigation tunnel and water spray quenched the flame front before it reached us."

"And you've been using this out in the Hinterland colonies?" Allenson asked.

Morton must have detected the disapproval even though Allenson tried to keep his tone neutral. The captain stiffened and his tone became defensive.

"It's getting nasty out there in the Hinterlands, General, with neighbor against neighbor. Sometimes we had to smoke Home Worlder guerrillas out of their lairs. Would you have me send in men instead of stereophonics and pay the resulting butcher's bill?"

"No, Captain, you're quite right to think of your men. I just hadn't realized how far the conflict has spread beyond professional armies."

Allenson had focused all his attention on the Cutter Stream Army. He had not given much of a thought to what else was going on but he should have anticipated nasty developments. When civil war broke out people started to choose sides or at least pretend to. Politics is a useful cloak to cover the paying off of old scores. Atrocity begets atrocity in an evil spiral of retaliation until no one can be neutral.

He had hoped to avoid this by keeping the conflict low key and between professionals. Maybe he had been naïve. He would have to look into this later after they escaped from this bloody place.

"The Brasilians will think we're dead so let's keep it that way. We'll stay in the *karaz* until we reach the foothills and then sneak out the way we went in."

"Captain Morton returned from Insubra with some excellent news," Allenson told Ling, shooting a warning glance at Morton.

Allenson wished to avoid the chiding he would get from his chief of staff if it became common knowledge that he had swanned off into the wild yonder on a mission more suitable for a junior officer. He wished to avoid Trina finding out even more. In his experience wives were inclined to be more forthright when pointing out the errors of their husbands than chiefs of staff were to their generals.

A brief moment of confusion flicked across the unmarried Morton's face.

"Would you like to tell Colonel Ling of your conclusions or shall I?" Allenson asked, unable to resist teasing Morton.

"Um, why don't you, sir?" Morton replied.

Morton clearly didn't understand how to interpret what he saw on Insubran. That alone justified Allenson's decision to undertake the reconnaissance personally. At least that was the excuse he used to himself to justify slipping the leash. He voiced his conclusions.

"Very well, the Brasilians aren't regrouping but pulling out. Captain Morton observed them moving men and essential material from the tramps to the assault ships and dumping nonessentials to make room. The ships are rigging for a long voyage, perhaps down to Port Brasilia or maybe even back to the Home World."

"But that means . . ." Ling began then trailed off.

"That we've probably won, Colonel," Allenson said, trying to keep the exultation he really felt out of his voice. "It's too early to run up victory flags but the loss of Oxford even when garrisoned by regulars will jolt the status quo in Brasilia."

Ling looked like a man who had just checked his lottery numbers and found a match to the jackpot prize but couldn't quite believe it.

Allenson continued.

"The enemy now has just two options. They can reintervene in force. That'd cost a fortune in logistics and denude them of troops at home. Brasilia can't support an army as large as Terra can. It lacks the population. It would hand Terra a golden opportunity if Brasilia sent their army across the Bight."

"And their other option is to negotiate our independence," Ling said with satisfaction.

Allenson nodded.

"Exactly! We'll have to give them a face-saving way out, guarantees of protection to their citizens' lives and assets and so on, but that's okay. We're hardly the maniacs of the Golden Horde trying to set up human hives."

"Heaven forbid," Morton said. "Anyway we'll need inward investment to grow."

Allenson spent the next few weeks rebuilding Oxford, which had taken something of a pounding. He shuddered to think of the damage inflicted by a full-scale urban assault. The city would have been destroyed brick by brick.

He expanded Morton's Canary commandos and used them as a fire brigade to damp down trouble in the Hinterland colonies. Morton had carte blanche to act as a police force in crushing terrorists and criminals of all persuasions whomsoever they claimed to be supporting. Allenson wanted to send a firm message that the government, not anarchy, ruled in the Stream. To be more exact, the army ruled until the government finally got its act together.

The Canaries proved equal to the task, crushing incipient warlords and self-proclaimed freedom fighters. Allenson hammered home a simple message. Freedom from Brasilia didn't meant freedom from civilization. Morton proved himself admirably flexible and nonideological. Allenson soon developed enough confidence to cease trying to micro-manage the Canaries' activities.

That left him time for politics and the delicate task of prodding the

Assembly at Paxton into declaring independence. He hoped that the success of the army would embolden the delegates. It didn't. They found it impossible to make critical decisions.

Independence wasn't just a matter of a simple statement of intent. It involved the creation of administrative and legal structures. That implied agreeing on a constitution. And so the debate ran on.

Allenson used Todd as an emissary. He shuttled backwards and forwards from Nortania with private letters from Allenson to individual delegates and returned with their replies. It would have been easier if Allenson could go himself and steer the discussions to a reasonable conclusion but he hesitated to leave the field army.

He put it about for official consumption that he was needed in case the Brasilians returned. Actually he thought that unlikely. He was really more concerned at something resembling a *coup d'état*. Buller had been somewhat cowed by the success of Allenson's softly-softly strategy. Nevertheless, Trina was convinced that he and Redley were plotting. They certainly were as thick as thieves.

Now that the crisis was over, various people with a grudge hoped to go back to proper soldiering. By that they meant democratically run militias overseen by good chaps who understood the Trinity way of doing business. People like Masters and Wilson.

All in all, Allenson was glad when Hawthorn returned.

"How was your holiday?" Allenson asked when Hawthorn finally made an appearance.

"Very pleasant, thank you," Hawthorn replied, without elaborating.

"Where did you go again?"

"Nortania, Mogadosh to be precise."

Allenson cocked his head as a thought surfaced.

"I seem to recall Trina noticed something about Mogadosh." He dug around in his filing system before finding a news record. "Here it is."

A brief report flicked on in a hologram above his desk. It reported the death of Sar Falco, a wealthy biochem company owner. A mysterious explosion and fire at his holiday villa in Mogadosh had also killed his wife and a number of employees. Foul play was suspected by the local authorities, who announced their expectation of early arrests.

Allenson looked at the picture of Falco attached to the news clip.

"I remember him. He was a delegate to the Assembly. What a shame. He was a useful ally as I recall."

"Really?" Hawthorn replied, with a complete lack of interest.

Allenson looked at the date.

"This must have happened while you were there?"

"Did it?"

Hawthorn used a finger movement to slide the hologram around so he could see it. A small motion detector on Allenson's desk correctly interpreted the gesture.

"Can't say I remember but I was probably busy at the time. I met this interesting woman who—"

"Yes, yes," Allenson cut in to forestall a long account of Hawthorn's amorous adventures. "Trina attached a note at the bottom. I didn't pay any attention at the time . . ."

His voice trailed off as he read.

"Apparently the gossip is that he was killed by Brasilian agents in retaliation for his support for the independence movement. Who would start such a ridiculous rumor."

"I can't imagine," Hawthorn replied

"I mean, why would the Brasilian secret service start knocking off individual delegates?" Allenson asked.

Hawthorn shrugged.

"Who knows, perhaps it was a private matter that had nothing to do with politics," he said casually.

Too casually, in Allenson's opinion; something about all this smelled fishy. Before he could inquire further, Hawthorn pushed a plastic file across the desk.

"I have some bad news."

Allenson sighed and picked up the file, which unlocked on contact with his DNA.

"Give me the bottom line."

"The Brasilians are recruiting mercenaries in the Home Worlds to launch a full scale invasion of the Stream."

Allenson's jaw dropped. That made no sense at all.

"What, but why? We're not worth the aggro—particularly as I've let it be known that we're willing to negotiate."

Hawthorn nodded to the plastic chip.

"They have a good reason. Details in there if you want to look them up."

"Summarize," Allenson said.

"You remember the whispers of a war-winning wonder weapon?"

Allenson groaned.

"Don't tell me it's real."

"No, not exactly. But the Brasilian Navy has discovered a naturally occurring mineral that will revolutionize engineering and warship design. The only known source is in the Hinterlands."

"Oh gawd," Allenson said. "Strategically that makes us worth fighting for. Brasilia can't afford to let Terra or some other Home World get control of this stuff, whatever it is. Are you absolutely sure the intelligence is reliable?"

"The Terran Exoworld Directorate is convinced. So apparently is the Terran Advocate General's Office."

"The Terrans gave you this information?" Allenson asked disbelievingly.

"Not exactly," Hawthorn replied blandly. "I stumbled across a Terran spy ring in the colonies while following a trail looking for Brasilian spooks."

"Quite embarrassing, really," he confessed. "The information was in the files. The chief spook had urgent instructions to drop everything and locate the mineral."

"So we can expect Terran involvement at some stage," Allenson said, more to himself than Hawthorn.

"Possibly, but first we have to fight off a Brasilian-led mercenary invasion."

"Then your softly-softly strategy is a complete bust," Buller said.

"So it would seem," Allenson conceded.

"I told you it would be," Buller said, with the air of a hypochondriac finding out he really is terminally ill.

Allenson allowed Buller his gloomy satisfaction. It would be impolitic to explain why the strategy had failed. The less people knew about a pot of gold at the end of the Hinterland rainbow the better it would be for everyone.

"Recriminations are pointless," Ling said. "I am more interested in where we go from here."

"I am open to suggestions," Allenson replied.

He looked around the room, meeting the eyes of his senior officers one by one. They all looked away except Todd.

"I have a suggestion."

"You!" Buller exclaimed with a snort. "You're only here to keep the minutes."

"I would like to hear your thoughts," Allenson said, ignoring Buller.

"They'll attack Port Trent."

"Why do you say that?" Ling asked. "Why won't they just reinvest Oxford with their new model army?"

"Because Oxford was a defeat," Todd replied. "They'll rationalize of course. They'll argue that you don't reinforce failure and that the hostility of the locals contributed to the disaster."

"All true," said Allenson.

Todd continued. "But the real reason is that soldiers are a superstitious lot. Oxford has bad Karma for Brasilia. They'll want to try a new approach."

"And Port Trent is the most important port in the Stream and also has strong Home World sympathies," Allenson said.

"Precisely."

"In which case we should get there first and fortify the city," Ling said.

"And what happens if wonder boy here is wrong?" Buller asked.

Allenson looked at Buller. "Then we haven't lost anything. I don't have a better suggestion, do you?"

Buller refused to answer so Allenson continued.

"Very well, the bulk of the army will move to Trent. We'll leave a small garrison at Oxford just in case. Please arrange that, Colonel Ling. I want Port Trent fortified under Colonel Buller's supervision. Colonel Hawthorn will be responsible for suppressing sedition."

Allenson caught Hawthorn's eye.

"Minimal visible force, please, Colonel. I don't want the Trent Home Worlders frightened and desperate enough to mount a countercoup."

He looked around the room again.

"You have your orders gentlemen: if you would stay behind, Colonel Hawthorn."

Allenson went to the side table and poured three cups of coffee. One of the perks of being general was that you got to drink real coffee. He carried them back carefully so as not to scald himself and deposited one each in front of Hawthorn and Todd, who rightly assumed Allenson would require his services.

"No need to record this conversation, Todd."

"What's on your mind?" Hawthorn asked.

"We are in a tricky situation legally moving the army into Port Trent," Allenson said.

Hawthorn guffawed. "Is that so? Is it any more or less dubious than fighting a war to take Oxford?"

"Actually, it is," Todd said. "I hadn't considered that point, Uncle. At Oxford it could be argued that here we were just restoring the legitimate civilian authorities."

"And more importantly we were enforcing law and order rather than challenging it," Allenson added.

Hawthorn shook his head in wonder.

"I doubt if the niceties of the law will save you if Brasilia wins. They might admire your rhetoric and all around gall but they'll shoot you just the same."

He considered.

"Shoot us just the same—although I may get away into the Hinterland while they're dealing with you."

He grinned at Allenson who grinned back before explaining.

"I'm trying to avoid a bloody revolution and factionalism. I want a political war for independence. I want to keep as many people as possible on our side and attract new colonists from the Home Worlds after we win. We must be seen to uphold order and stability. Most people will acquiesce with that, whatever their private political loyalties."

"What does that mean in practice?" Hawthorn asked, trying to prod his friend to get to the point.

"It means we don't go into Port Trent like a conquering army. I want you to make a public example of *anyone* who steps out of line."

"Anyone!" Allenson repeated again for emphasis. "Use civil or military law as relevant to the perp."

Hawthorn nodded.

"Understood, no favoritism."

"Being a Home Worlder or expressing loyalty to Brasilia is not a crime," Allenson said for clarification

"But inciting violence is," Hawthorn said.

"Precisely."

Allenson paused to sip his coffee.

"Then there is the problem of the new Brasilian governor."

"Couldn't we just shoot him?" Hawthorn asked.

Allenson assumed his friend was being deliberately provocative but you never knew with Hawthorn.

"No."

Hawthorn sighed.

"Arrest him and throw away the key."

"No."

"House arrest?" Hawthorn asked hopefully.

"Certainly not."

"You're not making my job any easier here!"

"You'll manage, you always do. I suggest you put an armed guard around the Governor's Palace to ensure his safety. They should ostentatiously make records of who goes in and out . . ."

"For the governor's own protection," Todd said with a grin.

"Exactly," Allenson replied.

"Now I come to consider the matter, I think the governor should have a Special Projects bodyguard every time he leaves his palace," Hawthorn said with a pious expression.

Todd said, "That should clip his wings a bit."

Allenson pushed a rebellious lock of hair out of his eyes.

"Let's hope so."

★ CHAPTER 20 ★

Digging In

When Hawthorn arrived at the Port Trent waterfront, the mob had heavy cables attached to the Mother of the Nation statue. They bolted the cables to the back of a heavy tractor. The driver incompetently slammed it into gear with a thump that caused the machine to rock on its suspension. The tractor surged forward until the cables tightened with a twang, then it promptly stalled. The golden statue swayed but remained upright. The mob jeered and howled. Stones glanced off the tractor's ceramic mudguards.

Hawthorn looked around for the civilian police. They stood in groups well clear of the riot. He walked across the road toward the man whose platinum braid marked him out as the senior officer. He would have run but his leg was still stiff from the haul through the Continuum to Trent. The ache did nothing to improve his temper.

"Who are you?" Hawthorn asked.

Startled the man responded automatically.

"Chief Supervisor Brent—of the magistrate's office."

The official looked Hawthorn over and drew himself up to his full quite impressive height. He sucked in his stomach.

"And who the hell are you?"

"Colonel Hawthorn, Commander of Special Projects of the Cutter Stream Army."

A loud cheer from the mob interrupted the conversation. They pulled the incompetent driver out of his cab and boosted a replacement into his seat. The new man got the engine going immediately and the tractor rolled forward to take up the strain. He gunned the engine and applied power through the clutch until the statue swayed once more. The tractor driver played it like a fish on a line, letting it rock back then reapplying power. The Mother of the Nation swayed forward until he had it rocking rhythmically.

One final burst of power and the statue toppled. The waterfront handrail sliced through the statue's head like a guillotine and the head fell into the water with a splash. The eyes that gazed to the horizon were lost to the fish and the mud.

The rest of the statue shattered like a china vase hit by a hammer. The gold exterior was microfilm-thin over cheap ceramic. The mob surged forward to smash up and steal the remains.

"They'll be looting shops next. Why aren't your deputies stopping them?" Hawthorn snarled, putting his face close to the chief supervisor, who recoiled.

"They're your people," the Supervisor said, presumably meaning they supported the revolution.

"No one who destroys or loots property is 'my people,'" Hawthorn replied. "Sort it."

The chief supervisor's eyes hardened. He nodded with satisfaction. He touched his collar and gave the necessary words of command. Uniformed officers fanned out from their various bolt holes.

The supervisor touched his collar again and some sort of communication device appropriated public address systems. His voice boomed across the waterfront.

"This association is illegal under section nine, subsection seven of the code civilis. Disperse immediately."

The rioters' response involved jeering, rude gestures and threatening moves with various improvised weapons. The cops didn't seem to expect anything else. They pitched in with electroshock batons and sublethal ion pistol shots without bothering to wait for the rioters to comply. Presumably the disperse order was necessary for some legal reason but otherwise was not serious.

Hawthorn slung his heavy rifle off his shoulder and switched it on. He held it at the high port position, not pointing it anywhere in particular, but holding it ready.

A rioter reached under his coat. He produced a stubby two-handed weapon with a short barrel and a long downward-pointing ammunition clip just in front of the trigger. He fired from the hip. Leaping flame erupted from the muzzle, accompanied by the harsh chatter of a cheap automatic firearm. The gunman sprayed bullets indiscriminately knocking down two rioters and a cop.

The rifle swung in Hawthorn's arms. He fired without seeming to take aim. The gunman's chest exploded in steam and cooked flesh. The blast flung the man backwards, to crash onto the pavement. He lay like a broken doll, torso at an impossible angle, indicating his spine was shattered.

"Nice shot, gov," said one of the Special Project troopers.

"It's sir, not gov," Hawthorn said wearily.

"Yes, sir."

"Spread out behind the magistrate's deputies and shoot anyone using a lethal weapon."

"Yes, gov."

"By anyone I mean rioters," Hawthorn added for clarification.

Experience had taught Hawthorn that Special Project Troopers tended to have literal minds. He didn't want any screw-ups involving a trail of dead cops.

By the time Allenson arrived at Port Trent, the civilian authorities had the situation back under control. Allenson kept the regular army off the streets, letting just Hawthorn's security troops in their distinctive badged uniforms support the magistrate's deputies. Port Trenters could hate the security troopers all they liked because they would be gone after the war, one way or another, but he wanted to keep the regular army aloof from politics. Nevertheless he made it known that he would not hesitate to intervene if the deputies were attacked by armed insurgents of any political persuasion.

Allenson's desk in his new office in Port Trent drowned in a sea of petitions, requests and unwanted advice. He was unsuccessfully trying to delegate to Hawthorn and Ling, who were putting up a fine defensive action when Todd rushed in without knocking.

"They've done it!" Todd said, waving a datapad triumphantly.

Allenson groaned inwardly.

"Who's done what?" he asked, cautiously.

"The Assembly," Todd replied triumphantly, "have voted to form a new state independent of Brasilia. It was your victory at Oxford that tipped the balance. It put some backbone in the waverers. I came back from Paxton as fast as possible so you would get the news first."

A muted wah-wah-wah noise from outside penetrated the office double glazing. It sounded like the cry of a multitude of the faithful at prayer.

Hawthorn rose from his chair and walked to the window.

"Not quite fast enough it would seem, young Todd. The Independence Movement is staging an illegal victory march up Stanton Street to celebrate. Home Worlders are throwing bottles."

He winced.

"There goes the across town omnibus. The Home Worlders have set it alight to block the road."

Allenson held out his hand and Todd passed the datapad over.

"I see they have drafted a Bill of Separation and Proclamation of Equality," Allenson said, perusing the pad.

"Really? What does it say?" Ling asked.

"It starts by stating that we have no choice but to dissolve the political bonds between the Stream and Brasilia . . ."

Hawthorn sniffed. "Tell that to the Home Worlders."

". . . and then goes on to list our reasons, starting by declaring that we hold certain truths to be self-evident . . ."

Hawthorn said, "If they were that self-evident we wouldn't have spent months rotting outside Oxford or be facing whatever happens here."

"Let's see," Allenson said, ignoring his friend. "All people created equal."

"Including indentured servants?" Ling asked, lifting an eyebrow.

"It says *all* and gives no exceptions," Allenson replied.

"That will go down well among the Manzanita Better Families," Ling said with a grin.

"Certain unalienable rights," Allenson continued, skipping through the paragraphs. "Life, liberty and security, consent of the governed, no taxation without representation—Trina will be amused to see her phrase recycled—justice for all, and so on. I think it's a fine document. No doubt there will be a few rough edges to smooth off in later drafts but this will do admirably for the moment. We'll distribute it unabridged among the troops."

Ling made a note on his datapad before looking up.

"It will soon leak out to the people if we do that."

"Let it," Allenson replied. "Better still, let's publicize it ourselves among our new citizens. This document changes everything, gentlemen. The Brasilian governor and his officials are now unwanted guests in a foreign land. I want them treated with all civilized norms. Equally I want them off-world on the next trans-Bight ship. It also means that Home Worlders have the choice of accepting citizenship or applying for foreign resident rights. Anyone agitating against the elected Assembly is an enemy alien and can be arrested and deported. Is that clear?"

Ling nodded, but Hawthorn was intent on the view outside the office.

"Colonel Hawthorn?" Allenson asked gently.

"What? Oh yes, crystal clear," Hawthorn replied. "Look I think I had better get down there. Someone has just lit up a lasercarbine . There it goes again. I will draft security proposals for you to sign later."

He rushed from the room.

"Never a dull moment, this independence lark," Ling muttered, rising from his chair.

"Right, Allenson, let me outline my preparations," Buller said.

He flicked up a hologram depicting a three-dimensional map of Port Trent and its environs. Trent Bay formed a rough north-south orientated isosceles triangle with its opening to the ocean at the base. Many rivers running southeast drained into it from the forested highlands of the continental mass to the west. The east bank of the bay was formed by a large flat alluvial peninsula called the Douglas Hundreds. This provided the wide protected anchorage for Continuum ships which had made Port Trent rich by colonial standards.

Port Trent sat on the south bank of a northward loop of the Valerie River where the estuary widened into Trent Bay at the cone of the triangle. The Valerie was the largest river in the drainage basin, rivaled only by the Joanne to the south. Port Trent's commercial docks ran south from the city along the upper west bank of Trent Bay.

Buller got up from his chair and walked to the hologram; unlike the other officers, he hadn't bothered to stand when Allenson entered the operation's room. He pointed to a red line that ran around the western suburbs of Port Trent from the Valerie to the coast below the docks.

"This will be the path of our main defensive line to protect the city. Ideally I would build two or three circumventions to give us defense in depth. There just isn't time so one will have to suffice," Buller said. "Fortunately the river estuary and bay act as blocking terrain to the north, east and south. We only have to fortify the west."

The use of circumvention in this context struck Allenson as an unfortunate choice. He knew Buller meant the word simply as a synonym for surround but in the military histories he had read it was often used to mean entrap. That was always the issue in a siege. Sometimes it wasn't clear who had who trapped until the dust settled. He shook himself out of his customary pessimism when something on the map caught his eye.

"What's that?" he asked Buller, pointing to a second red line across the Douglas Hundreds. It lay just to the south of the neck of the peninsula where it joined the mainland.

"I intend to dig a second line in there to defend the Douglas Hundreds."

"In case the Brasilians land on the peninsula?" Allenson asked.

"Of course not, the Douglas Hundreds' fortifications will point north for the same reason that Port Trent's face west," Buller said, not bothering to keep the sarcasm out of his voice.

A number of the junior officers in the operations room developed a keen interest in their work stations or the ceiling. Allenson let his breath out slowly. He kept his face impassive until he was certain he had a grip on his temper.

"And that is?" Allenson asked.

"Because the Brasilians will need to build up a bridgehead somewhere safe from counterattack as they unload. They will be relying mainly on small civilian ships to bring in their equipment. We control the only port capable of docking a trans-Bight ship. That narrows their options considerably, so they will land somewhere well inland."

Buller waved his hand vaguely across the inland regions to the west.

"Why won't they land on the Douglas Hundreds itself?" Allenson asked.

"You haven't been there have you, Allenson. Know why they call it the Hundreds?"

"No doubt you can enlighten me," Allenson said.

Buller looked at him suspiciously, probably rightly sensing sarcasm. Allenson kept his expression bland.

"It's the market garden of Port Trent. There's hundreds of small agricultural plots growing fresh produce for the city. They're irrigated by a spider's web of streams fed from a canal off the Valerie. Not exactly good military going if you see what I mean. It's also close to the city so we could move forces in faster than they could unload."

Allenson frowned.

"I see. So why waste resources fortifying it at all?"

"To stop the Brasilians just walking into the peninsula. I don't want them to set up a base there for two reasons: we may need the food grown on that peninsula if the siege drags on, and artillery positions onto the peninsula could interdict the port. They could do to us what we did to them at Oxford."

Allenson considered. Buller seemed to have thought matters through. It did make sense that the Brasilians only had two options for a landing zone and of the two the inland choice was by far the superior. Nevertheless doubts assailed him. Again the old maxim that if the enemy only has two choices he will inevitably select the third gnawed at his mind. He studied the map again but could not see a third option.

There was no effective defense if the enemy used a fleet of specialized assault ships to drop right in on the city. This whole war was based on the assumption that Brasilia wouldn't risk diverting resources on that scale across the Bight. Allenson saw no flaw in Buller's plan, so he signified agreement.

"That all seems sensible. For the sake of clarity let's christen the primary fortifications the Trent Line and the secondary the Buller Line."

Buller visibly preened.

"You have my permission to carry on, Colonel Buller."

He turned on his heel and left the room without waiting for a reply. It was not so much an intended snub as recognition that Buller was as incapable of appreciating courtesy as he was of giving it.

Todd followed Allenson out.

"One can see why the Brasilian high command found it unnecessary to employ Buller despite his undoubted military skills," Todd said when they were the other side of the door.

That night Allenson was required to attend an evening function in full regalia for the great and the good of Port Trent society. Venceray served again as host. Allenson had a distinct feeling of déjà vu. This time the man wore a crimson jacket and bottle-green corded trousers piped in yellow ochre to link the clashing colors into a single outfit. A transversely positioned triangular hat in yellow topped the effect. The tall and gaunt Venceray looked like a particularly poisonous stick insect in full mating display.

Allenson allowed himself to be steered from dignitary to dignitary, glad-handing all the way. The rictus he adopted in what he hoped looked like a welcoming smile caused his face muscles to ache after about the fifteenth introduction. Todd trawled along behind, surreptitiously recording each conversation. Allenson might need to feign remembrance of the platitudes exchanged at some later meeting. Fortunately nobody looks at a mere aide, so his action went unnoticed.

"You won't remember me," said a woman with gold feathers arranged in a crown which did nothing to hide the fact that she had a face like one of Paxton's draft animals. "But we met at your last reception in this very hall before you took up your command at Oxford."

Actually Allenson remembered her very well. She had been one of the first to sidle out of the by a side door to go to pay her respects to the new governor.

"I just knew you would beat those awful Brasilians, General. I never doubted your victory," the woman gushed.

Allenson tightened his rictus grin. After a few more lies Venceray disengaged him. Next up in the queue was a man who stood out simply because he wore the nondescript outfit of a Heilbron Ascetic.

"That man of yours in charge of security," the Ascetic began, scowling at Allenson, "seems to be some sort of aristo sympathizer. He has treated some of Our People rather roughly."

The capital O and P were clearly enunciated.

"Colonel Hawthorn is quite right to enforce law and order,"

Venceray replied before Allenson could select an appropriate answer. "Your People should learn to respect the property of their betters."

"Just what I'd expect from you, Venceray, being a bit of an aristo yourself," sneered the Ascetic.

Allenson smoothed the argument over with a firm commitment to look into the matter, a promise he had not the slightest intention of keeping. That was the primary advantage of political promises. They were an alternative, not a prelude, to action.

Todd retreated to an alcove to examine his datapad. Allenson kept a watch on him from the corner of his eye as he exchanged pleasantries with an elderly man and his daughter. He didn't want to stare and draw attention to his aide. The daughter kept her head lowered and gazed up at him through her fringe. Allenson found this somewhat disconcerting and wondered if she had a neck condition.

Todd returned and passed Allenson a note without comment. He glanced at it before screwing it up and putting it carefully in his pocket. It wouldn't do to lose it. Someone might pick it up and read the contents.

"Something important was come up?" the elderly man said, cocking his head to one side like a bird that has just spotted an unusually interesting worm.

"Nothing serious," Allenson replied. "Just the usual bureaucratic palaver. It'll keep."

The note was from Ling. It warned him that a fleet had been detected by Morton's Canaries assembling in the Continuum above Port Trent. The itch to rush out of the Hall and back to the operations room was almost overwhelming, but there was nothing he could do that Ling wouldn't already have underway. The last thing these people needed to see was an anxious general.

Next up to the crease was a short man who was as wide as he was tall. He was stuffed into a lime-green suit with transverse bands of steel gray. These clothes and his disconcerting habit of swaying when he spoke gave him the appearance of a child's spinning top. Allenson had to fight the urge to give him a prod to see whether he would bounce back upright by gyroscopic action.

He addressed Venceray, rather than Allenson.

"A bunch of bloody plebs broke into my warehouse and lifted ten cases of imported wine, Venceray. They left a note saying that they had as much right to it as Home Worlder snobs. They sprayed Leveler slogans all over the place."

The short man appeared to be as disturbed by the slogans as the loss of his property.

"Like what?" Allenson asked, genuinely curious. He hadn't come across levelers before.

"Property is theft and so forth. Calls for cancellation of debts and a redistribution of wealth."

"Indeed!" Allenson raised an eyebrow.

"I know," Venceray said, soothingly. "One wouldn't care if they even appreciated what they had stolen. The average pleb can't distinguish imported wine from tractor fuel."

"I don't care whether my customers appreciate the stuff or not. They can feed it to their pigs for all I care—provided they pay me," the short man said, oscillating more furiously from foot to foot.

"The new authorities are committed to protecting private property," Allenson said firmly. "I can't promise we'll always catch criminals, but we'll try. Perpetrators will be punished."

The oscillations slowed.

"Good chap," the short man said. "Only reason I went along with this independence nonsense was because I thought we could trust a Manzanitan gentleman not to have any truck with Levelers."

Wine and other socially-smoothing beverages flowed and the dignitaries coalesced into groups of friends, giving Allenson some peace. He was selecting a canapé when a sharp-eyed woman addressed him.

"The sea food is very good but unless you have a well calloused stomach lining you might want to stick to the mince."

"Thanks," Allenson replied, changing his choice. He liked sea food but the stronger varieties sometimes didn't like him.

"You're very relaxed," she said, taking a canapé and biting into it with even white teeth.

"It is a social occasion. Why shouldn't I be relaxed?" Allenson replied.

"Possibly because my people have sent me word that a Brasilian counterattack is under way?"

Allenson smiled. "You are very informed Lady . . . ?"

"Esmeralda."

"But your people aren't entirely accurate. They haven't started landing yet."

"So we have time to finish our party and beat the Brasilian fleet," she said. "Another glass of wine?"

Another half hour or so and Allenson detached himself from the festivities. He left leaving the more hardened topers relentlessly pouring vintages down their throats. Todd arranged a small buggy fleet outside. They sped to HQ with an escort from Special Projects clearing the way.

The lights were dimmed in the control room. The situation holograms hung like slabs of tinted glass suspended in midair. There was a stillness in the room, an air of anxious expectation like the atmosphere in the fathers' waiting room of a maternity hospital. Whatever their supposed function everyone in the room had their eyes fixed on the central display, which tracked the movements of the Brasilian fleet.

The operational control room was really Port Trent's civilian traffic control center. It possessed better equipment than anything the army could supply. An aide next to Ling slid out of his chair for Allenson to sit down.

Ling nodded to Allenson and picked up a hologram marker.

"They have a rendezvous set up in the Continuum equivalent to about twenty-five kilometers above the surface one thousand klicks to the northwest. They've held position now for nearly four hours while stragglers arrive."

The Brasilian fleet's behavior was consistent with a pack of civilian ships of various cruise capabilities and crew competencies. That answered one question. Allenson had been almost certain that the Brasilians would be forced to use ad hoc transport but it was nice to have it confirmed that they would not be facing a crack assault fleet.

"I suspect this is a navy flagship coordinating the invasion," Ling said pointing to a blip on the hologram that was transmitting a strong beacon signal.

Allenson flirted with dispatching Morton's Canaries stiffened by a couple of light infantry regiments on light frames; a swift hit and run might panic some of the merchant skippers. He reluctantly abandoned the idea. It was too risky.

He had no idea what defenses the fleet employed. For all he knew they were hanging there as bait waiting for a rash countermove. He couldn't risk a reverse at the start of the battle. The morale impact would be disastrous. He sighed, remembering simpler times when he had a lot less to lose than an entire nation.

They sat and watched the hologram for the next hour but no more stragglers arrived.

"Some of their ships haven't turned up," Ling said, grinning.

"It would seem so," Allenson replied cautiously.

He didn't elaborate his suspicion that the Brasilian inactivity was a trap in case Ling thought him hopelessly paranoiac.

"Energy readings increasing," said an excited voice.

"Thank you, Lieutenant," Ling said calmly.

Allenson intently watched the cursors representing the Brasilian ships. They moved, slowly at first but with increasing speed. Ling keyed a side screen that showed the geographic coordinates and velocity of the fleet. They were descending towards the surface, moving southeast towards the city.

"It seems that Buller was right to predict a landing to the northwest of us," Allenson said.

The ships kept coming, not particularly quickly but resolutely. After a few more minutes the navigation system plotted an extrapolation of the fleet's vector. Ling displayed the predicted landing zone. At this stage the ninety-five percent reliability estimate illuminated an area of about fifty kilometers diameter that encompassed most of the area around Port Trent.

The prediction zone shrank as the fleet approached and the prediction certainty hardened. The landing zone centered more and more directly on the city.

"They will no doubt change vectors when they reach their landing zone to a near vertical descent in case we have defense systems," Ling said.

"No doubt," Allenson said.

He wondered whether he was reassuring Ling or the other way around. The Brasilians must know that the colonials had no weapon systems capable of hitting ships except for the short-range point defense cannons in Port Trent itself. If they thought otherwise they would not be employing civilian transport. Unless it was a complex bluff. Maybe they had a naval assault fleet pretending to be merchantmen. Maybe they hoped to lull the Streamers into a false sense of security until they dropped right on the city.

But that was nonsense.

The Brasilians wouldn't need to bluff if they had that strong a force. Unless . . . he shook his head, the endless speculation getting him nowhere. No doubt the Brasilian commander was just being cautious. Your thinking changed when one wrong move could lose the war in an afternoon. You saw danger everywhere.

He smiled, remembering when he could take chances and damn the consequences. Allenson was suddenly aware that everyone in the room was watching him. He saw expressions of awe from the younger officers. They interpreted his half smile as *sang froid*. If only they knew!

"Energy blip, the fleet is part phasing and changing course," a young female voice said.

Game on, Allenson thought. The predicted landing zone flickered then changed location. Allenson expected it to move northwest as the Brasilian fleet descended.

It didn't.

Ling leaned forward to gaze at the hologram.

"What the fornicating hell are they up to?"

★ CHAPTER 21 ★

Hurry Up and Wait

The Brasilian fleet flattened their descent. The predicted landing zone moved out over the Douglas Hundreds. The ships crossed the city dephased at a height of around three thousand meters with all their lights on. A frustrated lasercannon operator triggered a wild and pointless burst. He may as well as waved at the ships for all the good it did.

"Makes you wish for a decent strategic defense system," Ling said with a grunt of disgust.

"May as well wish for a state of the art battlefleet while you're on," Allenson replied. "What puzzles me is where the hell they think they're going."

The fleet descended steeply until it disappeared from Port Trent's tracking system somewhere over the south of the peninsula.

Allenson touched a key.

"Morton?"

Captain Morton's head and shoulders formed above the console.

"We've lost contact with the enemy somewhere over the southern Hundreds. Get a team in the air and find them," Allenson said.

"On my way, sir."

Morton's arm reached forward and his hologram winked out of existence.

Allenson took an injector out of his pocket into which he had preloaded a *Nightlife* stimulant. He hadn't been sleeping well lately. The tube hissed when he flipped off the safety and pressed it against his wrist. Within seconds his weariness dropped away. The lights in the control room shone starker and the holograms sharper. He felt like an athlete on the balls of his feet waiting for the starting pistol to crack. There would be a price to pay later.

"Now what?" Ling asked.

"Now we wait," Allenson said, sinking back in his chair. "It's going to be a long night. Put the army on alert, First Brigade to be ready for deployment at one hour's notice."

"They already should be," Ling replied.

Allenson noted that his chief of staff had his hands behind his back. He probably had his fingers crossed.

"Remind them again," Allenson said. "Just in case."

Ling nodded.

The night dragged on with no word from Morton. The clock on Allenson's datapad ticked over. Each second lasted for at least a minute. Partly that was the situation but partly it was the Nightlife. Ling had put his chair back and closed his eyes. Allenson should have tried to get some sleep but the wide-awake juice did its job.

Oh well, too late now, as the man said, stepping into the empty lift shaft. He could take a sleeper and then redose on Nightlife later. He could also go barking mad.

Allenson chuckled out loud at the absurdity of it.

Ling woke up startled.

"Any news?" he said, stabbing at his console.

"Sorry Colonel, I didn't mean to disturb you. It's just that sometimes life is just too ridiculous to take seriously."

Ling looked at him as if he had taken leave of his senses. Allenson hastened to explain.

"You know the old army joke: hurry up and wait. Can you imagine how the troopers on standby are cursing us?"

"Yes, sir," Ling said, doubtfully.

The junior officers tittered sycophantically, any joke made by a general being considered hilarious no matter how weak it would have sounded from a second lieutenant.

At that point the console chimed and Morton's head and shoulders appeared.

"About bloody time," Allenson said under his breath.

"Sorry sir," Morton replied.

The gain on Allenson's console must be extraordinarily sensitive.

"Never mind that, Captain, where are they?"

"They've landed on one of the islands making up the reef to the south of the Douglas Hundreds peninsula."

"What?" Allenson replied. "I didn't know there were any islands there."

"They're very small and uninhabited so they probably wouldn't be shown on your maps," a local officer said over Allenson's shoulder. "Waves go right over them when a tornado hits."

He keyed up a small-scale map of the area showing a rocky archipelago.

"One of them's inhabited now," Morton said. "The invasion fleet's a ragbag of merchantmen and one assault ship running point defense. I lost two men before we knew it was there. The Brasilian Navy have all communications around the island jammed. That's why we had to wait until I got back to the mainland to report. I'm sending the data now."

A red cross appeared on an island about five hundred meters off the point of the peninsula. Another hologram opened to show a movie of the landing site. The assault ship sat on its skids on a flat plate of broken reef that had partially collapsed under the large vessel's weight.

Small tramp ships perched on rock outcrops nearby. At least two had toppled over into the shallow water. Allenson wondered how the Navy had gotten merchant owners to take such a risk with their property. The method of persuasion probably involved naval petty officers equipped with lasercarbines and bad attitudes standing behind the merchant skippers during the landing. It would never have occurred to him to use that level of ruthlessness—but then Allenson had to live in the Stream after the war. The Brasilian admiral didn't.

Larger merchantmen had landed in water channels between the outcrops. One of them had broken its back on a hidden reef just below the waterline. Men disembarked from the merchantmen and the assault ship deployed equipment using its cranes and lifts.

He toyed with ordering an immediate fast strike by First Brigade while the Brasilians were vulnerable. The problem was the scene was already an hour old. If the Brasilian commander knew his stuff, and there was no reason to assume he didn't, then he would have prioritized the deployment of point defense systems to boost the cover provided by his ship. That was probably what was being unloaded from the assault ship in the recording.

The damaged merchantmen wouldn't slow down deployment all that much. In the Brasilian's shoes, Allenson would just blow open the hulls where necessary to create new unloading hatches.

He decided to stick to the plan and wait for the Brasilians to attack Trent's fortifications. His raw troops would perform much better in fortified positions. The thought reminded him of something, the Buller Line across the Douglas Hundreds faced the wrong way, but did the line matter anyway?

He resisted the urge to send Buller a "told you so" message. Allenson had approved the defense layouts, which made them his responsibility irrespective of their originator.

"There's something wrong," Ling said.

He had been rerunning the video clip and checking it against maps and picture of the archipelago.

"Colonel Buller was convinced that the Brasilians would land on the mainland rather than the Douglas Hundreds because they would be trapped in the peninsula in a maze of canals, right?"

"Yes," Allenson replied.

"But surely all those issues still apply to their landing zone only with polished knobs on. Have a look at that island chain."

Ling keyed up a picture.

"It's a mass of shallow low-lying coral reefs separated by deep water channels. It's going to be a nightmare to transport troops across. Those reefs have never been surveyed so the Brasilians won't be able to use anything much bigger than a shallow-draft lighter. They'll be moving in penny packets and then only onto the Douglas Hundreds. Only a maniac would try to cross the mouth of Trent Bay in a lighter. One ocean storm and . . ."

Ling made the gesture with his hand of a knife cutting a throat.

"We can send light troops by frame down into the Hundreds to intercept each landing party as they come ashore. With locally superior numbers we can cut them to ribbons and defeat them in detail."

Ling's voice rose in excitement. Someone in the control room started to cheer and then thought better of it.

Allenson's mind raced.

"But why are they doing this? The Brasilian military are not stupid. Okay, inexperienced about conditions this side of the Bight, but they know a great deal about positional warfare, including defended landings. What are we missing?"

Ling said. "Perhaps it's simply that they underestimate us."

"Perhaps, but after Oxford I would have thought they might do us the curtesy of taking the Stream Army seriously . . ." Allenson's voice trailed off.

They called this the loneliness of command. Staff propose but only the general can dispose. For good or ill, only the general has the responsibility. Allenson scanned and rescanned the map of the area, searching for inspiration and eventually he came to a decision.

"You see this area here," he said to Ling, pointing to a compound about two thirds of the way down the Hundreds.

"Slapton," Ling confirmed.

"The ground seems to be drier."

"That's why the warehouses are there. It's somewhat higher than the rest of the peninsula."

"Excellent. We'll dig in a couple of line regiments. It'll take the Brasilians some time to get that far and we'll have plenty of warning of their approach. Let's see if we can trap them in the south of the Hundreds. Use First Brigade, our most reliable troops."

"Very good, General, but First Brigade is currently manning the Buller Line."

Allenson thought about it.

"Unfortunately those fortifications face the wrong way. Let's not abandon them at this stage in case this is part of some colossal feint and they're going to make a second landing on the mainland. It's probably a waste of time, but we have the manpower just sitting around in Port Trent. Marching will keep them out of trouble."

"How about the Eleventh then? They're mostly new recruits."

"Why not, some regular soldiering experience will do them no harm. Get them moving immediately."

Ling grinned.

"Hurry up and wait. That's the army way."

Ling busied himself at his console, patching through a secure call to Colonel Kaspary.

Allenson flicked through the holograms again. The doubt worm insisted that he had missed something. His decision was a compromise. All books on military strategy warned against compromise as delivering the worst of all worlds, but it was damn easy for an academic to urge bold strokes from the comfort of an armchair. Allenson lacked the luxury of hindsight to guide him.

Every military disaster that ever happened started as a bold decision that looked like a good idea to someone somewhere. You never won big from a compromise but you rarely fecked up on a grand scale either. He comforted himself by the thought that strategically he didn't have to win but survive. It was the Brasilians who needed a tactical victory. Let their commander stake all on a bold thrust while Allenson awaited events.

He smiled at his own torturous thought processes.

Hurry up and wait, that *was* the army way, but mostly one merely waited.

And Allenson waited—and waited—and waited. The mills of the Home World military might grind fine but by God they ground exceedingly slow. The Brasilian commander continued his ponderous build up and preparations. It seemed likely to Allenson that the enemy would move slowly and deliberately reef by reef onto the Hundreds.

He imagined that the Brasilian infantry would move forward, keeping all the while under the umbrella of their point defense cannon and dig in. The cannon would then be brought forward to the new position and the whole grisly process repeated.

Step by step like an invalid on crutches they would advance to the Hundreds and there was not a damn thing he could do about it. The Brasilian commander probably prayed each night that the rebel forces would be desperate enough or rash enough to strike at his line and be fried by the lasers.

The problem was that the Brasilian strategy made no logical sense when you factored in logistical requirements. They desperately needed to capture a port to resupply their army. It may have been a small force by Home World standards but their men still had to eat and their equipment would need fuel and spares.

They couldn't have carried enough materiel in their ragbag

improvised fleet to keep them going for more than a few weeks, maybe two months at most, which meant they would need resupply. How many tramp ships could the Brasilians seize to cast ashore on the Hundreds' treacherous barrier reefs? Damn few of the vessels would survive a single trip, let alone half a dozen, and by now the word would have gone out among the merchant skippers. Many ships would disappear before they could be requisitioned. Bad news was the only thing that traveled faster than light.

What kept Allenson awake was that he had no idea what the Brasilians intended. In the small hours when his confidence was at its minimum he imagined ever more unlikely and fabulous fiendish tricks from the enemy. He desperately needed information.

Hawthorn's spy network drew a blank because the Brasilian forces were fresh in from across the Bight. He hadn't had time to infiltrate them or subvert anyone. Morton volunteered to personally lead reconnaissance intrusions into the Brasilian landing zone but their security was superb. The Canaries lost so many men without useful result that Allenson forbade further missions. They had no more luck with drones. The police and civilian models available in Port Trent were utterly incapable of penetrating an assault ship's automated countermeasures.

So Allenson waited and worried. The only good thing that could be said about the delay was that it gave plenty of time for Kaspery's First Brigade to dig in at Slapton. He now had defense in depth throughout the Douglas Hundreds based on two solid defensive lines. He ordered continuous and aggressive patrolling to control the dead ground.

This was imperative in the case of the First. They had to locate and eliminate each Brasilian beachhead when it came ashore before the enemy could dig in and reinforce. In the case of the Eleventh it was really just a case of live ammunition training, as they were safely behind the fortifications manned by the First. He just hoped that the soldiers of the Eleventh didn't shoot each other too often.

Allenson had been in bed about two hours when his pad chimed on the emergency line. He struggled up from sleep, having taken a knock-out before retiring. He sat up, slapped the pad to turn off the alarm and stared bleary eyed at the screen. He had three goes at touching the communication key before making contact.

Trina stirred beside him.

"What is it?"

"Go back to sleep. It's just Ling."

"Does he know what time it is?" Trina asked, consulting a clock sculpted to resemble a mythical snake-beast attached to her side of the bed.

"I'm sure he does. Go back to sleep."

"Fat chance if you're going to hold a conference in the bedroom."

Trina swung her legs out of bed and reached down for her robe. Pulling it on, she disappeared out of the bedroom door.

"Sorry to disturb you, General," Ling said, clearly embarrassed. He had obviously overheard the matrimonial exchange.

"I'm sure you have a good reason," Allenson replied, his tone implying that Ling had better come up with a good reason.

"Well," Ling began uncertainly. "It may not be significant but Kaspary reports that he has lost contact with one of his patrols."

"Where?" Allenson asked.

"Down in the southern tip of the Hundreds."

Allenson could have wept. There could be a million reasons why a patrol had gone off the air, starting with communication failure and ending with the possibility that the bastards had found a comfortable spot and were taking a kip. He was so tempted to bite off Ling's head but what stopped him was the possibility, a faint possibility but a finite one nonetheless, that some subterfuge of the enemy was responsible. He didn't want to become the type of commander whose staff concealed matters to avoid a bollocking.

He took a deep breath.

"You were right to inform me immediately but as you say it probably isn't significant. Let me know if there are any—"

Allenson stopped because Ling clearly wasn't listening. He had his head turned away from his panel and was conversing with someone off-screen out beyond the sound isolators around his 'phone.

He waited until Ling turned back.

"Sorry, General, another report from Kaspary's headquarters. The forward patrol base has also gone off air."

A cold chill flowed over Allenson as if he had walked under a liquid nitrogen shower. The officer of the watch in the forward patrol base would have been chosen because he could be guaranteed to stay awake. He would have multiple communication devices at his disposal. They couldn't all have failed.

"Where is Kaspary now?"

There was another pause before Ling replied.

"He's leading a reconnaissance in force down to the coast."

Allenson nodded. Kaspary was a good man, which was why he was in charge of the First, but in this case Allenson wished Kaspary had sent a subordinate and stayed on the line. A mind worm sneered at him for hypocrisy as Allenson would have done exactly the same in Kaspary's place.

Trina marched back into the bedroom, holding a mug in each hand. White vapor trailed out into the chilly night air. Allenson smeled the complex herbal aroma of tea.

"I've got to go," he said, pulling himself from the bed.

He pulled open the drawer of his bedside table and held a Nightlife capsule against his wrist. Trina pursed her lips, but mercifully she did not comment.

The stimulant shot through his bloodstream, erasing all hint of tiredness. He felt alert and keyed up. Only the overbright edge to the colors in the softly lit room and the tinny harshness of every slight sound hinted that his body was being tuned beyond normal operating limits.

"Drink this before you leave. It will do you more good than those damned chemicals," she said, holding out a mug.

Allenson took it. He didn't want a drink, but it was a minor enough concession to matrimonial harmony. He gulped down the hot tea, scalding his tongue and throat. The wide-awake made it taste like copper sulphate, but to his surprise he did feel better after a few more sips. After a few more sips it even began to taste like tea.

"Don't you ever sleep, Ling?" Allenson asked, sliding into the chair beside his chief of staff.

"Sleep, right, I remember that luxury. These days I live on wide-awakes."

"Those things are only a short-term solution," Allenson replied disapprovingly. "You can't rely on them for any length of time."

"No, General," Ling replied, face devoid of expression.

"So what've we got?"

"Our communications are being screwed by saturation interference, but I've got intermittent contact with Colonel Kaspary. He's taken a whole regiment with him . . ." Ling checked his pad, "the Greenbelts, and is moving by frame low level and part phased down the center of the peninsula."

Ling keyed up a hologram map with a moving red line showing Kaspary's projected path.

Allenson nodded. "Good man, Kaspary, he won't full phase in case the Brasilians have a trap set up in the Continuum."

"Yes, sir, but of course that restricts his speed."

"You said we'd lost contact with some of our people. Has it been reestablished?"

Ling shook his head. "No, sir, in fact the problem is spreading."

Ling touched the console and overlaid the silent zone over the map. It formed an amorphous orange shape that ran across the bottom of the peninsula and up the coast, facing the mainland like a twisted amoeba. The zone curled around the red line representing Kaspary's forces as if the metaphorical amoeba was reacting to a needle probe.

Allenson found the graphic extremely disturbing.

"Contact Kaspary and order him to withdraw back to the Slapton Line. Do it now."

"One moment, General, we have to keep jumping frequencies to sidestep the interference. It's a bit hit or miss," said a young woman's voice behind him.

"Lieutenant Fendlaigh," Ling whispered in Allenson's ear. "Our communications geek."

She hunched over a console, long pale brown hair hanging from below a green cap displaying the badge of the army's engineering section. Hard brown eyes peered through a gap in hair like a child's pet hamster gazing out of its straw nest. Her fingers danced on her console like a concert pianist in the middle of a solo.

Thirty years ago Allenson would have dedicated a poem to her, probably a very bad one if past experience was any guide.

"Got him," she said triumphantly, pushing back her hair with her left hand while she fine-tuned something with her right.

"Kaspary," Allenson said, forgetting her. "Report please."

Kaspary's head appeared above his console. The man's eyes were wide and he'd lost his helmet.

"We've contacted the enemy. They seem to be raiding in some force."

The hologram flashed white and Kaspary ducked momentarily.

"I've ordered A Company to debus from their frames and take up ambush positions to pin the Brasilians. B and C Companies are still mounted and I've sent them to probe wide out to the left and right. I'm going to try to turn the Brasilian flanks and pocket them."

Kaspary's head disappeared. A gently flashing soft green light on the blank hologram indicated that they still had communications contact. Kaspary had turned off the feed at his end.

Allenson resisted the urge to call him back. The colonel was busy. He hardly needed some old fool of a commanding officer nattering on in his hear distractingly when he was trying to fight a battle.

"I've patched into helmet feeds," the communications officer cut in.

She really was first class. Allenson made a mental note to remember her name and to mark her down for advancement.

"Put them up," he ordered.

New holograms opened above the command console. The quality was patchy and the images winked in and out as she made and lost connections. The troops were on night vision, so the images were in shades of blue. Synthetic colors could be overlaid but they added little to resolution and could be positively misleading.

White streaks marked out incoming laser fire, a burst like a time lapse photograph of a meteor shower marking a heavy weapon. The hologram winked out. Allenson hoped that was because the feed was lost when the trooper threw himself face down rather than the other obvious explanation, that the soldier's head had been blown off.

Heavy weapons with a raiding force implied vehicles of some sort. Allenson's paranoia went up a notch.

"Find me a feed showing the Brasilians," he ordered the communications officer.

"All the engagements on the feeds are at long distance," she said, voice shrill with excitement. "But the range is closing, hang on."

Her fingers danced across the console and a hologram popped up.

It looked like a giant bathtub on wide tracks, the front square and sloping forward. The tank moved slowly over the muddy surface, gaining just one meter forward for every two meters of track wound underneath the hull.

The helmet camera was attached to the helmet of a trooper lying in ambush behind a canal. The waterway was not particularly broad, but had syncrete-supported banks suggesting depth. The tank tipped into the canal with a splash and floated. Its tracks churned the water to foam as it swam the few meters to the other side.

The forward-sloping tracks gripped the syncrete and the machine pulled itself from the water. Its tracks bit and slipped in succession, making the hull judder like a dog shaking itself after a swim.

"They've got amphibious armor," Allenson said. "The water's no protection at all."

★ CHAPTER 22 ★

The Loneliness of Command

The hologram showed a viewpoint down the sight of a single shot heavy laserrifle. The weapon was normally used to take out bunkers but at the moment it was aimed at a blunt armored prow grinding slowly towards the observer. The hologram whited out when the gun fired. In the aftermath a blue-white splash on the armor plate showed where the hit failed to penetrate. The whine of the rifle's recharging capacitors was clearly audible over the feed.

The tank paused and then turned by braking its right track. It spun ten or twenty degrees and slid. The left track sliced through the wet topsoil to kick a slice of turf across the ground like pudding slapped by a sharp knife.

The turn revealed a tribarreled lasercannon mounted on the left rear side of the open topped vehicle. White streaks zapped out of the 3-D hologram when the tribarrel spun. Ling automatically ducked. Allenson was too focused on the picture to react.

The Streamer fired his heavy weapon again. This time the pulse flashed on the suspension between the tracks on the flank of the armored box. A green flare of burning metal and ceramics spurted from the hit and the suspension caught fire.

Smoke rolled up to mask the tribarrel just as it fired another burst. The explosive flashback blew out the back of the tank. The tank's frontal armor clanged down to make a ramp and men ran out, one on fire. He dropped into the wet mud, rolling in a futile attempt to put out the flames.

An internal explosion outlined the waving arms of a black figure propelled by the blast wave to the top of the ramp. The concomitant backdraft sucked the enemy soldier down into the blazing hulk.

The hologram devolved into a confusing mess of white streaks and explosions. Then it winked out.

"I'll try to get the signal back," said the communications officer in a disappointed voice.

"No, show me a map of the whole peninsula," Allenson replied. "Overlay the locations of troops with whom we still have contact."

A rash of blue dots sprang up.

"Now put up the positions of units with which we have lost contact."

Yellow dots.

". . . and the location of known enemy forces."

Red triangles.

Allenson picked up a marker pen and pointed it at the hologram.

"You see these yellow dots along the west coast behind the Slapton line? My guess is that we have already been outflanked. I expect to see yellow dots and then red triangles on the east coast next. The Brasilians would have found the going easier in the sheltered waters of the Bay than on the open ocean side and so would have made faster progress."

He paused, rubbing his forehead.

"We've been outplayed, gentlemen," Allenson said wearily, momentarily forgetting that some of his officers were ladies.

No one was stupid enough to raise the point in the current situation.

"The enemy strategy is clear. They will pin Kaspary's First Brigade into the Slapton line; then use their amphibious capability to outflank and surround before chopping into the defenses from the rear. They'll slice the Line into segments and defeat each part in detail."

Ling said, "We could send the 11th south to hit the Brasilians in their rear."

"That would mean abandoning the Buller Line," Allenson replied.

"I could move troops from the Trent Line to take over the Buller," Ling said hesitantly.

"Yeees," Allenson replied, unconvinced. He really didn't want to strip Port Trent's defenses in case the Brasilians had another surprise up their metaphorical sleeve.

Allenson gazed at the map, head cocked to one side. There was absolute silence in the control room. This was the loneliness of command. Oh sure, you got to wear a fancy uniform and strut up and down while everyone saluted and laughed sycophantically at even your weakest attempts at humor. But there would come a time when you had to pay the price: when you sat in a headquarters and everyone waited upon your decision, when you could lose the war "in an afternoon."

He noticed an installation marked on the map at the western end of the Slapton Line.

"What's that," he said indicating it with his pen.

Ling peered at it.

"I don't know, sir."

"That's Slapton Ferry," one of the locals in the control room said. "No one lives there. It's not much more than a dredged deep-water cutting with a jetty. It was built to load and unload lighters but most stuff goes by frame these days."

"Contact Kaspery again," Allenson said to Ling. "Order him to retreat northwest with his advanced regiment to fall back on Slapton Ferry, then tell the commander of the 11th to move one of his regiments south into the Brasilan rear. Leave the other two to keep working on refacing the Buller Line, just in case."

A half-formed idea floated at the back of Allenson's mind. If all went well it would stay a mere phantom. If matters went against the Stream Army then he believed he might just have taken out an insurance policy. But he needed someone trustworthy to help him set it up. He took out his pad and keyed in a private number, activating the sound damper so his conversation was private. An icon showed when Trina picked up

"Trina, round up all the lighters you can get your hands on."

Trina's smile vanished and she slipped into business mode instead of asking pointless questions.

"Where do you want them?"

"Slapton Ferry and don't wait until you can assemble a convoy. Get each one moving as fast as possible."

"Understood."

She touched a key and cut the link.

Trina looked up Slapton Ferry and blinked when she discovered its location. Putting the why questions out of her mind for the moment, she concentrated on the how. She dug through the Port Trent Chamber of Commerce list to find contact details. The first proprietor she pinged failed to pick up, so she left an auto to keep trying and pinged the next. A pair of bleary eyes looked out of her console.

"Do you know what time it is?" the man said.

"Chowtrees Lighters?" Trina asked.

"Uh, yes," the man said.

"I'm Lady Allenson of Pentire. How many lighters have you available for immediate hire?"

The man perked up.

"Two available right now and a third is undergoing a motor service. My lads can get it back together in a couple of hours."

Trina nodded.

"Very good, I want you to send them empty to Slapton Ferry and await further instructions."

The man stared at her. One could almost see his mind revolving.

"That's on the Hundreds."

He paused.

"Why do you want them?"

"That's my business," Trina replied.

"The Brasilians are over on the Hundreds aren't they? Here, I don't want my boats anywhere near a warzone."

"You will be indemnified for any damage or loss," Trina said.

Actually she had no idea whether that was correct but right now she didn't care.

"And how about any lost earnings?"

"They're not earning anything at the moment are they?"

The man's eyes flickered.

"No, I want double the usual hire rate, half paid in advance and indemnification."

"I don't have time for this," Trina said calmly.

"Your problem," the man said.

He obviously thought he had her over a barrel.

"As I don't have time to negotiate, I will simply give you my terms which are normal hourly rates and indemnification. You will agree or I will send a Special Project detachment to requisition your vessels and man them. In that case no monies of any kind will be paid for any reason but you will get your barges back, assuming Special Projects don't run them aground or something. Most troopers are none too careful with kit in my experience."

"You can't do that!"

"Just watch me."

She got her barges.

Dawn broke before she had finished. An owner of one of the larger lighter fleets had told her to commit an unnatural sexual act. She got the distinct impression that he was no friend of the new administration.

When Trina was satisfied that matters were on the move so far as they could be, she pinged Hawthorn and informed him of her actions. She happened to mention the recalcitrant boat owner. Hawthorn ventured to suggest that he was confident the owner could be persuaded to change his mind after he paid him the compliment of a personal visit to explain the situation.

Trina grinned. People like Hawthorn were a liability in the normal run of things but he definitely had his uses when push came to shove. She also took the opportunity to explain her anxieties to Hawthorn. Trina knew her husband better than he knew himself and she could predict his actions before he thought he had made up his mind.

By nine o'clock the control room was deathly still. What do you say when a disaster slowly unfolds in front of you? Allenson waved away the aide who tried to serve him breakfast. Ling indicated that the aide should leave the tray on the side. While Allenson watched the monitor, Ling poured a mug of cafay and placed it at Allenson's elbow.

Red triangles poured around the Slapton Line and sped up the flanks to the Buller line, neatly bypassing the green regiment Allenson had ordered south. The regiment promptly disintegrated when the troops realized the enemy was in their rear.

The green square signifying the unit dissolved into a swarm of green dots representing individual units at company or even section level. Green dots fled on for the safety of the Slapton Line, back to the

Buller line or merely dodged randomly in zig-zag circles, bouncing off advancing Brasilian tanks like ricochets in a pin-ball machine.

Under relentless Brasilian pressure the troops of the 1st stationed at the eastern end of the Slapton line abandoned their position. They became hopelessly intermingled with green units from the 11th.

The only regiment maintaining cohesion was the Greenbelts. They were under Kaspary's direct control and had a purpose other than just waiting to be attacked. Information flowed into the control room and orders flowed out with little discernible impact on the growing chaos.

"All this technology and I have no more control over the battle than an ancient general standing on a hill waving colored flags," Allenson said.

The first green dots slipped from the Buller Line in the direction of the city as the panic spread to the remaining troopers of the 11th.

"There's nothing to stop the enemy taking the Buller Line on the bounce and rolling straight into the city," Allenson said tonelessly.

"I could send the 5th Brigade from the Trent Line to advance into the Hundreds," Ling said.

Allenson shook his head.

"There's no point in reinforcing failure. We'd just lose another brigade."

"Then let me send them into the city. The Brasilian tanks will be useless there and we can make them fight for every street and block."

Allenson's lips pursed.

"And Port Trent will be left a shattered ruin with extensive civilian casualties. It wouldn't matter who won the battle then as we would most decisively have lost the war. No keep the 5th back as a reserve so we can salvage something from this mess."

Allenson rubbed his eyes, feeling very tired and very old. Ling diplomatically inched the cafay forward a centimeter or two. Allenson automatically picked it up and took a gulp. It was cold, but he felt suddenly thirsty and drank it anyway. Ling signaled an aide and a fresh mug magically appeared accompanied by baked bread and cheese.

"You're starting to act like my wife, Colonel," Allenson said, between mouthfuls.

"I believe the duties of a chief of staff and wife have similarities but only up to a point, sir," Ling said, deadpan.

While Allenson ate, Ling studied the changing depositions of Brasilian units.

"I may be wrong but I think the Brasilians have ceased advancing," Ling said.

Allenson carefully put down his bread and studied the hologram. The red triangles had stopped their rush north on the edge of the Buller Line.

"Are they regrouping for an assault?" Ling asked.

"But they're not concentrating," Allenson replied, in wonder. "In fact they seem to be doing quite the opposite and dispersing across the peninsula."

The two men stared at the hologram until Ling cleared his throat.

"You know," he said hesitantly. "It looks to me that they might be digging in."

"Thank all the gods of lost battles for over-cautious generals," Allenson said. "They're digging in to prepare for a systematic assault. They must be waiting for artillery to come up."

Allenson laughed with relief.

"Now we have a chance to save the army."

He sprang up and pulled on his jacket, all fatigue a lost memory.

"But where are you going?" Ling asked.

"Where I might be useful because there's nothing I can do here that you can't do just as well if not better."

He paused at the door.

"Sorry, Colonel, but for the moment I leave the loneliness of command to you."

"Bloody super," Ling replied. "Go with him, Fendlaigh, and take a field set."

Allenson left the control room at the run. Actually doing something, as opposed to watching other men fight, made him euphoric, like discovering exactly where a splinter was located in one's softer tissue and extracting same.

He slowed as he left the building, partly to key the voice communications icon on his pad and partly because generals shouldn't be seen to run. It implied that all was going to hell in a frame with a broken pedal. It was especially important not to convey such an impression when all was actually going to hell.

"Sar," Boswell answered instantly.

"Uh, right," Allenson said. "You're there."

"Yes, sar, was there anything else, sar?" Boswell asked.

"Ah, yes, how soon can you bring my frame round?"

"Your official general's carriage or your barge?"

"The barge. Where we're going I need reliability and robustness rather than cute decorations."

"Very good, sar."

"So how long?"

"Perhaps you should look up, sar."

Allenson raised his eyes to find the barge parked outside his headquarters with Boswell up front in the driver's position. Someone had bolted ceramic ablative armor around the pulpit to the front and sides to reduce the driver's exposure. The faint shimmer coming off the barge's extended pylons indicated that it was energized and ready to fly.

Todd leaned over and helped him up into the rear compartment. Hawthorn leaned casually against the other side. He methodically checked the charges on extra power loads for his rifle and stowed them carefully in a pouch strap that he wore over one shoulder.

"Nice of you to join us," Hawthorn said with a smile.

"And what the freaking hell are those for?" Allenson asked.

Two long tribarrels on flexible gimlets were clamped to the front corners of the barge's rear compartment, pointing out to the port and starboard flanks. They were manned by men in Special Projects uniforms wearing helmets with reflective full face visors. One half turned and gave Allenson a cheery wave which he half returned before thinking better of it. Thick braided power cables coiled down to a large power supply cemented against the front bulkhead.

"Oh, I thought they might come in useful," Hawthorn said.

"I've no intention of looking for trouble," Allenson said defensively.

"Of course not," Hawthorn said sadly. "But somehow you'll stumble across it. You always do."

Allenson bridled but decided not to pursue the matter.

"There is a possibility of danger," he said to Boswell, "and you're not signed up to be a soldier. Maybe you should stay behind. Lieutenant Allenson can drive."

Boswell answered by activating the field. Fluorescing blue balls rolled down the barge's pylons. It lifted as the Continuum field bit on reality.

"Sir? Sir?"

Lieutenant Fendlaigh ran unsteadily out of the headquarters building, her slight figure burdened by a heavy rucksack over each shoulder.

Boswell looked at Allenson, who indicated he should kill the field and the barge settled back onto the ground.

Hawthorn hauled Fendlaigh aboard before she could mount the ladder and she ended up in his arms. He smiled at her, eliciting a blush. Allenson coughed and made the introductions. Fendlaigh stepped back into officer mode and started to unpack her gear.

Allenson nodded to Boswell, who lifted the barge off the ground once more, climbing steeply to avoid Port Trent's administration buildings.

"Hang on, I haven't said where we're going yet," Allenson said, taken by surprise and having to grab a rail to steady himself.

A trooper held out his hand but quickly retracted it when Allenson glared at him.

"Slapton Ferry, where else," Hawthorn replied.

★ CHAPTER 23 ★

Slapton Ferry

The sun came up, bathing Port Trent in pastel light. Filtering through kilometers of air it stained the few clouds in the sky bright satin pink like drapes in an upmarket brothel.

The barge dropped down to near water level where waves ran up the bay, breaking and rebreaking into white foam as the swells tumbled into shallower and shallower water. Whipped by the wind, the foam quickly blew away to add to a sea mist hanging over the water. There was little sensation of speed within the continuum field. Allenson couldn't even feel the chill air whipping past as the barge maintained its own microclimate, but he estimated their speed at barely eighty kph.

Boswell made a course correction, so Allenson moved to the right-hand side of the barge to see why. They passed close on the port side of a lighter ploughing slowly through the waves. It was not much more than an open rectangular box with a cut-off prow to facilitate loading and an engine compartment at the rear. The two-man crew stood in an open pulpit at the back, huddled up in warm overcoats and fur caps with side flaps that tied under the chin to protect their ears.

Light and riding high in the water, the lighter corkscrewed with every large wave. As it did, the wind caught the bow on the rise, trying to push the vessel off course as if the weather conspired against the voyage. The stream of white foam emerging from the drive at the stern twisted backwards and forwards as the helmsman fought the helm to keep his clumsy vessel on a heading.

Allenson waved to them as the barge passed but was ignored. The men's faces were in shadow but he could readily imagine their feelings as they watched him swan past in his warm shell. Frankly he was surprised they didn't make rude gestures.

The lighter slipped behind them and soon became lost in the sea haze, except for the squared off bow that occasionally reared up over a particularly heavy swell.

"We'd make much better time in the Continuum," Allenson said.

"Assuming we didn't run smack into a Brasilian trap," Hawthorn replied.

"Or we could go faster at a higher altitude," Allenson continued.

"And we could be shot down by some sort of air defense system."

"Is it likely that the Brasilians would have a mobile version of the type of equipment needed to detect and hit targets at this range?" Allenson scoffed.

Hawthorn glared at him.

"I don't know, Allenson. Just like I don't know if we might attract the attention of some sort of Brasilian hot-shot with eagle eyes and a marksman's badge to go with his long range cannon. Now why don't you just sit down and get some sleep and leave the rest of us to get on with our jobs?"

Allenson smiled and held up a hand to indicate surrender and sat. He leant back and closed his eyes to show he was willing, although there was no chance of him snatching any sleep.

Hawthorn shook him awake.

"We're closing on the coast."

"Right, thanks."

Allenson struggled to free his mind. His head felt heavy and he had trouble concentrating, so Hawthorn seemed to be talking to him from the end of a long pipe. He fumbled in his jacket pockets for a Nightlife. He eventually found one on the second attempt in a sleeve pouch. Pressed against his wrist, it released a cold chill that flowed through him. It sharpened his vision like bringing a lens into focus.

"General," said a female voice. "I have contact with Colonel Kaspery in voice only on a tight band. Apparently, the Brasilians have been mortaring the location of broad band transmitters and the 1st are running out of relays."

Allenson nodded. He supposed he should have expected that.

"Put him on Lieutenant . . . ," what was the damned girl's name?

"Very good, sir, on your pad now."

"How's it going Kaspary?" Allenson asked.

A damn fool question but he couldn't think of a better way to phrase it. He could hardly start by inquiring after the man's family or his views on the weather.

"Not good but not awful either, sir. We're falling into a pattern where I ambush their leading units with half my force while sending the other half back to find the next defensible position. The Brasilians deploy and force back my first detachment which passes through the second and so on. I can't stop them but each contact slows them down and buys time."

"Time's what I need, Kaspary. Time's the most valuable gift you can give me."

"Yes, sir, but I lose a few more troops every time. Pretty soon I won't have enough left to split my force."

"Do your best. I'm on my way to organize an evacuation. When you can't delay their vanguard anymore fall back on Slapton ferry. I'll be waiting."

"Understood, out," Kaspary said and the line went dead.

Hawthorn's men switched off the safeties on the tribarrels and swung them on their gimbals to check for freedom of movement. Someone, probably Hawthorn, had trained them well. It was too late to discover a problem with the mechanism when you were under fire.

Allenson automatically leaned out but could see nothing but seaspray. Boswell had the barge moving at fifty kph or so right down on the water. Air displaced by their passage left a wake like a speedboat. It meant they couldn't see far, but by the same token nothing could see them except at minimal range.

The lasercannon burst came out of nowhere. A red flare of burning calcium gushed from the top of the right-hand gunshield. It lit up the helmet crown of the trooper serving the weapon. His head exploded, his body falling back into the cargo bay.

The rest of the laser burst flared into the sea mist above and ahead of the barge. A fraction of a degree to the right and the burst would have missed the barge altogether. A fraction of a degree to the left would have left a burning wreck crewed only by the dead and dying.

That was the logic of warfare. Random choices decided who live and who died. Choose to get into this car and you lived, that one and you died—died pointlessly and no amount of cleverness or skill or bravery could shave the odds in your favor. It was what drove normal men mad after too long in the combat zone.

Allenson scrabbled for his carbine, which he'd placed on the floor. He'd just got his hand to it when he was bowled over by Todd racing forward. He cursed and got to his feet. Looking out over the side he saw a squat flat vessel to starboard lying low in the water. It churned the sea to foam with its tracks.

The barge flew on straight and steady, giving the Brasilian gunner in the amphib a perfect deflection shot. He ceased fire to take aim. Allenson found himself staring straight into the tribarrel. The amphib lurched over a swell as the gunner fired and the burst cut into the sea short of the barge. Energy hot enough to sear the skin on Allenson's face reflected off the surface. The water exploded into steam that almost immediately condensed white in the cold air, temporarily screening the barge.

The respite would only be momentary. Allenson screamed at Boswell to take evasive action, but the man was frozen in shock. Todd reached the pulpit and pushed the servant out of the way. He hauled the barge through a tight turn so that it emerged from the artificial fog on an unexpected trajectory. The Brasilian gunner fortunately knew his job and fired automatically onto their predicted bearing, so the shots went wide. They would all be dead in a flaming wreck if the barge had continued straight and level.

Hawthorn took a tight two-handed grip on the trigger handles of the barge's starboard gun. He flipped up the safety lever with his thumb and depressed the fire-tab. Astonishingly, the weapon was still operational. The tribarrels streamed fire into the sea about seventy five meters to the side and behind the barge.

He held down the trigger, walking the laser stream onto the slowly moving amphib. Steam exploded and condensed around the lumbering craft. Hawthorn fired continuously, pumping laser bursts into the steam.

Hawthorn kept the triggers down until red flared through the condensing white water vapor and black smoke coiled within it like a nest of cobras in a snowstorm. First one then another barrel overheated and cut out. Hawthorn only let go of the grip when the final barrel fused with a despairing phut of burned out components.

Smoke curled away from the gun. Todd brought the barge back on course.

Boswell leapt down into the cargo bay, his eyes wide with shock. His mouth worked but no words emerged.

"You did well, Boswell. Now sit down and rest," Allenson said gently, steering the servant to a bench.

Fendlaigh appeared with a medical kit.

"Shut your eyes," she said.

Allenson did as he was told and she sprayed his face with analgesic synthetic skin.

"When you've finished I believe I could use some of that," Hawthorn said in an over-controlled voice.

He held out badly burned hands for Fendlaigh to treat.

"Mind your arc," Hawthorn snapped to the port gun trooper who had his head turned to look back into the barge.

"I'll give you a cell-growth booster as well, sir," Fendlaigh said to Hawthorn, holding the kit against his wrist.

Allenson grinned the grin of a maniac.

"You've wrecked our gun, Hawthorn,"

"I suppose you are going to charge it to Special Project's budget," Hawthorn replied gloomily.

"I think under the circumstances we might combat-loss it," Allenson replied. "Anybody broken or lost anything else? We might as well get maximum use out of a combat-loss report."

Hawthorn had turned away to watch the starboard arc. He cradled his rifle in his arms so his burned hands were free.

"Do you think he'll be able to hold that gun?" Fendlaigh asked, talking softly so only Allenson heard. "His palms and fingers are a mess."

"He'll manage," Allenson replied. "He always does."

Slapton Ferry turned out to be an artificial harbor dug out of the mud flats. A change in water color showed where a narrow channel had been dredged to permit lighters to get right up against the foreshore. A curved breakwater of stabilized mud blocks on the side facing down the bay shielded the harbor from wave action. A one-track road connected the single short platform serving as a dock to a cluster of prefab one-story buildings a few hundred meters inland on drained ground that was slightly higher than the surrounding marshes.

A line of buoys marked the solitary channel through the shallow haven. Lighters milled around outside the breakwater looking for a suitable spot to anchor while they waited their turn to go in.

A brightly painted yellow boat was tied up to the dock. Troopers wearing flashes from a variety of different regiments churned in confusion over the shore and lighter, which rocked dangerously while the crew waved their hands impotently.

"Discipline's broken down completely," Allenson said.

"That's fixable," Hawthorn said, his voice as bleak as the winter wind.

It was hopeless trying to land on the dockside amongst the tightly pressed soldiers. Todd passed over the dock and up to the factory where there was a hard stand. Troops piled out of the way as the barge came down. A rush to get aboard started as soon as the field was turned off. Todd straight-armed a woman who tried to climb over the front. The scramble only stopped when Hawthorn gave a snarled order and his trooper triggered bursts from their remaining lasercannon across the heads of the crowd.

"Link my pad to the station's audio," Hawthorn said to Fendlaigh.

"Attention! Form up in your regiments around the station at attention. Anyone failing to comply will be regarded as deserting in the face of the enemy and summarily shot," Hawthorn said.

The activity around Slapton Station ceased. None of the troops moved. They just stared uncomprehendingly at the barge. Hawthorn nodded to his trooper and the man fired another burst skyward and troops ducked and recoiled. One or two who had retained their weapons half raised them.

"To me," Allenson said to Fendlaigh. "Give me vocal."

"This is General Allenson," his voice boomed around the station and echoed off the buildings in ghostly audio images. "I've come to get you people out of here but I can't do it if you prance around like a bunch of Terran dancing masters at a fine arts festival."

A small titter of amusement drifted across the hard stand. It was a rotten attempt at humor but as Allenson had often noted before, a general's jokes are always funny.

"So form up in your regiments and let's have some discipline and try and act like soldiers of the Cutter Stream Army."

There was a silence.

"You heard the general: The Reds form on me. Sergeant Nolan, I see you there. Get our people into rifle sections if you want to keep your stripes," a young man in an officer's uniform who was standing by the entrance to one of the warehouses shouted so loudly that Allenson could hear him in the barge.

It broke the spell. Men and women began to remember they were soldiers and started moving purposefully, clumping into groups with identical unit badges.

"Thank you gentlemen—and lady," Allenson said to the barge crew, remembering to nod to Fendlaigh. "I think we can make this work now. I couldn't have got this far without your efforts."

"Don't be ridiculous, Allenson," Hawthorn snorted. "I can stop people doing things but only you can persuade them to act. You'd have found a way whether we were here or not."

"Take over if you please, Hawthorn, and get this place in order. Keep everyone up here until you hear from me. I'm going down to the dock."

Allenson jumped down from the barge. A cold wind tugged at his clothes, bringing the sharp fresh tang of the sea. He sought out the young officer whose intervention had been so useful. He had formed a small group of soldiers into two lines and was inspecting them.

"General present," snapped the sergeant when he noticed Allenson.

The troopers jumped to attention. It was a bit ragged and one had lost his rifle but at least they were soldiers again and not an armed mob.

The young officer spun on his heels and snapped off a salute.

"You are?"

"Ortiz, sir, second platoon of The Reds, we're part of First Brigade, General."

"A fine body of men, Ortiz."

"Yes, sir," Ortiz said sourly.

Actually they were anything but. However, all things were relative.

"You and your men will accompany me to the foreshore, Ortiz, where we will restore order."

"Yes, sir."

"Sergeant Nolan, at the double, weapons live," Ortiz said without turning his back on Allenson.

"Carter where's your rifle?" boomed Nolan.

"Lost it, sarn't."

"Lost it, bleedin' lost it? No one in my platoon loses their bloody rifle. You bloody well find one smartish my lad or you'll be on my list."

Ortiz and Allenson walked down to the dock. Nolan lined his men into a column and marched behind them. Disordered troops parted for them, moving off the stabilized road into the mud to allow The Reds passage. It was that or be trampled. Allenson affected not to notice men wearing jackets with red facings surreptitiously attach themselves to the rear of the column. By the time they reached the landing stage their small force had doubled in size.

The babble of sound and constant movement at the dock stilled at their arrival. Ortiz muttered something to Nolan and the sergeant spread his men out into a line right across the back of the platform, rifles ostentatiously held at high port.

Allenson switched on the amplifier in has pad.

"Everyone—and I mean *everyone* who is not a crewman of the lighter—will leave this area immediately and report to Colonel Hawthorn at the Station. Form yourself into your units and await further orders."

There was the sort of silence you find at the center of a storm before the wind swings the other way. Allenson continued in a more conversational tone.

"Lieutenant Ortiz, you are to consider anyone who fails to obey my order as deserting in the face of the enemy and deal with them accordingly," Allenson said.

The troopers filed off the lighter in a sullen group.

Allenson spoke into his datapad, "Send the first batch down, Hawthorn, walking, if you please, in an orderly column."

"Understood," Hawthorn replied succinctly.

The first batch of troops appeared a few minutes later. They may have started in an orderly column but they broke into a ragged trot upon sighting the lighter.

"Get these people into line, Sarn't," Ortiz said loudly. "Anyone who shoves goes back up to the factory."

"You heard the officer," Nolan said. "You there, that man with the squint. I saw that. Back you go."

A man protesting volubly was forced back by the threat of a raised rifle butt in the hands of one of Nolan's troopers: a huge woman with pockmarks across her forehead. This particular man hadn't been any more unruly than the rest but Allenson supposed an example must be made of someone and he would do. Anyone who thought life should be fair had no business in the army.

"How many people can you carry?" Allenson said to the light skipper.

"We're licensed for forty," the skipper said.

"Not what I asked," Allenson replied.

The man considered, "Perhaps sixty?"

"Detail the first seventy for evacuation, Lieutenant," Allenson said, adding ten percent or so for luck. In his experience vehicle captains of all sorts tended towards conservative estimates unless being paid by the unit.

The lighter skipper gave Allenson a dark look but held his tongue.

"Count of seventy, Nolan. They walk slowly, one at a time onto the lighter and sit where they're told. Any trouble and the miscreant goes back up to the station."

The evacuation proceeded. Allenson realized after the first lighter had cleared the dock that he had no way of signaling the next one in. Fortunately the lighter skippers showed no inclination to hang around a war zone and sorted themselves out by some hierarchical system of ranks known only to the trade of lightering. One succeeded another in a smooth efficient procession so Allenson happily let them get on with it.

As the evacuation continued, civilians, mostly displaced farmers, got wind of what was going on and started to turn up. The first few were not a problem but as their numbers increased they tended to disorder the waiting columns. Allenson was obliged to make them form a line of their own on a first come first served basis, feeding them onto the lighters a few at a time.

It wasn't long before the inevitable happened. A florid faced man in a business suit left the back of the civilian column. He made his way briskly to a gray-painted lighter with yellow flashes that had just pulled up at the dockside. Allenson intercepted him.

"Get back in line," Allenson said.

"That's mine," the man said.

He gestured at the barge with one hand while using the other to turn back a lapel to show a badge in the same gray and yellow.

"You can't stop me getting on my own boat."

"I can and will," Allenson replied coldly. "That lighter is under military control and this is a combat zone. Get back into line and wait your turn or I'll send you back up."

He had half-turned away when the man grabbed his arm rudely and pulled.

"Listen soldier-boy. You've got no right to tell me what to do. If you think that poncy backwater colony aristo accent impresses me then—"

Allenson backhanded the man across the face. The lighter owner sat down hard on his rounded butt, face now florid for reasons other than over-consumption of rich foodstuffs. A small riverlet of blood trickled out of the corner of his mouth from where his lip had been crushed against his teeth. The man wiped the blood of with his hand and stared at it in horrified fascination,

"I don't have time for this crap," Allenson said, recovering control with great effort. "And I don't have time for you. I will shoot you if I see your fat face again in the next hour. Now get out of my sight."

Allenson shifted his attention back to filling the lighter. One of Ortiz's troopers moved the now silent lighter owner on using the toe of his military issue boot. From the enthusiasm he put into the task Allenson surmised that he had personal issues with florid-faced men in business suits. No doubt his views were based on past experience.

The next lighters loaded without incident. A constant stream of boats arrived in the bay to wait their turn. Allenson made sure he exchanged a word or two with each skipper as he pulled in. He recognized one matelot as having made an earlier trip. The man grinned when Allenson thanked him for coming back.

"Not sure I rightly had much of a choice, squire. Lady Allenson is meeting the returning lighters with some bloke called Krenz in tow. Very persuasive, she is."

He reflected.

"'Course it helps that she is also offering twenty percent bonuses for the second trip, thirty for the third and so on."

"I see," Allenson replied faintly, now understanding why the queue of empty lighters off Slapton Ferry was not diminishing.

He blanched to think about how he was going to lose this particular cost in the budget. Oh well, a problem for another day.

As the day wore on Allenson noted that the type of soldier forming the columns changed from more disciplined regulars to frightened and confused conscripts. A greater percentage of them carried the badges of regiments of the Eleventh rather than the First Brigade. Frightened men and lethal weapons make a dodgy combination. With hindsight, an issue was inevitable. It came in the form of a panicky shout from a packed lighter about to cast off.

"That man there, yes you. Why are holding a bloody grenade? It's not live is it?"

"Don't know, Corp, it might be."

"Shit! Get rid of the fecker."

"Nooo . . ." Allenson screamed but it was too late.

A small gray object arced out of the lighter on a trajectory leading to the dock where the next line of evacuees waited patiently. It hit the stabilized soil with a ceramic clink.

You could spot the veterans and regulars among the waiting soldiers right away. They were the ones who immediately flung themselves face down. Their inexperienced comrades remained upright gawping. Allenson was among those taking cover so he didn't directly witness what happened next but it was easy enough to reconstruct.

The grenade bounced off the foot of a prone trooper. It rolled gently back towards the lighter, sparking off mass panic. A wave of men hurtled from the landward side of the lighter towards the opposite wale, in the process bowling over the protesting skipper. The overcrowded lighter promptly capsized, dropping its passengers into the water.

Allenson lifted his head at the howls of fear and screams for help. The grenade sat innocently about two meters from his nose, a gray cylinder about fifteen centimeters long and four centimeters diameter. It didn't look right. There should be fine-spaced indentations to act as guides for the blast that would transform the casing into a shower of lethal splinters.

His stomach lurched when the cylinder gave a faint click followed by a loud pop. Thick yellow vapor rushed out of a valve arrangement at the top. The air filled with smoke.

"It's a feckin' marker flare," Nolan said, his voice thick with mixed emotions of relief and anger.

Allenson jumped to his feet. He kicked the flare off the dockside into the water, eliciting further screams. It flared briefly below the surface before dying. The sea wind whisked the yellow smoke away to reveal chaos.

The activity churned up the mud, staining the water brown and releasing foul odors.

"Stand up you idiots," Allenson broadcast through his datapad. "The water is only waist deep. Why do you think we are only using shallow-draft lighters?"

Sheepishly, drowning men found their feet and waded towards the dock to be lifted from the water by their comrades. A half dozen or so had managed to drown. Bodies floated faced down. More victims were probably trapped under the overturned lighter.

Allenson surveyed the mess soberly.

"You men, don't bother climbing out of the water. We don't have time for salvage operation so someone has to drag the wreckage out of the way. Guess who's volunteering as I don't see why the rest of us should get wet. We'll pass you some ropes."

It took thirty valuable minutes to clear the channel for the next lighter. Allenson sent the waders back up to the station to dry off before they re-joined the queue. He made it look like a punishment. The real reason was that he was concerned they would suffer hypothermia out on the Bay in an open lighter.

As it turned out he was wasting his time. The sky darkened, filling with black clouds, and the first spots of rain pattered lightly onto the pools of water in the surrounding marshes.

"Some hot cafay, sir?" Boswell said, proffering a thermos flask.

"Where did you spring from?" Allenson asked.

He waved a hand.

"Never mind, just pour the cafay."

Allenson warmed his hands on the cup and sipped at the contents. It tasted vaguely metallic but was wet and hot. Its temperature was its most important quality when he tipped it down his throat.

"Thank you, Boswell."

"Sorry I lost my head on the frame, sir, when we were shot at."

"Your first time in a fight?"

"No, sir, but it's the first time anyone has shot at me with a sodding great cannon."

Allenson laughed humorlessly and turned his coat collar up against rain that had become more insistent.

"Don't worry, you'll get used to it in time."

"Yes, sir," Boswell said doubtfully. "Another cup?"

Allenson looked at his drink, surprised to see it empty. Had he really gulped a cup of burning liquid down so quickly? Apparently so.

"I believe I will."

He held out the cup.

The chain of lighters cycled through Slapton Ferry smoothly under Ortiz's control but it all took time, too much time. Allenson was amazed that the Brasilians had left them alone this long. Surely they must have scouts out who had spotted what was going on. His enemy was professional, but fortunately methodical, and geared to a war of materiel and position rather than maneuver.

He didn't underestimate the Brasilian military, but they moved step by step like a sleepwalker, consolidating each gain before preparing for the next advance. He supposed you had to work like that in the Home Worlds, where the concentration of troops per kilometer of line was so high. Generals who stuck their necks out got their heads cut off. Here in the emptiness of the colonies it was different.

There were no lines of any length or permanence. Small armies clashed when they collided at strategic points and, if a position fell, the next defendable place might be as far as a frame ride away. A war ebbed and flowed over around fortified bases and cities like a flash flood rushing to pool around boulders and high ground. And like a flash flood an army's fortunes could recede as quickly as they advanced.

Allenson's musings were interrupted by the ringing of bells. Now he knew he was seeing things.

A farm servant drove a herd of quadrupeds through the swamp towards the ferry. The clanging came from bells affixed to collars around their necks. The animals were lithe, scrambling surefootedly through the mud and leaping from tuft to tuft of grass.

"What the hell do you think you're doing?" he heard Ortiz shout at the rustic.

"Bringing my flock to the ferry like I always does at this time o' year," the drover replied.

"Well you can't. The ferry has been requisitioned. Don't you know there's a war on?"

"Nowt to do with me. My animals have to go to market now or I won't get the best price," the rustic said with what to him was clearly inarguable logic.

Allenson began to think he was starring in some sort of theatrical farce.

"Hey shoo," Ortiz said, waving his arms at the beasts, which looked up startled.

They shied away nervously from the waiting line of troopers.

"Don't you be scaring them," warned the drover.

At that moment the black sky split with the white flash of an electrical discharge. A peal of thunder followed scant tenths of a second later. The storm was right on top of them and the rain came down in determined sheets.

It was all too much for the flock. The animals turned about and scattered into the marsh, chased by the outraged rustic. Allenson's datapad chimed and he switched it on. Rainwater poured down the screen, distorting the hologram, but he recognized Hawthorn.

"The first of Kaspary's men are trickling in. He'll be with us within twenty minutes or so with the rest of his regiment's survivors."

"Understood," Allenson said.

They were all out of time.

★ CHAPTER 24 ★

Plots and Plans

Up to this point Allenson had given no thought to how many men might be left behind to be put in the bag by the advancing Brasilian army. He had driven the evacuation as fast as possible and that was that. Nevertheless he was pleasantly surprised to find the station almost completely empty when he reached it.

Hawthorn greeted him at the administration block that was serving as a headquarters out of the rain. Inside a handful of men wearing the red and black slashed badge of Kaspary's Greenbelts sipped hot drinks.

"Where is everybody?" Allenson asked.

"The odd trooper still turns up but we've shipped out those who maintained enough cohesion to make it here," Hawthorn said. "They're probably the only ones worth saving anyhow."

"How many bayonets does Kaspary have left?"

Hawthorn shrugged.

"Perhaps two hundred."

"So damned few," Allenson replied softly.

He didn't bother to subtract the number from the Greenbelts' theoretical establishment to work out the casualties. He hadn't the time or mental strength. Later would do, maybe never if it slipped his mind.

He was fooling himself, of course. Casualties suffered as the result of his orders never slipped his mind. He just couldn't deal with it now.

"Then there's the wounded," Hawthorn said casually.

Allenson just looked at him.

"You probably noticed that I only sent walking wounded down to the lighters," Hawthorn said.

Allenson hadn't noticed.

"Where are they?" he asked.

"In the warehouse opposite."

"Show me," Allenson ordered.

"Why, Allenson? There's nothing you can do. Let the medics get on with their job."

"Show me!"

Hawthorn took him to a newish one-story warehouse that was in noticeably better condition than the others. It was as silent as a temple inside. Sedated troopers were laid out in rows, burnt skin and the stumps of amputated limbs encased in solidified therapeutic foam.

A woman watched when he walked past her. She had no hair and her eyes stared out of foam skin covering her face and head. A breathing tube ran through the foam in the area of her mouth. Orderlies carried a corpse to the back of the warehouse where bodies and body parts were stacked under disinfectant slime. People in combat uniforms clearly marked by the diagonal red and white stripes indicating medics moved silently up and down the aisles checking their charges.

A woman hurried over to Allenson and held out her hand.

"Dr. Sal'Framagh, I'm in charge here."

"Thank you for the care you're giving my men," Allenson said.

"It's what we're for," she said briskly.

"How did these people possibly get here with such terrible injuries?" Allenson asked.

"Their comrades bring them in mostly, but some make it under their own efforts. You would be surprised what people can do *in extremis*."

"No," Allenson replied, "I wouldn't."

"They would never have survived the lighters," Hawthorn said, gesturing at the recumbent figures.

"No, I can see that," Allenson replied.

He pulled himself together.

"Doctor, I have no right to ask, and it certainly isn't an order . . ."

"But you want to know if medical staff will stay with the wounded until the Brasilians arrive to take over their care," she said.

"Yes."

"Some of my unmarried personnel have already volunteered. I will be staying myself, of course."

"Of course," Allenson said gently.

He uttered some meaningless platitudes.

"I want all those people to receive public commendations," Allenson said to Hawthorn once they were outside.

The history books would record that General Allenson was the last one out of Slapton Ferry that night and they were almost right. When the barge lifted and started back to Port Trent the last of Kaspary's rearguard was still boarding a lighter.

Allenson had precious free time to think about the strategic situation on the way back instead of simply reacting to events. The problem was the more he thought the less he liked the options. He managed to snatch a couple of hours sleep but took another Nightlife after they landed at his Port Trent headquarters just after dawn. He called an immediate meeting of his staff, which gave him just enough time to snatch breakfast.

He had to force himself to eat. Allenson was not exactly a gourmet at the best of times but everything tasted metallic and was difficult to swallow. Nightlife side effects were showing. There were other stimulants that mitigated the impact but he was loath to go down that road as he could end up taking drugs to moderate unwanted effects of the drugs he had taken to counter the first set of side effects.

On the other hand he was incredibly thirsty, another symptom of the drug. While he breakfasted he searched through his datapad for an old document; something he had read a long time ago and only half remembered. When he found the file he was soon so lost in it that he forgot how bad the food tasted.

Buller, Ling, Hawthorn and the staff were present when he entered the conference theater. Looking round he noticed that Buller was no longer a shoe-in for the worst dressed officer in the room award. He and Hawthorn now also competed for that honor.

"If you would bring us all up to speed on the situation, Colonel Ling," Allenson said after seating himself.

Ling walked to the podium in the center and activated a hologram showing a three-dimensional map of the area.

"The Brasilians are massing all along the south of the Buller Line. They have the Douglas Hundreds completely sealed off. We must assume that any of our troops still there are lost."

"The terrain hardly offers suitable concealment for guerrilla operations," Hawthorn said.

"Quite."

"What forces do we have manning the Buller Line?" Allenson asked.

Ling spread his hands expressively.

"The equivalent of a handful of scratch-built companies; most of the garrison has fled back to Port Trent. We're trying to round them up now."

Hawthorn snorted.

"The Brasos can walk in any time they like. Good thing they don't know that."

Brasos was a new one on Allenson, but it was only a question of time before his men found a derogatory nickname for the enemy. It was what troops did to offset the uncomfortable feeling that the enemy was three meters tall.

"Options, gentlemen?"

There was a silence.

"Anyone?" Allenson asked again.

Ling coughed.

"Well, if nobody else has any ideas. . . . As I see it we have three choices," Ling said.

He ticked them off on his fingers.

"We can evacuate the scratch companies as soon as the attack starts, heavily reinforce the Line with fresh troops from the Trent Line and make a fight of it, or we can compromise and feed in just enough troops to bleed the Brasilians with a view to eventually pulling back."

Buller shook his head.

"No compromises. They're just a way of avoiding making a decision and inevitably turn out badly."

"I agree," Allenson said. "I suspect that we might be bled dry faster than the enemy. Equally, I distrust allowing the Brasilians to suck us into a set piece battle where they hold all the cards. I remind everyone that the fortifications on the Buller Line face north."

Buller cleared his throat but said nothing.

"I choose option one, then, Colonel Ling. Clear the line out, if you please."

Ling made a note on his pad.

"That does offer the Brasilians the possibility of bypassing the Trent Line by crossing the Valerie in their amphibious armor. Then they could attack Port Trent directly."

Buller rubbed his hands together.

"Excellent, we'll stop them in the city itself. I can make every building a fortification and every street a firetrap."

"I believe you," Allenson said softly. "But tell me, Colonel, if you were the Brasilian general how would you crack such a nut?"

"Not easily," Buller replied. "You isolate sections of the city block by block using heavy cannon fire and reduce each block with artillery, but that's the beauty of it, you see. The defending troops dig into cellars and trenches and occupy the rubble as soon as the bombardment stops. At some point the enemy has to cease so he can send in his infantry. The attackers have all the disadvantages in the resulting firefight. Rubble makes a great defensive position. We'll bleed them with attrition as they clear out each section of city. Their materiel superiority will be at a discount in an urban battle. It'll be man against man, rifle against rifle."

"And the civilians?"

Buller looked at Allenson uncomprehendingly.

"What about them?"

Allenson pointed out the obvious.

"They'll be massacred in the crossfire. We can't evacuate the largest city in the colonies. We haven't got the resources or anywhere to send them."

"Civilian collateral damage worries people," Hawthorn remarked to Buller in the tone of someone reporting an inexplicable but reliably robust observation. "Personally I don't understand why a civilian death is worse than a soldier's but there it is."

"We won't contest the town itself. We'll declare it an open city and the Brasilians will have to respect that and forgo bombardment," Allenson said. "They're welcome to dissipate their strength moving troops into the urban areas and police them if they so desire."

"You have another plan?" Ling asked.

"I do. Have any of you gentlemen ever heard of Julius Caesar?"

Allenson was greeted with blank looks.

"Well I'm not surprised. He's all but forgotten now but once he was a very important man, a warlord who conquered half the world and made himself king. His descendants ruled for the next two millennia."

"Is this relevant?" Buller asked rudely.

Allenson nodded.

"I believe so," Allenson said. "Caesar faced a situation not unlike the potential one we have here. His enemies occupied a city and had an army in the field. Caesar built a double walled fortification around the city facing inwards and outwards and allowed his enemies to dash themselves to pieces on it. We have the outer wall on the Trent Line already so all we need to do is build the inner and the Brasilians are very kindly giving us the time."

"We'll be trapped within the Trent Line if anything goes wrong," said Ling, fulfilling his chief of staff role of devil's advocate.

"That's what Caesar's enemies thought," said Allenson with a grin. "But he used his fortress wall as a base for sallies to defeat his opponents in detail. Any further comments?"

Silence reigned.

"Take responsibility for fortifying the inner face of the Trent Line, if you please, Colonel Buller."

"I'll get right on it. I take it I can requisition whatever resources I need?"

Allenson nodded.

The meeting broke up after that with no further discussion.

"Buller was unusually cooperative," Allenson said to Todd after they left the theatre and were alone. "I expected more of a protest when I turned down his plans for a bloodbath."

"Victory has many fathers but defeat is an orphan," Todd replied cynically.

"You think we're about to lose?" Allenson asked.

"I suspect Buller thinks so, as too much depends on imponderables outside of our control. We have next to no information on the Brasilian Order Of Battle so how can we possibly assess their capabilities?"

"How indeed," Allenson replied, "but keep that thought to yourself."

The problem was that Todd was absolutely right.

Back in his private quarters Allenson prepared a report on the situation for the Assembly at Paxton. He created three copies in secure plastic folders to be carried independently by three of Morton's commandos riding one-man frames. The Brasilians would be lucky to intercept one of the Canaries but there was no possibility of them capturing all three.

As an afterthought he added a summary by visual record to emphasize the importance of his conclusion.

"It is my belief that in the long run Port Trent may prove indefensible against the forces deployed against it. I intend to hold the fortified Trent Line as long as possible but then retreat to Brunswick rather than lose the army."

The Brasilians launched a massive attack on the Buller Line. It was preceded by a ferocious artillery barrage that fell upon vacant fortifications, a hammer blow to crack an empty shell. The Brasilians took another three days to regroup before spilling out of the Douglas Hundreds along the east bank of the Valerie in their amphibious carriers. They moved up their artillery and created new supply dumps in expectation of having to make a contested crossing.

Allenson withdrew all military forces back into the Trent Line, leaving only paramilitary police to keep order in the urban zone. Apart from a few probes to confirm that Trent was indeed demilitarized, the Brasilians stayed out of the city, rather to Allenson's regret. It would have been helpful if the Brasilian Army embroiled itself there but one cannot always hope to face an incompetent commander. The perils of urban warfare would be entirely familiar to a Home World general.

But all this granted precious time to fortify the inner face of the Trent Line and create a string of forts like beads along a string. Then the unexpected happened. In response to his dispatch a delegation from the Paxton Assembly dropped out of the continuum in a fast yacht.

Political interference in his conduct of the campaign was probably inevitable, Allenson thought, but decidedly unwelcome. Nevertheless he scheduled a meeting for the next day, giving the Assembly delegates just a night to recover from their journey. He took the opportunity that evening to look through the biographies of the delegates to gauge their likely reactions. He was pleased to see that Stainman led the group. As politicians went, Stainman had always struck him as having a sound grasp of reality.

He gave some thought to the composition of the people who would meet the delegates. Ling and Todd with other members of the army staff would attend in full dress uniform, supposedly to supply information and keep notes. Mainly Allenson wanted them there to overawe the politicians and dissuade the amateur armchair strategists among them.

Hawthorn and Buller would have to be included on the dual basis of keeping your friends close but your enemies closer. By the same principle he invited Venceray and his political opponent, Carhew, a lean and hungry-looking lady who represented the trade guilds. They attended as delegates for the civilian politicians of Port Trent.

When the politicians were conducted into the meeting room by junior officers, the military commanders were already in place. Allenson rose from his chair and personally greeted each politico in turn before they were shown to their seats.

Allenson took immediate control of the meeting by acting as chairman. He introduced Ling and asked him to take the floor. From the podium Ling took the delegates through the military situation while Allenson stood supportingly at his elbow. Complete silence met the completion of his crisp, clean exposition while the politicians digested the unfamiliar military terms and concepts.

"Any questions?" Allenson asked, walking forward.

Silence descended.

Carhew stood up.

"You've pulled out of Port Trent, so you don't propose to defend us?"

"No, I don't propose to fight *in* Port Trent, Sar Carhew. I *am* defending it by occupying the Trent Line. The Brasilian Army can't just ignore my force."

Venceray shook his head.

"Sit down, Carhew, Allenson's right. We can't give the Brasilians any excuse to smash the city."

"Just the argument I would expect from a Homer sympathizer like you," Carhew said to Venceray.

"Gentlemen, the decision is mine and I have made it," Allenson said without raising his voice but there was a whiplike edge that stopped the argument before it got out of hand.

"I don't understand why you're not defending the river," said Greasebe, a delegate with whom Allenson had no previous dealings.

"Because I can't," Allenson replied, irritated at having to point out the obvious. "Wherever I positioned my troops the Brasilians would just pin them with artillery fire. Then they would cross the Valerie in their amphibs on our flanks and roll up our line, unit by unit."

Greasebe frowned, not really understanding the point.

Allenson continued.

"To counter that strategy all I could do would be to spread my troops ever more widely along the river. Eventually the line would be so thin that the Brasilians could punch through anywhere they chose. Modern firepower may favor the defender tactically but modern mobility favors the attacker operationally because they can mass at the contact point to overwhelm any static defense."

"Yes, I see that," Stainman said thoughtfully. "So you intend to sit tight in the Trent Line and hope the Brasilians lose a battle of attrition by throwing themselves against the fortifications."

"Fortifications are a valuable force multiplier," Allenson replied, "but I think we can be a little more proactive than that."

He took control of the podium and drew arrows and troop locations onto the strategic hologram.

"The Brasilian amphibs are not seaworthy enough to cross the Bay, so I have placed my most inexperienced regiments from the 11th garrisoning the southern forts. My best troops, the First Brigade, are up in the northern forts close to the river. My battle plan assumes that the Brasilians have a limited amphibious lift capacity and can only move a section of their army at any one time."

He paused to pour himself a glass of water and sip it, making the delegates wait.

"The most mobile unit in the Army, the Canaries, will form a dispersed tripwire along the riverbank. They will offer only token resistance to an invasion before retreating north back into the continental mass. The Brasilians will then find themselves advancing into a vacuum. I believe the temptation to press inland to outflank the

Trent Line before waiting for their whole army to cross will be irresistible."

Light dawned in Stainman's eyes.

"It's a trap."

Allenson smiled at him.

"Precisely. When the vanguard are beyond direct fire support from the Brasilian artillery, we hit them with a full frontal attack from First Brigade. Simultaneously, the Canaries assault them in the rear to spread confusion."

"It's a bold plan, but what are the chances of pulling it off?" Stainman asked.

Allenson focused on him.

"The most optimistic results from strategic modeling suggest that we can destroy a subsection of the opposing forces and drive them back across the river. The most pessimistic outcome is that the Brasilian vanguard holds long enough to be rescued by reinforcements. Either way we will have given them a bloody nose and blunted their attack."

He stopped and looked around the room, meeting each delegate eye to eye.

"Any questions, sars?"

"Your plan depends on some key variables working out right," a young delegate called Peeki who was dressed in a fashionable purple suit observed.

"Such as?"

"Well suppose the Brasos have enough amphibious transports to move the whole army in one go?"

"Those transports had to be transported all the way across the Bight from the Home Worlds. How many could there be? Besides, if they had more they'd have used them in the Douglas Hundreds."

Stainman looked worried.

"I see that but suppose the Brasilian commander is more timid than you anticipate. Suppose he just moves his whole force over the Valeria before advancing one meter,"

"In that case we do nothing and we've lost nothing," Allenson countered, "but I don't expect that to happen. The temptation of a quick bloodless advance to gain ground cheaply will be too strong."

He took another sip of water.

"Well if that is all, sars—"

"Not so fast," Carhew said. "I understand from the Paxton delegates that you intend to cut and run to Brunswick and leave us in the lurch here in Trent."

"I wouldn't put it like that," Allenson replied.

"How would you put it?"

"If the force multiplier of defending fortifications moves the attrition rate to our advantage such that the Brasilian army has to call off the siege, then well and good. If it doesn't then Port Trent will fall. In that case it would be idiotic to allow the field army to fall with the city and I intend to break out and regroup at Brunswick."

Uproar followed. Amongst the more incoherent cries of outrage Allenson managed to decipher the following points.

"But they'll simply follow you . . ."

"They'll advance straight on to Paxton . . ."

"We can't lose Port Trent. It's unthinkable . . ."

"Silence!"

Hawthorn stood up.

"This is an army, not a political debating chamber."

"I doubt that the Brasilian Army would be able to immediately follow us," Allenson said. "In my experience, Home World armies are powerful but extremely ponderous. Home World warfare depends on strength, not speed. We should have plenty of time to fortify our reserve base at Brunswick and repeat the whole process again. We attrit the enemy by making them attack fortifications and then we jump to Trinity. With every move we drag their army farther from its logistics base at Trent. Brunswick, you will recall, lacks a trans-Bight port."

Another sip of water.

"By the same reasoning the Brasilians can't make an overwhelming strike on Paxton. They will have to strongly garrison Port Trent or I will take it back from them and cut their supply line. No Home World commander will risk that."

"What do you think, Colonel Buller?" Peeki asked.

Buller just shrugged and kept his council. Allenson smiled cynically, as he suspected Todd had read Buller correctly. The man didn't want to be proved wrong and the best way to achieve that was to say nothing. Predicting failure would make him look ridiculous if

Allenson's strategy was successful and might make him look like a
Jonah if it failed. Equally, he wouldn't want to have been seen to
support the plan if it failed.

"Well," Stainman said. "I think that covers everything. I am obliged
to tell you that the will of the Assembly is that you defend Port Trent
vigorously. We fear it will never be recovered once lost. There are
many in the city who would welcome the Brasilians but obviously we
can't afford to lose the city and the army."

In other words, you're on your own, Allenson thought.

Not that *that* changed anything.

The politicians wanted to tour the Line to see the preparations with
their own eyes, but Allenson dissuaded them on the grounds that an
attack was expected at any moment. He saw them back to their yacht
personally, accompanied by Ling and Hawthorn. He did this partly
out of politeness and partly to stop any of them having a private
meeting with Buller or some other dissident officer.

"Would it be unkind to hope for a Brasilian gunship intercept?"
Hawthorn asked, as the yacht made a low level full transition into the
Continuum.

Ling snorted.

"Now, now, we should respect the people's representatives,"
Allenson said mildly.

"Really?" Hawthorn replied. "I'll take your word for it."

"You'll join me for lunch, gentlemen?" Allenson asked. "If you
have time, that is. Don't let me detain you if you have urgent duties."

He added the codicil because a general's offer of hospitality was
normally unrefusable.

Hawthorn chose the after-luncheon cafay to drop a depth charge
into the conversation.

"I wonder which of our respected representatives will be the first
to leak your battle plan to the Brasos?" Hawthorn asked casually.

Allenson's jaw dropped.

"You don't really think one of those people was a traitor, do
you?"

"I wouldn't be at all surprised," Hawthorn said darkly. "In my
experience the only sure thing you can trust a politician to do is save
his own skin. Actually in this case, I'm less worried about politicos

themselves than those they'll tell to show how important they are. This'll include their friends, their wives, their wives' friends, all the servants present at the conversations and the servants' friends and relatives."

He grinned and tipped a generous measure of plum brandy into his cafay.

"Well, I suppose so, but hopefully the matter will be decided long before the information leaks anywhere that matters," Allenson replied.

"No matter, I've already made sure that the Brasilians have received a full description," Hawthorn said casually.

Ling inhaled his cafay and choked.

"You've what?"

Hawthorn smiled.

"I've passed the information in a leak through one of their own people."

"Why?" Ling asked, showing commendable restraint.

"They have reason to think I've already turned this particular agent."

"I see," Allenson said, and he did. Light was beginning to dawn.

"They also have all sorts of conflicting information flowing in through their other agents and intelligence assessments. In fact, I've made sure of it."

"In war, truth is so precious that it must be protected by a bodyguard of lies," Allenson murmured.

"What?" Ling asked.

"Nothing, just remembering an old quote I read somewhere," Allenson replied.

Hawthorn topped his cafay cup up with more brandy.

"I've arranged for the body of a Canary officer to be washed up on the Brasilian side of the Valerie. Rather stupidly he was carrying an unsecured datapad just full of orders."

"I hope I have a cunning plan?" Allenson asked.

"Indeed, you simultaneously intend to launch multiple seaborne and frame raids across the Bay and Valerie as I recall," Hawthorn replied.

"Bold, not to say completely reckless," Allenson said, with a grin.

An aide entered the dining room and handed a note to Ling. He glanced at it poker-faced and motioned that it be passed on to Allenson. It was brief and to the point.

The Brasilian offensive had started.

★ CHAPTER 25 ★

Clash of Arms

The control was tomb-silent but crackled with psychological pressure. Aides slid quietly between the consoles and exchanged terse comments in hushed tones.

A crushing artillery barrage soaked the nonexistent colonial fortifications on the east bank of the Valerie thirty kilometers north of the Trent Line. The impressive display of military might was a mighty blow expended on a vacuum. After ten minutes the barrage shifted inland and to the flanks to seal off a section of bank from possible Streamer counterattack. Amphibians waddled into the water and began to churn across the river.

Allenson watched from such cameras hidden on the east bank that had survived the barrage. He fidgeted and rose from his chair.

"I'm going up to the north fort to join Kaspary."

"Very good, General," replied Ling, who was getting used to his commander's urge to be in the front line.

Ling casually touched an icon which flashed acknowledgment.

Allenson discovered to whom Ling was signaling when he stepped outside to find a frame. His barge was already ready with Todd in the pilot's podium. Allenson pulled himself over the side and was unsurprised to find Hawthorn, Fendlaigh and a security squad already aboard with two Special Project troopers manning a laser tribarrel each side, or rather womanning the port tribarrel. Fresh gleaming ceramics showed where repairs had been made after the vehicle's previous adventure.

He was surprised to see Boswell.

"Are you sure you want to come with us?" Allenson asked. "Your duties don't include combat."

Boswell's expression was strained but he nodded his head resolutely.

"Quite sure, sar."

Todd lifted off before Allenson could sit down and flew northwest until he had cleared the fortifications. This didn't take long, as they consisted largely of underground bunkers linked by tunnels and trenches protected by long, shallowly sloping stabilized-earth scarps. Then he turned northeast, running low, parallel to the Trent Line but out of sight of the defenders.

It would have been too damned dangerous to fly directly over the line. No matter what identification signals were used some idiot would be bound to panic and open fire, triggering a free for all.

Todd approached the north fort circumspectly, making sure he had contact and clearance before moving slowly into the ditch behind the counterscarp. He parked amongst a variety of requisitioned civilian frame transports. A trooper gestured to them from an opening cut into the scarp opposite. Allenson, Hawthorn and Todd followed the guide along a trench into the fort.

Trenches zig-zagged off confusingly. The twists and turns confused Allenson's sense of direction. Corners were protected by fire positions from which defenders could rake adjacent lengths of trench. The trooper led them unfailingly to the roofed bunker that served as Kaspary's headquarters.

Colonel Kaspary was a thin man with a goatee beard. He had the habit of stroking it when he concentrated. He dressed in a deep blue dress uniform that must have been smart when crisply pressed. Now it was creased and stained.

Allenson shook the man's hand.

"I wasn't expecting to see you here, General," Kaspary said, lifting an eyebrow questioningly. "I assure you we are quite ready to attack."

"I have no fear of that. The Fighting First is my best brigade," Allenson raised his voice so that his words could be heard by all the surrounding soldiers.

"With your permission, Colonel, I hoped to accompany you, if I won't get in your way."

"Of course you can and welcome," Kaspary replied, even managing to look as if he meant it.

No other answer was possible, but Allenson knew that the arrival of one's superior just before combat was the very last thing any commander needed. He shouldn't be here but he just had to come. It would be intolerable to wait back in the control room while people fought and died following his orders. He needed to reassure Kaspary.

"You are still in complete charge, of course."

It might have been Allenson's imagination but Kaspary seemed to relax slightly.

He sat behind Kaspary at his console, watching events unfold. The first batch of Brasilian troopers bailed out of their vehicles and dug in on the east bank while the amphibs recrossed the river to pick up a second lift. It took thirty minutes for the tanks to make the round trip and heave themselves out of the water.

"So what are they going to do now?" Allenson asked. "Go back for a third lift or press on through?"

The barrage ceased and the Brasilians did—nothing. The amphibs waited on the east bank, their troops still embarked.

"They seem to be waiting. I wonder what for?" Kaspary asked, stroking his chin.

"Maybe they want to see how we will react. Our apparent passivity must be puzzling," Allenson said.

"I'll expect we'll soon find out."

Kaspary was right. But the answer came in a wholly unexpected way and from a wholly unexpected source.

"Colonel," a voice said from a console in the corner.

"Hmm?"

"Urgent priority contact from Colonel Ling."

"Well, put it on."

A hologram opened by Kaspary showing Ling's head.

"Colonel Kaspary, do you have General Allenson with you?"

"Here," Allenson replied, leaning forward so he would be within the reception zone visible to Ling.

"South Fort is under attack," Ling said.

"What, how?" Allenson asked.

South Fort was way down the line alongside the Bay.

"We don't know," Ling replied. He sounded tired. "There was no preparatory bombardment or warning of frame activity. Just a message that Brasilian commandos were storming the counterscarp."

"Right, I'll deal with it."

The link snapped off.

"Colonel I'll need one of your regiments and some transports," Allenson said. "We can't afford to lose South Fort."

"Take the Cinnerans; they're the closest to establishment strength. Do you still want me to try to ambush the Brasilians?"

"Not unless you get an unmissable opportunity. You'll have to decide as the situation warrants."

"Very good, sir," Kaspary said seemingly unruffled by the loss of one third of his force. He showed the nerve that had made him the only man to keep his head in the Douglas Hundreds' debacle.

Allenson shot out of the bunker without further conversation. He pointed to the trooper who had been their guide. The man leaned casually against the side of the trench. He gazed in astonishment at a general who ran. A running general was an offense against the natural order of things, his expression seemed to say, akin to a talking animal or water flowing uphill.

"You! Take me back to my barge. At the double, man, what are you waiting for?"

The trooper took off and Allenson's entourage followed. The strange procession ran through the trenches, leaping over boxes and other obstacles. When they reached the barge, transports in the ditch were already filling with soldiers in combat uniforms with purple facings and lapels. These must be the Cinnerans.

Allenson embussed and waited impatiently, tapping his fingers against the ceramic hull. After a geological aeon, his pad lit up with a face in a combat helmet.

"Major Shong, sir, commander of the Cinneran Regiment awaiting your orders."

"Lift now, Major, and follow me."

Allenson made an up gesture to Todd and the barge part took off. One by one, a disparate collection of transport frames followed, weaving around one another. Miraculously, none collided.

"Have you been briefed?" Allenson asked Shong over his pad.

"Sort of, sir. I understand there's been some sort of attack on the most southerly fort of the line and I'm to place myself under your command."

"You know as much as I do, then."

"I don't under how Brasilians could just pop up by the Bay like that," Shong said.

"Nor do I, Major, but I know where they're going. You and I are going to evict them."

The shortest route south took them across the chord of the Trent Line on the city side of the defenses. Garbled reports from Bay Fort indicated that it had not yet fallen but that heavy fighting was ongoing. Panic stricken calls from junior officers manning bunkers insisted that a large Brasilian force was already inside the complex.

Despite her best efforts Fendlaigh was unable to establish a coms link with the fort's command bunker. This was not a good sign. The few videos she managed to capture showed confused firefights, although she did manage to isolate an image of a heavily armed Brasilian commando in body armor using a grenade launcher.

Hawthorn handed Allenson a multishot laser carbine.

"Keep it on auto and even you should be able to hit something with this. Just try to avoid making it me," Hawthorn said lugubriously.

"You're all heart," Allenson replied.

"Do you intend us to fly straight into the fort?"

Allenson shook his head.

"It's tempting but we have no idea what's there. Just a couple of Brasilian point defense cannon would cause carnage."

"We could make a short Continuum hop and surprise them," Fendlaigh ventured.

"If I was the Brasilian commander I would anticipate such a move. I'd have a unit of gun frames waiting in ambush in the Continuum. No, we'll swing round to the south, come in low over the sea and land on the coast. Hopefully they'll not notice the frame activity in the confusion. Even if they do we'll be below the line of sight horizon for all but the last few seconds."

Allenson's barge led the frame convoy in the loop over the sea despite Shong's protests. A single rifle shot glanced off the bottom of the hull indicated that they had stumbled across the enemy. The woman on the port gun returned fire with a series of short bursts from her tribarrel. Something exploded with a flash that gave rise to a column of boiling black smoke.

The Streamer frames raced through a convoy of gray-green assault boats.

"So that's how they crossed the Bay," Allenson said to himself. "How could I have been so recklessly stupid as to assume that amphibious tanks were their only water transport asset?"

"Don't beat yourself up," Hawthorn said firing a snapshot from his rifle at a fleeting target. "It was a reasonable assumption given that they didn't use them in the attack on the Hundreds."

Further laserfire, explosions and smoke marked the passage of the Cinnerans through the Brasilian flotilla. The assault boats were soon left behind and the frames grounded on a gravel beach. Troopers poured out and Allenson jog-trotted up the slope onto a plain of dry scrub. He used his datapad to examine Bay Fort, which was only five hundred meters away. Little showed above ground—but that was to be expected.

Gaps had been punched in the razorwire around the fort. Scorch marks indicated the use of some sort of thermic lance or charge. An explosion in the fort vented a cloud of greasy orange smoke.

As soon as the last Cinnerans had made it up the slope, Allenson gave the order to move out at a fast walk. Hawthorn and his Special Project troopers formed a ring around Allenson and his aides. They passed through the wire, using the holes in the razorwire so thoughtfully provided by the Brasilian commandos.

The first small arm shots lit up the scrub. Allenson kept the advance to a walk. He wanted his troops to be still capable of fighting when they reached the scarp. A handful of Cinnerans fell, but the loss rate was acceptable. He suppressed any emotion about the fact that soldiers were dying because of his orders. That was what happened in war: people died. No loss rate was acceptable to the families and friends of the victims, but how could it be otherwise?

A flicker in the sky caught his attention. It turned into a puff of gray smoke about three meters above the ground forty or fifty meters in front of him. He heard the sharp crack of an exploding grenade. Another one soared over his head to explode amongst his troops. Three Cinnerans folded in on themselves and collapsed.

"Spread out," Shong ordered, circling his hand over his head for emphasis.

"Charge," Allenson added.

Walking was no longer an option. Now that they were within grenade range, losses would rapidly become unacceptable. Allenson put his head down and concentrated on running over the uneven ground. More cracks followed and something tugged at his sleeve. The security trooper alongside him pitched face down. The back of his head was missing.

Allenson ran up the slope of the fort counterscarp holding his carbine out in front in both hands for balance. He pitched over the edge into the ditch, landing hard and rolling. A Brasilian commando leaned over a wall of sandbags and fired a burst of searing white laser pulses from his carbine.

Theoretically laser shots were invisible unless aimed right at your eyes, in which case they were only visible for a microsecond before your optic nerves, retinas and brain cooked in rapid sequence. In practice dust and water vapor in the air degraded the beams, scattering high intensity light. That was very visible, especially at minimum range.

Allenson had no idea where the laser pulses went. They didn't hit him, which was good enough for the moment. He rolled onto one knee and fired back from the hip, holding down the trigger of his carbine.

Laser pulse hits lit up the sandbags and stabilized walls of the scarp face. Sand fused in blue flashes of ionized silica, and brown puffs of soil spurted from the wall. The Brasilian commando ducked. Allenson held down the trigger, only releasing it when an amber hologram showed that his gun was in danger of meltdown.

The commando popped back up as soon as Allenson stopped firing. A jet of red steam sparkling with an orange-yellow twinkle of burning ceramics shot out of a hole in his armor. This time he went down and stayed down. Hawthorn moved carefully past Allenson. His hunting rifle whined as it recharged its capacitors.

Hawthorn gestured with his left hand and two security troopers took up a position each side of the tunnel entrance behind the sandbags. One of them signaled one-two-three with his fingers and they tossed grenades into the tunnel simultaneously before flattening themselves against the wall. Two explosions sounded and a blast of dust shot out of the tunnel entrance. The troopers ran inside, carbines at the ready, before the dust settled.

Allenson followed but the tunnel was empty. It emerged into deep zig-zag trenches that made up the fort proper. Allenson pinged Shong on his datapad.

"Sir?"

"Situation report, if you please, Major."

"All sections report that they are in with light casualties. We've encountered only a handful of defenders. A couple of sections are held up by defensive fire from bunkers so I've ordered my men to spread out and try to outflank. My leading units are reporting explosions to the north."

"Very good."

Allenson cut the connection and indicated the advance to continue. Hawthorn led, putting his datapad around each sharp turn first to check for surprises before venturing around the corner. Eventually he stopped and held up a hand. Allenson moved through the troopers to join him.

"There's a bunker at the end of this section," Hawthorn said.

"Manned?" Allenson asked.

Hawthorn shrugged.

"We won't know unless someone sticks their head around the corner and waves," Hawthorn said. "Any volunteers, No?"

He smiled grimly.

"Shrenk, Brown, get out of the trench and crawl across the top to the bunker. See if you can drop a charge through the fire slit but stay low."

One trooper made a stirrup out of his hands. The second put his boot in and was propelled upwards. His head had barely cleared the parapet when a heavy laser pulse exploded on the lip of the trench, spraying molten soil into his face. The trooper fell back into the trench, breath bubbling through roasted and swollen lips.

Hawthorn flipped an inoculator out of a pouch and shot the trooper full of sedative.

"See if you can stabilize him, Frensa."

A trooper took off the wounded man's helmet and sprayed analgesic artificial skin onto his face.

"Looks like we're going to have to do this the hard way," Hawthorn said. He leaned his rifle against the side of the trench and turned to Allenson. "Lend me your carbine."

Allenson passed it over.

"What have you in mind?"

Hawthorn ignored him.

"Shrenk, I'll keep their heads down while you carry the charge down the trench and lob it into the bunker. Stay on the right-hand side to give me a fire lane."

The trooper called Shrenk swallowed hard but unclipped the charge from his webbing without comment. Hawthorn flattened himself by the corner with his back to the rest of them.

"On the count of three," he said, putting his left hand behind his back.

He extended one finger at a time.

Allenson relieved Shrenk of the charge. The man looked surprised but offered no resistance. On the third finger Hawthorn leapt across the trench to the far side of the turn and opened fire in short bursts. Allenson ran like a man avoiding his creditors, holding the charge against his chest like a football. He'd been good at sports at college. He trusted that he hadn't lost the knack but each footfall seemed to take forever.

Laser pulses flashed across the bunker's firing slit in one second bursts as Hawthorn nursed the carbine. For a vital second nothing happened, then laser streaks lit up the left side of the trench. The defender in the bunker automatically targeted Hawthorn as the greatest threat but he'd shot too quickly.

Hawthorn fired again, peppering the fire slit and eliciting streaks of return fire from the bunker. Again they passed by Allenson's left shoulder but this time Hawthorn failed to return fire.

A voice shouted from inside the bunker and Allenson saw a flash of light reflect off the barrel of the gun turning in his direction. He threw himself headlong as if he was going for a touchdown. Something burnt a line down his back, then he was sliding along the ground face first under the arc of fire. He rolled over until his back was against the wall and pulled his ion pistol out of its holster.

Officers carried pistols as a mark of rank and occasionally for disciplinary purposes. One never expected to actually use the things in combat. A carbine held horizontally in one hand slid out of the bunker's firing slit. The hand tried to angle it downwards to sweep the dead ground in front of the bunker with fire.

Allenson took very careful aim. He was a lousy shot but at this range he could almost touch the target with the pistol's muzzle. He fired at the hand and smelled the sweet tang of roasting flesh. There was a cry and a curse from inside the bunker.

The carbine clattered to the ground as the hand withdrew. Allenson discharged the pistol once more in the general direction of the firing slit to discourage further attempts on his life.

He pulled the safety cap off the charge and gripped the cord that uncoiled from the fuse. It then occurred to him that he hadn't asked the length of time the fuse was set for. If it was too long the bunker's residents would have time to push it back out. This would be most unfortunate for one General Allenson. Too short and it would go off in his hands, also not a desirable outcome.

Three seconds was usual. He gambled on Shrenk being a creature of habit. Soldiers tended to be, particularly when dealing with lethal devices. He pulled the cord and counted: one thousand, two thousand, then he thrust the charge through the firing slit and dropped back to the ground.

He got to three thou . . . when the air smacked him against the trench floor, which retaliated by pushing back hard. There was a loud bang and a cloud of dust emerged from the firing slit.

Troopers piled down the trench at the run. The first one to reach Allenson's prone body stood on him to get into a suitable fire position. The trooper unloaded his carbine into the bunker in long bursts, sweeping his gun from side to side.

Allenson didn't complain. He doubted that anyone had survived the blast in that confined space but it never ever hurt to make sure.

Hawthorn lay prone at the far end of the trench. Allenson's gut contracted. Hawthorn lifted his head, got up and dusted himself off. He ambled down the trench, his limp noticeably worse.

"You're going to need a new gun," he said to Allenson and held out the carbine.

A laser shot had deflected off the side, ruining the weapon. That explained why Hawthorn had stopped firing.

"You have the luck of the devil," Allenson said with feeling.

"He's supposed to look after his own," Hawthorn replied with a grin, reaching down and helping Allenson up.

He switched the grin off.

"Speaking of which, you just can't help yourself, can you? Shrenk was supposed to make the run."

"Don't be too hard on him. I really didn't give him much choice in the matter."

"Yeah, I can imagine."

They sorted themselves out into a skirmish formation and proceeded without incident. They came to an excavation containing the central bunker that acted as the fort's headquarters. A massive blast had collapsed the roof, taking out the whole structure. A leg stuck out from under the rubble. A trooper pulled at it to see if he could free the body.

Why the man felt the need to do this Allenson had no idea. The victim could not possibly be alive. A fact demonstrated when the limb came—being unattached to a torso. The trooper flung it down as if he held a poisonous snake.

Cinnerans joined them from other trenches that radiated out in all directions. All roads led to Rome or in this case led to what was left of the command bunker. Allenson tried to contact Shong but failed. None of the Cinnerans he questioned could offer any light on Shong's whereabouts.

A soldier in Streamer Army uniform shot out of a tunnel from the north side.

"Don't shoot," the man shrieked when the rifle's barrels turned in his direction.

He held both hands in the air and had lost or abandoned his weapon.

"Who are you?" Allenson asked.

"They're right behind me, hundreds of them. It's every man for himself," the man sobbed, ignoring Allenson's question.

There was another exchange of fire somewhere in the northern zone of the fort.

The man shrieked and pelted into one of the tunnels on the south side of the command bunker. More troopers emerged from the north and ran through Allenson's group. Many had thrown away their rifles, helmets and other equipment. Their uniform flashes indicated that they were Eleventh Brigade troopers.

Todd grabbed at one of them.

"Let me go," he squealed before wriggling free.

Cinnerans began to edge back into the southern trenches.

A burst of fire from the entrance to one of the eastern trenches downed two Cinnerans. Hawthorn punched a shot into the bronzed visor covering the face of the Brasilian commando who'd fired.

"Hold your ground," Allenson ordered.

It was too late. If Shong had been there, maybe he could have rallied his men. The Cinnerans didn't know Allenson or Hawthorn. Once the retreat started it turned into a rout until only Special Project troopers remained.

"Back the way we've come," Allenson said bitterly. There was nothing else to do.

"Slowly, in formation," Hawthorn said. "I'll shoot the first man or woman to run."

The security troopers did know Hawthorn. They didn't flee but acted as rear guard, stopping to fire and throw grenades whenever Brasilians pressed too hard. In the end they were outflanked. The trench structure gave a great deal of protection but Allenson knew that the game was up when they took fire from a side gallery.

He ordered the troopers to make a run for it. They passed through a tunnel in the scarp that led into the main defensive ditch where the high counterscarp trapped them. Allenson tossed a mental coin.

"This way," he said, leading the group east along the ditch towards the city-side of the fort. That seemed a slightly more likely place to find an exit ramp. Hawthorn hung back with a couple of troopers as a rear guard. Every so often he lobbed a grenade to keep their pursuers from being too keen.

The chest of the security trooper walking on Allenson's right suddenly lit up with multiple laser hits. They came from a heavy crew-served weapon in a bunker positioned to fire down the ditch. It was designed to halt any enemy trying to break into the fort but it just as adequately stopped anyone from breaking out. Allenson threw himself tight to the wall to be out of the weapon's line of sight.

That was the thing with lasers, very accurate but they only shot in straight lines.

Hawthorn joined Allenson.

"If that bastard had waited another few seconds he could have mown us all down," Allenson said.

"He doesn't need to," Hawthorn replied. "They've got us well and truly trapped. Do we rush the gun or the enemy section behind? May as well do one or the other right away. Our situation ain't likely to improve any."

"Neither," Allenson replied. "We wouldn't stand a chance. You and I might prefer to go down fighting but we have a duty to the others."

He gestured at Todd and the troopers.

"We'll surrender and hope the Brasilians are taking prisoners today."

Technically, shooting soldiers trying to surrender was a war crime but trying to give oneself up in the combat zone was always a tricky business. Most successful surrenders took place before the battle or well after it when tempers had cooled. Allenson was sure of one thing. Trying to surrender after gunning down some of the attackers wasn't an option.

War is full of the unexpected. Chaos rules the battlefield and it doesn't always work to one's disadvantage. As it happened, they weren't required to test the Brasilians mood.

Allenson's barge skimmed over the top of the counterscarp in a flicker of part-phased frame field. With the advantage of height its lateral tribarrels fired long bursts down into the ditch at targets out of sight of Allenson's group. A loud whoosh and flash indicated that the starboard gun had found something vulnerable in the bunker to the east.

The barge dropped into the ditch. Allenson's people flattened themselves against the scarp wall as the vehicle took up most of the space.

Boswell beckoned them from the pilot's podium. The woman manning the port gun lifted her visor and winked at Allenson. She held out a hand to help him over the side. He thought she had the most attractive and welcoming smile of any human being he had ever met.

The barge lifted and pivoted on the spot as soon as everyone was aboard. The gunners raked the ditch again as they climbed. Allenson had no idea whether they had targets or were just laying down fire on general principles. He found he didn't much care.

Todd made his way up the cargo hold to where Allenson sat. He kept one hand on the rail as the barge made a number of abrupt flight changes.

"What now, Uncle?" Todd asked.

"Now we go back to the control room and try to salvage something from the shambles."

★ CHAPTER 26 ★

Forlorn Hope

Allenson entered the control room with the air of a surgeon about to carry out a last-chance operation on a dying patient. No one spoke, which was just as well as he was in no mood for small talk. He joined Ling at the main console and patched through to Kaspary, Morton and Buller who popped up as holograms.

"South Fort has fallen to a Brasilian commando raid, but I reckon that lot have shot their bolt. They've taken significant casualties and have no land transport. The attack was a distraction, but strategically pointless provided we don't overreact and do something stupid. We mustn't allow ourselves to be drawn into a war of attrition by trying to recapture the fort."

Allenson turned to Kaspary's hologram.

"Situation report, if you please."

"Morton reports that Brasilians are digging in on the east bank of the Valerie but that scouting parties have started to venture inland. I don't think it will be long before they try a reconnaissance in force. When they do I'll hit them with an attack by however many troops I can move by frame. It would help if you could return some of my lift capability and the Cinnerans if you have finished with them, sir."

"I have some additional information that might be important," Morton said.

"Go on," Allenson replied gloomily thinking that it was exceedingly unlikely that he was going to find the news to his advantage.

"The Brasilians have acquired lighters from somewhere and have started to move their heavy artillery across the river."

"But I gave orders that all lighters were to be concentrated under our control," Ling said angrily. "There shouldn't have been a single vessel left in the Hundreds or the Valerie. I'll find out who screwed up and I'll have their head."

"Don't waste your time," Allenson replied, shaking his head. "Lighters could easily have been hidden by a traitor with Home World sympathies or just some businessman who didn't trust us with his assets. Whatever, it doesn't matter now."

Allenson looked at the hologram of Buller, a move that would be replicated by Allenson's hologram above Buller's console.

"And how do you rate our chances once the enemy have their artillery in place?"

Buller shook his head.

"Zero! Our only hope would be to mount a raid and destroy the tubes or ammunition while they're in transit or being emplaced. Of course, the Brasilian commander will expect such a countermove and be waiting."

Siege warfare was like a board game where all the moves and countermoves had been worked out millennia before. Action and reaction were entirely predictable from the first turn.

Allenson replied. "I concur, we can't win this round. They'll methodically and slowly smash our forts to pieces one by one. If we stay here we'll lose the army as well."

He took a deep breath.

"Right, gentlemen, we evacuate to Brunswick starting immediately while we have the strength to overwhelm their pickets in the Continuum. We'll do it in three waves by brigade, first the 11th, then the 5th. I want the 1st to go last. Once the enemy work out what we're doing they'll start to concentrate substantial blocking forces in the Continuum so the 1st may have to fight their way out. Major Morton?"

"Sir?"

"Your Canaries will sweep ahead of the first evacuation wave. Try to take out as many of the Brasilian pickets as you can. We want to keep the enemy in the dark about our intentions as long as possible."

"Gotcha, General," Morton said far more cheerily than the situation warranted.

"Colonel Buller will go with the 11th in the first wave. Do what you can to fortify our Brunswick base, if you please, Colonel. Colonel Ling and the staff will evacuate with the 5th. Please organize the evacuation, Colonel Kaspary."

Buller asked the obvious question.

"What will *you* be doing while all this is going on?"

Allenson answered without looking up from his datapad. His people had their orders and his mind had already shifted to the next problem.

"I shall be trying to confuse the situation by giving the Brasilian commander the idea that we intend to make a fight for Port Trent. I intend to impede their advance with a blocking force."

Allenson looked up.

"I will need to hang on to your Cinnerans a little longer, Colonel Kaspary."

Kaspary nodded but didn't reply.

Various people wasted more time trying to talk Allenson out of commanding the Forlorn Hope, as the blocking force was promptly nicknamed. Allenson had none of it. He was utterly exasperated by people telling him that he was too important to risk. As far as he could see, Kaspary, Ling, or even Buller could do as good a job as him. God knows, they couldn't do worse. It never occurred to him to wonder whether any of his subordinates could hold the army together.

That afternoon, Allenson, accompanied by Todd, put on his dress uniform in all its splendor. He joined a parade on the flat area outside the Central Fort that served as a ship park. Hawkins had the Cinnerans lined up at attention alongside the survivors of the 11th who had garrisoned the South Fort. They had started as two companies of Seerwood Foresters but there were not enough troopers left to fill out more than a couple of platoons.

Fortunately Cinneran losses were light, which was just as well as they had been understrength to start with. Now they were at about fifty percent of establishment. Unfortunately the casualties included Major Shong, whose corpse presumably lay somewhere unrecovered in South Fort.

Allenson ignored the Foresters and addressed the Cinnerans.

"Colonel Kaspary put you people under my command because,

and I quote him, you were the best regiment in the 1st, meaning you were the finest regiment in the army. Well God help the colonies if that's true. You broke and ran before a handful of Brasilian light infantry."

Actually, the Brasilians were elite special force commandos but that didn't need to be explained.

"But I'm going to give you a second chance to redeem yourselves. The army is evacuating Trent. You and I will guard their rear in the position of most honor."

The position of most honor was also the position of most danger, but that point didn't need dwelling upon either.

"There will be no more routs: Colonel Hawthorn?"

"Sir!"

Hawthorn snapped crisply to attention. Allenson hadn't been aware his friend even knew the right moves.

"You and your men will accompany us. You will shoot the first man who displays cowardice in the face of the enemy."

"Yes, sir," Hawthorn replied unemotionally.

He grinned at the assembled Cinnerans, whose officer at the front of the parade took two steps forward and saluted.

"That will not be necessary, General. No man here will run."

There was a murmur of approval from the ranks.

"You are?" Allenson asked.

"Captain Braks, sir, in acting command of the regiment."

"Very good, Captain," Allenson replied, but he didn't rescind his order to Hawthorn.

"What about us, sir," asked an officer from the Foresters.

"I'm sure your people did their best, Lieutenant. You'll evacuate with the rest of the 11th."

"With respect, sir, I would like a return crack at the Brasos. We'll do better next time."

Allenson considered.

"Well, if any Forester feels the same way he may volunteer to accompany the Cinnerans under your command."

About half volunteered, which was less than Allenson had hoped but more than he had expected.

Allenson retired to his quarters and minutely examined topographic maps of the region to the north of Port Trent. The Brasilian artillery had crossed the Valerie several kilometers upriver, an unnecessary precaution as there was no possibility of the Stream Army interdicting the operation. He looked for a blocking position, somewhere he could hold up the enemy for a reasonable time—preferably without losing a regiment in the process.

He understood the thought processes of the Brasilian commander as if he could read his mind. The artillery was the weapon that would win the battle for Port Trent. Therefore it must not be left vulnerable to any risk, however small. Time was on the Brasilian side. Accordingly the commander played safe and did things by the book.

In a Home World army, that was almost more important than winning. One couldn't be criticized in defeat provided one did things properly. On the other hand doubts would always hang over a general who won using unconventional tactics. Some people might suspect he was not *sound*.

The Brasilians would protect the artillery with their main force as it moved south into position to reduce the forts one by one. Light infantry would be sent ahead to seize key strategic points and create a road lined by friendly troops.

He considered letting the Brasilian lights flow past a concealed blocking force; then spring an ambush on the main column, but reluctantly rejected the idea. The light infantry would merely return and counterattack his rear, trapping his people against the main column. Ambushing the Brasilian light troops would have to suffice.

If he had read the Brasilian commander correctly the man would halt the main column in any case once the ambush was sprung until the situation had been clarified. This would achieve Allenson's purpose of delaying the Brasilian attack on the forts in the most cost-effective manner—cost effective, that is, as measured by troops lost versus time won for the evacuation of Trent to proceed.

So he pored over the map looking for a suitable ambush position. It would have to be somewhere guaranteed to be on the Brasilian march route, somewhere that offered his people concealment and cover but left the enemy exposed. But somewhere not so obvious that the light infantry commander would automatically deploy into combat formation in the expectation of a trap.

The route was easy enough to discern. There was only one all-weather stabilized road that ran south parallel to the Valerie. It meandered well inland along the edge of the river's flood plain. He rejected as too obvious a perfect ambush position where the road crossed a tributary on a bridge.

The road swung west just north of the Trent Line to connect with a second stabilized road that came in from the agricultural areas. A small town had grown up at the junction, as is the way of things. The buildings would give his men concealment. The flat fields around the town would leave anyone moving down the road completely exposed, like toy soldiers on a table top. When things got too hot the town structures would also give cover for his men to run for it.

He touched an icon on the map and the town's name was displayed. It was called *Kismet*.

The door opened.

Allenson clicked off the map and turned to greet his wife. He spoke quickly to avoid questions that he did not want to answer, such as why he was personally leading the Forlorn Hope. Trina was too bright to bullshit about the blocking operation. She would grasp that it had every possibility of turning into a suicide run. In vain would he explain that he had a plan to get away, albeit along a very dodgy avenue of escape.

"Trina," he said in feigned delight, moving to embrace her. "I'm glad to catch you as I've a very important task for you my dear."

"You have?" she asked.

"We are abandoning Port Trent, as you've no doubt heard. I need you to organize the evacuation of the soldiers' families."

She frowned. "As noncombatants they would be safest moved independently of the army."

"If you think that's best, my dear," Allenson said, hoping he looked as if this hadn't already occurred to him.

"I will need to hire a suitable ship and give the Brasilians reasonable notice of our passage. They may wish to inspect the vessel to ensure it is not being used to shift military equipment."

Allenson nodded agreement.

"Possibly, but I expect your word will suffice, which is why I need you to be in charge."

"Other civilians will also want to get out when they learn about the evacuation," she said, eyes defocusing as she thought the matter through. "I'd better get on it without delay."

"As you say," Allenson said, grinning at her retreating back.

He had been married long enough to know that it was better to deflect his wife with something for her to do rather than meet her inevitable objections head on when he intended something she would consider stupid.

The lasercannon crew ripped up the floorboards of the front room of the house in Kismet to lower the gun to ground level. They cut a horizontal gunport in the wall and positioned the weapon well back. From there it could fire up the road without giving away its position, at least for a while. Allenson nodded approvingly before letting himself out into the front garden. There, a section of infantry from the Foresters dug in.

It had taken a degree of persuasion and some not so subtle hints of forthcoming violence to get the inhabitants of Kismet to leave for the city. One old man had to be forcibly put onto the tractor train. Allenson found the whole matter distasteful. He lied and told the people they could return when it was safe. Well, it was not a complete lie in that they could return, but there probably wouldn't be much left of their town to return to.

He scanned the ground to the left and right with binoculars. The Cinnerans were dug into camouflaged trenches that ran out at forty-five degrees to the road. They had crew-served heavy weapons positioned on the far end of each line. The Foresters dug in just in front of the town. The troops had wanted to occupy the buildings. Allenson knew from bitter experience how little protection a wooden building offered from heavy laser pulses or mortar rounds so he vetoed that.

He urged the men on and then they waited, sleeping in the trenches. Allenson slept badly, disturbed by nightmares filled with burning houses and people. When he awoke his mind and body were sluggish so he took a stimulant.

Allenson gave strict instructions that all equipment was to be switched off. He took it as read that the Brasilians scouts would be using some sophisticated detection equipment. Inevitably some soldiers would forget or ignore the order but he hoped that any energy signs would be assumed to come from the town.

Mid-morning, the first Brasilians were spotted by an observer located up on top of a grain silo. It took a few minutes for the trooper to climb down and run to where Allenson had set up a headquarters with Todd and Fendlaigh beside a kitchen garden wall.

The Brasilians were well spaced in an irregular formation. They walked beside the road but not on it. The two leading men each side of the road had rifles slung over their backs. Their hands were occupied carrying detection wands, probably looking for mines. The enemy soldiers were professionals, no doubt from some sort of elite pathfinder unit.

They moved slowly as they neared the town, stopping two hundred meters out to scan the buildings. A third man moved up to the front to confer with the two on point.

"That'll be the officer," Hawthorn said, observing the trio through his rifle's optical site.

They appeared to be arguing.

"Something's spooking them," Allenson said.

"The town's too quiet," Hawthorn replied. "Where are the kids playing in the street, tradesmen going about their work and women doing domestic chores?"

"You could've maybe mentioned this sooner," Allenson replied.

"Oh sure, so you could use the townspeople as bait?" Hawthorn asked.

"Of course not," Allenson replied hotly, imagining the carnage among panicked women and kids when the firefight started.

Hawthorn wore a cynical grin.

"Okay, point taken," Allenson said.

The Brasilian officer ended the debate by pointing vigorously at the town. The wandsmen reluctantly advanced, followed by the rest of the unit. Allenson let them come in another hundred meters before switching on his datapad. One of the wandsmen stopped and pointed his device directly towards Allenson's position.

"Fire," Allenson ordered.

Hawthorn caressed his rifle's trigger. The officer dropped like a rag doll. The green troopers of the 11th opened up with a ragged volley from their laserrifles. Most pulse streaks zipped high, but with that many shots fired some had to find targets. Both wandsmen went down.

"Aim low, damn you," the Forester's lieutenant screamed.

One of the wandsmen got onto his hands and knees and began to crawl away. Hawthorn fired again and the man's jacket caught fire. This time he stayed down. All the Brasilians then dropped so it was impossible to distinguish casualties from those merely taking cover. They began to return fire, shooting at the windows and doorways in the buildings behind the Foresters.

A porch oil lamp exploded, spewing burning oil along the ground and into a Streamer's foxhole. He screamed and jumped up, clothes ablaze. Laser pulses lit up his jacket and he collapsed. At least he stopped screaming.

The open area to the left exploded in flame when the Forester's lasercannon opened up. The gunner did it by the book. A one second burst, shift the gun five degrees and repeat. Brasilians threw themselves out of the burning vegetation. They rolled over on the ground to extinguish the flames licking at their uniforms. Burst after burst slammed into the long grass.

The Cinnerans still held their fire as they'd been ordered. That was why they were on the wings. Allenson doubted the Foresters could hold to the necessary fire-control. The job of the Cinnerans was to wait until the Brasilians walked right into the trap and then lay down enfilading fire.

A few Brasilians eventually detected which house held the cannon. They fired back with their rifles, marking the building for their comrades. A light automatic squad weapon took up the refrain. It raked the house. Small explosions like the hacking coughs of a lungworm victim sounded from the Brasilians' skirmish line. Seconds later, grenades exploded harmlessly in and around the buildings at the edge of town. By chance a few dropped short into the Forester's position.

One fell into a slit trench. The concentrated detonation threw out a limbless torso.

The firefight spluttered on fruitlessly, slowly winding down.

The analytical part of Allenson's mind ran pointlessly in the background of his consciousness when it had nothing more useful to do. He pondered on the series of chaotic chance events that placed that man and grenade into juxtaposition. If the man had chosen another trench, or if the grenadier had been a better shot, or if the wind blew at a slightly different angle or . . . if the soldier had never been born. There was no end to the "ifs" that made the odds astronomically unlikely that that particular man would die in that place.

One of the houses caught alight, wooden clapperboards burning fiercely. The Forester's lasercannon stopped firing, hopefully simply because it was masked with smoke. One of the disadvantages of laser weapons was that they had low penetration.

The Brasilians took advantage of the drop in firepower to rise to their feet and retreat. They proceeded section by section, laying down suppressive fire on the general area of the Foresters. The Cinnerans on the wings continued to hold fire. They were Allenson's ace-in-the-hole, a card only to be played when it was most advantageous.

No terrain was ever truly flat and a few centimeters could mean the difference between death and safety on a battlefield swept by direct fire weapons. Most of the enemy infantry made it to where they were concealed behind a low ridge. Allenson ordered a ceasefire.

A wounded Brasilian trooper crawled slowly and agonizingly on his elbows back towards his comrades' position. His legs trailed behind. A Forester fired a shot at the wounded man which missed by several meters.

"I said cease fire," Allenson yelled, turning his datapad to full volume. He switched it off and spoke to Hawthorn. "I suppose I was over optimistic in hoping that the Brasilians would walk completely into the trap."

"You know," Hawthorn said conversationally to Allenson, "I may have made a mistake taking out that Brasilian officer right at the start. He looked the sort of gung-ho chinless incompetent who might have ordered his men to charge the town. We could have got the lot of them then. Those Brasilian NCOs are regrettably efficient."

He sighed.

Two Brasilians burst from cover and ran to their wounded comrade. Seizing him under the arms, they dragged him to safety. No one fired.

Hawthorn carried on musing.

"Of course, those self-same NCOs might well have shot their own officer in the back if he ordered them to commit suicide. It probably didn't matter that I killed him first."

"Right," Allenson said weakly.

"Hell of a way to go, shot by your own men," Hawthorn said.

The day wore on. Every so often the Brasilians lobbed a grenade in the general direction of the Foresters. None caused casualties, but it kept the Streamers pinned down in their slit trenches. Hawthorn sniped at anything showing over the ridge, but was doubtful that he had a kill. It was more a question of reminding the enemy that they were still under observation.

The grassland shimmered when the plain heated up. Allenson's troops began to run out of water. Eventually Allenson asked volunteers to sprint from trench to trench distributing bottles.

What happened next was quite unexpected. Firefights started on the wings; little spurts of combat that fizzled out almost as soon as they started.

Allenson snarled.

"The bastards have worked their way round to outflank us. I bet there's no more than a couple of men still in front just firing the odd grenade and waving helmets in the air to keep our attention."

"Yeah, a good plan. Pity they ran straight into the Cinnerans," Hawthorn replied with a grin. "Don't tell me you planned that."

"Actually, no," Allenson replied. "But don't tell anyone. I'd hate to lose what little reputation for competence that I have left."

The firing died away after a couple of minutes.

Allenson signaled Braks. There was little point in maintaining communication silence with the Cinnerans. The enemy knew just where they were.

"Report if you please, Captain."

"We've repelled probes, sir, on each wing. The enemy backed off as soon as we fired without making much of a fight of it."

"Very good," Allenson replied, "await further orders."

"That's curious, those are veteran troops," Hawthorn said. "Not the sort to give up easily."

"They're in no hurry. Why risk getting killed when the war is going their way," Allenson said. "It's not like they have much emotional investment in this war. They'll just pin us down and wait for the heavy infantry to bring up mortars. Then they'll blast us out."

"Excellent," Hawthorn said.

"I intend to be gone before that," Allenson said.

"Find out how the evacuation is going," Allenson said to Fendlaigh "You can switch your equipment on now."

When she didn't answer, he turned.

The young woman knelt with her back to him. She leaned forward over her communication array as if trying to protect it with her body.

"Fendlaigh?" Allenson asked again.

He went to her and touched her shoulder. She fell onto her back, sightless eyes staring at the sky. There wasn't a mark on her but she was still dead, her equipment smashed and burnt. Allenson couldn't remember any particular explosion close by but the Brasilians had fired volleys of grenades. The blast had killed Fendlaigh by stopping her heart, collapsing her lungs or simply turning her vital organs to jelly. A blast that left her uniform and skin unmarked.

Allenson reached down and closed her brown eyes. There was no particular reason to but something about them disturbed him.

"Shame, that," Hawthorn said dispassionately. "Now we won't know when we can leg it."

"No," Allenson replied, mind churning as he ran through the options.

Hawthorn was right. They were in deep trouble. He had no way now of getting in touch with Kaspary. Allenson knew how long the evacuation to Brunswick was planned to take but when did anything that complicated run to plan? A messenger would take too long, even assuming they got through. He daren't just assume that all three waves made it out according to the timetable. He could lose the army if he quit the blocking position on that assumption.

His duty in these circumstances was to stay and buy Kaspary as much time as possible. That meant sacrificing the Foresters and the Cinnerans. Military logic dictated that exchanging two understrength regiments for an army were an excellent exchange. His soul revolted at sacrificing the men under his command. It occurred that he wouldn't have to worry about it for long as he would also be dead. He would make sure of that but it still didn't sit right.

He forced himself to calm down and assess the problem rationally.

As tradition dictated, a Brasilian mortar barrage opened up when the sky lightened. It plastered the Streamer positions identified by the enemy pathfinders' probing attacks the previous day. The mortar fire ceased as the sun came up. Brasilian heavy infantry attacked out of the sunrise, supported by suppressive direct fire. It was a perfect set-piece attack carried out by well-trained troops.

Of course the charge carried the trenches. It would have carried them even if Allenson had not taken the precaution of withdrawing his people back into town. The Brasilian blow fell upon a vacuum. He ordered the Foresters to the rear with instructions to guard the transports. This was a useful role, but his main reason was to protect their fragile morale by giving them something to do. They had performed well yesterday, but he had little confidence in their skills for what was to happen next.

The noise of battle died away when the Brasilians discovered the Streamer positions abandoned. An ominous silence hung over the town. Allenson awaited events, his mouth dry. He crouched down beside a plum tree in the garden of a one story house. His line of sight extended down one of the lanes between the houses for a bare thirty meters.

Kismet had grown organically from a farming hamlet. It had never been subject to the rigors of town planners. Each house was placed haphazardly at the whim of whosoever had caused its construction. Vehicle lanes and footpaths curled between and around houses and kitchen gardens.

The Cinnerans were dispersed in small fire teams through the town. They had orders to contest a position only until outflanked or heavy weapons were brought up to blast them out.

A loud explosion sounded from beyond the town's boundaries.

Hawthorn grinned evilly.

"There's always some idiot tempted to pick up shiny loot."

Some of the Special Project soldiers had showed an inventive mastery of the art of making booby traps.

A second explosion sounded a few minutes later.

"And an even bigger idiot incapable of learning from other people's disasters," Hawthorn said with satisfaction.

Allenson was too agitated to answer. His biggest fear was that the Brasilians would simply screen and bypass Kismet with their main force. This would render his road block ineffectual. He thought they wouldn't. The Brasilian Army had shown itself to be highly competent at a set piece attack, but cautious and reluctant to take risks.

It was part of the cultural makeup of the Home Worlds, but especially when all the troops and logistics had to be hauled across the Bight. In theory Brasilia had infinite replacements to throw into the war, but military power declined as the square of the distance of the supply chain. It was a very long way to the nearest Brasilian base.

But there was always the risk that the enemy would behave out of character, so the booby traps left behind in the abandoned trenches were a psychological prod. He wanted to make the Brasilians angry: angry enough to want to settle accounts.

For whatever reason, the enemy took the bait. Mortars and heavy weapons mowed down the empty eastern buildings. Once it stopped, Cinnerans would move forward to set up fire positions in the wreckage to greet the advancing Brasilian infantry.

The noise of battle recommenced. Allenson listened in on the Cinneran command channel. It was difficult to make sense of the terse reports and orders. They were using sound only on the assumption that the Brasilians would be monitoring their communications and video might give away too much.

Black smoke rolled over the roofs, drifting to the west in the prevailing breeze. It didn't take long before Allenson could smell the fumes from burning wood and plastics. Fortunately most of the acrid fumes went over his position.

Laser weapons in a town of wooden buildings were bound to cause fires. The smoke thickened as the minutes ticked by. Allenson fancied he could hear the roar of flaming buildings. Something was wrong.

He contacted Braks, who was up with the leading teams.

"What's going on?" he asked.

There was no reply so he waited a few minutes before trying again. Braks was no doubt busy with his own problems. This time he got an indirect answer by monitoring the Cinneran channel.

"This is viper nine."

Viper nine was Braks's identifier.

"They're using flamethrowers. Stay out of the houses."

Allenson relayed the message to everyone.

"Lead units filter back," Braks said.

"Looks like we're next," Hawthorn said to Allenson.

Allenson and Special Projects were part of the second line.

Hawthorn muttered something to his datapad and his troopers took up fire positions on the west side of a small open area probably used for markets or as a vehicle park. Lanes curled away to the southeast and northeast.

The tension in the air tingled like the static before an electrical storm. The pressure didn't ease as the minutes clicked by. A Cinneran slid out from a tight alley directly opposite and ran across the square. He was followed by a number of others who appeared like weevils out of the unlikeliest places.

The NCO stopped to talk to Hawthorn.

"They're right behind us."

"Okay, off you go to the next position," Hawthorn said.

The NCO waited.

"Yes?" Hawthorn asked.

"Watch out for flamethrowers."

Hawthorn nodded, without taking his eyes from his rifle sight.

It was a few minutes before Allenson spotted movement at a window in a house opposite.

"In the yellow-framed house," Allenson said softly.

"Yeah, noticed him a few seconds ago. They're infiltrating the buildings opposite."

Allenson shut up. This was Hawthorn's show.

A shadow detached itself from a fence on the right-hand side of the square and scuttled along the front of the houses to stop in a doorway. More followed, all moving forward in a chain. Allenson slowly turned his head to find the same was happening on the left.

Still Hawthorn waited.

Brasilian soldiers appeared in the doorways and windows of the houses opposite the Special Projects position. When there was no response the soldiers jumped out and doubled across the square.

"Sloppy, very sloppy," Hawthorn said. "Someone's in a hurry."

He let the enemy get two thirds of the way across and then fired. A Brasilian folded from the waist and tumbled over his feet. The Special Project troopers opened up with carbines set to full auto. At urban distances, anything the carbines lost in accuracy or punch was more than made up for by rate of fire. Allenson fired with the rest, pumping short bursts into the open ground.

Brasilians fell as if a giant knife swung across the square at knee height. The survivors turned and ran back but were easy targets. The Brasilians at the edge of the square tried to give covering fire, but they were in a poor position for a firefight and took losses. They rapidly faded back into cover themselves.

Hawthorn touched his datapad and bombs hidden in the houses to the north and south of the square exploded. Wood, clay, and body parts cascaded into the air.

The handful of assault troops who had made it back into cover shot angrily into the colonial positions. The Special Project troopers kept down until the ineffectual fusillade died away.

They had ten minutes or so before the next assault. That gave time to treat the wounded and get them back. The Brasilians received reinforcements and this time they did it by the book. The attack was announced by a stream of rifle fire into the Streamer positions accompanied by the cough of grenade launchers.

Wooden buildings and fences shattered under the explosions. A ten centimeter long splinter punched through Hawthorn's jacket.

"Bastards," he said conversationally.

He pulled the splinter out, staining his shoulder with blood before he could apply a spray. Then he sighted down his rifle and fired. Allenson had no idea where the shot fell, but from Hawthorn's expression he exacted some measure of revenge.

The Brasilian suppression fire abruptly stopped.

"Here they come, people," Hawthorn yelled, rising to one knee.

Brasilian assault troops charged in as dispersed a formation as the limited space permitted. They screamed as they ran, discharging automatic weapons in the general direction of the defenders. Brasilians died in clumps but more came on showing awe inspiring discipline. They released so much fire that some of it hit home. Hawthorn's people started to die.

"Shit!" Hawthorn said.

He fired and a Brasilian fell forward, skidding along the ground on his face. He had a tube gripped under arm and a bulky pack on his back. Hawthorn took careful aim and fired again. The downed trooper exploded. Plumes of fire curled and twisted into the air. Men burned when touched by the orange and yellow ribbons. They died twisting and screaming in pain.

Over on the left a loud whoosh sounded. A line as bright as a solar flare sprayed out from the lead assault troops to splatter into the Special Projects position. Whatever the Brasilians were using as an accelerant clung to wood and flesh. It ignited both with fierce intensity. A Streamer trooper rolled along the ground trying to put out flames that wouldn't extinguish.

"Fall back," Hawthorn screamed, the order repeated by the NCOs.

He and Allenson scrambled through the house behind. They made it through milliseconds before the flames.

The flamethrowers were the clincher. No position, however strong could be held for long before the defenders were burned out. The only upside was that it turned Kismet into a sea of flame. Burning houses thickened the air with smoke black and turgid from the residues of partly consumed organics. Each breath tasted of solvents and bitter minerals. It lay heavy in the lungs causing hacking coughs that brought up stained phlegm. But the thick smoke rolling across the town also concealed the fleeing Cinnerans and masked the vehicle park.

When Allenson climbed into his barge, he noted that cocked and loaded spring guns were stacked on the floor. He ordered the frames to stay together, but inevitably vehicles lifted prematurely in small flotillas. They phased straight into the Continuum as soon as they were clear of the ground.

Allenson held his barge aloft part phased until the last vehicle lifted. His barge orbited so his gunners could take turns pouring laser pulses into the burning town to stoke up the flames.

They fully phased into a Continuum dark with the shadow of the world's gravity well. Yellow trails indicated the tracks of the other frames. The gunners switched off and depowered the lasercannon, which were worse than useless within a Continuum field. A laser pulse couldn't escape the field. It would simply bounce around burning everything in its path until completely converted into heat that also couldn't get out. The crew took up spring guns, which shot ceramic bolts that could pass through the field.

The other frames had the sense to wait in the shadow of the world until they could form a convoy for self-protection. Allenson placed his barge at the front and surveyed his fleet, if it could be dignified by such a term. Barely any two transports were the same model and few boasted hull mounted spring guns. With little hope he gave the signal to move out.

Fast, light, enemy attack frames appeared all round them as soon as they left the shadow zone and moved into the open Continuum.

★ CHAPTER 27 ★

Outrageous Fortune

A frame field permitted only limited electromagnetic radiation in the visible spectrum to pass through. Anything else was too dangerous. The raw energy of the Continuum would rip apart an unprotected vessel, dropping the wreckage into the harsh vacuum of realspace. Communication between frames was limited to that spectrum. Often this meant hand gestures and colored lights.

Allenson flashed the signal to tighten their formation. There were dangers in approaching another frame too close. If the fields touched, horrible things could happen, but they had to take the risk.

They couldn't run, so they had to fight. Their only hope was to fend off the light Brasilian fighters until their crews were exhausted. The heavier colonial transports had larger crews and more staying power. Brasilian frames moved in, attacking in waves to discharge harpoons from multibarreled swivel guns before retreating to reload.

Each wave got in a little closer. Allenson's troops died. So far they hadn't lost a frame but sooner or later a harpoon would hit something critical. Then he might have to decide whether to slow the whole convoy down to support a lame duck or to leave them to their fate.

More frames appeared in the distance, flickering in and out of sight through the multicolored streamers in the Continuum created by the high density of maneuvering vehicles. Allenson's heart sank. They would have been pressed to escape their current opponents, but Brasilian reinforcements eroded even that slim chance.

He seriously considered giving up. Surrender had always been a potential outcome and the chances of it being accepted by the Brasilians were much higher while the colonial formation still had enough cohesion to pose a threat to attackers.

Allenson reached for his pad as the next wave of Brasilian gunboats swept in, to signal his surrender, when they abruptly checked and swung about. The new frames weren't Brasilian reinforcements but Kaspary's men. They hit the enemy frames like the wrath of God and the surprised Brasilians scattered like minnows before pikes.

Within seconds not a single Brasilian frame was visible. The First Brigade gunboats gave up the pursuit almost immediately and reformed behind Allenson's convoy. Kaspary had obviously been most forceful on the need for combat discipline. It was all too easy for victorious troops to hare off into the Continuum after a fleeing enemy until he turned and massacred the dispersed chasers.

The combined convoy laid course for Brunswick. Allenson sat down to rest his eyes and fell asleep at once. Brunswick was but a short hop from Trent and the barge had already landed on the Brunswick base when he woke.

The long sleep should have done him good but somehow he was more tired than ever. He dragged himself out of the barge and contacted Ling to set up a debriefing. He leaned back against the barge hull, watching the Brunswick light which showed a red shift tinting the clouds pastel pink. He wondered whether the effect was caused by the sun or something in the air. He could look up the answer on his pad but he just couldn't find the energy.

An incoming message from Ling indicated the place and time for a meeting. He hadn't got long enough for a shower or change of clothes so he merely injected Nightlife to clear his head. Hawthorn noticed and pursed his lips but refrained from comment, which was just as well because Allenson was all out of diplomatic niceties.

He had the strangest illusion when he walked into the meeting room that Fendlaigh was manning one of the hastily set up podiums, but Fendlaigh was dead. He closed his eyes and when he opened them the terminal was unoccupied. What he saw as a woman was nothing but a shadow created by a packing capsule leaning up against the wall.

Ling, Todd and the other brigade commanders were already seated. They rose when he entered but he irritably waved them back into their seats before taking his own place.

Allenson got each of the brigade commanders to give a report, including Kaspary.

"I seem to recall I ordered you to proceed to Brunswick with all haste and leave the Forlorn Hope to make our own way," Allenson said, looking at Kaspary.

"Ah, yes, well, I was just watching the rear to shepherd in any stragglers from the third evacuation wave when I noticed combat in the distance."

"Indeed," Allenson replied. "That was fortunate."

Kaspary was lying, of course, but it sufficed as an explanation.

"Colonel Buller not coming?" Allenson asked.

"He sends his apologies but regrets he is tied up improving the fortifications," Ling replied smoothly.

"Indeed," Allenson replied again, thinking he was beginning to sound like an automated receptionist. Ling was also lying but Allenson really did not feel like taking any more shit from Buller so he let it go and changed the subject.

"I take it that our defenses are inadequate."

"That's one way of putting it," Ling replied.

Allenson said, "Well, I shan't require them to withstand a major attack. All they have to do is stop us being rolled over by a *coup de main*. If and when the Brasilians turn up in force we shall immediately evacuate to Trinity."

"Then why are we here at all?" asked the commander of the 5th.

What was the damned man's name? It was on the tip of Allenson's tongue but he couldn't seem to dredge it out of his memory. Terril? No Ferril, that was it.

"Because we needed somewhere a short hop away from Trent to reorganize and await reinforcements. I want the Canaries to go back to Trent and spread the word among the backlands that we need fighters. Our support is much stronger amongst the rural communities than the city. As soon as we have replaced our losses we relocate to Trinity."

"Won't the enemy just follow us?" Ling asked.

"They may well come as far as Brunswick, but not as far as Trinity. World hopping is not in their military manual."

Allenson reflected for a moment.

"Actually, I doubt they could follow us that far even if they wanted to. The Brasilian military machine is frighteningly strong but very ponderous."

"I agree," Hawthorn said, surprising Allenson.

Hawthorn rarely contributed to strategy discussions but he had another comment to make.

"And you should go to Paxton in the meantime, Allenson, to report to the Assembly. The politicians will be getting jumpy."

Allenson opened his mouth to refuse.

"Good idea," Ling cut in. "You will have to go back sometime to hold our masters' hands and now would seem propitious—while things are quiet."

"Certainly no one else would suffice," Todd added. "The politicos will only be reassured by you personally."

Allenson had the distinct feeling of being ambushed. He glanced around suspiciously at his comrades but was met by level stares and open expressions utterly lacking in guile. That settled it, the bastards *were* plotting against him but he couldn't quite see any flaw in their argument. He should report to the Assembly and now was as good a time as any.

"Very well, gentlemen," Allenson said, with bad grace.

"Who will command in your absence, Colonel Ling?" Ferril asked.

Allenson shook his head.

"This is not time to start shuffling people around and I won't be gone long. Colonel Ling is too valuable as chief of staff and Colonel Buller has enough on his plate. The senior brigadier will assume command in my absence. Who would that be?"

"Colonel Kaspary, sir," Ferril replied.

Both Ferril and Ling looked relieved.

"Then Kaspary it is," Allenson said.

Allenson was playing games. He knew damn well Kaspary was senior, which was why he commanded the 1st. The reasons for his choice made sense and were politic but he would have found some way to appoint Kaspary whatever the situation. He couldn't trust Buller not to get all his people killed in some foolhardy venture. Ling had proved to be a valuable chief of staff but he was an unknown quantity as a combat commander. Kaspary was a proven fighter and he had enough confidence in his decisions to modify orders in the light of circumstances.

"Before I leave, Colonel," Allenson said to Kaspary, "I would like to make a short inspection of the base fortifications. Accompany me, if you please."

"Very good, sir, I will notify the base commandant."

The tour of the defenses turned into a depressing task. Allenson examined a rampart that might have held up a Brasilian commando for all of ten seconds, provided said commando was somewhat elderly, heavily wounded and agoraphobic. The bunker behind it had walls so thin that an energetic five-year-old could have poked a hole with his pen.

A single fence of razor wire ran across the front of the rampart with a sign attached to one of the poles. Curious, Allenson walked around to look at the message which read, "Keep Out, Private Property." Someone had peppered it with shotgun pellets.

"The whole area had been popular with bird hunters before we built the base here," said the elderly major who had been base commandant before the army arrived. "There was a certain amount of resentment when we fenced it off."

"Are these typical of the fortifications?" Allenson asked.

"Not entirely," the commandant replied. "In some places there is still just a fence."

"Oh dear God!"

"But Colonel Buller has started work in those zones," the major said, clearly trying to inject some good news.

A thought occurred to Allenson.

"What sort of birds did the locals hunt?"

"Water fowl," replied the ex-commandant.

"You mean this is a marsh?"

"Only for a few weeks in the wet season when it's on the migration route."

"So that's why it was gifted to the army by the Brunswick Commercial Council," Allenson said. "The land was valueless."

He had unhappy memories of the last time he fortified a flood plain.

Hawthorn and Todd insisted on accompanying Allenson back to Nortania, Todd by declaring that an aide's place was with his principal and Hawthorn citing security. They took the barge. Boswell piloted and a squad of Special Project troopers came along for the ride. No one seemed in any great hurry despite Allenson's irritation at the time lost. The barge landed not in Paxton, but at a villa complex a couple of kilometers outside of the city. Trina greeted him there.

"What's going on?" Allenson asked Hawthorn, after he had extricated himself from his wife's clucking attentions.

"On?" Hawthorn replied, looking puzzled.

"You know what I mean."

"Trina thought that it would be advantageous for you to rest for a couple of days and collect your thoughts before meeting the Assembly."

"I see, but how did you know she had taken this villa?"

Hawthorn coughed.

"Well, actually I suggested it, for security reasons," Hawthorn said blandly.

Trina and Hawthorn had never exactly been close. Allenson was astonished to find that they were apparently in communication: astonished and disconcerted. His wife and best friend together made a near unstoppable force if they decided to maneuver him. He was not sure he liked that development but he was too tired to argue about it.

He had only been at the villa for forty-eight hours when Todd rushed into the room he was using as a study. He was working on his report but the words wouldn't come and the numbers he tried to marshal made no sense. The symbols squirmed on the screen as if they were trying to escape.

"Uncle, I've just been notified that Colonel Kaspary has phased in over Paxton and wants to speak to you urgently."

"What the hell is he doing here?" Allenson asked, horrible possibilities gnawing at the fringes of his mind.

Todd looked down.

"Brunswick's fallen and the army's been destroyed."

Allenson's heart stopped. The world became monochrome and contracted until Todd's face floated bodiless at the end of a long dark tunnel.

"Uncle, Uncle?"

Todd sounded worried and his face was screwed up in some strong emotion. His voice echoed as if it was coming from the end of a vast hall. Allenson tried to speak but his tongue would not move.

Then it went black.

Allenson dreamed the weirdest dream. He lay in a bed in a strange white room that smelt of death. Todd was there, not his nephew but his elder brother.

"But you're dead, Todd," Allenson said, stating the sheer bleedin' obvious.

"Of course I am, Allen," Todd replied. "I'm only in your head, you know. The smell of the treatment room pulled me out of your memories."

That made sense, but then Todd always made sense. His advice was invariably good.

"'Fraid I've made a bit of a cock-up, sorry," Allenson said, but Todd had gone.

He went back to sleep.

Voices arguing in the corridor outside woke him. It sounded like Stainman and Evansence from the Assembly. Trina gave them hell but they kept demanding to see him.

"Who the feck let these people in," Hawthorn's voice cut through the conversation. "Out! I'll tell you when the general is available."

It went quiet so he drifted back to sleep. When he woke again, Trina sat by the bed.

"Good morning," she said.

"I slept all night?" he asked.

"You slept for three days. The doctor diagnosed complete nervous and physical exhaustion. The genosurgeon kept you under while she flushed out your system."

"I see," Allenson said.

"I doubt that," Trina replied. "How could you be so bloody stupid?"

"What?" Allenson asked, surprised by her vehemence.

She fished around in her bag and held up a tube of Nightlife.

"Ah," Allenson said.

"Ah! Is that all you have to say?"

"Sorry," Allenson proffered.

"These things are for partying kids, not mature generals."

"I had to cut through the fatigue. People depended on me."

"I depend on you. You would be no use to anybody dead, would you?"

"I suppose not. Sorry," he tried again.

"How are you feeling?" she said, somewhat mollified by his contrition.

"Pretty good," he replied.

Oddly enough it was the truth.

"I dreamt Todd, my brother, was here, and Hawthorn."

"Hawthorn *was* here."

"Really, so I didn't imagine the assemblymen either."

"They wanted to see you and wouldn't take no for an answer from me. Fortunately I anticipated something of the sort. I arranged for your friend to be on hand to underline my wishes."

"He can be most persuasive," Allenson said with a grin.

She nodded.

"I didn't think you were particularly fond of him but the two of you seem to have reached an accommodation."

"We have a shared objective," she replied.

"Indeed?"

"To try to keep you alive and healthy despite your best efforts."

She grimaced.

"I never doubted Hawthorn's loyalty and affection for you, Allen, but having him around was like storing a box of unstable explosive in the cellar. It mightn't mean you any harm but one day it'd still bring your house down round your ears."

"So what changed," he asked, curious.

"In times of trial, explosives have their uses. I would have preferred a life that had no requirement for the Hawthorns of this universe, but if that's what it takes to be your wife then that's what I'll do."

"Tell me about the estate," he said, changing the subject.

He listened happily as she discussed the various small defeats and successes that marked the progress of his demesne like milestones along a road. A terrible weight had gone from his soul, leaving calm, like gentle weather after a great storm. He had been afraid of failing his family, the army and his people but now it was complete. He had done his duty, given his best shot and he had failed. So that was an end to the matter.

★ ★ ★

Allenson discharged himself the next morning. He returned to the villa Trina had rented and made an appointment to see the leading assemblymen that afternoon. When he lunched with Trina she kept darting sharp glances at him. No doubt she was curious about what he planned and puzzled by his good humor. He couldn't resist teasing her a little but eventually came clean about his intentions. They had her blessing. Indeed, she cried with relief.

After lunch he went to his room, where Boswell waited with a new dress uniform. He donned it and let Boswell fuss around getting various embellishments into the correct position. Servants set great store by such matters.

Trina saw him off at the door. She had wanted to go with him but he had politely, albeit firmly, declined.

"Your uniform doesn't hang right. I think you've lost weight," she said, eying him critically.

"Army food will do that," he replied.

The villa came with a suitable carriage. Boswell brought it around to the front door. Allenson boarded and they were off. He flipped through his report on the short journey but found nothing he wanted to add. He put the report aside. For good or ill it would have to do.

Hawthorn and Todd waited for him in the vestibule of the Assembly Hall. They went into the meeting room together. Allenson reflected that the last time he had been here the Assembly had made him captain general. A somewhat ironic thought to surface given the current circumstances.

Allenson stopped dead. Dead bodies sat in the ranks of chairs. Some missed limbs, some had smashed skulls, while a few were completely unmarked like poor Fendlaigh. Blood and tissue smears desecrated the walls as if some giant had sneezed while suffering a nose bleed.

Allenson shut his eyes tight. When he reopened them, the corpses had vanished. Evansence, Stainman and a half dozen others sat in a semicircle in front of a single chair.

"Please sit down, General," Evansence said, gesturing at the chair.

Allenson glanced at it disdainfully. The set up reminded him of a court with himself in the position of the accused. He had offended most of the assemblymen present at one time or another during his term as captain general. Now it appeared that they intended to put him in his place. They were too late. He intended to put himself back in his place. It just wouldn't be the same place as they had in mind.

"That won't be necessary, sars. I'll keep this short. My report is in here. It tells you everything you need to know."

He handed Evansence a plastic folder.

"This is intolerable," said an assemblyman called Roiter, his face turning florid. "You are in the presence of your superiors, sar. Sit so we can examine you."

Hawthorn chuckled.

"My superiors," Allenson raised an eyebrow. "I think not. Good day, gentlemen."

He nodded at the assemblymen and turned.

"Where are you going?" Evansence squeaked.

"Why home, of course," Allenson replied, turning back. "My strategy has failed so I have offered my resignation."

He gestured at the folder. Evansence still held it but seemed to have forgotten its existence.

"No doubt you will wish to appoint a fresh mind to the task."

"Like whom?" Stainman asked, looking thoroughly alarmed.

Allenson considered.

"That's not really my decision, but as you've asked my opinion I suggest Kaspary or Ling. Both are good men who will serve faithfully."

"And no one's heard of them," said Assemblyman Distan.

"Some consider Colonel Buller would make a suitable captain general," said Allenson.

"Colonel Buller for one," Hawthorn said.

"Unacceptable," Stainman replied.

Allenson shrugged.

"Well, no doubt you will give the matter some thought, sars."

He walked to the door in complete silence. There he paused.

"The other alternative would be to ask the Brasilians for terms."

"Terms!" Assemblyman Distan said weakly. "Their terms are likely to include hanging the lot of us as rebels."

"That's possible," Allenson conceded. "But the Brasilians aren't barbarians and this war must be costing them a fortune. I'm sure something acceptable could be thrashed out. For what it's worth, my advice would be to open negotiations while you still have some cards to play."

There was a dead silence as the terrible reality of their position sank into the assemblymen's minds like acid eating through a rusty plate. Something about the Hall struck Allenson now that his business was done.

"Why is this place so quiet?" Allenson asked.

He wondered where the rest of the assembly and their aides and servants were.

"The rest of the Assembly has evacuated to Agnew," Evansence said, looking thoroughly miserable. "We stayed behind to meet you."

"Agnew on Munchausen?" Allenson asked, surprised.

Munchausen was a quiet rural backwater of a world known mainly for its mushroom crops. Agnew was little more than a market town although it had an agricultural polytechnic. No doubt the Assembly planned to relocate to the college buildings.

"You can't just go home and leave us in the lurch," Stainman said.

"I promised my wife," Allenson replied.

"But what about your duty to the Colonies," said Assemblyman Chung.

"Are you refusing to accept my resignation?" Allenson asked.

"Absolutely," Evansence replied.

Roiter verbally pirouetted through one hundred and eight degrees, from accuser to supplicant. "It's your duty,"

Allenson blinked. He walked back to the delegates and thought the matter through before replying.

"I must warn you there are conditions."

"Name them," said Stainman.

"Very well, I will have to build a new model army and I will have to use it like a rapier against the Brasilian's club tactics. We'll never match them for strength so we have to substitute speed."

At that point, a private hologram signal flickered on the edge of Allenson's vision indication an incoming priority message on his pad. He decided to read it. The delegates could wait. With any luck they would take offence and fire him. He really didn't care.

The message was from Trina. It expressed her love and wished him good fortune. Allenson smiled, lost for a moment in his private life.

Stainman coughed.

Allenson dragged himself back to the task in hand.

"Where was I? Oh yes, my conditions for withdrawing my

resignation. I can't keep referring back to you on Munchausen to ratify every political decision. The place doesn't even have a proper port. Accordingly, you must grant me plenipotentiary powers."

There was a chorus of outrage.

"Very well." Allenson turned to leave.

"Stop!" Stainman said sharply.

His voice silenced the committee and caused Allenson to pause.

"Make out the necessary documents and we'll all sign them," Stainman said to Evansence.

"Do we have the authority?" asked Roiter. "Shouldn't this go before the Assembly?"

"Of course it should and it will—right now," Stainman replied. "The motion is to give Allenson plenipotentiary powers, all in favor?"

He raised his arm and looked around the empty meeting room. The rest of the committee held up their hands

"Anyone against?"

No one moved.

"The ayes have it by six votes to none. The Assembly has voted according to the constitution. The motion is carried."

"They'll have our heads if this goes wrong," Chung said.

"I fancy the rest of the Assembly's opinion will be the least of your problems if Allenson fails," Hawthorn pointed out with a malicious grin.

The committee squirmed.

"Very well, sars, on that basis I will continue to serve," Allenson said.

Chung led the rush to the door. The assemblymen had a fast packet boat to Munchausen to catch. Allenson found himself alone in an empty hall with Todd and Hawthorn.

"The king is dead, long live the emperor," Todd said obliquely.

Hawthorn shook his head and laughed out loud.

"Amazing, they try to give you a Grade A bollocking and by the end are begging for your help."

"This wasn't actually the outcome I intended," Allenson replied. "I meant what I said about resigning and going home."

Hawthorn chuckled.

"I know. They believed you. That's why they were so terrified. They had the look of small children who tell daddy to go away; then are horrified when he opens the front door. Under the bluster they know *you* are the army of the colonies. You're the only thing standing between them and a Brasilian firing squad."

"Be that as it may, the tricky bit is still to come," Allenson said.

"What's that, Uncle?" Todd asked.

"I have to explain to my wife that we're not going home yet."

★ CHAPTER 28 ★

Restoration

The next few weeks were inordinately busy, but eventually the situation stabilized enough for Allenson to chair a strategy meeting for his senior officers.

"So how much of a force do we have left, Colonel Kaspary?" Allenson said, in his role as chair of the Recruitment Committee of the New Model Army.

"Precious little," Kaspary replied. "Casualties amounted to somewhere between one third to a half of the army at Brunswick, mostly as Brasilian prisoners. Another one third or more deserted in the rout. Many of the militia reckoned that their term of service was up so they just went home, their obligations completed at least to their satisfaction. We have about twenty percent left of which about half are from the 1st."

He said the last with a certain amount of unit pride that softened his expression for a moment.

"I take responsibility for the Brunswick debacle." Kaspary slid an envelope across the table. "My resignation, sir."

"Declined," Allenson replied, ripping the envelope in two. "Don't look like that, Colonel. If the Assembly refused my resignation I see no reason to accept yours."

There was no answer to that so Kaspary didn't try to make one. Hawthorn filled the gap in the conversation.

"My agents tell me Brasilian officials are granting Loyalty Certificates to any residents of Trent and Brunswick who present themselves and take an oath to the Government of Brasilia."

"There's a lot of Home World feeling in both colonies anyway," said Ling.

"What are they offering?" Kaspary asked.

"The usual, peace and security," Hawthorn replied. "Many people will settle for that."

"We will consider a response in due course but we have more pressing issues . . ." Allenson replied.

The door was flung open and Buller lurched in. He was sweating and his collar was soiled where it had rubbed on his stout neck. From the evidence of his jacket he had garnished his breakfast with blackberry sauce. He flopped down in a chair without bothering to proffer an apology for his lateness.

Allenson continued as if nothing had happened.

"Our primary task is to rebuild the army, gentlemen. Desertions cost us more troops than combat losses and sickness combined. We did our best to transform militia into regulars but failed. I propose to start again with a New Model Army of professional soldiers. They will answer direct to the Assembly through the powers that our masters have chosen to delegate to me."

Allenson paused to let the implications of the power change sink in.

Buller tilted back his head and stuck out his chin aggressively. "I propose we reform our people as guerrillas and adopt a scorched earth policy. We burn out anyone who supports the Brasilians and assassinate their officials in the bloodiest manner possible. We can pick off individual soldiers while avoiding serious battles—"

"We have discussed this before, Colonel," Allenson replied, eyes as hard as granite chips. "The Brasilians will respond in kind to terrorist tactics and our civilians will bear the brunt of it."

"So much the better," said Buller. "Every farmer they hang and farmer's wife they rape will add to our support: nothing like a good massacre or two to whip up a bit of patriotism, what?"

"I said no!"

Allenson voice was cold and final.

Buller flushed and lost his temper.

"You never learn, Allenson, that's the trouble with bloody amateurs. You tried matching colonials against regulars and got your clock cleaned. How the hell you weaseled out of being sacked for the mess you've made I'll never know. Suppose you have old friends in the Assembly who pulled strings."

Hawthorn's eyes blazed and Allenson had put his hand down hard on his friend's shoulder to keep him in his seat.

"One more word, Colonel, and I'll have your commission."

Buller choked but shut up.

Ling hurriedly jumped into the conversation.

"The Lower Stream want a local commander to oversee preparations for their defense in case the Brasilians move their way. I've told them such a move is unlikely but they're insistent."

Ling spread his hands apologetically.

Allenson said. "Very well, you will command the lower Stream militias, Colonel Buller."

"It'd be best if you took up your commission immediately," Hawthorn said, enunciating each word clearly and unemotionally. "Your orders can be sent on."

Buller looked at Hawthorn and rose without speaking. Hawthorn's eyes tracked him across the room like point defense sensors until he was the other side of the door.

"Thank you, Colonel Ling, I do believe you defused a difficult situation there," Allenson said.

"My pleasure, sir."

Allenson continued as if Buller had ceased to exist.

"I intend to create new line regiments and we will need to look at the officer corps. I want people with combat experience but we must also be prepared to train promising material."

"Officers who do their jobs with the field army are disadvantaged for advancements against their contemporaries," Ling said, "who find reasons to go home and lobby their local politicians."

"That stops now."

Allenson rapped the table with his knuckles.

"All militia commissions are rescinded. Only new commissions granted by the Assembly in the form of ourselves will be recognized. You may make it clear to any interested party that I don't give a rat's arse for the opinions of any politician when it comes to promotions. Advancement by merit only will now be the order of the day. Once we have regimental cadres for The New Model Army sorted, their first mission will be to go back home and find recruits to fill the ranks."

"We have lost most of our heavy equipment, sir," Kaspary said.

Allenson said, "You can leave that to me. I have been in touch with the Terran War Directorate. They took a bashing in the last war and show little inclination to repeat the experience, which suits me just fine."

"We don't want to exchange the devil we know as a master for the devil we don't," Hawthorn said.

Allenson replied, "Quite, however they appear willing to supply us with state of the art weapons and logistical equipment."

Kaspary rubbed his hands together.

"With a new unified command structure and top of the range gear we actually stand a chance."

"I bloody hope so," Hawthorn said gloomily. "If I have to hang I'd rather it not be alongside Buller and a bunch of politicians. One has one's standards."

Allenson examined the credentials of the small slender Terran diplomat sitting opposite him very, very carefully. Hawthorn would already have gone over his diplomatic accreditation with microscopic attention to detail, but an additional show of caution might be beneficial to negotiations. It also gave him a chance to assess the negotiator.

The word that came to mind was "slippery." The man oozed charm like hydraulic fluid from a leaky valve. One got the impression that if one tried to pin him down he would slip from one's grasp like a bar of soap.

"These seem to be in order, Sar Preson," Allenson said, handing the plastic clip back. "But I notice that you are here in your capacity as deputy to Director General Suntalaw. I was under the impression he held the portfolio for Terran internal, not external, affairs."

"That is so," Preson replied with a smile that showed perfect genosurgeoned teeth decorated in cream and powder blue whirls. "However, DG Suntalaw has also been given the portfolio for the Exoworld Directorate on a temporary basis by the Central Policy Bureau."

Central Policy Bureau was a euphemism for the Terran advocate general himself. The other members were pensioned off nonentities who could be relied upon to rubber stamp whatever the AG proposed.

"Indeed," Allenson raised an eyebrow. "What happened to Lady Fancisco of Exoworld?"

"Alas, she was taken unexpectedly ill and is being treated by the advocate general's personal physicians."

Which probably meant that if she wasn't dead yet she soon would be. No doubt she had would sign a full confession implicating several politicians against whom the AG needed leverage. Frankly Allenson wouldn't give much for Suntalaw's chances either, long term. Holding both the internal and external directorates in his sweaty grasp gave Suntalaw total control of Terra's various security apparatus.

Some might wonder whether such power might be used as a springboard for a coup against the advocate general himself. Many Terran bureaucrats and politicians had bet that they could beat Advocate General Ferroman to the draw but none had yet succeeded. Allenson suspected that Suntalaw might be one of the people implicated by Fancisco's imminent confession.

But none of this was his problem

"I see you are offering to supply us with military equipment and subsidies in the form of favorable import credits for Terran commodities. What do you require from us in exchange?"

Preson made a moue and languidly waved a hand.

"Terra supports the rights of free peoples everywhere. We regard it as our privilege, nay duty, to support the colonists' struggle to rid themselves of Brasilian tyranny."

"Quite," Allenson replied, almost managing to keep a note of sarcasm out of his tone. "But is there nothing more practical we can do to show our appreciation of your support?"

"Well there might be one small matter you could assist us with," Preson said, after apparently searching his memory.

"Indeed?"

"But yes, now I recall," Preson became more animated.

He gazed at Allenson with transparent honesty.

"One of our prospectors discovered a mineral found in the Hinterland, some sort of exotic metal I believe, to which Terra would like exclusive access. The stuff is valueless but attractive."

"I see, so why do you want it?"

"Oh, I believe there is a plan to make unique jewelry, medals, badges of rank, that sort of thing."

"How odd," Allenson replied.

"Why so?" The charming grin again.

"Because Brasilia also has found a unique heavy element in the Hinterland, only this one is extremely valuable. It will revolutionize Continuum travel, or so I'm told. Naturally, I don't concern myself with such matters."

It was Allenson's turn to flash the teeth and wave languidly to indicate an aristocrat's proper disinterest for technical details.

"Surely some mistake," Preson said desperately.

"No doubt, but for the sake of argument let's assume that this magic metal actually does exist, purely hypothetically you understand."

"Of course."

"Then the Stream's policy would be to export it to all the Home Worlds partly to generate income, but mainly to keep the balance of power. Of course, to do that we have to win our independence, otherwise Brasilia gets the unbihexium. Then we are all in a precarious situation. You know, I really think that Terra will find it in her interests to support us generously."

Allenson beamed at the negotiator, but Preson's face was a perfect blank.

"On that basis I will gladly accept Terra's kind offer of free support. Rest assured if we find any unique material in the Hinterland suitable for jewelry you have my personal assurance that Terra will get exclusive access."

Allenson switched his pad off with an air of a man reaching closure.

"I fancy Advocate General Ferroman will wish to hear your report personally upon your return home, so please convey to him my warmest thanks and well wishes."

Preson's face reflected a funereal pallor. Allenson made a mental note to get the visual spectrum on his office lights checked.

Allenson had been pretty sure that the Brasilians would pause and regroup on Brunswick. He doubted they would press on to Nortania or swing back to attack the undefended Heilbron colonies but there was always that nagging doubt. He had been wrong so many times now that it was almost anticlimactic when the enemy behaved exactly as he expected, if not quite exactly as he predicted. Days passed to weeks and the Brasilians showed no plans to go anywhere.

He seized upon the opportunity to rebuild the army. Volunteers poured in from all over the colonies, motivated by a mixture of patriotism and the offer of decent equipment and regular pay. The troops who escaped Trent and Brunswick, those that hadn't deserted, were pretty solid. Many of the new recruits had prior military training from one source or another. Some of them were probably deserters reenlisting under new identities. Allenson had passed the word not to investigate the backgrounds of promising recruits too assiduously. Some stones were better left unturned.

Allenson read through the latest intelligence reports. The material was massive and anecdotal, which made it difficult to interpret. Nevertheless, he drew some very comforting conclusions. However, intelligence data was usually fragmentary at best and often misleading or even contradictory. It was so easy to cherry pick material to support a preconceived view and overlook contrary indications.

He needed a second opinion from someone clever, someone cynical and pragmatic, someone who didn't care enough about outcomes to let his opinions taint his analysis. Most of all, Allenson needed someone lacking ambition or fear who would tell him the unvarnished truth. In short, he needed his friend Hawthorn. He reached for his pad.

Allenson was struggling in trying to get some sense from a supplier who had delivered five hundred combat boots for one-legged soldiers with only left feet when Hawthorn knocked and entered. He gratefully dispatched the correspondence to Trina with a request that she look into the matter, something he should have done from the start.

Boswell followed right behind with two mugs of cafay on a tray.

When he left Allenson got down to business.

"The Brasilians are consolidating their hold on Brunswick," Allenson said, gesturing at the plastic file with the intelligence reports.

"True, they've spent an inordinate amount of time refortifying our old base outside the capital, Palisades. God knows why, we were hardly in a position to storm the place," Hawthorn replied.

"What I don't understand is why they have scattered their regiments in penny packets across the world," Allenson said.

Hawthorn produced a hip flask and poured a generous splash of brandy into his cafay. "When you put it like that, I suppose it explains why they fortified the base."

Allenson looked quizzically at his friend.

"So a small garrison could hold off an army until relief arrives from the outlying garrisons," Hawthorn explained.

"The enemy is always three meters tall," Allenson said, shaking his head at the idea that the shattered colonial army could launch a full blown offensive at the Brasilian base.

"I suppose the garrisons are to hold down the rural population," Hawthorn said. "If you look at appendix seven in the report it seems that the Brasilian units on Brunswick are having trouble with their supply line. They are relying on the locals for food."

"I expected that, as Brunswick lacks a port capable of handling the necessary quantity. Nevertheless it raises the question of why they haven't pulled the bulk of their forces back to somewhere like Port Trent?"

"No rational reason that I can think of, unless it's about imperial prestige. Where the Brasilian soldier plants his boots, he stays," Hawthorn said, expertly mimicking the upper class accent that was *de rigueur* for senior officers in the Brasilian military.

Allenson's butterfly mind wondered whether the accent was a necessary qualification for admission to Brasilia's Gravelwick Military Academy or whether successful candidates were given voice training. He forced himself to get back to the matter in hand.

"You're beginning to sound like Buller now," he told Hawthorn with a grin.

Hawthorn gave a glare of mock outrage.

"I shall have to call you out if you continue to hurl base accusations like that."

Allenson just smiled, so Hawthorn continued.

"However, the policy does seem to be working to our advantage. The troops are garrisoned among the locals. This policy is less than popular, especially as the soldiery are no more fastidious than any other occupying army about helping themselves to whatever they fancy from whatever the civilians have available. It hasn't been helped by the replacement of Brasilian regular regiments with mercenaries. They are even less likely than the regulars to stint themselves when, ah, requisitioning."

"Indeed," Allenson's interest perked up. "So despite the Loyalty Certificates, Home World enthusiasm is cooling rapidly on Brunswick."

"I'd say so," Hawthorn replied.

"Tell me about the mercenaries," Allenson said.

Hawthorn shrugged, "What's to tell? They're recruited from Cornuvia, a not particularly wealthy Home World within the Brasilian sphere of influence. I've no reason to think that they'll be any better or worse than any other mercenary army."

"No," Allenson said slowly.

He was sure he'd read something interesting about Cornuvia but he struggled to lift the memory from out of the morass that he was pleased to call his mind. He recalled that the world was mainly known for mining but he was sure there was something else. Now he thought about it, he hadn't read about Cornuvia, he'd heard about it. Trina had mentioned something about the world over breakfast some months ago. He hadn't been listening and they'd had a fight over him ignoring her. He would have to approach her delicately on the matter, very delicately.

Another month passed with no move by the Brasilians. Comedians on the entertainment circuit coined the struggle for independence The Phony War. One did a passable imitation of Allenson himself as a senile military commander who kept forgetting which world he was on, all such jolly fun. Allenson passed word that he thought the parody amusing in order to defuse attempts by patriots to force the comedian to desist. As he surmised, the joke soon ceased to be fashionable when it had the public approval of the powers-that-be.

Allenson was in the habit of chairing briefing meetings attended by all his senior and middle ranking commanders from the combat, security and logistics divisions so there was nothing unusual about the meeting he called one windy and wet Nortanian morning. Not until he dropped the bombshell.

"Gentlemen, we move against the main Brasilian army on Brunswick in forty-eight hours."

Some of his closest confidants suspected something was up, of course, as their responsibilities made up pieces of a puzzle that when put together pointed to his plan. But secrecy had to be maintained.

He worked on the assumption that anything of interest known to more than ten people on Nortania would be on the Brasilian general's desk two days later, that being the average journey time between Nortania and Brunswick.

There was a stunned silence, followed by a babble of sound that was a mix of anxiety from the senior commanders and excitement from their juniors. Allenson held up a hand for silence.

"I have decided on this for the following reasons," he counted them off on the fingers of his left hand.

"My first reasons are military. Firstly, it is vital that we regain the strategic initiative. Up to now we have allowed Brasilia to dictate events. That has to stop because we are being forced into a losing war of attrition in a series of set-piece battles that favor Brasilian military methods. Secondly, our troops' expertise with our new Terran-supplied equipment has probably reached the optimum balance between training and boredom. Our army is probably as good as it is ever going to get. Thirdly, the enlistment period of many of our veterans of the Port Trent and Brunswick campaigns is almost up."

Ling coughed.

"You wish to say something, Colonel?"

"There's nothing to stop us asking them to reenlist, sir."

"No but will they? In particular, will the most energetic and restless types who are the backbone of The New Model Army? Most of our senior NCOs are drawn from this group and I refer you to my previous comment about boredom."

He looked around the meeting room from face to face, but no one added anything further.

"My final reason is political. Sooner or later our masters in the Assembly will decide that it is safe to come home from Munchausen. Back on Nortania I have no doubt they'll wish to oversee the army personally. Anyone think that is a good idea?"

The question was rhetorical. It didn't require an answer.

"Accordingly I am resolved to attack. Questions?"

"Do we have the lift capacity?" Ling asked.

"Trina," Allenson turned to his wife.

"Around half the army have access to personal frames of one sort or another. In addition we have the barges that took Brunswick produce to Port Trent and Paxton; the ones Colonel Kaspary used to evacuate Brunswick."

"That can't be many," said Flamant, one of the new brigade commanders.

"You'd be surprised. There was a great deal of trade along these routes in peacetime. From my experience in shipping," Trina emphasized this for those who weren't aware of her background, "I estimate that we will have sufficient lift capacity to move the remaining troops, artillery and essential supplies in two tranches."

"Of course, those personal frames will have wildly different specs and I wouldn't bet on many being in great condition," Hawthorn said.

"Agreed," Allenson replied, "which is why the first wave will consist of barges escorted by Morton's Canaries and selected ad hoc units of Hinterlanders in possession of one- and two-man fighting frames. I will be leading this wave, of course."

"Of course," Hawthorn replied, rolling his eyes towards the ceiling.

Allenson ignored him. If the first wave was wiped out the disaster wouldn't be any greater simply because the commander in chief went down with it. One more major defeat and the army was finished. Who could build a New New Model Army or even want to try in those circumstances?

"The troops on personal frames will follow immediately so that the vanguard at least should arrive with—or just after—the barges. Individual Stream soldiers will be scattered all over the world if they don't have someone to follow. The frontiersmen can shepherd in stragglers once the barges have landed and the troops have set up a perimeter."

"But won't the Brasilians be patrolling the Continuum in force?" asked Flamant, who seemed to have decided to adopt the role of Devil's advocate.

"Morton?" Allenson asked.

"The enemy have patrols out but not in any great numbers and their routine is haphazard. They seem pretty halfhearted about the matter."

"They're convinced that they crushed the Stream Army at Trent and Brunswick," Hawthorn said.

"Not entirely untrue, of course, but we've come a long way back from that state of affairs," Allenson said. "The barges will return immediately after unloading for the remaining troops."

"I suspect there will be a delay to recharge the barge capacitors," said Blount.

Blount had no direct military experience. Allenson had appointed him commodore of the barge flotilla because of his shipping expertise. His career had spanned captain, ship owner and factor. He demonstrated an unflashy competence in each role.

"That's what worries me," Kaspary said. "We'll be taking one awful gamble trying to keep such a disparate force together. Even without the inevitable unexpected factors that will delay the second lift. We might as well put our army through a sausage grinder as arrive in penny packets to be mopped up in detail by enemy attacks. They would have all the advantages of interior lines."

"It'll work as long as everybody does his job," Allenson said sharply, "and I have every confidence in the people in this room. Besides, I expect to achieve strategic surprise."

"How so, some scout is bound to see the invasion fleet and sound the alarm?" Morton asked.

A conspiratorial grin crossed Allenson's face. He knew something the others didn't.

"We'll take the enemy unawares because they think we're finished and so will have trouble accepting that they're under attack, and because their troops are dispersed all over Brunswick . . ."

He paused for dramatic effect.

". . . but mostly because we'll be attacking on Kobold Day."

★ CHAPTER 29 ★

Invasion

A murmur went around the meeting.

"Someone has to ask so it might as well be me. What in the name of all that's holy is Kobold Day?" Hawthorn asked.

"All that's unholy you mean," Trina replied.

"I remember my wife telling me about Kobold Day. . . ."

"Humpf," Trina interrupted.

"Perhaps you should explain, my dear," Allenson said smoothly.

"Kobold Day is a week-long semi-religious festival held in midwinter all over Cornuvia, which is where the mercenaries that make up the bulk of the Brasilian Army come from," Trina added, noting blank looks around the meeting room.

"Cornuvians primarily earned their living from mining when the world was first colonized. They were dumped there by a transworld corporation that went bust three or four hundred years ago. Conditions in the mines were terrible. Most of the work was done by hand with pickaxes and the like so the death rate was ghastly. The miners had a superstition that misfortunes such as cave-ins and the toxic effects of the arsenical ores were caused by hostile supernatural goblinlike creatures called kobolds. Kobold Day was an attempt to placate the beasts. I don't know whether they still believe in kobolds, or whether they ever really did, but they still celebrate Kobold Day."

"I don't see how this helps us," Flament said, wriggling impatiently on his chair.

"Perhaps this short video will demonstrate," Trina said. "My friend

Lady Fieldings' youngest son, Oswald, backpacked around Cornuvia on his gap year before college. Let me show you some clips he made of Kobold Day. There's no sound for some reason so I'll give a commentary."

She touched her pad and a three-dimensional hologram of abysmal quality filled the room. The colors were bleached out and the images flickered. When the hologram settled down it showed a square surrounded by buildings. Garish streamers flew from every available surface.

An extraordinary figure clad all in black danced into view. A long black mask painted with staring red eyes and teeth concealed his face. It was what he had around his waist that attracted all eyes. A large hoop suspended from his shoulders supported a black skirt hanging to the floor. Silver runes posed at various angles decorated the skirt.

A long pole stuck out of the front of the hoop at forty five degrees. From the top some kind of animal skull leered out at the cheering spectators. The prancing figure grasped the pole in both hands so he could waggle it obscenely while gyrating his hips.

"That's the 'Obby 'Ound," Trina said. "It supposedly represents some sort of fertility god."

A second figure, a woman, leapt around the 'Ound waving a silver club. She wore a skin-tight suit of red with a yellow high-coned hat fastened to her head. Purple chiffon streamers attached to the peak of the cone fluttered in the wind

"That's the Teaser," said Trina. "I don't know what she represents."

A column of men wearing black scarves with plastic glowing antlers on their heads followed the pair. Behind them danced a troupe of women wearing red scarves and hats that looked like large red flowers.

"I believe the symbology is obvious," Trina said, primly. "At dawn on Kobold Day the people dance in and out of all the houses led by the 'Ound and Teaser to scare away kobolds."

The clip ended and was replaced after a few blurred seconds by a shot of someone's feet. Then the image settled on a three-meter sausage turned on a spit over a trench of burning charcoal.

"The Cornuvians chuck any food that is on the turn into a giant sac made from stitched together animal gut and roast it for the traditional Kobold Day lunch."

"Good God," someone said.

Another clip showed a woman in rags clutching a trident and shield being paraded around the square on a silver painted throne.

"That's the consort of the Lord of Misrule."

The final clip showed people lying in reclining chairs pouring a liquid into their open mouths from a sort of miniature watering can.

"The rest of the clips are all like this or of the celebrants falling over, vomiting or fighting. Traditionally the Cornuvians imbibe great quantities of a special Kobold Day alcoholic drink made from distilling fermented apple juice. It took Lady Fieldings' genosurgeon two weeks to detox young Oswald when he returned from his adventure."

"And this is just one day?" Hawthorn asked, chuckling.

"Oh no, the name is misleading. Kobold Day goes on until the festival goers run out of alcohol or stamina, whichever fails first. I believe it usually lasts for at least a week and maybe two."

"They won't find many apples on Brunswick," Kaspary said.

"I doubt that will be a problem," Trina replied dryly. "The Cornuvians don't appear too fussy. I believe any drink with a high enough alcohol content will do."

"And Kobold Day starts tomorrow," Allenson said.

"So we shall invade Brunswick on the third day when everyone has had a chance to get well and truly rat-arsed," Hawthorn said, laughing.

The Continuum was in a good mood when the invasion flotilla left Nortania. Barely a ripple of blue and green energy disturbed the deep background indigo. Allenson elected to travel on a three-man fighting frame, where the crew sat in tandem.

Todd and Hawthorn announced that they would be riding with him. Allenson protested that he would prefer them to have their own transport. It would be advantageous in case of mishaps to spread the army's leadership as widely as possible. Trina weighed in on their side. Allenson gave in when even the ever-loyal Ling pursed his lips and shook his head.

Hawthorn rode in the bow with a heavy spring gun mounted on gimbals. It was generally acknowledged that he was the best shot. Todd took the rear as befitted an ex-wheelman with a university blue who could provide some grunt in the pedaling department. It did not escape Allenson's notice that this left him sandwiched in the middle in the place of maximum safety. However, the reasons for the crew layout were entirely logical so he kept his observation to himself.

Allenson placed his frame at the head of the barge flotilla where he could keep an eye on his flock. Hinterlanders on one- and two-man fighting frames forged ahead and to the flanks to provide security. Kaspary brought up the rear, having drawn the short straw. He had the responsibility of shepherding the motley group of private frames. All they had to do was follow the highly visible yellow wake that the barge convoy trailed through the Continuum. Allenson suspected that even this might prove challenging for some of the participants.

The flotilla had an easy crossing to their layover point on a sparsely inhabited world called Notorious, named after the number of settlers lost trying to colonize the place. Large horned herbivores roamed the most habitable and agriculturally rich continental plains. Large, fast, vicious carnivores preyed on the herbivores.

One day when the economics was right a suitably armed colonization program would exterminate the megafauna and open the world up for farming. That was currently a long way off. Land was cheap in the Stream and so mudgrubbers, as the settlers were known, found easier worlds to cultivate.

None of this bothered the Streamer Army overmuch as they regrouped and rested on an island. In any case, they were heavily armed. Everyone got a decent night's sleep, once the few amphibious monsters in the immediate vicinity had been fried. Well, almost everyone. Allenson's fertile subconscious kept inventing new ways the army could chance upon disaster and fed them through into his dreams.

It didn't seem to help that so far it had all gone well. One or two barges had to turn back on emergency pedal-power after battery failures and a few of the private frames managed to get lost despite Kaspary's efforts, but that was only to be expected. Deep in the underlying strata of Allenson's convoluted mind a stubborn abyssal layer kept insisting that a malevolent universe was lulling him into a false sense of optimism before setting him up for a major pratfall.

The advantage of a naturally pessimistic outlook is that one is rarely disappointed by the vicissitudes of fate. Allenson was almost satisfied on some visceral level when Continuum conditions turned nasty not long after they left Notorious. Conditions deteriorated with terrifying speed. The deep indigo of the Continuum clogged with multicolored streamers of energy until it became a churning maelstrom of greens and yellows shot through with dancing red whirlpools.

Pushing through the turbulence demanded more and more power until all three on Allenson's frame were pedaling hard.

"Do we press on?" Hawthorn asked over his shoulder.

Looking back, Allenson could see the barges pitching and tossing as the steersmen tried to keep them on course. Visibility had decreased sharply. He could not see what was happening to the screen of Hinterlanders up front or the private frames at the rear. He checked the course on the frame's navigation. The storm conditions would make the calculator's estimates of distance covered less and less accurate but so far as he could tell they were about half way.

There was no world listed closer than Notorious or Brunswick to shelter. He could try to find a coherent energy stream and run down it until they reached somewhere habitable but it was as big a gamble as continuing or turning back.

"We go on," Allenson replied, decision made.

So they did, for hour after hour until Hawthorn screamed a warning. Todd rammed the tiller over just in time to avoid a single-man frame that shot out of a red-brown petal of energy off their port bow. It raced down their starboard side and vanished into an explosion of silver and yellow stars.

Allenson had a split second stop-frame view of the driver hunched over his steering column. He pedaled furiously, his mouth wide open to gulp air. The desperation and terror in the Streamer's eyes caught Allenson's attention.

Todd turned their frame back on course. There was nothing the crew of one frame could do to help another in the Continuum. Their fields were little bubbles of isolated reality that could not be allowed to touch without inviting catastrophe.

The silver and yellow explosion might just have been the wash displaced as the one-man frame punched through a sharp energy gradient. It more likely indicated the vehicle dropping out into realspace due to some equipment failure. If so, the driver was already dead from asphyxiation and decompression. Airtight frame hulls were expensive and largely pointless. All they did was prolong the crew's agony if a machine malfunctioned and fell out of the Continuum. It wasn't as if anyone was going to find you in the vast dark realspace ocean where the fastest traveler was a photon.

Todd guided Allenson's frame to Brunswick pretty much as planned. One upside of the filthy conditions in the Continuum was that Brasilian patrols must have run for cover. They didn't spot a single enemy frame.

Ground zero was a shallow wooded valley about five klicks outside of the market and service town of Teneyk. Allenson had intended to rendezvous in the Continuum to allow stragglers to catch up, then descend into the valley en masse to overwhelm any defense. The conditions made that impossible. He planned to land in the dark just after midnight but they had been so seriously delayed that the sun was high in a bright blue sky on their arrival. Fortunately they saw nothing when they phased in, no Brasilians but no Streamers either.

When Todd switched off the field, the biting cold of a Brunswick winter rolled over Allenson like a tidal wave. It seared his lungs when he inhaled and condensed water vapor into a white mist when he exhaled. The shock was all the greater because conditions inside the frame field had become unpleasantly hot and steamy so they had all stripped to the waist.

The first thing Allenson and Todd did was to break out and don warm clothing. Hawthorn, seemingly oblivious to the temperature until Allenson chucked him a shirt and parka, checked the area around them using his rifle's sights.

Todd unclipped the beacon from under their frame and plugged it into the vehicle's battery. He watched the winking light pattern of the machine's small control panel until satisfied it worked satisfactorily.

Almost immediately a barge slid down the valley, part phased. Hawthorn watched it carefully, his rifle switched on and held at high port. It looked like any other Brunswick produce carrier. That meant it was probably Streamer but Hawthorn tended to err on the side of caution.

The barge landed and Stream troopers jumped over the sides. A young lieutenant dashed up to Allenson and threw a parade ground salute. Allenson winced, hoping he wouldn't do it again. There was no reason to think that the woodland along the side of the valley harbored enemy snipers looking for officers to pick off but it was a stupid risk to take. There was more than one reason Allenson was in standard rifleman's combat fatigues rather than in a full dress uniform complete with obligatory dead chicken on the helmet.

"Lieutenant Arkright reporting, sir!"

The officer would have saluted again but Allenson grabbed his arm.

"Where did you spring from, son," Allenson asked, reflecting that he was beginning to sound like the army's grandfather.

"We landed farther up the valley, sir. I wasn't sure if we had the right place but then we picked up your beacon."

"Very good, Lieutenant, just in case someone less friendly picks up the beacon I want you to take your platoon down to where the Teneyk road passes by the mouth of the valley and dig in. Block all movement along the road."

"Yes, sir."

The lieutenant started to dash off, but Allenson called him back.

"Order your men to put on warm weather gear first. I don't want anyone down with frostbite."

"Yes, sir," the lieutenant hovered and looked unhappy.

"Something wrong?" Allenson asked.

"Where do I get warm weather gear from, sir?"

"You didn't bring any?"

"No, sir, no one told me to."

Allenson gaped at the boy before pulling himself together.

"No matter, off you go."

The young officer dashed away.

"No one ordered him to," Allenson repeated to Hawthorn who had come up during the conversation.

"I heard."

"It never occurred to me to give such an order. What part of the term 'midwinter festival' did my commanders fail to grasp when it came to personal kit? The clue is in the name."

"I guess everyone in the command line assumed the same thing you did; that it was obvious."

"And so campaigns are lost." Allenson said, looking to the heavens just in time to see three barges descend.

More barges came in over the next hour, Commodore Blount's in the first dozen. Before reporting to Allenson Blount went from vessel to vessel to ensure that recharging had started. The landing zone soon hummed with the background rasp and hum of chain saws and small ceramic wood-fired generators. Allenson concerned himself in setting up a secure perimeter and getting automatic air defenses online.

After two hours, the first private frames and Hinterland fighting frames began to trickle down. They tuned up in dribs and drabs, their crews utterly exhausted. Allenson wondered how many had failed to make it. Kaspary arrived accompanied by a cluster of frames that he had rounded up. The result was better than Allenson had anticipated. Despite the turbulence in the Continuum at least two thirds of the first wave were safely down. Only half had thought to bring warm clothes.

Allenson gave the landing force another two hours to sort themselves out into combat units and get some rest before calling a staff briefing for the senior commanders. Fortunately all made the trip safely. He daren't leave it longer as the sun would be setting in five hours or so, although at this latitude his pad informed him that he could expect a long twilight from the clear skies.

"There's no chance of any barges returning anytime soon for the second wave even if they could get through the Continuum storm," Blount said. "Their batteries are completely exhausted. Most of them only made it by rotating teams of emergency pedalers. We don't have sufficient generators in working order to recharge enough vehicles in one go so I'll have to do them in two tranches. I take it you still want them to go back in a single convoy for protection, sir."

"I do." Allenson turned to Major Pynchon. "How do we stand for artillery?"

"As most of it is Terran-supplied one-shot, self-contained, rocket mortars, I took the precaution of dispersing our tubes throughout the flotilla. We are still unloading, sir, but I would expect to have around two thirds of our compliment."

"Excellent, that was well done, Major."

Pynchon nodded his thanks to Allenson for the compliment.

"A change of plan, gentlemen, we're not going to wait for the second wave. We attack Teneyk immediately with what we've got while it's still light. Major Morton, you will stay here until you receive my signal. Then you and the Canaries will lift and act as a blocking force in the Continuum. No one gets in or out of the town."

"Gotcha, General," Morton said, face flushed with excitement—or maybe it was the cold.

"Colonel Kaspary will lead the Hinterlanders on foot to screen our advance. Take out any Brasilians outposts on our line of advance but silently, please. Let's not give the bastards any warning. Major Flako's regiment will remain as camp guard . . ."

Flako protested, but was quickly silenced by his brigade commander. Allenson continued as if he hadn't heard. Overenthusiasm was a permissible fault in a junior officer.

"The regiments will assemble in column in order of their numbers, the artillery support regiment to the rear. We march out in twenty minutes. Is there any commander who thinks he or she can't meet that deadline?"

He looked around the group. One or two looked uncomfortable and avoided eye contact. The brigade commander of the 2nd, a Colonel Percival, met his gaze boldly.

"Well?" Allenson asked.

"I think it's too hasty and we should take the time to fortify the camp first."

"Your opinion is noted, Colonel. Who is your senior regimental commander by the way?"

"Major Tannelle, sir," Percival said, pointing to a stout woman.

"Very well, you are relieved of command, Colonel." Allenson said. "Major Tannelle?"

"Sir."

"Are you confident you can get the 2nd's regiments into the line on time?"

"Yes, sir."

"Any other questions?" Allenson asked.

"You will be leading the attack, sir?" Flament asked.

"Of course. I will be with the lead regiment."

"The general will be just behind the lead regiment where he can oversee operations," Hawthorn added for clarity.

"Thank you, Colonel," Allenson said testily.

He had intended to be at the front but could hardly publicly overrule his head of security in such a matter. That would set off an alarm among the other officers that he might try to manage their jobs as well as manage Hawthorn's. He bestowed a crushing glance on his friend, who remained utterly uncrushed. Todd assumed a bland expression.

"You will notice that only nineteen minutes are left, people, so I suggest we all get on with it," Allenson said.

It was childish to want the last word but Allenson felt like a child whose treat had just been snatched away.

The Hinterlanders moved out in loose dispersed fire teams within five minutes. The line regiments took a little longer.

"Thirty-five minutes," Allenson said, checking his pad. "They've got to be sharper. Hell they *should* be sharper after all that training."

"Seems pretty good to me," Hawthorn replied. "I expected it to take an hour. How long do you think it takes a Home World battlegroup to be ready to march?"

"They have the luxury of operating to a different tempo," Allenson replied, but he took the point.

The line regiments marched in column along the Teneyk road. This kept everyone together and maximized distance covered for energy expended. It was a suicidal formation if they were shelled or attacked from the air. That was not worth guarding against. The battle was lost before it started if the enemy knew where they were and had heavy weapons available to interdict them. Everything depended on speed and surprise.

It was like a desperate gambit in a game where only one distribution of cards could give you a win. You assumed the cards had been dealt that way and played accordingly, even if the odds were against you. Allenson had done his Kobold Day best to stack the deck. But an unlucky sighting by an alert enemy patrol and a competent artillery officer could undo everything. As the old saying went, if you can't take a joke you shouldn't join the army.

The column made at a steady three kilometers an hour. That was half the normal light infantry march rate. His people were already tired from the crossing and adrenaline can only do so much. The troops would have to fight like tigers when they reached Teneyk. They would only get one chance to take the town by *coup de main*. To get bogged down in a siege was in the long run to be overwhelmed by attrition.

About one klick out from the town they came across a barn. A halfhearted effort to fortify had been made by throwing up earthworks and piling sandbags around the entrance. Weeds and small yellow flowers grew on the heaped up soil.

The regiment in front of Allenson deployed from march into a semi-battle formation—semi because they were still far too clustered for combat. Allenson hurried to the front and moved in to investigate the building with the lead platoon. Hawthorn, Todd and the Special Project troopers stuck to him like glue.

The front door was open, revealing a man in Brasilian army fatigues sitting with his head down on a table. He might have been asleep were it not for the congealed blood. A trail led from under his chin to where it had pooled on the table. Hawthorn gave a signal and his troopers moved cautiously in, carbines at the ready.

The barn wasn't that big so they were back out within a couple of minutes.

"Anyone in there?" Allenson asked.

The lead trooper shook his head.

"No one, leastways no one alive."

The Hinterlanders had obviously dealt with the matter. Allenson studied the man at the table again. There was no sign of violence or a struggle, apart from a slit throat. He might have been executed while unconscious. A small still-civilized part of his mind protested but he crushed the thought. Kaspary's men were in no position to take prisoners.

Allenson allowed a flicker of optimism to light his normal gloom. Maybe the Cornuvians in the town would be similarly Kobolded. He didn't go in to check his hypothesis by examining the other bodies. He had seen more than enough corpses in his lifetime and anticipated witnessing many more in the near future.

He called over the communications officer, a young studious-looking lieutenant with his equipment in a backpack, and ordered him to signal Morton. The transmission was disguised as a routine civilian message, in case anyone was listening. Allenson hadn't learned the officer's name and had decided he wouldn't unless the lad survived until the next day. Somehow he doubted he could keep this resolution.

Hawthorn left a security trooper outside the barn to prevent the following regiments from wasting time carrying out their own investigation when the regiment moved out. Flament kept them in loose formation and Allenson didn't interfere.

★ ★ ★

The inertial navigator in Allenson's pad reckoned they still had half a klick to go when they came across Kaspary's Hinterlanders in a dispersed line in front of a low, lightly wooded ridge. The road turned aside to the right and disappeared into a gap in the downs.

Kaspary was easy to find because he sat on a flat-topped rock outcrop near the road.

"Teneyk's just over the hill, General. The road goes through a cut in the hills where the Cornuvians have a timber blockhouse."

"Very well, we will attack immediately."

"With just one regiment?" Flament asked.

"Exactly so, Colonel. No doubt the other regiments will march to the sound of the guns. The longer we wait here the more likely we are to be spotted."

Allenson pointed to various terrain features as he laid out the plan of attack.

"Third Company will go over the ridge on the left flank under your direct command, Colonel Flament. The Second will attack frontally and First Company will take the right flank and clear the blockhouse. The Hinterlanders will circumnavigate the town and cut the road leading out on the far side."

"Where will you locate your HQ, sir?" Kaspary asked.

"I will be with the First," Allenson replied in a firm voice. "The blockhouse blowing up will be the signal for the Second and Third to commence their assault over the brow of the ridge. Any questions? Very well, gentlemen, positions please."

Allenson joined the officer commanding First Company, a rather lissom brunette of the indeterminate age that rejuvenation treatments brought.

"I won't interfere with your command, Major Rainhav, but I will be coming with you."

Her expression suggested she was less than delighted to be accompanied by her captain general. Allenson quite understood why. Even if he managed to restrain himself from micro-officering her company there was always the possibility that he would get his fool head blown off. A dead general was not something likely to enhance her reputation or facilitate promotion. She was, however, far too intelligent to protest.

"Of course, sir, you're very welcome," she said.

He moved away to allow her some privacy to give her subordinates their orders.

"Don't worry, I'll keep the old man out of your way and out of trouble," Hawthorn said in a stage whisper behind his back.

The major choked back a scandalized laugh.

Allenson decided that his dignity was best served by yet another temporary bout of deafness.

Rainhav gave her briefing in a few short sentences. Her three platoons jog-trotted along the road in column loudly singing a marching song that Allenson recognized as a variation of "I Don't Want to Join the Army." There were as many variants of the song as there were regiments in Brasilia and its colonies.

They pounded around the edge of the wooded hill and Allenson got his first view of the town. Teneyk sat in a low bowl surrounded by hills. It was much as he anticipated, an unremarkable market town of wooden, mostly one-story, bungalows. It possessed a central square, sided by two-story structures that housed the few government officials and mercantile leaders. Warehouse and workshops were placed to the perimeter to keep powered ground carts away from the living areas.

The town center was laid out on a grid pattern but the other buildings had been built haphazardly, creating a maze of back alleys. It was strangely quiet. Each wooden house possessed at least one stone chimney but smoke trickled from only a handful despite the cold.

Of more immediate worry was the blockhouse partly cut into the hill on the immediate left-hand side of the road. It was a suicidal defensive structure as there was no way of evacuating or reinforcing it in the event of an attack. The door actually faced outwards. The firing slit facing up the road was far too big, almost window sized. Allenson had the distinct impression that it was intended more as a customs post to regulate traffic than as a serious fortification. On the negative side, it was built from shaved tree trunks rather than wooden panels.

Rainhav didn't hesitate. She waved her arm and her troops increased their pace and volume. This provoked no reaction from the blockhouse. The range shrank to thirty meters before a head poked out of the firing slit. It gawped at the approaching Streamers and a hand combed tangled hair. At twenty-five meters and closing, the head ducked back inside.

After a few seconds a second head appeared. This sported NCO stripes on a helmet and was marginally more alert. He took one look before disappearing and uttering an incoherent yell.

First Company took this as the signal to disperse. The time for subterfuge was over. Troopers dropped on one knee and discharged their laserrifles. Pulses sparkled off the blockhouse, making little impression on the logs.

Three of Rainhav's people put their heads down and ran full sprint for the building. Supporting fire from the rest of the company ceased when the runners blocked line of sight to the firing slit.

A laserrifle appeared in the slit and fired, dropping one of the sprinters. It was immediately answered by the slap of Hawthorn's heavy hunting rifle. The remaining sprinters made the side of the bunker. Hawthorn fired again through the unwisely wide slit. Someone screamed.

The door of the blockhouse opened a fraction. A hand clutching an ion pistol emerged. The owner of the arm tried to angle it around the blockhouse to take a shot at the sprinters without exposing his own body. It proved an impossible task.

One of the sprinters fiddled with a package before posting it through the slit; then both dropped flat. They must have used a ridiculously short fuse because there was an impressive blast before they hit the ground.

The bunker heaved like a man taking a massive breath before an equally massive exhale. Smoke, dust and fire shot out of the slit. The bunker's door blew clear of its hinges. It came to rest on the far side of the hill in a tangle of splinters and burnt meat.

Game on.

"Charge," Allenson yelled, starting forward.

★ CHAPTER 30 ★

Decision

Quick as Allenson was off the mark, Hawthorn's security detachment was faster. They surged in front of him. Each one fired a short burst of laser pulses from his carbine through the blockhouse doorway as he passed. By the time Allenson reached the structure it was well alight. Black smoke billowed out from the entrance and through cracks in the roof.

The Second and Third Companies poured over the ridge, yelling battle cries or just screaming. One lost his footing in a steep section and tumbled end over end. He was brought to a halt by slamming into a tree.

Still nothing moved in the town.

Allenson overhauled the troopers in front of him to reach the front of the charge. Hawthorn yelled something he didn't quite catch.

First Company was in the town proper before Cornuvians tumbled out of the buildings. The enemy wore a variety of brightly colored civilian overcoats over Brasilian Army battle suits. First Company poured up the road while Streamers from the other companies infiltrated into the commercial zones.

A couple of Cornuvians staggered out of a bungalow door on Allenson's right. The one in front sported a purple parka and a lemon-colored yellow feathered boa that was surely intended to adorn the neck of a dancing girl. He was armed with a bottle of yellow liquid and scratched his crotch with his free hand.

Allenson dropped to one knee and triggered a long burst from his carbine. The laser pulses chopped the man into the dirt. The feather boa burst into flames. Allenson was so surprised at hitting the target that he was late shooting at the corpse's colleague. That man backtracked with remarkable alacrity and dived back inside.

A head appeared at a window, provoking a hail of fire from the security troopers around Allenson. He had a snapshot glimpse of the face and naked breasts of a wide-eyed woman before laser-hits reduced her to burned meat. The timber planks around the window burst into flames under the onslaught.

Cornuvians shot back from the windows. A Streamer curled over and dropped. A security trooper hurled a small cylinder through the open door. Allenson felt as well as heard the thump of a thermic blast. A bright flash illuminated the interior of the bungalow, followed by roaring flames.

They pressed on.

A bright orange pulse from some sort of over-charged energy weapon shot over Allenson's head. He had no idea what if anything it hit. Streamers pumped fire into the windows of any structure in the general direction of the shot. Paint burned off. Wood cracked, spitting flames. Wooden buildings were more a liability than an asset in a firefight. They offered little protection against laser weapons and turned into death traps when they inevitably caught fire.

At a corner they ran smack into a gaggle of Cornuvians running the other way. The two groups interpenetrated and inextricably mingled. Something struck Allenson hard on the left shoulder. He lost his balance, stumbling sideways over a Streamer who rolled under his legs.

Allenson fell on one knee. He let go of his carbine with his right hand and placed it on the ground to steady himself. He felt the familiar sensation of combat-time when the universe slowed down. His senses focused down onto whatever microscopic event his hind-brain thought critical.

A silver combat dagger stabbed the rolling Streamer between the shoulder blades.

Sunlight shining through the clear cold winter air glittered off the serrations of a double-edged blade. A ferret-faced woman grinned at Allenson, showing a single blackened front tooth. She allowed herself the luxury of enjoying the sensation of killing. She twisted the knife before withdrawing it from the fallen Streamer's back. Jagged edges tore at his flesh, releasing red blood in slow spurts.

Allenson used the time the woman wasted in sadism to drop his useless one-handed hold on the carbine. It fell slowly as if in a half-gee gravity field. By the time she attacked he was already upright and balanced. He leaned forward with both feet firmly on the ground.

She thrust the blade in a vicious upward lunge aimed at his belly. He twisted to one side and deflected it with his left forearm. Momentum carried the woman past. He completed the turn, hitting the back of her neck with the heel of his right hand. He put his whole body weight into the blow. He struck not so much at her but a point ten centimeters beyond her.

She folded around his hand. The impact propelled her forwards. Her body leaned forwards and her head rotated back to gaze at the sky. With both arms flung out she looked like a devotee of a religious cult who had achieved an orgasmic revelation.

The woman pitched away like a rag doll and disappeared into the melee. The last glimpse he had was the silver dagger trailing a spatter of blood droplets as it rotated free in the air. Allenson hadn't shed a tear over Fendlaigh. He wouldn't waste a moment's compassion on some psychotic mercenary.

Rather than look for his lost carbine, Allenson drew his ion pistol. It would have been foolhardy to try to find the carbine in the middle of a rat-fight. The pistol was probably more use at point blank range anyway. He touched the activation switch on the side with his thumb when the barrel was clear of his body. He spared a millisecond to check a red hologram winking above the gun. It signified that the weapon was live and set to full power.

A Cornuvian ran at him with a rifle. Allenson lightly caressed the trigger to no effect. He cursed his inability to shoot straight. He adjusted his aim. An orange dot shot right across the charger's body and disappeared. The Cornuvian ran right up to him, reversing his rifle to drive the butt into Allenson's face.

At this distance not even Allenson needed an aiming sight. He extended the pistol and fired at less than a meter range. A needle-thin high intensity laser ionized the air between the target and the gun. That created a path for a short but massive electrical discharge that followed almost too quick for the human eye to see. The Cornuvian twisted in muscle spasms and fell backwards. He voided his bladder when he lost control of his body.

Ion pistols were often used for policing, as the discharge intensity could be set to stun rather than kill, unless the unfortunate victim suffered from a weak heart or some other defect. High intensity yielded only two or three shots before the power supply was exhausted. Such a short range weapon was only ever used *in extremis* anyway when two or three shots decided the fine line between death and survival. It was a last ditch weapon but occasionally an exceedingly useful one.

As it happened Allenson didn't need to fire again. Close combat melees rarely last long and the few surviving Cornuvians broke and ran. Very few made it back to cover. Their fleeing backs made an irresistible target. One or two tried to surrender but were slaughtered out of hand by Streamer troops hopped up on a lethal cocktail of adrenaline and fear.

The uniforms of the cluster of soldiers around him included unit badges from the Second and Third Regiments. Reinforcements had arrived without him noticing.

"You want to live forever, people? Advance!" Allenson yelled, waving his arm and jog trotting down the alley.

It was vital to keep the momentum going while the Cornuvians were dispersed through the town. If the enemy got the chance to organize and take up defensive positions they would soon realize how few were the attackers.

How does a seventy kilo dog equipped only with teeth bring down a hundred kilo armed man—by all-out attack.

Urban warfare is nasty and brutal, a series of ambushes and short-range firefights. It is the ultimate infantryman's battle. Only infantry can comb through a town, driving the defenders out of their hidey-holes. Such terrain usually favors defenders. Preparatory bombardment merely smashes up buildings. The rubble forms a natural fortification for the defenders who creep out of cellars and bunkers like rats after a fire.

But wooden buildings are more to the attacker's advantage. They are easy to set on fire using laser weapons. Grenades turn wooden planks into showers of lethal splinters.

The Cornuvians should have set up defensive fortifications on the ridges around the town perimeter. Presumably no one had ordered them to and most soldiers are not particularly keen on hard physical labor. Once the attack started in the wood-built town their only hope was to burn down buildings to create firelanes and dig in.

Allenson wasn't giving them time. Tempo was the often unremembered key component of battle. It could be as important to the outcome as combat and logistics.

The Streamers came upon mercenaries wheeling a lasercannon out of a garage filled with agricultural gear. They shot down the surprised crew in a flurry of laser bolts. Allenson stopped to examine the gun. It was mounted on a tricycle carriage of two large front wheels and a much smaller one at the rear. It was intended to be towed by a ground vehicle with the rear wheel off the ground or propelled under its own power by a small motor.

He briefly considered turning it on its previous owners but reluctantly dismissed the idea. He had no idea how to start the motor. Presumably neither did the Cornuvians or they wouldn't have been trying to push it. Maybe it was malfunctioning or maybe it wasn't but he didn't have time to find out.

Tempo. They had to press on.

The ground floors of the two-story buildings around the central square were made from stabilized earth slabs. The enemy had knocked loopholes in the walls. One building's defenders put out enough fire to gun down the first Streamers who tried to rush the building with grenades.

Allenson's group found cover. They bombarded the structure with laser fire but their small arms couldn't penetrate. He was still considering the problem when Hawthorn threw himself down alongside.

"I do wish you wouldn't go off on your own like that," Hawthorn said with a deep sigh. "It makes it very difficult to look after you."

Allenson replied with a comment that would have won admiration from a drill sergeant. Hawthorn grinned and stuck his head up to examine the enemy position. He withdrew it sharply when a shot nearly incinerated his hair.

"Tricky," Hawthorn said. "What are you going to do?"

"We can't just bypass and cut off the square's buildings," Allenson said, thinking out loud. "We don't have enough people to form a perimeter and continue the assault. We can't ignore them either as they offer a secure fort for the Cornuvians to rally."

The communications officer crawled into position behind them, sliding his pack across the ground.

"Sorry sir, I couldn't keep up."

The young man seemed close to tears.

"Never mind, you're here now. Find out where our artillery is."

The officer busied himself with his gear. After a while he lifted up his head.

"They're still on the road, sir, about a kilometer out."

"Tell Colonel Pynchon to make all haste and set up on the hills surrounding the town."

"Yes, sir."

"What is your name?"

"Shevent, sir."

Allenson nodded, then spoke to Hawthorn.

"I can't wait for Pynchon. Pass the word, maximum suppression fire to make the bastards get their heads down, then we rush the place."

"They'll be heavy casualties," Hawthorn said.

"I know," Allenson replied curtly.

People were going to die because he screwed up again. He should have had the mortars on barges ready to rush them forward. He hadn't for fear of point defense weapons but the Cornuvians didn't seem to have any, or at least none ready to go.

He gave the fire order using his datapad as a loud hailer. There was hardly a need for secrecy as the enemy would soon know what was coming.

A hail of fire swept across the street, peppering the building opposite. Flakes of earth spun off the outer wall and the defensive fire slackened. There was no better time so Allenson rose to one knee and raised his arm. Naturally, he intended to lead the assault himself.

A line of continuous heavy laser pulses formed a continuous bright streak. It ran from somewhere behind Allenson's right ear to the corner of the building. Earth blew out and the corner collapsed. The wooded story above creaked and leaned but maintained structural integrity.

There was a phut, phut noise like a city delivery van on the move. A second burst chewed up another five meters of wall. This time the top story gave up its unequal struggle with gravity. The whole end fell off onto the rubble below in a rending crash of splintering wood.

"Charge!" Allenson cried.

They cleared the building of the handful of defenders who chose to make a fight of it in record time and sniped at those that fled out of the other side to cross the square. While his men consolidated the position and regrouped, Allenson returned to congratulate the little group of Streamers by the cannon on its tricycle undercarriage.

"'Tweren't nothing sir," the Streamer in the gunner's seat said when Allenson offered heartfelt praise. "This little beauty has a petrol engine just like the tractor on my uncle's farm. They can be a bit tricky to start if you don't set the throttle and choke just right. Them Cornuvians flooded the carb. Bloody amateurs."

He spat.

"Right," Allenson replied, nodding as if he had a clue what the man was talking about.

"Heads up, someone's lifting." Hawthorn's voice came in clear over Allenson's datapad.

A barge rose, shimmering in its Continuum field from somewhere across the square. It accelerated, turning its nose away as it climbed. Troops packed the open luggage racks. Streamers shot their rifles at it without much effect. A second vehicle, some sort of container transporter, followed.

The tribarreled nose of the cannon lifted. It spun on its gimbals as the gunner stared down at his sight on the controls. The barge was a good five hundred meters off and starting to dephase when the cannon spat.

Bright streaks connected with the rear of the barge. It exploded, spilling flaming debris and bodies into the air. The main hull rolled end over end and tumbled to the ground where it set light to something.

The acrid smell of ozone formed by ionized molecules of oxygen recombining in unstable arrangements filled Allenson's nose.

The transporter slammed back down out of line of sight so hard that Allenson heard it strike the ground. The driver presumably preferred to risk broken bones rather than be incinerated, a decision that Allenson could well understand.

That did in the Cornuvian morale. They fled their positions.

The cannon was soon left behind as the Streamers harried the retreating enemy. The little petrol motor could only propel it at a slow walk. Allenson told the crew to keep it in air-defense mode. Only one small frame managed to make the jump into the Continuum, weaving and twisting to avoid the searching streaks of light.

Allenson stayed close to Shevent, trying to direct the attack, but it was all happening too fast.

"I've got Colonel Kaspary for you, sir," Shevent said.

Allenson leaned over to take the screen.

"The enemy are pouring out of the back of the town. 'Fraid I can't hold them. I've had to pull back to avoid being overrun."

"Very good, Colonel. Harass them and try to slow them down but stay clear. Allenson out."

Allenson handed the screen back to the young lieutenant.

"How fast can you run with that gear?" he asked.

"As fast as you need, sir."

"Very good," Allenson replied, wondering if he had ever been this young and keen. "Let's go."

Allenson jog trotted down the high street that bisected the town. The odd crump of a grenade or zip of a laser still sounded from deeper into the side streets but the road was clear. Every so often they passed little clusters of Streamers checking out houses and sheds, but they reached the row of outhouses that marked the edge of town without mishap.

The Cornuvians were nowhere to be seen.

"Get Colonel Kaspary," he said to Shevent.

Allenson climbed onto a shed and surveyed the area with binoculars. Beyond the town the land sloped gently away. The road passed between orchards and various crops that showed up as splashes of green and bright blue.

"Patching through to your datapad," Shevent said.

"Where are they, Colonel," Allenson asked.

"You see that patch of trees with orange blossoms flanked on each side by blue fields."

"No," Allenson scanned fields. "Wait, yes, got it."

"They've dug in there. We've got them pinned down with sniper fire."

★ CHAPTER 31 ★

To the Victor the Spoils

It took another hour before Pynchon arrived and set up his tubes. The light had started to fade. After a few ranging shots, Allenson had him drop a ten minute barrage onto the Cornuvian position. It was impossible to monitor the effect, but he could imagine the impact of the high explosive rockets dropping almost vertically onto the shallow pits that was all the Cornuvians would have been able to dig. Some of the rockets hit trees, adding sprays of wood splinters into the hell of blast and red hot spinning metal fragments.

A couple of the missiles malfunctioned and dropped short, adding to the general shambles that the battle had inflicted on the town. The shorts undoubtedly caused Streamer casualties. Allenson cursed. It was a rum do to survive the battle only to be mown down by friendly fire. No doubt the bloody Terrans had supplied them with second grade missiles or those past their use-by date.

When the artillery stopped he contacted Pynchon.

"How many rockets do you have left?"

"We've used about half," Pynchon replied. "I can give you two more five minute barrages or about an hour of harassing fire."

Allenson considered his options. That was just enough rounds for preparatory fire to keep the Cornuvians' heads down while fresh troops from Second and Third Brigades mounted an assault. Even so it would be bloody. Damned few of the mercenaries would survive close assault but the Cornuvians would defend themselves with the desperation of cornered rats. Mercenary casualties he could live with but Streamer losses were a different matter.

He keyed his pad. "Shevent, put me through to the Cornuvian combat frequencies and broadcast in clear."

"Ready sir," Shevent replied.

"This is General Allenson of the Cutter Stream Army to the commander of Brasilian forces. You have fought well, but your situation is now hopeless. I can bombard you with artillery all night if necessary until you are plowed under. Surrender now and I will extend quarter as laid down by military law."

There was a long pause before a reply. When it came it was not what Allenson wanted to hear.

"Go to Hell!"

Allenson's mouth set in a hard line. He prepared to gamble on another throw of the dice.

"Pynchon, another five minutes at maximum intensity."

The rocker barrage renewed. Some of the warheads worked over old craters, throwing loose earth into the air, but others struck new positions. Unfortunately, the bombardment left him precious little ammunition to support an assault. If this gambit failed he would have to either accept heavy Streamer casualties in a frontal assault or let the Cornuvian survivors escape. Neither option was particularly optimum or palatable. He pressed the icon on his pad to broadcast again in clear

"My previous offer stands."

It occurred to Allenson that when Hawthorn had too much money in the pot and a weak hand he invariably raised the bet. He touched the icon again.

"But now I require you to surrender your equipment intact."

He held his breath waiting for a response. There was no answer so he tried once more.

"Come, sir, you have done all that honor demands. What is the point of further slaughter?"

"Very well, damn you," the Cornuvian commander replied. "We'll surrender our equipment undamaged, what's left of it."

Allenson let out the breath he hadn't realized he was holding. That was the drawback with mercenaries. No matter how professional, they were never really committed. It wasn't that they couldn't or wouldn't fight, but that they had no particular interest in the strategic outcome. One couldn't expect them to sacrifice themselves for a cause because they had no cause.

A Brasilian line regiment might have fought to the finish to tie up Allenson's army for as long as possible or just for the sake of regimental tradition.

The Cornuvian commander came back on, jolting Allenson out of his daydream.

"Except that I intend to destroy our communication equipment with army encryption codes. I cannot permit you to obtain those."

"Agreed," Allenson replied.

The Brasilians would change the codes anyway. He could easily allow the Brasilian commander this sop to his professional pride.

He would let Colonel Flament take the surrender. First Brigade deserved the honor as they had borne the brunt of the fighting. He jumped down from the low roof and stumbled. He suddenly felt drained. He would have fallen if Shevent hadn't caught him.

Conditions in the Continuum were still bad the next day. Allenson decided to march the prisoners back to the landing zone under the guard of First Brigade while the Second and Third combed the town for wounded and for useful military equipment. Allenson promised draconian punishment to any soldier stealing from civilians.

As it turned out civilian casualties were light because most of them had already fled Teneyk to outlying farms and civilian properties. The empty town had already been comprehensively looted of anything of value by the Cornuvians.

A message drew Allenson to a warehouse on the side of the town from where they had made their initial assault. There he found Hawthorn waiting.

"I thought you might be interested in seeing this particular batch of booty yourself," Hawthorn said, beckoning him inside.

Combat frames were lined up in rows, twenty or more of them, being poked over by Streamers.

"There's another warehouse full next door," Hawthorn said. "You always were a lucky bastard, Allenson. Imagine if we hadn't overrun this sector in the first few minutes and they got them into the air. But I suppose you create your own luck."

"I gambled and it came off," Allenson replied, but he realized how close to disaster they had come.

He examined the nearest frame, which was a five-seater in a 2+2+1 configuration. Two gunners sat at the front, the primary pedalers behind and the driver in the back. Each gun position had a heavy single-barreled auto-fire laser mounted on gimbals. They were designed perfectly for colonial warfare.

"The batteries are all charged ready to go," Hawthorn said. "Apparently they're a traditional Cornuvian frame called a coracle for some reason."

"Lieutenant Shevent," Allenson yelled.

"Sir?" Shevent said, raising his head from behind a packing case.

"There you are. Call in our barges to pick up captured equipment and we'll escort them back using these—coracles," he said, stumbling over the unfamiliar word.

"Yes, sir, ah, there's something happening," Shevent said.

"Indeed."

"Yes, sir, I've been monitoring Brasilian army channels and there's a mass of communications. Cornuvian units are pulling out all over Brunswick and falling back on the main base at Palisade."

"How do you know? Don't tell me we got the encryption codes after all?" Allenson asked.

"Ah, no sir, they're broadcasting in clear."

"The Brasilian HQ is sending out orders unencrypted?" Allenson asked, suspecting some complicated trap.

"Not exactly, sir, I don't know what the HQ is instructing. That is still coded. The Cornuvian outlying garrisons are talking to each other in clear. They have unilaterally decided to pull back rather than be overwhelmed one at a time by our supposedly superior forces."

Hawthorn snorted, "The enemy is always three meters tall."

Allenson listened in to the Cornuvian signals himself. They sounded genuine, but he decided to stick to the plan to retreat out of Teneyk that afternoon before the enemy could mount a counterattack, even if it mean leaving some of the spoils behind. He had pushed Lady Luck hard enough already. She had a habit of turning nasty on people who took her for granted.

They got back to the landing zone without incident. But once there a civilian carriage rotated around the circuit the wrong way and wandered into the flow of clumsy overloaded barges. Allenson noticed other civilian frames and ground vehicles in the camp as his barge came in to land.

He barely climbed out when an overweight man in a voluminous purple silk suit with bilious green ribbons waddled over and shook his hand.

"You must be Allenson. Jolly good show, sar, couldn't have done better myself."

"And you are?" Allenson asked, trying to retrieve his hand.

"Filmby."

"Have we met?" Allenson asked, hand still going up and down.

"I have the honor to be chief actuary of the Teneyk Chamber of Commerce," Filmby said grandly, as if that explained matters. "I have some ideas about what you should do next."

"The general is very busy," Hawthorn said, jumping out of the barge.

"I do not believe I know you, sar," Filmby said, drawing himself up to his full unimpressive height.

"Colonel Hawthorn, Security," he turned. "Trooper, escort this civilian back to his carriage before he gets hurt."

"Let's be having you, squire."

The black clad soldier gripped Filmby by a pudgy purple arm and marched him off. Special Project troopers surrounded Allenson. They cleared a path through the cheering civilians who converged from all points of the compass. For once he didn't object to the troopers' presence.

"You can let him through," Hawthorn said to a trooper who was blocking Todd.

"Uncle, you'd better come quickly. A situation is developing with the prisoners."

Allenson followed Todd at the run, security troopers in tow. He feared the worst when he saw the flash of laser weapons lighting up the dusk sky.

He hadn't envisioned capturing so many enemy soldiers, so had failed to bring anything to pen them in. The Cornuvians sat on the ground guarded by a platoon from First Brigade. At least that must have been the idea but the Streamer soldiers had their backs to the prisoners. They faced down a mob of angry Brunswickian civilians.

"You Home Worlder bastards aren't so high and might now, are you," screamed a woman's voice.

A hail of stones and clods of earth soared into the prisoners. Something hard hit a Cornuvian in the face and drew blood.

"What the hell's going on here," Allenson asked, dashing up to the noncom in charge of the Streamer platoon.

"Some of the locals are feeling their oats now that the Cornuvians are helpless. They intend to get their own back," the noncom said.

"String the buggers from the trees," cried a voice from the crowd.

"Who fired?" Allenson asked.

"I did, sir, over the heads of that lot," the noncom said, gesturing at the crowd of civilians.

He raised his head defiantly as if he expected disciplining.

A civilian dressed in rough farm laborers' clothes ran up to Allenson, waving a fence post.

"Those boogers have got it coming," he said. "Out of the way soldier boy or I'll crack your skull while I'm on."

Allenson wasn't about to bandy words with an oaf. He just picked him up by the lapels and hurled him back into the crown. The action released a howl of anger and protest.

"Colonel Hawthorn," Allenson raising his voice loud enough to be heard over the mob. "These Brasilians are my prisoners and I have personally guaranteed their safety. I'll be damned if I'll let a bunch of louts impugn my honor by making a liar out of me."

"Quite right," Hawthorn replied, observing the mob with distaste. Allenson continued.

"This landing zone is under military law and this is an illegal assembly. It will disperse. Your men will arrest any unauthorized person still within one hundred meters of the camp in five minutes. Furthermore you have my permission to shoot the next man or woman who threatens violence against the prisoners or our men."

"Very good, sir," Hawthorn said in response. His troopers spread out.

The mob went very quiet but held their ground. A young man with a bright blue neck scarf pushed to the front and half turned to address the crowd. He held a bottle in his left hand half raised as if preparing to throw.

"They wouldn't dare. They're bluffing! I say we—"

The youth stopped speaking when an orange spot appeared in the center of his chest.

Hawthorn held his hunting rifle casually at waist height. The orange sighting spot was rock steady on the young man.

"Bluffing! You really think so?" Hawthorn asked with genuine amusement. He smiled at the man in the blue scarf, who froze. "There's an easy way to put it to the test."

The youth lowered his arm and backed up, but the orange spot tracked him all the way. Eventually, he dropped the bottle and ran.

"Pity, now I suppose I'll have to make an example of someone else," Hawthorn said waving the barrel of his gun.

The mob dispersed.

"Or perhaps not."

Hawthorn waved his men forward and they ran behind the crowd, slamming gun butts into the backs of the tardy.

"Good work," Allenson said to the noncom in charge of the prisoner guard detail. "I'm pleased that you acted to protect our prisoners."

He had half expected his troops to side with the mob against the Cornuvians.

The noncom spat on the ground.

"Wasn't going to let no bunch of worthless drunks rough up the Brasys now they're helpless. Reckon that lot weren't so ginger when the Brasys had guns. *We* took 'em fair and square and a damn hard fight they gave us."

He turned to look at the prisoners who watched Allenson intently.

"They've given us no trouble, sir. Not a bad lot really, just a bunch of poor bloody infantry like ourselves, begging your pardon, sir. I prefer their company to a bunch of bloody civvies."

Allenson nodded agreement.

"Don't let yourself be overrun. Shoot if anyone tries to disarm you."

"Not a problem, sir."

Allenson walked away with Todd while Hawthorn and his men cleared the landing zone.

"I've been speaking to the prisoners, Uncle," Todd said. "You know most of them only joined up under duress because their families are in debt. They personally are getting damn all out of this."

"My information is that the Brasilians are paying handsomely for their services," Allenson said. "I wonder where the money's going?"

"Mostly to the oligarch families who control Cornuvia," Todd replied. "I reckon most of the prisoners would be happy to be written off as dead and become Streamer citizens. Some may even join up, soldiering being what they know."

"That is most interesting," Allenson said.

The next morning Allenson paraded the regiments due for release in front of the captured equipment. Altogether it made a tidy haul. The nifty little gunships were the stars of the display. The men cheered and whooped so enthusiastically when he climbed the makeshift rostrum that he eventually had to hold up a hand for silence.

He turned a blind eye to the civilian overcoats that had been purloined to keep out the cold. Such acquisitions were not looting but military requisitions, to be paid for in the fullness of time should the rightful owners come forward.

Hypocritical?

Perhaps. One may be as precious about military law as one wants, but no army is ever going to balk at doing whatever it needs to survive. He wasn't going to have his soldiers freeze on some legal technicality.

"Fellow Stream citizens . . . fellow soldiers," Allenson started, to be immediately interrupted by more cheers.

"We did not fight for money or for glory but for liberty."

He paused for effect.

"Liberty we have won."

More cheers.

"We have struck our oppressors such a blow as they will never forget."

Frantic cheering.

Actually he doubted whether the average Brasilian had heard of Brunswick or gave much of a toss one way or the other, but that didn't matter.

"Everyone here today has done their duty and may leave the army with honor. Indeed, they will leave with my thanks. I consider any man or woman who fought with me at Brunswick a brother or sister whatever their station in life. It will be enough for anyone here when challenged in times to come about what they did for their country to simply reply: I . . . fought . . . at . . . Brunswick!"

He dragged the last words out until they were drowned in cheers.

"As for me, I shall go on with the struggle until the last enemy soldier is driven from our worlds. That I pledge. Any person here who has the stomach for it is welcome to march with me. Colonel Kaspary will be opening a recruitment desk and inviting men and women to reenlist. It has been a privilege to serve with you and I can think of no better companions for the ordeal ahead. I thank you all for your courage."

With a last salute he stepped down from the rostrum before his own high-blown rhetoric caused him to throw up. War is nothing but blood, sweat and tears—but sometimes the alternative is worse.

Allenson went to oversee the loading for the evacuation. He intended to be long gone when the Brasilians brought their ponderous military might for a counterblow. He soon realized his presence was more of a hindrance than a help. Matters would run much more smoothly if he just let his officers and noncoms get on with it.

He sat on a tree stump chewing a remarkably taste-free slab of military ration-packed bread. Two birds squabbled on the ground. From their brightly colored yellow and red plumage he assumed they were male. Female birds were normally camouflaged for egg-sitting. The birds hopped around in a circle beak to beak. They shook their wings and chirped angrily. Every so often one would drive the other back with quick thrust. The victim would soon rally and return to the fray.

Winter was the time of year when male birds laid claim to territory. Territory to attract a mate in the spring. Territory to provide food to feed the chicks in the summer. The winner would prosper and transmit his genes into future generations. The loser may as well not have existed. It all came down to territory in the end.

He tried to tell himself that it was different for people. They could leave their achievements as a cultural legacy for future generations. His intrinsic honesty and self-awareness made him reject the lie. Who in the modern world remembered the achievements of the leaders of the Third Civilization, let alone the Second or the First?

Only gene replication mattered in the long run.

Kaspary's arrival broke his reverie. He scared the birds so they flew off, no doubt to continue the fight somewhere else.

"How many reenlisted?" Allenson asked.

"A good two thirds," Kaspary replied in momentary delight before his face fell. "Three thirds would have been better, of course, as the Stream really needs all of them and then some."

Allenson clapped him on the back.

"Two thirds is excellent. You have to learn to be patient, my friend. I discovered many years ago in the Hinterlands that sometimes all you can do is continue pedaling until you find somewhere safe to land and take a breath."

He was not faking optimism. They had just won their first offensive victory. A war of independence, a civil war in effect, is quite different from formal battles between established states. In civil conflict momentum is everything. Most people are fairly indifferent about the political issues involved, reckoning that they can adjust tolerably well to the rule of either side. Victory goes to the faction that builds sufficient impetus to convince waverers to join the winners while the joining is good.

One of the brightly plumed birds was back, strutting up and down and whistling a song of triumph. There was no sign of its competitor. Allenson broke off some of the bread and tossed it to the creature who pecked at it lustily.

To the victor went the spoils.

The End